To Luke, a fellow musician and music lover — Enjoy the story! Best, Roger L. Trott

Getting In Tune

A novel by
Roger L. Trott

coral press

ISBN10: 0-9708293-6-1
ISBN13: 978-0-9708293-6-8
Library of Congress Control Number: 2008921450
Manufactured in Canada.
1 3 5 7 9 10 8 6 4 2
First Edition

Cover Design: Linda Root
Author Photo: Corey J. Ball

www.coralpress.com

For Lisa, who supported me in all ways possible while I submerged myself in the fiction of my often misspent but wonderfully memorable youth.

This book is also dedicated to the loving memory of my mother, who overcame her best instincts to let my band practice in her living room, to my father, who always kept plenty of good books around the house, and to the guys in the band (you know who you are), who, for better or worse, made me what I am today.

1

THE RINGING in my ears seemed to be coming from deep inside my head, a piercing sound interrupted only by percussive thunderclaps of pure pain.

Ring. Bang! *Ring*. Bang! *Ring*. Bang!

Trying to shield myself, I shoved balled-up fists into both ears, but it didn't help. Pete Townshend, wielding his cherry-red Gibson SG like a tommy gun, loomed above me, windmilling power chords from *The Real Me*. I winced at the stack of Hiwatt amps pointed right at my head and strained to watch his bloody fingers attack the strings.

But what was that annoying ringing? Feedback?

The ringing suddenly stopped, but the pounding continued until Pete paused and looked down at me. "Look, mate, it's simple." *Bang! Bang-Bang!* "C minor, B-flat, F. Down the neck. Bloody easy. Sounds hard, but John and Moonie are doing all the work, see."

Bang! Bang-Bang!

A grin spanned his mug; tears of pain ran down my own.

"It's *this* chord, man," he insisted, showing me his twisted version of a C minor. "You play it like you mean it, you turn it inside out and shake it, and the birds'll come rushing up, right? And the joint'll be packed, and everyone'll think you're the Ace Face. It'll be just like the Marquee in '64, mate."

I tried to speak. I tried to tell Pete that I didn't believe, like he did, in the Universal Chord, the harmonizing combination of notes, pure and easy, that would connect us to everyone else. Or maybe I did. I wasn't sure. But I knew I believed in the other angle, the dark corner of the quadrophenic personality that we shared. *Can you seen the real me? Can you? Can you?*

7

Pete rubbed his big geezer nose and shook his head. "C'mon. You'll suss it, mate, just like the Who always did. Just bang these chords. And then John does his bass run and Roger comes in. Like this."

Once again his arm swept around in an arc, and I cowered.

Bang! Bang-Bang!

And then the ringing started again. I jerked away and my eyes popped open.

Shit, the phone.

I blinked away layers of twisted dreams and squinted at the alarm clock. Ten o'clock in the morning. Townshend disappeared, but the phone kept ringing. I knew Mick wouldn't answer it. The last time I'd seen him, he was passed out on the couch with the TV test pattern reflecting on the lenses of his glasses.

Struggling against a mess of sheets, I shoved out of the water bed and staggered into the kitchen. I stumbled over a growing pile of empty beer cans next to the refrigerator and searched the cluttered tile counter for the phone. The ringing continued to assault my brittle, dehydrated brain. I flung aside a week-old newspaper with Jimmy Carter's smiling face on the front and grabbed the phone.

"Hel—" I coughed, clearing stale Budweiser from my throat. "Hello."

"Daniel Travers? That you, man?"

I didn't recognize his voice, but the nasally twang sounded vaguely familiar. Was it Pete himself calling to finish his tutorial?

"Uh, yeah?" I answered cautiously.

"Hey, this is Rick Astley with Big Country Productions. How you doin'? Didn't wake you up, did I?"

Tightening my grip on the phone, I steadied myself. No dream, this was real. Rick Astley worked for a talent agency in Denver and booked rock clubs throughout the western

U.S. He was Big Time. I remembered talking to him a couple of months earlier after sending him one of our demo tapes. He hadn't seemed interested in us then.

"I've been up for a while," I lied with another dry cough. "How're you doing, Rick?"

"I'm cool, man. Hey, how's your band? What d'ya call yourselves? The Killjoys? Where'd you get that name, any-how?" He sounded like he was speeding on caffeine. "You guys been playing much lately?"

"Yeah, sure." I struggled to keep up with Rick's DJ-like patter. No time now to get into the band's name. With my free hand, I brushed long strands of hair away from my mouth.

Rick took a sucking breath and was off again. "Listen, Danny, one of my bands canceled out on a gig I booked for 'em next week, and I was hoping you guys could fill in. I listened to your tape again, and I think you're ready for the job. You interested?"

Wow. I tried to think. What would Townshend do? He'd do it. No doubt. Maximum R&B, on and on, mate.

"Danny-boy? You there?"

Danny-boy? "Sure. What's the gig?" I braced my hand against the green Formica of the kitchen table. Bread crumbs stuck to my palm.

"This is the deal: It's five nights at the Mai Tai Hotel in Puente Harbor, up in Washington. The gig starts next Tuesday and runs through Saturday night. You get a flat $750 for the week. You want it?"

"Next week?" Holy shit. I squinted at the TONY'S MUF-FLER SHOP calendar tacked to the wall. "You're talking about November 2? *Next* Tuesday?"

He laughed. "Let me spell it out for you, man. November 2, 1976. Five days from now. Got it?"

I swallowed and tugged at the elastic waistband of my boxers. Maybe four years of playing the boonies of Northern

California would finally pay off. But now my brain really locked up on me. Where the hell was Puente Harbor? Did we have any other bookings that week? Would the Blue Bomb, our '66 Dodge van, get us there in time? Shit, the damn thing sometimes broke down just backing out of the driveway.

Astley's voice cut through my foggy thoughts. "Danny, you still with me? You want the gig?"

"Sure. But where's Puente Harbor?"

"Look, it's not too far from—where are you?—Reedley?"

"Creedly."

"Crudly?"

"Right," I said, giving up. "We're a couple hundred miles north of San Francisco."

"Yeah, well, you just head north up I-5 and turn left at Seattle. You'll figure it out. It may take you a couple of days unless you bomb straight through."

Beads of sweat inched their way out onto the skin above my eyes. "Look, Rick, we want the gig for sure," I said, already fearing the band's reaction, "but I need to talk to the other guys to make sure everybody's free. Can I call you back later to confirm?"

"Sure, man. But I need to hear from you today or by no later than first thing tomorrow. You guys would be doin' me a big favor, and I'd remember it."

Big Country Productions could book us anyplace. This was it, the break I'd been waiting for. My hungover brain tried to burn through the vapors in an effort to get itself around what was happening. The door to my future had been suddenly flung wide open and the light was blinding. *Can you see the real me?* My heart slammed against my eardrums.

"You tracking me?" Rick asked, clipping each word. "I need to hear from you by tomorrow morning, right, man?"

"Right, right," I spit back at him. "But what's this place—the Mai Tai?—what's it like?"

"Piece'a cake, man. Great place to break in on the Northwest circuit. That's why I'm giving it to you guys. Hendrix played there before he became big. And Heart played it when they first started out."

"Hendrix and Heart?" My pulse kicked even higher. "So it gets a pretty hip crowd then? We could do some of our originals?"

"Uh, probably not a good idea, friend. You guys aren't big enough, yet. Just stick to the covers." He then paused, and when he started again, his cadence shifted, slowing as if he needed to better consider his words. "Look, the Mai Tai gets the usual rock club crowd, you know? Locals, cruisers, maybe a few chopperheads, people like that. You play some hard rock, stuff they know, and they'll dig you."

I pushed down my disappointment. I knew we were ready to do our own stuff. But something else he'd said caught my attention. "What's a chopper—" I started to say.

"Hey, get back to me by tomorrow, O.K.?" He now sounded impatient. "I've gotta get goin'."

"Yeah, sure. We're playing a gig tonight. I can talk—"

"Cool. Call me by ten. If I don't hear from you by then, I'll have to give it to someone else, O.K.?" Then the line went dead. Wait, did he mean ten o'clock his time or my time? Was Denver in a different time zone? Did it matter? My head continued to pound, and I dislodged another strand of hair from the corner of my mouth. And what the hell was a chopperhead?

✳ ✳ ✳ ✳ ✳

I SAT SLUMPED in a cracked kitchen chair, trying to regulate my heartbeat while gazing around at the kitchen of the decrepit house Mick and I rented for $95 a month, when Mick shuffled in, weaving his way toward the counter, his way-too-long blue-flannel robe sweeping the floor behind him.

"Who the bloody hell you talking to so early?" he said, squinting at me, fingers sorting through his tangled black shag of hair. "What time is it? It wasn't me mum, was it?" He struggled to the stove, fumbled with the knobs, and finally turned on the heat under a rusted teapot.

For some reason, Mick's accent sounded particularly fake this morning, perhaps because Townshend's had been drilling away at me all night. The chords from *The Real Me* suddenly banged against my brain, and I pushed them back, but I could still hear them echoing around in my skull.

"You're not gonna believe it," I said. "Remember when I sent out tapes to those talent agencies? The one in Denver just called and wants us to do a weeklong gig in some town in Washington. Next week."

Mick's eyes widened, blinked, and then returned to their usual squint. "Sod off, mate."

"I'm not kidding. It's some place Hendrix once played."

The eyes widened again. Without his glasses, Mick's pupils swam in a watery sea of red instead of their usual ponds of glass-muted brown. He searched the pockets of his robe for his black-framed glasses, without which he was legally blind. Mick claimed he didn't need the thick, corrective lenses, but I knew he was full of shit. Even so, I could never tell how much he could see, with or without the glasses. He slipped them on and leaned against the counter.

"You're daft, Daniel," he observed with what we both knew was great insight. "And where are your bloody clothes? Please, nothing kinky for me today, thank you. Too early. And I need a cuppa first."

I ignored him, gazed out the window, and focused on a brittle orange leaf clinging to the limb of an old oak behind the house. Slowly, as I watched the leaf pull away from its mooring and blow happily away, I fully realized the opportunity being offered to me: I could leave Creedly behind. Unlike Townshend, I had no true guru or avatar like his

Meher Baba to guide me through life, but I did have ol' Pete, and he'd just have to do. A smile worked its way through the fumes of last night's six-pack.

"You know what this means, don't you?" I said.

Mick, in the middle of spooning instant coffee into a plastic 49ers mug, glanced at me. "We're going on holiday in our undies?"

"We're getting outta this stinking town."

He snorted. "Oh, sure. For a week, maybe."

"Maybe forever, if we're lucky."

"Uh-huh." With shaking hands, he poured lukewarm water into the mug, dropped in two aspirin, and stirred the coffee with a dirty fork. "Before you start picturing yourself on the cover of *Rolling Stone*, you might want to consider that the others might not be so keen on the idea. I'm not even sure I'm up for it."

"Are you outta your mind? This fuckin' town is a dead end."

Mick shook his head in response and shuffled off toward the living room. "I'll be in here dying on the couch if you need me." But the blue robe with the cigarette burns in the sleeves reached the door before its occupant stopped and looked back at me. "Did you say Hendrix played there?"

"Yeah."

"Well, bloody hell."

2

I HAD EXPLAINED the gig to the band and now there was silence. From my seat in the top row of the gymnasium, I looked at Rob, Sam, Mick, and Yogi perched on the bleacher seats around me. We had arrived early for the dance at Creedly High School and had already set up our gear on the gym's stage. We were ready to play, but first we had to fully discuss the Puente Harbor gig. In anticipation, I had screwed down my brain with two cross tops—the small, white amphetamine tablets I kept in the vial in my pocket—but they weren't helping.

As if I didn't have enough to worry about, Pete Townshend wouldn't get out of my head.

Can you see the real me? Can you? Can you?

Good question. I was lucky enough if I could make it through every day without splitting into four pieces, without shooting off in every direction, trying to manage everything that came into view. Talk about your quadropheniacs. I was a mess, but nobody knew.

I had seen the Who in '73, in that acoustically abysmal barn of a concert hall in south San Francisco called the Cow Palace. With Mick and Rob, I had waited in line for five hours just to get inside. And then we had sat on the cold concrete floor for another couple of hours before the bands came on. But once the Who hit the stage, man, it didn't matter. My heart ran up my sleeve and into my throat every time Townshend's legs splayed out and his arm swept around in a brutal attack on his guitar. He played in a way that let everyone know he was one fucking angry, dissatisfied, alienated geezer. And when Keith Moon—drunk, PCP'd out, jet-lagged, whatever—toppled backward off his drum set, Townshend did the coolest thing: He asked some kid to come out of the crowd to play drums on the last few songs. Pete understood. He might be one alienated son of a bitch, but he was one of us.

I'm not one to do the hero-worship thing. I know most of those celebrities and rock stars are screwed up. But as I watched the Who that night, I realized Pete was different: He was *totally* flawed, and he knew it, and he screamed and jumped and bashed his way through it. *Love me anyhow, I dare you*, he seemed to say. He didn't try to pretend he was anything other than what he was. I saw it; I felt it. He was searching for something, and he got into my head that night and wouldn't leave me alone. And now he didn't care that I had a hangover—I'm sure he'd had plenty. No, Pete continued to bang away. *Can you see the real me?*

As the Who defined Townshend's yin and yang, my band—Rob, Mick, Sam, and Yogi—framed the four corners of my closed-in, polar-opposite, quadrophenic world. I bounced among these four poles like a pinball, trying to keep the band together. Sometimes I didn't know where I left off and they began. And it wasn't like I'd absorbed their good parts, just the negative self-doubting stuff that drove me out of my head. And, believe me, I had enough of my own stinking shit to deal with without taking on theirs. But that was the deal. Pete explained it to me one night. *That's what you accept when you're part of a band. If it's not, then that band's not gonna happen for very long. And when it comes apart, if you really care about it, your guts go with it and there's nothing, nothing left.*

And so I now sat on the top row of the bleachers in my white coveralls and black work boots, Pete Townshend angry in my head, trying to figure out why those four parts of me wouldn't come together, knowing why I didn't believe in the Universal Chord. I'd read somewhere, probably *CREEM*, that Townshend had ended up with a nervous breakdown trying to find the unifying combination of notes that made up the lost chord; here I was, on the verge of a breakdown just trying to unify four guys.

While I considered where I next wanted to move a discussion that could soon turn into an argument, my gaze kept wandering around the nearly empty gym. There, hanging from the ceiling, were all the Creedly championship banners; there, all around us, were the now empty bleachers still ringing with cheers for the basketball team; and there, down on the plywood stage, was Yogi's drum set, roughly occupying the spot where I'd been grudgingly handed my diploma nearly three years earlier, and where my brother, Kevin, had received his diploma the year before they shipped him off to Vietnam. That memory made me wince, and I forced my mind to swing back to the here and now; but I couldn't shake the weird feeling that, in this echoey hall of mixed memories, my future was once again about to be decided.

Two girls on stepladders were draping yellow and black streamers along a banner above the stage that read CHS HOMECOMERS—SHAKE YOUR BOOTY. Yeah, right: KC & the Sunshine Band. That was something Pete and I both knew: The music was changing, and rock 'n' roll was going down unless something came along and kicked its butt. From what I was hearing on the radio these days, mainstream rock had become a load of self-satisfied crap, mired in its own excess, bloated, bankrupt, and out of gas. Yeah, something needed to save rock 'n' roll, and it better come along and do it *fast*.

Rob, sitting backward with Sam on the row below the one occupied by me, Mick, and Yogi, suddenly leaned forward and waved a hand in my face. "You still with us, Daniel?"

I looked down into the angular Scandinavian face of our tall hippie bassist, a battered tan Stetson propped on his head, his long blond hair tucked behind his ears. He was wearing his favorite tie-dyed T-shirt, and his long fingers—

the fingers that made difficult bass lines easy for him—were tapping away on a knee of his ragged Levi's.

"Yeah, I'm listening," I told him.

"Like I was saying, this Puente Harbor gig sounds cool in *theory*, but where the hell is this place?"

"I looked it up," Mick said, breaking in before I could answer, "and it's not bloody likely that Yogi's babysitters will let him get that far away. The bleedin' place is practically in Canada."

One of Rob's eyebrow's twitched high. "No shit?"

"It's just a little northwest of Seattle," I clarified, shooting a sideways glance at Yogi's chubby, wide-eyed face, a face framed by protruding ears and short rust-colored hair that was already receding at the temples. He was twirling a drumstick and humming to himself. He had apparently missed Mick's snide remark. I looked back at our bassist.

Rob's watery pale-blue eyes—bloodshot undoubtedly from an afternoon reefer—narrowed. "Ah. All the way up there?"

"It's not that far," I said. "A one-day drive, maybe two to be safe."

"Don't lie to us, mate," Mick said. "It's on the Olympic Peninsula, right across the Strait of Juan de Fuca from Victoria. But I doubt any of you wankers know where *that* is."

"Fuca?" Yogi said, the drumstick stopping in mid-twirl. "Is it really pronounced that way?"

From the bleacher seat next to Rob, Sam hunched his linebacker's shoulders, threatening to bust open his swirling paisley shirt, and pointed a finger toward Mick. "I know where Victoria is. And knock off that stupid accent."

"*Vic-tor-i-a,*" Yogi suddenly sang out, oblivious and off-key. "*Vic-tor-i-a.*"

Shit. This was already going worse than I had expected. I checked my watch—still forty-five minutes until the dance started. "It's a good gig," I said, trying to regain control of the conversation. "Astley said it could get us on the club circuit. Look, I've got to call him first thing tomorrow morning or we lose it. You guys really wanna play proms forever?"

"Who said we'd be doing this forever?" Mick said. "And we've got a good thing here. I'm getting laid; I'm getting high. Why go play for some poofters in Canada?" His voice, seemingly reinforced by the loudness of his bright-red polyester shirt and signature chartreuse scarf, echoed off the hard surfaces of the gym. Scanning the room, I saw that the dance committee's adviser, a cranky woman who had been my sophomore English teacher, had entered the gym and was talking to the two girls hanging the streamers. If they hadn't heard Mick already, they soon would.

"Let's take this outside," I suggested, and I was a little surprised they so easily followed me. We clambered down off the bleachers and went through a side door leading to the athletic fields behind the gym. After I pulled the door shut behind me, the five of us were alone and in the dark, except for the pale light of a moon streaming through tattered clouds. The guys gathered in a circle, breath condensing in the sharp October air. I lit a Marlboro and tempted its smoke into my lungs. As I did, I noticed my hands were shaking from the cross-tops I'd taken earlier.

"Look," Rob said, flipping away stray strands of hair that had slipped from behind his ears, "Mick has a point. I mean, why burn all that energy driving to Washington for—what was it? Seven-hundred, eight-hundred bucks?—when we can make as much playing around here? That kind of bread will barely cover the narcotics." He laughed, but I knew he was partly serious.

"There's no place like home," Yogi now sang out through the darkness, audibly clicking together the heels of his black high-tops.

I leaned back against the cold brick of the gym wall and kicked at tufts of damp grass. The cross-tops burning through my system cut both ways, and the elation that I'd felt earlier in the day now ate at my stomach. To make matters worse, Townshend's jagged chords jumped back into my head, stabbing at my nagging hangover. C minor, B-flat, F.

I had expected Rob's reluctance. After knowing him for so long, I could usually anticipate his reactions, and what I had learned over the years was that contrary to his hippielike appearance, Rob was dug in and avoided risks.

I'd known Rob Verlaine since early in our freshman year of high school, where I'd first met him late one day, literally bumping into him when we both turned a hallway corner from opposite directions. Rob had dropped the small stack of albums he was carrying.

"Hey, sorry," I said, expecting an angry reaction.

But Rob looked at me with those translucent blue eyes and gave me a lazy smile, which I later learned hid more than it revealed. "It's cool, man. Don't sweat it."

I helped him gather up the albums, glancing at the covers as I did: Grateful Dead, Quicksilver Messenger Service, Jefferson Airplane. Not my favorite bands—too '60s spacey, too San Francisco psychedelic—but groups I respected for their dedication to the music. "Where you heading with these?"

With his free hand, Rob rubbed at the bridge of his prominent nose. "Just got 'em. I'm heading home to sort out the bass lines. Lesh and Casady play some pretty trippy stuff. Seriously, man." He started to shamble off down the hallway.

Immediately sensing something intriguing in his taste in music, his peace-love-and-understanding demeanor, and his assumption that I'd know the names of the Dead and Airplane's bassists, I caught up with him. At the same time, I realized that an opportunity had presented itself for moving my guitar, which I'd been banging on in private since Kevin had left for Vietnam, out of the bedroom.

"Hey, hold up a second," I called out as he slowed to a stop. "I play guitar myself. How about I join you?"

Again the smile. "Well, I'm kind of doing it to explore my artistic inner self, you know, but if you're hip to that, sure."

And it was that simple, the beginning of a musical partnership, but one that would grow more complicated each day it existed, because neither Rob nor I was that simple.

So Rob's reluctance about taking the gig didn't surprise me, but the reluctance of the others, especially Yogi's, did. What did he have to lose? But then I remembered Mick's crack about Yogi's babysitters. I looked at our drummer and asked, "How about you? You're up for it, right?"

Yogi's blank brown eyes stared back at me from across our little circle. Our roly-poly drummer was still living at home, where his uptight parents controlled him. Watching his Charlie Brown face, I couldn't tell if he was mentally working out the problem of confronting them or thinking about something entirely different. It was always hard to tell with Yogi.

I continued to peer through the darkness at him. Even in the cold, he was wearing his usual green-striped tank top to free up his arms when he played, and his tennis shoes were untied, ready to pull off, along with his socks, to give his feet a better feel for the bass drum and hi-hat pedals. He didn't look much like a rock star, but he was a hellacious drummer, and he was right for us, even if the other bands in town hadn't wanted him. I needed him, but to my benefit, Yogi thought it was the other way around.

"How about it, Yogi," I repeated. "You're with me, aren't you?"

He pulled a Baby Ruth bar from a side pocket of his baggy jeans and ripped it open. "Well, I'd like to, Daniel, but you know, well, you know how it is."

"Come on," I said softly, knowing that he was referring to his folks. Although Yogi was only a year younger than the rest of us, he still seemed to approach life like an adolescent, letting others make decisions for him. Behind the unfocused eyes, he was a smart guy, able to tear down and rebuild a car engine, repair our amps and lighting equipment, and work his way through complex electronic schematics. But something was holding him back. I wasn't sure what—maybe a lack of confidence caused by his overprotective mother. He'd never considered moving out of his parents' house, and, as far as I knew, he'd never dated anyone. In many ways, he was like a beaten-down puppy, seeking an owner he could trust. At this moment, I knew he was looking to me to guide him, an unwise choice but one that worked to my advantage.

"Look, Yogi," I said to him, "you owe me one."

I didn't need to say much more, because he knew what I meant. After all, I'd given him a chance to be something more than a misfit and a momma's boy. He stopped messing with the candy bar and finally looked at me. "I don't know. If you think—"

"You're the backbone of the band, Yogi. Don't let me down."

"Well, I guess," he said, "yeah, I guess I could. Nobody would miss me, would they?"

"They would, but it's our gain."

Yogi stared at me for a long moment, then said simply, "Whatever you say, Daniel." His momentary look of focus faded away.

I now glanced sideways at our shag-headed lead singer, bobbing up and down beside me on the toes of his blue Adidas tennis shoes, and instinctively knew where to probe. And I had him to thank. Mick's skill at manipulation, which I'd absorbed over the four years since he'd joined the band in high school, guided me to the right words: "So, tell me, Mick, what's the problem? You nervous about something?"

"There's no problem, mate. I just like it here. And I'm skint at the moment."

"Is it the money, or are you really afraid that your father won't let you go?"

"My dad?" His breath shot out in a cloud of moisture. "What does that old fart have to do with anything?"

Mick's accent had momentarily disappeared, and I smiled, knowing I'd hit my mark. "I dunno. I thought maybe you were worried about his reaction. I know he doesn't like you singing in the band."

Mick thumped the side of the gym wall. "Bollocks to that! I do what I bloody want, and he knows it. And you know it, too. So just shut the fuck up about that, O.K., mate?"

His angry rebuttal, with accent back in place, brought on a moment of silence. Sam, who had been gazing out into the murkiness toward the football field, leaned into the circle. "Look, Daniel, I think I'm with Mick and Rob on this one. We'd have motel costs on the way up and back. And gas and food. I mean, gas is over sixty cents a gallon now. I don't know about you guys, but I'm not rolling in cash at the moment. Even scraping together change to buy new sax reeds is tough right now."

"And I've got classes at the JC next week," Rob added. "Maybe we should pass on this gig. We've got gigs lined up here anyhow."

As I felt my opportunity slipping away, something clutched at my gut. Was I wrong? Wouldn't the music save me? My head tilted back onto the wall, and I found myself staring up at the dingy moon. My hands continued to shake, reminding me of the price I paid for trying to feel good. The trick, I knew, was to keep breathing. While studying the moon, I took a couple of deep breaths and considered my next move.

"Hey!" Mick suddenly bounced into the center of the circle, shattering my thoughts. Bobbing around like a boxer, Mick jabbed a finger in turn at Rob and Sam. "Oh, bloody hell," he said in a needling voice, "what a couple of poncy poseurs."

"What the hell you talking about?" Sam shot back, brushing Mick's hand away from his face.

"What's a poseur?" Yogi asked.

"Daniel's got it sussed," Mick said, ignoring them. "We're the best band around here. Why are we wasting our time playing for prom queens? Bollocks to the money. This is our chance, mates. This is what we worked for, idn't? I'm going!"

"Chill out, Mick," Rob said. "I thought you were against it."

"I'm bloody going," Mick insisted.

I smiled to myself and made a mental note that I should always follow my instincts, at least with Mick. Push one of his buttons and you'll always get a reaction, maybe not the one you want, but you'll get one. Mick could be unpredictably dangerous, but now, as I watched him bear down on Sam and Rob with energy that wouldn't subside until late into the night, I didn't care. He was going to Puente Harbor, and that's all that mattered.

Two down, two to go. I pulled my Army surplus jacket closer for warmth and looked across our little circle at Sam. He had absolutely nothing to lose. When he had failed to get a football scholarship after high school, his immediate choices had been reduced to playing in the band or working construction. Sam wasn't one to avoid hard work, but, hey, you choose. Besides, there just weren't jobs available in Creedly's stunned post-Vietnam economy.

Sam Estola had been well known at our high school. And in white-bread Creedly, Sam, with his dark Latin features, muscled body, and sweeping jet-black hair, was hard to miss. He ran with the jocks, played middle linebacker on the high school football team, and led the sax section in the school's stage band. And he had been, and still was, something else the rest of us weren't: Popular. Mick knew this, and it bugged the shit out of him. And as I watched Sam eye Mick, who was still bobbing up and down next to me, I realized the unspoken competition that existed between the two of them. If Mick was willing to go to Puente Harbor, I figured Sam would also go.

"C'mon, Sammy," I said, "aren't you ready to get outta here? See the world? I mean, Mick's ready to go."

"I dunno. I was thinking about working over the winter."

"You're kidding. Where?"

"My dad said he could get me on at his job site."

I sighed. This was new information. "Doing what?"

He avoided my eyes. "A gofer. Hauling sheet rock and shit like that."

I let the depressing concept hang in the chilly air for a moment. "Is that what you want to do? Haul sheet rock? And, anyhow, we'll only be gone for a week."

Sam gazed down at the grass separating us and cracked the knuckles of his thick, strong fingers. His straight hair, glistening black in the moonlight like the paint job on his Camaro, hung limp against the tops of his shoulders. Finally, he looked up at me. "What the hell. I don't want Mick calling me a poseur. And if he does it again, I'm gonna stick my foot up his ass."

Mick grinned and pointed across at him. "I take it back, Sammy old man, although the foot thing sounds interesting."

I turned my attention back to Rob, who had grown increasingly stubborn about everything since he'd started living with Candi six months earlier. Candi was a lot like Rob—Scandinavian blonde, smart, and attractive. But unlike Rob, she knew it and used it to manipulate him. And Candi, an overachiever who did everything she tried just a little bit better than everyone else, was one of those people who expected their definition of success to apply to those around her. Candi had high expectations for Rob, and I doubted that those expectations included him sticking with the band over the long haul. Even so, I liked Candi's quick wit and ready laugh, and I knew Rob really cared about her, but I was beginning to sense problems in the way Rob's face tightened whenever Candi's name came up in band discussions. I guessed that he was having trouble figuring out how to please her while keeping everyone else happy.

I thought for another long moment before speaking. The band was important to Rob, although I knew it was much more important to me. Rob appreciated rock music as an art form, finding the creative side of it fascinating, exploring how his bass could fit rhythmically and melodically into musical puzzles that changed shape with every song. But I feared that Rob was riding with the band as long as it was relatively painless; that he'd slide into the mainstream when the time was right.

In some ways, though, what Rob brought to the band was purer than what motivated the others. With Mick, the band was simply a vehicle for expressing his ego and attracting girls, even though I guessed that subconsciously his primary motivation was to prove that he could move the masses as mightily as his preacher father. Sam, on the other hand, was in it for no other reason than to have fun and earn a little extra money. Mick and Sam would stay with the band as long as the getting was good. Only Yogi, who saw the band as the only family that really cared about him, was in it for as long as I needed him.

But the problem at the moment was our bassist. "Well, Rob," I said, "it's up to you. We've always been in this thing together. You go or none of us go. And you know we'll do great up there."

Rob folded his arms. "Yeah, sure."

"We will. Look, we've worked hard to get this chance. Some of us have quit school to do this."

"That's cool, but I didn't, you know."

Mick thumped the wall again. "Oh, bloody hell—"

"Shut up, Mick." I lowered my voice. "Rob, I realize you're still dealing with school, but this gig is our chance to find out if we're really good. We've played every school and club around here until they're sick of us. Nobody can touch us. You know it and I know it, but we need to get out there where the big fish live. We've gotta swim out deeper into the ocean."

He petulantly flipped his hair, thankfully ignoring my inane analogy. "But why now? We can always do a road trip some other time."

"Maybe. But Astley won't give us another chance if we blow this off. If we don't take it, we'll all be stuck here. We can pull the money together for the trip. It won't cost that much. Yogi, Sam, and Mick are up for it—"

Rob's face tightened and his eyes blinked several times. He rarely let his emotions show, but he was now struggling to maintain control. I knew what was going on: His choice was down to pissing off the four of us or Candi. I had him cornered. And even though I felt bad about Rob's predicament, I wasn't about to let him off the hook now.

He started to say something but paused, and I could see him mentally backing off. "Christ, I didn't know the future of the universe depended on us doing a road trip, but if you guys feel that strongly about it, I guess I can do it." He pulled in a long breath. "But I need to call Candi first."

Victory was within my grasp. Time to back off a bit. "Fine. Call her and see what she says. Use that phone at the front of the gym. We'll wait for you out here."

For a long, awkward moment, Rob hung there before us, then he stuffed his hands into his pockets and pushed through the door into the gym.

"Yeah, ring up bloody Yoko," Mick whispered as the door shut behind Rob.

Sam stifled a laugh and murmured, "He's in love, man. Give him a break."

I looked over at Yogi, who, oblivious as usual, tapped out a beat on an imaginary snare drum with the half-eaten candy bar. I let my head fall back against the wall again, feeling the steady throb of my hangover.

After several minutes, Rob pushed back through the door. "She's cool with it," he said, forcing a grin. "No problem."

I tilted my head forward and released a breath. The four pieces had come back together, and I was whole again. "I knew Candi'd be O.K. with it," I lied, suspecting from the length of the phone call that it hadn't been an easy conversation.

"*Candi, ah, honey, honey,*" Yogi sang out, waving the remains of the candy bar. "*You are my candy girl, and you got me wanting you.*"

"Shut the hell up, Yogi," Rob said.

I let Rob's uncharacteristic outburst fade away before pulling open the door to the gym. "Now that that's settled, let's go tune up."

I let them file ahead of me—overhearing Rob's whispered "Sorry, man" to Yogi as they passed by—and forced a big breath of cold air into my brain before following them into the gym.

3

THE NEXT AFTERNOON, four hours after calling Astley to tell him we were on, I walked into the garage and wrote three words on the chalkboard we used for song arrangements. I stepped back, cleared my throat, and looked around at the guys, who had gathered to practice for the Puente Harbor gig. One by one, each of them stopped fiddling with cords, amp switches, and cymbal stands, and looked over at me.

Rob caught the words first and nervously laughed. "Man, that's a mind blower. 'Hendrix, Heart, Killjoys.' "

Mick snorted. "Bloody hilarious, Daniel. Why didn't you put us first?"

Sitting behind his mammoth cobalt-blue Ludwig drum set—two bass drums, two floor toms, four mounted toms, snare, hi-hat, and five bronze Zildjian cymbals—Yogi twirled a drumstick and grinned. Sam simply nodded, wiped his forehead, and continued plugging mike cables into the back of the P.A. head.

We were a good band, sometimes a very good band, almost certainly the best in the area, but I wanted us to be great. Now was the time for more motivation, more focus; and, as I knew well, fear was a great motivator. I tapped the chalkboard. "That's where we're going. But we need to get better fast, and we've only gotta few days."

"We get the point," Mick said, draping himself over his mike stand in a pose of utter boredom. "You don't need to act like a wankin' teacher. Let's get on with it."

"Just wanted to get your attention." I left the names on the chalkboard, strapped on my black Stratocaster guitar, and switched on my Fender Twin Reverb amp. I waited for the warm smell of the amplifier's tubes to come to me. The garage, cozy with sound-deadening blankets hanging from the walls and doors, began to hum with the low sizzle of P.A. speakers and guitar amps.

Rob plucked a bass string, adjusted his volume, and then ran through a quick scale. He segued into the riff from *Whole Lotta Love* before slipping into *Sunshine of Your Love*, buzzing a note against a fret and missing another. I glanced over and saw the strain on his usually placid face.

"Hey," Mick said, with a clap of his hands. He took a step toward the chalkboard and pointed at the words I'd written. "This is a good time to get rid of that daft thing."

"What are you talking about?" I asked.

He continued to point. "That. Killjoys, right? Our name's daft. Always has been. Who wants to hang out with a bloody killjoy?"

I groaned. We'd had this argument a thousand times before. As a name, the Killjoys was my idea, and I'd fought hard to keep it, talking the guys, especially Mick and Sam, out of supposedly cool but meaningless names like Asteroid and Vapor Trail. With names like those, we might as well call ourselves Aerosmith or the Eagles. What the hell did those names mean, anyhow? No, I wanted something edgy and contradictory, a name that said we weren't just another party band. I wanted a pissy name like the Stooges or the New York Dolls, and to me the Killjoys had that same kind of twisted attitude. Maybe the name didn't fit the cover songs we were playing now, but it fit the agitated, angry things that I was starting to write.

"C'mon, Daniel," Mick said. "Let's change it. They don't know us yet up in poofterville, right?"

"What do you suggest?"

"Well, how about Mick and the Micksters?"

I looked around at the other guys, who seemed mildly amused. "O.K., fine," I said. "I don't want to waste anymore time on this. How many in favor of Mick and the Micksters?" No hands went up.

"Hey, I was just pissing around about that name," Mick said.

I ignored him. "How many in favor of keeping the Killjoys?"

Yogi's hand went up. I glanced at Rob, who unenthusiastically raised a hand. Sam abstained by ignoring me. "O.K., we're still the Killjoys," I said, holding up my hand. "Let's get started with practice."

"Oh, bloody hell," Mick said under his breath. He continued to hang on the mike stand, morosely muttering while the rest of us finished setting up and tuning. "What's first?"

I glanced down at our song list. "Might as well start at the top. *All Along the Watchtower*."

He grimaced. "Oh, how bloody perfect. Jimi bleedin' Hendrix. What's next? *Crazy on You*? If so, you can count me out, mate. I might fancy scarves, but I'm no Ann Wilson."

I laughed, but as I did my eye caught the three names on the chalkboard and my legs went spongy. Maybe fear *wasn't* such a great motivator.

＊ ＊ ＊ ＊ ＊

LATE SATURDAY MORNING, a day before we were to leave, I stood on my mother's porch, hands in pockets, waiting for her to come to the door. The little rectangular window in the center of the door framed my reflection like an overexposed album cover shot, and I cringed at the image. My brown hair, frizzed and tangled as usual, puffed out sideways from my head. I pulled a rubber band from a pocket of my Army surplus jacket, and after tying back my hair studied the reflection again. It wasn't much better. My eyes were like dark stains on a bleached-out sheet.

I knew I wasn't a good-looking guy, at least not in any traditional sense. Besides my hair, which I kept freak-flag long and which tended to go haywire at any moment, my eyes were indistinct, the color of mud, and were usually streaked red by cigarette smoke. My cheeks were high and hollow, which would've been O.K. except that my chin disappeared soon after appearing below my mouth. And, considering the vertical deficiencies of my face, I was too tall—almost as tall as Rob. One of the few girls I had dated in high school once told me that I looked European, spouting some crap about me being pale, gaunt, haunted. I suppose she meant it as a compliment—though if she had, we sure didn't stay together long—but I didn't take it as much of a recommendation.

That's one of the reasons I needed Mick. He wasn't particularly attractive either, but that didn't matter to him. He had no problem prancing around in the spotlight. For me, being out front, toes inches from the edge of the stage, face lit up by the spotlights, was like being in one of those sweaty dreams where your clothes are missing. So, except for an occasional trip up to the microphone to add background vocals, I stayed well back in the shadows near my amplifier. My cross-tops—kept in a vial in my pocket—helped, but I needed ongoing motivation to overcome the fear. And that's why I continued to stand on the porch, waiting for Mom to open the door.

Looking sideways into the door's reflecting pane of glass, I rang the bell again, knowing from Mom's Plymouth sedan in the driveway that she was home. Finally, her face appeared through the window and momentarily merged with mine before the door opened.

"Pleasant!" she said, using my given name, the name of her father, the grandfather I never met. "I didn't expect to see you today." She wasn't kidding. Her dark hair, speckled gray, wasn't piled in its usual neat, tight bun. The apron over her housedress was stained with the ingredients of some long-past meal.

I slid past her into the entryway. She reached toward me and then pulled back. "Can you stay long, honey? I can fix you some lunch."

I shook my head. "The band's taking off tomorrow for a gig in Washington. I just stopped by to get something from Kevin's room."

She followed me through the entryway and into the kitchen, where I saw a half-empty fifth of Gilbey's on the counter beside the panda bear cookie jar I remembered from my childhood. I continued down the hallway to Kevin's room.

"You're going all the way to Washington?" she called from behind me. "The state? Why didn't you let me know? I thought you were returning to school."

"What gave you that impression?" I passed by my old room and then hers on the way to Kevin's bedroom at the end of the hallway.

"Well, honey, your grades were so good when you quit last year, I just thought. . . ."

I kept going down the hall.

"Will you be back in time for your birthday?" she said from behind me. "Remember the special dinner I'm planning for you."

"C'mon, Mom." I twisted the knob of the closed door to Kevin's room. "I didn't promise to come over that day."

"But Daniel, it's your twenty-first." Her voice sounded a little needy. "I thought you'd spend at least part of it with me."

"Look, Mom," I said over my shoulder, "we'll talk about it when I get back. I'll only be gone a week." I pushed through the door, swinging it partially closed behind me. She wouldn't follow me into Kevin's room. The smell of stale dust told me that no one had been inside for weeks.

"Have you heard from him recently?" Mom asked from the hallway, her voice strained.

"Who?"

"You know who. Your father."

"Oh, him. Not recently." I glanced around at the Who

and Kinks posters still tacked to the wall over the twin bed and knelt down in front of Kevin's red-white-and-blue footlocker. I flipped open the cover and quickly found the dog tag lying on top of the triangular-folded flag. The calluses on the fingertips of my left hand quickly passed over the tag's brail-like letters and numbers. Still attached to its chain, the tag slipped snugly over my head and ponytail.

I heard Mom pacing in the hallway. "What are you doing in there?"

I closed the footlocker and crossed the room to a low bookcase beside the bed. "I'm getting a record," I called back, flipping through the albums in the bookcase. Finding what I wanted, I slipped out Kevin's copy of *The Who Sings My Generation*. For good measure, I took his copy of *Happy Jack*. He wouldn't need them.

With the albums under my arm, I returned to the hall and started back toward the front door. Mom trailed me.

"Pleasant, I've been meaning to talk to you about something."

I kept moving. "Why do you keep calling me that? Nobody does, not even Dad."

"It's your name, honey."

She caught up with me in the kitchen, and I stopped. "Look," I said, "the guys are waiting for me over at the house. I need to get going."

She glanced away, but her eyes apparently caught the Gilbey's bottle because they quickly swung back to my face. "That's what I wanted to talk to you about. Why are you wasting all your money on that terrible house? It looks like it's ready to collapse."

"That's where I live. That's where the band practices." I shifted from one foot to the other and looked longingly through the window at the Blue Bomb, which I'd parked behind her sedan in the driveway.

Mom tilted her chin in that way that told me she

was about to drop something on me. I couldn't help but notice that we had the same small, squared-off chin, a feature that made our faces look unbalanced by our high foreheads. "Why don't you move back here, honey?" she asked. "I miss having you around. You could save money, and I could use your help with the lawn and the house."

"You mean, like, live here?"

"Your old room's still empty." Her voice went up hopefully.

But I couldn't do it. "Are you kidding? No way. I told you we practice at the house. I have to be there."

Her chin arched higher. I now noticed new wrinkles appearing around the corners of her mouth. "You won't be doing that forever. You'll need to get a job and save for when you go back to college. With your father gone. With Kevin. . . ." She paused and bit at her lip.

"What's that have to do with anything?" I gave my head a tight shake. "Kevin's been dead a long time. And he would've wanted me to play."

Her eyes flashed. "Don't tell me what I already know. I just meant that everyone's left me, and there's plenty of room for you here."

She kept staring at me as my teeth ground tight. I had to consciously relax my arm to keep from bending the LPs. "Look, if you'd let Kevin get the CO deferment like Dad wanted, maybe they'd both be here."

"Pleasant!"

I arched my head away from her, but her open hand caught my cheek. My free hand started to rise, but I stopped it. "I'm leaving," I said, moving toward the door. She touched my shoulder, but I flinched away. Looking back, I saw tears forming at the corners of her eyes. She moved to hug me. I tensed. Then she pulled back, and I turned away.

"That's why I don't come over here," I told her. "I can't solve all your problems."

She stopped at the entryway, and I could feel her gaze on my back as I went through the door.

After pulling the door shut behind me and crossing the lawn toward the van, I caught sight of Mom through the kitchen window, her arms crossed, head turned away from me. I started the engine but sat parked in the driveway for a moment, looking at the house. I shook my head. There was nothing I could do. It was too late.

I slipped the glass vial out of my pocket, tapped out two of my cross-tops and swallowed them dry as I pulled out into the street.

4

PLEASANT DANIEL TRAVERS. That was the name she
gave me, and I never forgave my father for letting her do it.
How could I? He could've altered my entire personality by
insisting on something normal like Steven or Michael. But,
no, he let me become Pleasant, and it wasn't long before I
knew I just couldn't get comfortable being in my own skin.

I suffered through seven grades of school, being mis-
taken by teachers for a girl and losing playground fights at a
pace that would've made Jerry Quarry proud, before coming
to the conclusion that Pleasant had to die. That's when my
middle name, Daniel, was elevated to the top of the charts,
and I was reborn, just like Tommy in Townshend's rock
opera. And later, for good measure, I added a B to replace
my now-missing middle name. The B stood for nothing in
particular, but it had symbolic and symmetrical importance:
Peter Dennis B. Townshend, born 1945; Pleasant Daniel
B. Travers, born 1955. The initials connected me to something better than my family heritage. And nobody called
me Pleasant anymore. Except her. Well, and Mick once in a
while when he got in a particularly foul mood.

Even with Mom's nagging "Pleasant" still ringing in my
ears, my mood had improved considerably by the time I got
back to the house. I knew it was because of the pills, but that
was O.K.. The guys had already broken down the P.A. and
were ready to load the gear into the van by the time I arrived,
but it was still almost dark before Rob jammed the last duffel bag of microphones and guitar cords into the back of the
Blue Bomb and slammed its doors shut.

Together, the five of us walked into the garage, now
lonely-seeming without the amplifiers and mike stands.

Rob glanced at his watch. "I need to split. Candi's cooking up something big for me tonight. She's calling it the last supper." He forced a laugh and started down the driveway.

"Hold on." I grabbed the sleeve of his blue work shirt. "Everybody's here by seven tomorrow morning, O.K.? And Sam, you're gonna pick up Yogi on the way over, right?"

Sam nodded and glanced at our drummer. "Be ready by quarter to seven."

"Hey!" Mick interrupted with a clap of his hands. "One of you needs to come by me parents' place tomorrow. I'm staying there tonight."

I shook my head. "Don't do this to me, Mick."

"What? Chill out, mate. Me mum just wants to cook me breakfast before we leave, and I need some clean clothes. Anyway, I'm leaving the car there while we're away."

I should have anticipated this move—Mick idolized his mother and wouldn't leave town without personally saying goodbye—but I hated letting him out of sight right before leaving. But no use arguing with Mick about his mother.

I turned to Rob. "Look, you're gonna be here on time, right?" He nodded. "Good. Now listen, Mick, we'll be by your house at seven-fifteen sharp. You'll be ready, right?"

"Sure, mate. I'll be there at the bleedin' curb with bells on me fuckin' sneakers."

"You'd better be."

He grinned and squinted at me through the thick lenses of his glasses. "Trust me, Mother Hen. Trust me."

✳ ✳ ✳ ✳ ✳

A LARGE CHUNK of a Big Mac disappeared into Mick's mouth. *"Ooh, baby I love your way,"* he gurgled along to Peter Frampton.

Sam slurped a milkshake and shook his head.

The big hand of my Timex told me that we had another half hour to kill before leaving for the party at Sam's friend's house. Rob and Yogi had taken off soon after we'd finished loading the equipment, leaving the three of us to entertain each other, and we weren't doing a good job of it. Even so, we made it through the last side of *Frampton Comes Alive* before finally heading out the door into the starless night.

After dropping Mick's Pinto off at his parents' house, he joined me in the Blue Bomb, and we followed Sam's black Camaro through town. With no idea of where Sam's buddy lived, we stayed close on his bumper. Creedly was a sprawling, messy town, often thick with traffic headed nowhere. Tonight was no different. We slowly wound our way past dozens of strip malls and weary subdivisions, crossed over the river that neatly divided Creedly into two parts, and picked our way through the syrupy cruise circling the dying downtown area before finally leaving the Saturday-night congestion behind. As I drove, Mick fiddled with the radio, switching back and forth between Creedly's two pop-rock stations, first landing on *Disco Duck*, then over to *Let Your Love Flow*, back to the first station for *You Should Be Dancing*, and finally to *Silly Little Love Songs*. When McCartney merged into Manilow's *I Write the Songs*, Mick gave up and switched off the radio.

"Bugger-all, Daniel," he yelled above the constant rattle of the van and its load of equipment. "You should really get an eight-track in this thing. You could get some Roxy or Bowie going, right?"

"I'm just glad it's running O.K.."

We finally chugged up into an area of cheap housing west of downtown and pulled up across from a ranch-style house whose peeling exterior paint and overgrown front yard distinguished it from its neighbors as a rental. ZZ Top's *Tush* blared from the opened front door.

Sam led us into the house and was immediately greeted by three buffed-up guys drinking beer in the darkened living room. Mick and I scanned the room for familiar faces before wandering into the glare of a kitchen jammed with people leaning against the counters, plastic beer cups in hand. I recognized a few of the guys standing around the kitchen table, former football players from high school, dudes whom Sam used to hang out with. One of the girls in the group had been a cheerleader. The kitchen dwellers glanced at us before returning to their conversations.

"The keg must be in the back," I guessed.

We pushed our way through to a sliding glass door leading to a patio. Sure enough, a keg of beer, iced down in a small plastic garbage can, had been set up on the covered patio. Clusters of girls and guys, mostly guys, some smoking cigarettes, some pushing wads of chewing tobacco between cheeks and gums, stood around the keg. We shuffled over to the garbage can, dropped a couple of bucks into a Folger's donation can, pumped the keg a few times, and drew a couple of beers.

"You want to stick around for a while or take off?" I asked Mick. "It looks like jocks and rah-rahs."

"Not so fast, mate." Mick slowly gazed around the patio. He was without his glasses, but that didn't keep him from locating and ogling a long-legged brunette, cold but fetching in short shorts, standing near the keg. "The lager may be cold," he said, "but the birds are hot."

"How do you know? You're blind."

"Ah, Daniel, me lad. I see what I wants to see."

I quickly drained my cup in an attempt to smooth out the jittery high and the cotton-mouth dryness of the uppers. "Don't forget that we've gotta get up early tomorrow." Even as I said it, I knew the mix of intoxicants wouldn't let me sleep for hours.

While we sized up the situation, I noticed a big block-headed guy, one of Sam's high school friends, walking toward us. He clapped a meaty hand on Mick's shoulder, causing Mick to slop beer on his favorite blue Adidases.

"Hey, I know you," the guy said loudly, looking down at

Mick with a blotchy face that seemed to lump and stretch like a ball of Play-Doh. "You're with Sam in the Killjoys, right? You're that freaky singer."

Mick disgustedly shook the beer off his shoes and looked up at him. "Yeah, that's me, ya big yob," he said with a snarl.

I started to edge away, but the guy apparently missed the insult. "Right," he said with a loud laugh, "Big Bob. Ya know me."

I breathed a sigh of relief and tried to drink from my empty cup. Someday Mick was going to get me killed.

"I saw you guys play at Alley's Lounge last month," Big Bob bellowed. "Man, you guys rocked. And you were fuckin' outrageous, like Jagger or somethin'."

Mick's face brightened a bit. Not only did he enjoy being recognized, but he also had a soft spot for anyone who acknowledged his brilliance and noticed the traits he shared with the Stones' singer. "Aye, you're Sam's friend, right? How're you doin'?"

"I'm right on, man." Big Bob slapped Mick's shoulder again. "Where're you guys playin' next?"

I left Mick and Bob together to continue their backslapping and walked over to the keg to get another beer, certain that one more would help the opposing drugs reach a tolerable balance in my nervous system. It was a science that I practiced nightly. By the time I wandered back across the patio, Mick was in the middle of telling Bob about our trip to Puente Harbor, which he was now calling "our tour of the Pacific Northwest."

While Mick and Bob talked, a group of three girls and two guys joined us. One of the girls, a sleek redhead in a tan down vest, gaucho pants, and Dingo boots, put her arm around Bob's waist, barely eliciting a glance from him. The taller of the two guys, a stringy dude with a spotty mustache, took a swig from a pint bottle of Southern Comfort and passed it over to Mick, who was now telling Big Bob stories of life on the road. I couldn't help but smile. Up to this point, the band's road life had consisted of overnight stays in small nowhere-and-gone towns in the mountains surrounding Creedly.

The girl who ended up next to me glanced my way a couple of times while Mick yapped on. I casually sipped my second beer and watched her out of the corner of my eye. She didn't fit the scene and definitely didn't fit the group she was with. Tall and thin, she was dressed all in black. She wore a black T-shirt that blended into a short-waisted black leather jacket hanging too long at the sleeves and dark straight-legged jeans ending at pointy-toed boots. Something was written on the T-shirt, but I couldn't read it. She wasn't from Creedly. No doubt.

I took another sip and stole a look at her face. Her short, straight blonde hair was cut sharply at the jaw the same length all the way around, and she wore little makeup except for black mascara beneath pencil-thin eyebrows. Her pale face was contoured by sharp, high cheekbones, a cute upturned nose, and a rounded chin. I shivered for some reason.

She caught me looking at her.

"Hi," she said, tucking her chin and rolling her brown eyes upward like a child who had just been scolded.

I tried to smile. "Enjoying the party?"

"It's O.K.." I waited for her to say something else, but she paused and then finally motioned with her head toward Mick. "I gather that you two, um, play in a band around here."

"Yeah, four years now." I watched her long fingers tug at the sleeves of her leather jacket. She seemed painfully shy.

"What . . . what do you play?"

"Me? I'm the guitarist." I took a step sideways away from Mick and the others. She edged away with me.

"No," she said. "I mean, what kind of music do you play?" She continued to watch me with tucked chin and upturned eyes. My heartbeat ticked up. I knew it wasn't the drugs.

"Uh"—I tried to unravel my tongue—"oh, you know, we basically do covers. Bad Company, Aerosmith, the Stones, Zeppelin." I took a gulp of beer. "Stuff like that."

She nodded, slowly shaking her bluntly-cut hair. "Hmm, traditional guy stuff."

"Guy stuff?" With a few words and barely a rise in her voice, she had put me on the defensive. Worse, she was right.

"You know, Jagger, Tyler, Plant." She smiled, but only slightly. "A bit, um, misogynistic, wouldn't you say?"

What the hell? Maybe she wasn't so shy. I took another gulp of beer, rolled misogynistic around in my head for a moment, and then looked sideways at her eyes. "Maybe so. But we also do some Roxy Music, T-Rex, Bowie, newer stuff, you know? And we're working on a few of our own songs, too."

"Does he sing them?" she asked with another tilt of her head toward Mick.

"Yeah, Mick's our lead singer. How'd you know?"

Her shy smile grew, but she kept her chin tucked. "Oh, I don't know. The attitude, maybe. He's from England?"

I grinned, and her smile faded.

"What'd I say?" she asked.

"Sorry. I couldn't help it. Mick's accent is fake. He grew up around here."

Her eyes widened. "Really? I *did* think he sounded a bit, um, fraudulent. But what's the point of that?"

"There's no point. He thinks he's Jagger."

She stared at me.

"I'm not kidding. He started faking the accent in high school after seeing *Gimme Shelter* about ten times, and he hasn't stopped since. And he's got those big lips, so Mick fits him. He just wandered into the garage one night when we were practicing, grabbed a mike, and said his name was Mick. His real name's Jack, but nobody calls him that anymore."

"Well. I see. He sounds . . . unusual."

I kept grinning. "That's one way to describe him. But he's good onstage, so we put up with him." By now we had almost edged off the patio and were standing by ourselves. "Speaking of which, you're a little different yourself, if you don't mind me saying."

To my surprise, she reached out and gave my arm a shy poke. "Thanks for noticing. You're not so average yourself, with all that hair. At least not around here. By the way, a lot of women would kill for your hair. Maybe not me, but a lot of them would."

I had to ponder that one for a moment, especially since I had been thinking of cutting my hair. Suddenly I was very interested in this curious girl who wasn't anything close to anyone I'd ever dated, not that there had been many. I realized that I hadn't stopped smiling, an unusual sensation that wasn't altogether pleasurable. "Where are you from? You can't be from Creedly."

"My," she said, batting her eyelashes at me, "you know how to make a girl feel special, don't you? You're right. I grew up in San Francisco, but I'm living in Berkeley now. I'm taking classes at Cal."

"Ah," I murmured. That explained a lot. Berkeley was only two hundred miles south of Creedly, but culturally it was worlds away.

"Betty's my cousin," she said, tilting her chin toward the chubby girl standing next to the Southern Comfort man. "I came up for the weekend to visit her. Betty's boyfriend is a friend of Bob's, and he invited us over."

"Welcome to Creedly. By the way, my name's Daniel."

"I'm Nita."

"Nita," I repeated. She extended her hand and I took it. My heart started beating erratically, the uppers kicked higher by a surge of adrenaline. I looked over Nita's shoulder at Mick, who had the pint of Southern Comfort up to his mouth, his face lit up like a pink house. Returning my eyes to Nita's face, I tried to think of something more to say. Any second she would fall back into the group with her cousin, and all would be lost. Maybe that wouldn't be a bad thing. Still, my heart continued inching its way up my throat. *Breathe*, I told myself. *Keep breathing*.

"Daniel," Nita said softy, interrupting my thoughts. She tucked her chin and looked up at me, her eyes swimming in the light from the porch. Forgetting my mantra, I held my breath and looked into those eyes. Uh-oh. I was in deep shit. She moved closer and whispered, "Would you like to, um, smoke a joint? I brought some good stuff with me from Berkeley."

I released my breath and laughed so loudly that I briefly caught the attention of Mick, Big Bob, and the others. Mick squinted at me and waved, but I turned away from him.

"Now what'd I say?" Nita asked, shrinking back a step. "Was I too forward?"

"No, no." I stifled my laugh. "That's not what I expected you to say."

"What, then?"

"I don't know, but that wasn't it."

"Well, do you?"

"I'd love to."

"O.K. then." Her chin came up. "Is it, um, cool to light up here?"

My grin faded. I looked around the patio. A friend had gotten busted at a party like this a few weeks earlier. Why take the risk? Plus, I wanted to get her away from this crowd. "My van's parked out front. It might be safer there."

She retucked her chin and tugged at her sleeves. "O.K. You're the local."

I led her in an arc around Mick's group, attempting to disappear into the crowded patio, but he saw me when we stopped to refill my beer.

"Daniel, where ya goin', mate?" he yelled across the patio with a stumbling step in our direction. "You need some help with her?"

I hooked Nita's arm and guided her quickly toward the sliding glass door into the house, blinking as we stepped inside the brightly lit kitchen. Sam sat on the other side of the kitchen table engaged in mouth-to-ear conversation with the former cheerleader I had seen earlier. He caught my eye, smiled, and raised his eyebrows while he watched me steer Nita through the kitchen and into the living room.

An Aerosmith album was playing in the darkened room. A muted TV was on, and a silent *Don Kirshner's Rock Concert* was beaming across the room. With Nita beside me, I stopped and watched Toni Tennille bounce along on-screen to Aerosmith's *Walk This Way*, and all notions of reality slid sideways through my brain. The balance of drugs was wrong; science had failed me. Was Nita even real? Was I? I glanced at this girl beside me, and she again tucked her chin and smiled back at me. Toni Tennille took a bow, and the world righted itself again.

＊ ＊ ＊ ＊ ＊

IN THE VAN, I turned on the overhead light and Nita pulled a thinly rolled joint, roach clip, and Zippo lighter from a small, black leather purse that I hadn't noticed before.

"You were ready, weren't you?"

She smiled in a way that made my chest hurt. "You never know what opportunities life will present." She glanced over her shoulder at the equipment jammed behind us. "So you really are in a band. I thought, maybe, it was just a line to get me into the back of your van. I know about you macho rock-star types."

I absorbed her remark without comment, figuring silence was the safest response, and turned off the overhead light. "We're taking off tomorrow morning for a club date in Washington."

"Really? You're serious, then. I like that."

"Well, *I'm* serious. I don't know about the others." I took the lighter and, shielding it with my hand, lit the joint for her. She took a couple of quick puffs to get it going and then took a long drag and handed it to me. I took a deep hit and almost coughed.

"This stuff's strong." I handed the joint back to her.

"I should've warned you. It's Hawaiian. You don't need much of it." She was right. I already felt a buzz coming on. Most of the pot we got in Creedly was cheap stuff from Mexico. Hawaiian weed was pretty exotic, at least by local standards.

"By the way," she said, "where are you guys going in Washington?"

"Puente Harbor. It's west of Seattle somewhere."

"Puente Harbor," she repeated. "I know where it is. My father lives in Seattle. He keeps sending me plane tickets to come up to visit, but I've only gone a few times. We drove over toward Puente Harbor once when I was up there."

"Then you know more about it than I do."

"So why do you do it?" she asked, handing the joint back to me.

"Do what?"

"Play music." Her chin dropped again in that way she had, and she looked sideways at me with a sly smile. "Tell me, is it really just a ploy to get girls?"

I took a smaller hit and exhaled. I was having trouble figuring Nita out, and the combination of the pills, beer, and now the marijuana wasn't helping. My personal science project definitely needed more work. I glanced at her and decided that a flip answer wasn't safe.

"I play in the band for a lot of reasons," I finally answered, hearing Rob's evasive, equivocating tone in my voice.

Her eyes stayed fastened on my face. "I'm curious why. I love the art of creating, of translating something that's inside you, but rock music seems so . . . exploitative." She paused. "That's not the word I was looking for."

"It's close enough," I said, but I wasn't entirely sure I knew what she meant. Exploitive of the musicians or the fans?

"So why, then?"

I tried to give her the obvious answer first. "The band's something that might get me out of this town." I handed the joint to her. "If we're good and lucky."

"But why's that so important to you?"

I stared at her as she took a hit. "Would you want to live here?" I raised my eyebrows. "You're in Berkeley. *Nothing* happens here. At least, nothing good."

She exhaled. "That's not a real answer. Your family must be here."

"My family? I have no fucking family." My hand searched for the outline of the dog tag beneath the fabric of my shirt as I absorbed the upward surge of adrenaline. I tried to push down the harshness but couldn't. "My dad's in L.A. My so-called mother's still here, but that's another reason to leave this bloody place."

I'd startled her. "Oh," she said, pulling in a breath.

Mick's voice had become mine, and I heard Pete Townshend whisper, *Can she see the real you?* God, what was the real me? What did he mean by that? I stared out through the dirty windshield and ground my teeth. The night momentarily lost its focus, and I felt myself slipping away again. . . .

"Daniel?"

I looked at Nita and refocused. "Sorry," I whispered, measuring my breath.

"That's O.K.," she said uncertainly. "I take it you don't get along with her."

"Do you with your bloody parents?" Uh-oh. Mick, again.

Silence. I looked at her and waited, smelling the leather of her jacket mingling with the odor of blue smoke.

"They're split up, too," she finally said. "Maybe we should get back to music."

"Good idea." I closed my eyes, searching for P. D. B. Travers. Keep breathing.

"Tell me why you really play. I want to know."

"I told you." I couldn't keep the edge from my voice, but she wasn't deterred.

"That wasn't an answer. At least, not the entire answer."

"How do you know it's not?"

She tugged at a sleeve and kept her eyes trained on my face. "Daniel, I paint abstracts. It's my way of staying in touch with my inner self. Do you understand? And when I do, when I put the brush to canvas, I sometimes feel something move through me. It's something exhilarating, like, I guess you could say, love might be. Something very pure. Is that what you feel when *you* play?"

I stared back at her across the interior of the van. *Love? Purity?* Good God. My head swam. I concentrated on the glowing end of the joint that was once again in my hand, opened and closed my eyes, and tried to sort through the various voices running through me. I knew she wanted to hear the truth, and I could sense that it was somehow important to her, but I wasn't sure I could articulate what I felt.

"O.K.," I said with a defeated sigh, already knowing that my explanation was doomed to failure. "This may sound silly, but when I'm playing, I can sometimes get to a place where I'm totally inside myself. Like I'm in a little world where it's just me and my guitar, and I'm someone else, floating around above it all."

I suddenly wondered, was that the Real Me? I paused and glanced at her, but she only nodded in response. I took a breath and went on. "And when we're onstage, when we're in a groove, I feel an energy that I don't get anywhere else, like I can almost reach out and touch people, and that they want to connect with me. It's the only time I ever feel that connection. I know it sounds stupid, but it's hard to explain." I suddenly realized that the fingers of my left hand were moving, as if trying to find Pete Townshend's Universal Chord.

And I also realized that I must have sounded like a complete idiot, but she nodded again and seemed to study my face. "Transcendency," she murmured. "I understand."

Transcendency? Could that be it? No, it wasn't that lofty, if I understood her meaning. But what else could I say? That I'm playing music because Kevin didn't stand up to Mom, and now I'm doing it for him? That Pete Townshend resides in my brain, and the only way I can accommodate him is to plug in and bash chords? That music and uppers are the only way I can keep from becoming a total freaking quadropheniac? No, the truth was no good.

I gazed across the space of the engine well separating our two seats. Then I heard Sam's voice in my head: "O.K., maybe you're right," he said for me. "I really do play just to get girls."

She laughed. "I knew it. You guys are all the same."

I breathed out more easily. As usual, marijuana had done its sneaky little job of making us think that things were all right. I mentally thanked Sam and handed the joint back to her. "You need to relight it. Sorry."

She reached down into the purse resting on the floorboard as I turned on the overhead light to help her. When she straightened, the front of her jacket fell open, revealing the words printed on her T-shirt: WATCH OUT, PUNK IS COMING.

"Where'd you get the T-shirt?"

"Do you like it?" Nita had the joint going again and handed it to me. "My older brother lives in New York, and he sent it to me. It's for a new music magazine called *Punk*."

"Punk?"

"Yeah. You know, punk music. Has it made it up here, yet?"

I turned off the light and took a drag on the joint. "Not really," I said, breathing out. "But I've been hearing some interesting stuff on KSAN lately. I can pull it in from San Francisco at night on my home stereo."

Her face became animated. "KSAN? That's what *I* listen to. So you've heard Jonathan Richman and Patti Smith and Richard Hell and Television?"

I grinned back at her. "And the Ramones."

"They're so cool."

"Nobody else listens to KSAN up here," I said, my heart pounding erratically once again. "You're the first person I've found who even knows about those bands."

She grinned. "Well, Daniel, we've got a little secret then. *They* don't know what's coming."

I grinned back at her. "Yeah, and I'm ready for it. Those short stripped-down songs, like what the Who used to do—they're the original punks, y'know?—anyhow, that's what I've been trying to write lately, but the band doesn't like doing 'em." That was an understatement. Yogi liked the song ideas I was bringing in, enjoying the opportunity to bash away, and Rob seemed slightly amused by the vitriol of the lyrics, but the other two saw that my songs would do nothing but drive our audience away. And maybe they were right. After all, how could you dance or party to a song that basically said "Fuck you and your empty-headed values"?

But Pete and the Who knew that rock music had to change to survive. And *I* knew it. From what I knew about punk bands, they saw it the same way: Tear that shit down, strip it away, build it all up new from the bottom. From London to the Lower East Side, they were ready, driven to do that, no matter what it took—what it cost. . . .

Of course they weren't here in Creedly. That left me by myself to ask the inevitable question: What about me? Was *I* ready?

"No," I said, feeling euphoric and agitated at the same time, "the rest of the band doesn't really understand what it's all about."

"Then you'll have to educate them. After all: 'Punk is coming.' " She giggled, stubbed out the roach in the ash tray, and looked toward the house. "Betty probably thinks you kidnapped me. We'd better get back inside."

"I guess you're right." With burning eyes, I gazed across at my new friend, her blonde hair somehow shining in the darkness, and I realized that I was higher than a Bee Gee on helium.

5

I AWOKE FIVE MINUTES before the alarm thinking about Nita, my eyes buzzed wide open by the thought that she was thinking of me this morning. Or was she? The more I thought about it, the more I figured, Not bloody likely. Even so, I rolled up onto the sloshy edge of the waterbed and reached for the bookmark with the phone number she'd pushed into my hand when I left the party. I stuck it inside a Graham Greene paperback that I'd been reading and, after climbing out of bed, jammed the book into a zippered side pocket of my suitcase.

Sam, with Yogi beside him, pulled up in his parents' faded brown station wagon a few minutes before seven. Sam didn't mention the party or Nita, but he gave me a quick wink and grin when he saw me. A few minutes later, Candi dropped off Rob in front of the house while we were loading my bags. With Rob barely out of the car, Candi pulled a U-turn and sped off. Not able to hide his look of relief, Rob ambled up the driveway.

"Everything O.K. with Candi?" I asked. We threw his bags into the station wagon.

"Yeah, she's cool," he replied, glancing in the direction of Candi's exhaust. "And *I'm* cool." He tugged at the brim of his Stetson, putting his I-don't-give-a-shit persona firmly back in place. "Let's get this show on the road."

After locking up the house, I slid into the van beside Yogi as Rob climbed into the station wagon with Sam. We drove the short distance to Mick's parents' house, and I parked on the street while Sam eased up the driveway. Yogi and I watched as Sam strolled up to the front door, where he was met by Mick's mother. After a short discussion, the door shut, and Sam, scowling and muttering to himself, walked over and stuck his head through the passenger-side window of the van. As expected, Mick had just gotten up and was running late. "I'll go in there and drag him out myself if I have to," Sam said, his dark eyes flashing. "I feel like shit, too, but I got up at six so we could hit the road early. I'm giving him a half hour, no more." He stared down the street for a few seconds before stomping back to the station wagon.

While we waited, I kept an eye on the front door, fearing that Mick's father might appear. An evangelical minister who led a fiercely loyal flock of followers, Mick's father had a reputation in town for his theatrical pulpit presence and unpredictability. I had never been within fifty yards of his church, but from a safe distance I'd once witnessed a baptismal session at the Sacramento River that had come perilously close to an organized drowning. And everyone in town had heard about his Elvis-like gyrations and the women swooning at his feet during altar calls. Half of his father's sermons apparently dealt with his son's sinful ways, and Mick worked hard to give him plenty of good material. Mick and his father might have hated each other, but they were alike in one way: From what I'd heard, Mick had stolen most of his stage moves from his old man.

Fortunately, it was Mick, with black-rimmed glasses askew, shirttail hanging from his jeans, and hair glistening wet, who finally emerged through the front door, his mother trailing behind him. Mick held a small suitcase in one hand and a brown lunch bag in the other, reminding me of a little boy being sent off by his mom for his first day of school. He remained on the porch while his mother gave him a smothering hug. Finally, he spun away and staggered toward the station wagon, his mom watching from the porch while he tossed his suitcase into the back of the station wagon. He crawled into the seat behind Sam.

With Mick finally settled in the car, Sam carefully backed the station wagon down the driveway. I started the van and edged away from the curb as Mick's mom waved. But before the station wagon reached the asphalt of the street, I saw it slow. The side rear passenger door popped open.

"Now what?" I sighed, stopping the van with its nose halfway into the street. I checked my side mirror for oncoming traffic.

Suddenly I heard Yogi gasp. "Oh, my God!"

I jerked around and saw Mick leaning out the car door, his head and glasses hanging inches from the surface of the driveway. His mouth opened and out it came: an awful, runny mess that hit the concrete and ran down the driveway. I quickly glanced back at the house, seeing Mick's mom holding a hand over her mouth as if muffling a scream. Suddenly the dark shape of Mick's father appeared in the doorway.

"Oh, shit!" I shoved the van into gear.

With Mick still hanging partway out of the car, Sam quickly backed the station wagon into the street, straightened up, and sped past us. I took one last look at the house, spun the wheel, and took off after the station wagon.

"Did you see their faces?" I said, starting to laugh. I watched Mick edge himself back into the station wagon, pulling the car door shut as he did.

Yogi giggled and sang out, *"Mama told him not to come."*

We caught up with the station wagon at the first stop sign. While Sam waited at the stop, Rob turned in his seat and looked back at us through the rear window of the wagon. He grinned broadly and flashed us the peace sign. Mick was nowhere to be seen.

I wiped tears from my face as we followed Sam the few miles to I-5, which we'd be on for the next 500 miles, and continued to laugh to myself while veering onto the northbound on-ramp. I thought about how little Mick had changed over the years, and as I did, I started to worry about him. Then I started to worry for all of us.

Mick's entry into the band, on a stifling Creedly night in August, came about a year after Rob and I had added Yogi to the mix, officially forming a group. That night we were working our way through *Jumpin' Jack Flash* in the garage of Rob's parents' sprawling ranch-style house, which was tucked into one of the better parts of town. His folks were out, so we had the garage door up, trying to catch whatever breeze might saunter by before one of the neighbors would invariably tell us to shut up. Rob and I had tried trading off the lead vocals, but neither one of us could come close to approximating the sneering tone needed for the song.

"I dunno," I said to Rob, who had just finished another attempt at the vocal. "I'm not sure this song's right for us."

"Like any of the others are?" Rob fingered his bass. "Look, man, I'm cool with kicking these things around for fun, but I never wanted to be a lead singer. And you've got a better voice anyhow."

"Rob's right," Yogi said, red-faced, sweat dripping down onto his snare drum. "You're like, um, that guy in Bread. You know, the *baby I'm-a want you* guy."

As usual, I didn't know what he was talking about, but I knew one thing: I would not be the lead singer. The thought of it turned my blood cold and made my sweat run even hotter. I shifted my guitar strap from one shoulder to the other, wiping my palms against the front of my sweat-splotched T-shirt. I let my eyes roam across the rock posters tacked to the garage walls, lingering for a moment on Grace Slick's face, before looking out into the gathering darkness of the street. That's when I first saw Jack Kelly. He was leaning against the garage door jamb, a smirk plastered on his face, puffy lips parted by the stub of a cigarette. A small, wiry guy about our age, he immediately struck me as someone clinging to a rung on the evolutionary ladder somewhere between Jagger and Steven Tyler.

He squinted back at me. "Nice go," he said. "At least the instrument part. But the singing's a bit wonky."

Wonky? Rob, Yogi, and I exchanged glances. I looked

back at the kid, taking in the dirty shag haircut, tight sleeve-less black T-shirt, and blistered cut-offs, and asked, "Who are you?"

"Me? I'm Jack, mate," he answered, now grinning, "but everyone calls me Mick, as in Jagger, right? Didn't mean to interrupt your show. Just passing by to pick up a pack of fags."

Yogi's acne-marked forehead wrinkled. "Did you say fags?"

"Smokes. Ciggies, right?"

"Oh." Yogi's expression faded to relief, and the bright smile came out. "Are you from England?"

Mick's grin increased in width. "Might as well be, mate. But I live a ways over there, right?" He gestured with his head to the south of us, where the neighborhoods shifted to solid middle class.

I didn't know what to make of him, the funky accent, his street-tough pose, but I knew we didn't need a critic hanging around while we mauled perfectly good songs.

"Well," I said, again shifting the weight of my guitar off my shoulder, "you're welcome to listen if you want, but maybe we should be getting on with it."

I turned to fiddle with the knobs of my amp, but I heard Rob clear his throat. Looking up, I saw that the kid had walked into the middle of the garage and was standing at the mike stand.

"Mind if I have a go at it?" he asked, bobbing on the balls of his tennis shoes and fingering the mike.

"What?"

"That Stones song, mate." He took the mike out of its stand. "I know the words."

"Uh"—I looked over at Rob, who shrugged—"you sing?"

"Bloody right," Mick spit out. "Gotta for the birds, y'know?"

I looked around at the guys again, but I wasn't going to get any help from them. I guessed that he might split if we let him embarrass himself, so I nodded at the kid and said, "What the hell."

I lit into the opening riff. To my surprise, the cocky little guy came in right where he should, with an angry, sneering vocal that, if anything, one-upped Jagger's. Looks flew around the room as my guitar, Rob's bass, and Yogi's drums quickly coalesced around his voice. By the second verse, Mick was working the wall across from us, bouncing and pointing and gesturing as if the faces on the posters were adoring fans. By the end of the song, he had already made us a better band, a realization that was not lost on Rob and Yogi, judging by their stunned expressions. I knew that we had found our singer.

* * * * *

YOGI AND I rattled and shimmied along at 55 mph, staying a comfortable distance behind Sam's station wagon. The Blue Bomb, which earned its nickname by blowing up at inopportune times, wouldn't go much faster, especially when fully loaded, so I settled in for the long haul. I turned on the radio, and we soon had *Reeling in the Years* humming above the sound of the van's slant-six engine, accompanied by the tippity-tap of Yogi's drumsticks on the dashboard.

Creedly disappeared in the rearview mirrors, and I felt good. No need yet for my mood-altering, cross-topped little buddies. Mick's spirited adios on his parents' driveway had loosened me up, and I figured that no matter what happened the rest of the trip, nothing could be more unexpected than that. I also thought about Nita again, and my pulse settled into a comfortable groove with the realization that nothing could be done about her, at least for now.

As we wound up the freeway past Shasta Lake and climbed the long grade toward Mt. Shasta, the scenery slowly changed from rolling oak-studded hills to steep-sided ridges, dotted with evergreens. Yogi offered me a powdered doughnut from a bag his mother had sent with him, and we were eating away when we started losing the radio station from Creedly. I finally turned it off when the static got annoying. In the absence of music, the numbing rattle of the van filled my head. *No vacancy here*, I whispered to myself.

Maybe my whispered words had been audible because Yogi turned his head and gave me a quizzical look. Powdered sugar ringed his mouth like clown makeup. I grinned and sighed. Christened Edward Leonard, Yogi had an awesome talent for searching out and destroying food—an ability that hadn't escaped Mick, who had gleefully compared him to the picnic-basket-stealing cartoon bear. My grin faded with the nagging realization that my future, at least in part, rested on the erratic skills of this grown-up adolescent. I shook my head and started thinking about the vial in my pocket.

A half-hour later we rounded a long curve at the top of another steep grade, and suddenly Mt. Shasta burst into view, rising straight up from the plateau surrounding its base. The sight of the massive mountain startled me, adding to my sudden feeling of gloom. The upper slopes of the mountain were still white from last winter's snow, and the 14,000-foot peak disappeared into clouds swirling around its top.

After passing through the town of Mt. Shasta situated near the base of the mountain, I picked up a weak radio station coming from somewhere north of us. Country-western—Conway Twitty, I guessed—but it would have to do for now. With the scenery spreading out in the desertlike sameness of the high plateau, Yogi slumped down into his seat and closed his eyes. The view of Mt. Shasta still dominated the reflection in my side mirrors, and I heard Yogi begin to snore.

I took one last look at the mountain in my mirror. I had been too young to join them at the time, but Kevin and my father had climbed to the mountain's top the summer before

Kevin was drafted. The memory jolted me. Had that been the last time I'd been happy, that summer? I know it was the last time for my father. My mom? Who knows? She had always been uptight and critical, but Kevin had at least kept her human. When Kevin left us—with my dad still arguing that he could get a conscientious objector deferment, and my mom still holding firm that it would be an unbearable embarrassment to the family—I didn't realize that the thread holding us together was about to snap.

Yogi took the wheel in Ashland, shortly after we passed into Oregon. I sagged down into the ripped passenger seat and tried to sleep, but the possibility of dozing off was way behind me, somewhere back on the other side of Mt. Shasta. Instead, my closed eyes found the image of Dad and Kevin, spilling into the house with their hiking gear and boots, laughing, triumphant. They had made it to the top. Kevin, I remembered, had flung his duffel bag to the floor and swept Mom into a swirling hug. She pushed him away, interested only in examining the gaping rip at the knee of Kevin's jeans. Kevin ignored her and found me, putting me into a headlock while telling me how he'd get me up the mountain the next year—carry me himself, if he had to.

Nearly four months later, Kevin had stood in virtually the same spot in the living room, his possessions in the same ragged duffel bag, telling me how he'd be back real soon to get me to the top of the mountain. I watched him move to the door to say goodbye to Mom and Dad. Dad, looking uncertain, reached out to shake Kevin's hand, but Mom shoved between them, concerned about a small stain on the leg of Kevin's khakis. Watching her dab at it furiously with a wet cloth, my brain had imploded, all notions of what love and family meant collapsing inward. Kevin was on his way to boot camp and the swamp of Vietnam, but Mom was more worried about how his clothes looked. That's when it started, or when it ended, or maybe both.

Even now, as that image of her trying to clean the spot from Kevin's pants danced across the back of my eyelids, the memory caused every vein in my head to contract.

Opening my eyes, I glanced into the side mirror. I knew the mountain was behind us, way too far back to see, but somehow I saw the white outline of Mt. Shasta etched into the glass. I shifted my gaze back to the road ahead of us.

6

TRAVELING ALONG Washington's Highway 101, now two days out of Creedly, with Rob dozing beside me in the passenger seat of the van, I followed the station wagon between the misty beginnings of the Olympic Range on our left and the open water of Hood Canal on our right. As we moved north with Olympia and the long miles of I-5 behind us, the sunlight weakened and the air cooled. I tried to recall Nita's face, but it seemed like years since she had turned at my van and walked back to the party. I wondered what she saw in me, if she'd seen anything at all. . . .

The closer we got to Puente Harbor, the more I fretted and worried. This was the part of my personality that I'd come by naturally. The anxiety, the depression, the burning in the pit of my stomach—it was all mine. One of the great things about Townshend, as I'd found out in that *Creem* piece, was that he went through the same thing. The problem for both of us was in thinking too much, analyzing, dissecting, then dismembering and ripping at every memory, good and bad. The problem was this compulsion for meaning, the notion that every action, every creation, hell, every breath must contain truth. Unfortunately life, in all its fractured, trivial detail, didn't work out that way; and so when our memories smothered us, our intentions degenerated, our creations failed, they had to be taken apart and then destroyed. Why did Townshend smash his guitar after every show? Why did he fight Daltrey onstage? Was it all just show? No, I figured that it had to be Townshend's overwhelming urge to destroy what he saw as his imperfect creation. And what did I have? For me, all the fury shot straight back at myself and the voices ricocheting around my head. . . .

Gripping the van's steering wheel, I felt a wave of dizziness come over me, and I realized I'd been holding my breath. O.K., O.K. . . . just let go and keep breathing. That was my mantra, but it didn't always work, just like Pete's embrace of the teachings of Meher Baba, his silent Indian spiritual master, couldn't keep him from sliding off into alcoholism and fighting with his bandmates. My personality being what it was, I'd gravitated toward uppers, the substance that pushed me furthest away from myself, toward where I would ultimately find the Real Me.

And lately I had something else. In my clearest moments I saw that the songs I was starting to write could do the same thing as the uppers. Like my pills, each song was an angry, bitter thing but also a perfect little gem of the self that resided within the Real Me, the part that might die if exposed to light. Blunt, brutal, nihilistic, they were about as close to the truth as I could get.

As I mulled all this over, I'd let the front right tire of the van drift onto the shoulder, kicking up gravel and dust. I pulled back onto the pavement but not before Rob jerked up.

"Hey, Daniel. You cool, man?"

"Just lost my concentration for a second."

His body relaxed back into the seat. "Just checking."

"Rob."

"Yeah?" He rubbed his eyes before flexing his fingers on the ceiling of the cab.

"I've been thinking." I cracked the window and lit a cigarette. The outside air temperature had cooled considerably since the last time I'd checked. "I'd like to play some of my songs—some of the new ones I've been working on—but I need you to back me up with the guys."

Rob's eyebrow went up. "You talking about the ones you showed us in practice awhile back? You want to play them this week?"

"Maybe. Yeah."

"Didn't the Denver dude say we should stick to covers?"

I glanced over at him. Rob wasn't going to tell me what he really thought about the songs. "I think we could sneak in a few originals. We're playing five sets. If we dropped one or two in, nobody'd notice."

Rob tugged at the brim of his Stetson. "Maybe so, but you know Mick. He won't want to sing 'em. You heard him at practice. He was griping about them having no melody."

"You agree with him?"

Rob shrugged.

I squinted through the rear window of the station wagon at Mick's bobbing shaghead. Rob was right. The songs were more like high-speed rants, driven fast by distorted guitar chords and bashing drums. Mick had little room to sing the lyrics, which were admittedly pretty pissy. When I'd brought in one of them, a song called *Thrill*, a few weeks back, Mick had mumbled his way through the words, eventually declaring, "This is about your bloody life, idn't it? *'They killed my brother, they messed up my mother.'* Who the shit cares?" Sam had pretty much the same opinion, telling me, "Nobody's gonna understand this, Daniel. People wanna shake their butts, not get kicked in the head by some bitchy song." Only Rob and Yogi had seemed interested, but they were willing to let the song go when the others protested. I felt the anger return when I recalled how quickly they had dismissed my song and the others I'd brought in earlier.

Rob suddenly grinned at me. "Maybe you should sing 'em."

"What?"

"You sang them in practice when you showed 'em to us."

"No way," I sputtered, my right hand suddenly at the dog tag beneath my shirt. The thought paralyzed me. I couldn't even introduce a song without stuttering. "I've heard my voice on tape."

Rob laughed. "You're not that bad, man. C'mon. It'd be cool. You'd reduce the Mickster to playing tambourine."

I eased off the accelerator. "Look, Rob, I'm not the lead

singer, O.K.? I don't have the voice. And I know I don't have the looks."

Rob shook his head. "You've gotta get off the speed, man. You're getting paranoid. Your voice is fine. And I don't know about your looks, but I don't think you'd scare off small children. Why are you so freaked out about singing a couple of songs? Hell, even Townshend sings some of his. And how about the way *he* looks?"

"Let's just drop it, Rob. I'm not singing them."

"Whatever, man. It's your call. They're your songs."

"Forget I brought it up." What was I thinking? Of course Mick wouldn't sing them. He didn't do anything he didn't want to do. My idea was an imperfect creation: Kill it quickly.

Rob settled back in his seat and returned the brim of the Stetson to its position over his eyes. I slipped a couple of cross-tops from the vial in my pocket and washed them down with a swallow of flat Coke. Twenty minutes later I felt better, but my quick surrender continued to eat at me. I knew from what I'd read that Pete Townshend would literally come to blows with Roger Daltry to get his way with the Who, as he did when he punched Daltry in the middle of a rehearsal for their *Quadrophenia* tour, but I wasn't up to battling Mick. I needed him to front the band. Without him, we were going nowhere. I was going nowhere.

I suddenly felt the need to change the conversation I was having with myself, and the jolt from the pills made me want to talk out loud. I looked across at Rob, who seemed way too relaxed for his own good. Maybe it was because he was away from Candi. For two days, he hadn't said a word about her, which had got me wondering about what was going on with them. I'd seen him sneak off to a phone booth outside a café near Portland the night before, but he hadn't stayed in it long enough to have a conversation.

At least on the surface, Rob and Candi seemed like a perfect match, kind of like a smarter version of Rod Stewart and Britt Ekland, but I was beginning to seriously worry that eventually Candi was going to play Yoko to Rob's John, as Mick had jokingly suggested a few nights earlier. And I wasn't sure who would win if Rob's choice ultimately came down to the band or Candi. But maybe I was worrying needlessly. And, anyhow, who knew what Rob was thinking? Would Rob even tell his best friend, who I liked to think was me, if something major was about to go down in his private life?

I glanced at him again. "Hey, Rob."

The Stetson slid back and he yawned. "Yeah?"

"So, what's up with—" I stopped myself. The cross-tops had a sneaky way of loosening my tongue, of getting me to talk about stuff that was better left unsaid, and I knew Rob wouldn't want to go where I wanted to take the conversation. He was already pretty touchy about Candi, and in my amphetamine-altered state, I figured the best I could do would be to piss him off. I lit another cigarette and slipped the match into the ash tray.

Rob pushed himself upright. "Yeah? What's up with what?"

"Nothing, man. It's not important."

Rob squinted at me, but I avoided his eyes. "You got something on your mind?" he asked. "You still thinking about your songs? I really think you should try singing them."

"No, it's not that." I took a drag on the cigarette to better focus my thoughts and decided that I shouldn't be afraid to ask Rob a simple question. "I was just wondering what was going on with you and Candi."

"With Candi? What do you mean?" Rob's voice had suddenly gone flat.

I glanced at him and then back at the road ahead of me. "I dunno. It's just that I've been getting the impression that things aren't too cool between you guys right now. Like maybe Candi's been giving you a lot of grief about going on this trip." I gave him another quick glance. "But if it's none of my business, just tell me to shut up."

Rob tugged at his hair, and his eyes rotated from me to the passing scenery. "Look, Daniel," he said into the glass of the window, "I'll be honest with you. Candi doesn't think the band's going anywhere, that we're just wasting our time. She just basically thinks it's a dead end for me."

I willed my pulse to slow and proceeded carefully. "So what do *you* think?"

His face turned back toward me. "Shit, I don't know. I'm just processing it, man. But I still like playing, if that's what you mean." He started to say something else but stopped.

"That's cool," I said, nodding. "But, look, I think Candi's wrong. I really think this gig's gonna lead to bigger things. But I feel for you. Girlfriends . . . shit." I shook my head.

"It's no big deal," he said, shrugging, but the strain on his face told me how badly he was being squeezed by Candi. And I still sensed that he was holding something back, not telling me everything about his problems with her.

Seeing Sam's station wagon slow to round a corner, I downshifted. We were now veering west along the top of the Olympic Peninsula. "I think we're getting close to Puente Harbor. Fifty miles, maybe."

Rob slumped back down and returned the brim of the Stetson to its position over his eyes. "Well, let me know when we're there."

I took that as my cue to let the conversation drop. We rode on in silence for another hour before the station wagon began to slow. I eased off the accelerator and looked ahead at a road sign: WELCOME TO PUENTE HARBOR—POPULATION 25,500.

"We're here," I announced.

Rob tipped his hat back and leaned forward. "About fucking time."

7

WITH THE STATION WAGON now following behind us, we rolled into Puente Harbor on the highway running east to west through town along the waterfront. Rob cracked his side window, letting a strong breeze coming off the Strait of Juan de Fuca fill the van. I shivered and glanced at the grimy industrial port buildings off to our right and the weathered motels and littered lots to our left. My spirits dropped. Was this it, the rest of the world? Thankfully, my little cross-topped buddies kept my spirits from being completely smothered by the damp malaise thrown off by the town.

To my eyes, Puente Harbor looked vaguely familiar, like one of those tired, old fishing villages perched lonely above California's north coast, only this town was bigger and messier. The community appeared working-class poor, and I wondered what kept it alive. It couldn't be the rock 'n' roll scene. Maybe logging and commercial fishing. Maybe spending by tourists passing through on their way to the Olympics or Victoria. The thought crossed my mind that the town seemed like everything else in America these days, broken down, kept barely alive by dying industries. It was obsolete, just like all those out-of-date American-made cars being pushed aside by Japanese imports.

Rob's head rotated from one side of the road to the other. "You sure Hendrix and Heart played here?"

"That's what Astley said. At the Mai Tai Hotel." I looked out across the harbor as the buildings gave way to open water. "What's *puente* mean, anyhow? Do you know?"

"Sam said it means bridge in Spanish." His eyes followed mine across the harbor.

"I don't see one. Figures." I turned my eyes back toward the town. "Man, this place looks grim."

"Maybe it gets better when you get into the main part of town." Rob sounded dubious. "You know where it is?"

"First Street. It's gotta be somewhere to the left."

We approached a major intersection with Washington Street, and I turned off the highway. Sam stayed right behind me. The late Monday afternoon traffic was light and few people were on the sidewalks. The street took us straight downtown, which was crowded with two-story brick and wood-sided buildings, including a hardware store, a hole-in-the-wall shoe repair business, a couple of coffee shops, a few glum-looking real estate offices, a Salvation Army store, and an old theater playing *Rocky*.

At the next intersection, I stopped at a red light and peered up at the cloudy hills rising from the backside of the downtown area. The highway and the main streets paralleling the highway ran across a narrow flat bordered on the south by rolling hills climbing toward the Olympic mountains and on the north by the Strait of Juan de Fuca. Most of the town's houses appeared to be clustered along a patchwork of streets cut into the hills, rising higher and higher until the homes and streets disappeared into the evergreens. Reaching these neighborhoods apparently required driving up steep roads or climbing sets of concrete pedestrian stairs that I now saw rising between buildings along the cross streets.

"This is it," Rob said, pointing at a street sign.

"What?"

"First Street, man."

I guessed about the direction and turned right. Luck was still with me. Within three blocks we found the Mai Tai Hotel, an imposing old structure, redbrick and three stories high, sitting placidly at the base of a hill on a street of half-deserted shops and old flop-house hotels. With darkness coming on fast, I parked alongside the Mai Tai, and for a moment Rob and I sat silently in the van gazing up at the decaying pattern of brick and mortar rising into the gloom of Puente Harbor.

Hearing the voices of Sam, Mick, and Yogi spilling from the station wagon behind us, I swung out of the van and nearly bumped into a utility pole. Stapled to the pole was a poster announcing an upcoming concert at the county fair-grounds: A big red Valentine with the name HEART scrawled inside.

"Hey, Rob, check this out."

He came around the van and looked at the poster. "Huh, that's a weird coincidence. Too bad they're playing the day we're leaving. Might've been fun to go."

My spirits rose. "I guess Astley was right about this being Heart country. Maybe they'll stop by and check out our show Saturday night."

"Dream on, man."

We joined the others, who had migrated to the front of the hotel, and looked up the three steps leading to the double-wide glass doors and large plate-glass windows. Closed blinds hid the interior of the hotel and bar from the sidewalk outside. Tarnished bronze lettering affixed to the brick front advertised its amenities:

THE MAI TAI HOTEL

QUALITY ACCOMMODATIONS

FINE DINING AND DANCING

Next to the door, a large, hand-lettered sign was taped to the inside of the window.

LIVE MUSIC

TUESDAY–SATURDAY

9:00 TO 2:00

$2 COVER, 2 DRINK MINIMUM

Right below the sign, crudely taped to the window with masking tape, was a photo backed by hot-pink paper. We crowded up onto the sidewalk to check it out. It was us. Our eight-by-ten publicity photo had been duplicated by Big

Country Productions, and our name and their logo were printed at the bottom of the picture. NOW APPEARING had been
scrawled across the top of the pink paper and FROM CALIFOR-
NIA was written across the bottom under our name.

For a few silent moments, we stared at the photo and it
stared back at us: five young guys trying to look tougher than
they were.

Mick, who had pulled the hood of his purple sweatshirt
up over his head, leaned closer and squinted at the photo.
Then he let out a whoop. "The Killjoys from California.
We're bloody stars!" He did a little hopping dance around
us before noticing that we weren't joining in. "What's with
you geezers?"

"Looks like a wanted poster," Rob observed, expressing
what the rest of us felt.

Leaving the photo behind, we straggled into the dark
lobby of the hotel and stood inside the doorway, trying to
get our bearings while our eyes adjusted to the darkness. I
squinted down at the stained red carpet covering the lobby's
floor and wondered why all the blinds were drawn.

The deep, narrow lobby contained a small check-in
desk, with old-fashioned wooden mail slots behind it.
Farther down the lobby, along the left side of the wall, I
saw soft drink and cigarette vending machines glowing in
the semidarkness. An elevator and stairs were cut into the
wall across from the vending machines. Foghat's *Slow Ride*
seeped through padded green swinging doors on the right
that apparently led to the bar.

Astley had told me that the place was owned by someone
named Mr. Tom, but where was he? The lobby was empty,
so I walked through an open doorway immediately to the left
of the check-in desk and found myself in a small restaurant.
Some sort of food stewed in a kitchen off the back of the
restaurant. I looked around. No Mr. Tom—no one else for
that matter.

I stepped back into the lobby where the other guys stood clustered in front of the desk. They looked uneasy, as if afraid someone might get picked off by a predator if he strayed too far from the herd.

In spite of my own nervousness, I grinned. "Loosen up, guys. It's not haunted. I'm gonna check the bar. I'll let you know if I see any ghosts."

I pushed my way through the heavy, swinging doors, and my eyes started spinning trying to take in an even-darker room. Before the doors had even swung shut behind me, I was hit by the odor of stale cigarette smoke and beer, and something that unexpectedly smelled like aftershave lotion. Was it . . . Old Spice, my dad's favorite?

My eyes adjusted to a surprisingly spacious room. I sensed the bar counter off to my left, but I stood just inside the doorway and took in the scene. Straight ahead, a maze of round tables covered much of the bar's worn, hardwood floor. Chairs were stacked upside down on the tables. On the far side of the jumble of tables, a large, rectangular area of floor, scuffed and stained, had been left clear. Apparently the dance floor. On the other side of the dance floor, a wide plywood platform rose a few feet off the floor. The stage. *Our* stage. A green neon sign advertising Ranier Beer glowed on the wall behind it.

The walls of the room held nothing else, or so it seemed. To my right, yellowed blinds covered the windows overlooking the sidewalk, and flat black paint covered everything else, including the ceiling, the restroom doors on the left, and the load-in doors to the right of the stage. A disco ball dangled over the dance floor. Except for the disco ball, it was like being in the hull of a dank, old ship.

Then I had a déjà vu sensation. And I knew what it was. The bar looked just like the Marquee must've appeared in '64 when the Who played it. Of course, I'd never been there, and maybe the Marquee was nothing like the Mai Tai, but

I had played the Marquee somewhere in my dreams, and I was certain it had the same smell, the same feel. The Who had used their Tuesday-night gigs at Soho's Marquee Club to build a huge following of Mods, young, style-conscious Londoners tripping on uppers and maximum R&B who adopted the Who as their own. Maybe we could do the same thing here at the Mai Tai.

Slam!

I looked left, toward the long wooden bar that dominated most of the room's back wall. Two young men and a woman sat together on bar stools playing liar's dice.

Bam! The man sitting nearest me again slammed the dice cup down on the lacquered top of the bar's wide counter and then tilted the cup to peer at the dice. He and his companion looked as if they'd just rolled off the same fishing boat. One wore a hooded gray sweatshirt, stained jeans, and heavy work boots; the other a faded red cap, flannel shirt, and blue overalls. His wind-burned face was partly obscured by bushy sideburns that almost met at his chin. The woman sat disinterestedly beside them, smoking a cigarette and peeling the label from a beer bottle.

A middle-aged Asian man was behind the bar. He contrasted sharply with his three customers. His hair was neatly cut, parted on the side, and his white Oxford shirt and grey slacks were nicely pressed. Not a wrinkle on him. A clean white apron was tied around his pencil-thin waist. He leaned against the back counter of the bar, arms folded and eyes half shut. I walked over to the bar, and he turned his head toward me.

"Can I getcha drink?" he asked without moving anything other than his lips. The woman's head turned my way.

"I'm looking for Mr. Tom."

"I'm Tom. Who're you?"

"I'm Daniel Travers with the Killjoys."

Mr. Tom tilted his head as if he hadn't heard me. I tried again. "I'm with the band playing here tomorrow night. The

Killjoys? Rick Astley of Big Country Productions sent us. He said that you'd give us rooms."

His expression suddenly changed. He smiled, but it was one of those here-today-gone-tomorrow kind of expressions. "Yes, yes. Killjoys. You're early. Good. Two rooms. Yes, yes." He stiffly extended his arm across the bar, and we awkwardly shook hands. A cloud of Old Spice drifted by my head. Now I knew who was drenched in aftershave lotion.

The guy with the bushy sideburns paused with the dice cup raised above the bar. "Always plenty of rooms here at the Mai Tai. Used to be the best whorehouse in town before the cops busted it. Now it's just the second best."

I forced a laugh that I knew sounded unnatural. Maybe this place was nothing like the Marquee. "We've never played a whorehouse before," I said, forcing bravado. "Might be interesting."

The guy smiled and went back to his game. As he did, the woman swiveled toward me, unraveling herself like a cat, and pushed back the long, black hair hanging over her left eye. Her face was gaunt, like a model's, and she had the sleepy-eyed look of someone who spent most of her time in bars. She was dressed in a white lace-up blouse that was anything but laced at the top. Farther down, she had on skintight jeans tucked into brown boots with thick crepe soles.

"Aren't you a little young to be in here?" the woman asked, her voice raspy, cigarette-burned, her sleepy-eyed gaze sharpening as her eyes moved up and down over me.

I wasn't sure how to reply, so I kept my mouth shut, already feeling that maybe I *was* too young to be in here. I took a closer look at her. Contrary to her world-weary appearance, she wasn't that much older than me, perhaps a couple of years. Unlike the two guys with her, who looked like the kind of semiharmless losers you'd find in any bar anywhere, she looked out of place. Maybe it was the calculating look in her eyes, like a tiger watching its prey without twitching a whisker, hungry but watchful. In a flash, I suddenly saw a younger and more lurid version of Mrs. Robinson sitting before me.

As if on cue, she leaned forward on the bar stool, letting the top of her blouse hang open. At the same time, she stubbed out her cigarette and moistened the filtered end of another with the tip of her tongue. "So you're one of Astley's bands, huh?"

"You know Rick Astley?" I said, surprised that she would know our agent, who was based three states away.

"Yeah, I know him," she answered sharply. "He comes by to check out the bands once in a while. And you guys better be an improvement over the last band he sent out. A bunch of lightweights. You guys are gonna have to rock if you wanna play this place."

The two men stopped their game long enough to look over at me and grin.

I glanced at Mr. Tom, but he seemed to defer to this woman. Her tone suggested that her role here was something other than a typical barfly. But who was she? As my eyes drifted back to her, I tried to think of a clever comeback but failed. The view down the front of her blouse was distracting. "Yeah, well, I think we're pretty good."

"I bet you are," she said, seeming to know where my eyes had gone. She smiled, an unnerving, leering expression that made me hold my breath for a moment. "And I'll be back tomorrow night to check you out."

Christ. Was it my imagination or was she coming on to me? I looked at the two guys again, both still grinning at me. Shifting my eyes back to the woman, I sensed, maybe hoped, that she was just one of those hard-ass kind of women who get off on playing head games with guys, especially in front of other people. Either way, she was making me nervous. To my relief, Mr. Tom finally cut her off with a wave of his arms. "Come, come, come. Rooms, rooms."

He pulled up a hinged side section of the bar and stepped through. With a sideways glance at the woman, I followed Mr. Tom out the bar doors and back into the lobby, where the guys were scattering to let him get through to the check-in desk. A cloud of aftershave trailed him.

"Two rooms. You boys get two rooms." He paused and smiled in turn at Mick, Rob, Sam, and Yogi. "You good boys?"

The guys glanced at me and nodded. "Yeah, sure."

Mr. Tom lifted two sets of keys from the pegs next to the mail slots. Keys hung from virtually all of the other pegs. He gave the room keys to me, and I waited, expecting to fill out a registration card. Instead, he motioned the guys over to the desk. He smiled again and raised his right hand, extending five fingers. "You play five night, five hours."

We nodded dumbly.

"Nine to two. Fifteen-minute breaks. O.K.?"

"No problem," I answered, "that's what we usually play at clubs. By the way, do we get paid after each night or at the end of the week? Astley said we'd get our rooms and $750 for the week, right?"

Mr. Tom either didn't understand me or chose to ignore the questions. "You good boys, O.K.? I lock the doors at three. You don't come back late. Elevator no good. Use stairs. You be good boys." I wasn't sure if it was a question or a command. He smiled again. And then he was gone, back through the swinging bar doors, leaving a vapor trail of Old Spice like some old buccaneer.

We walked outside to get our bags from the station wagon.

"Man, that was weird," Rob said. "I hope we've got this money thing right."

"Don't sweat it," I said. "I'm sure it'll get handled just like every other place we've played."

But something in the eyes of the woman sitting at the bar told me that the Mai Tai was unlike any other place we'd ever played before.

* * * * *

WE FOUND OUR two rooms after climbing the lobby stairs to the second floor. The rooms weren't next to each other, or, for that matter, even on the same corridor.

The floor was laid out like a T, with the stairwell located at the bottom of the T. We found the first room adjacent to the stairwell, and then we walked along the patchy green carpet, past five rooms on each side of the corridor, before reaching the hallway branching right and left. The other room was the fourth down the left corridor. The hotel's heavy, musty smell reminded me of an old lady's house that had been closed up for the winter, and I doubted that many of the rooms in between ours were being used.

The room next to the stairwell held a queen-sized bed and a roll-away, the other, two twin beds. Both rooms were "bleedin' grotty" in Mick's words: dark, grimy, TV-free, phoneless boxes. After touring the rooms, we stood in the hall discussing sleeping arrangements, but Rob quickly decided the matter. "I want one of the twin beds. Nothing personal, but I'm not sharing a bed with one of you guys." He turned and started down the hallway to the room around the corner.

"I'm with Rob," Yogi said over his shoulder as he fled down the hallway. "You'll be partying all night. I need to get my sleep."

"Arseholes," Mick yelled after them.

The three of us trooped down the hallway like children disciplined and banished to their rooms. We stood in the middle of ours, looked at the two beds, and then looked at each other. "Rob's right," Sam said. "I ain't sharing no bed." We flipped a coin for the beds, which we agreed would rotate among the three of us during the week. I won the queen; Sam got the roll-away for the first night. Mick was on the floor in one of the sleeping bags we'd been smart enough to bring along.

With my victory in hand, I walked into the bathroom to use the toilet, eyeing the unfamiliar facilities. An old porcelain sink, stained around the drain, stood next to a grungy toilet that flushed with a yank of a chain hanging from the tank. Mom would *not* like this place, I thought, which brought a smile to my face. I gingerly pushed aside the yellowed curtain hiding the shower stall and my smile faded. "Hey! You guys gotta check this out."

Mick and Sam pushed their way into the bathroom. I held the shower curtain back so that they could see the huge mildew spot growing in the middle of the back wall of the shower. The greenish center spread and diffused to a sort of blackish brown at the edges. The wall was starting to collapse inward at the center of the foot-wide stain.

"Somebody get a gun," Sam said.

I let the shower curtain fall back into place. "Nice accommodations, huh?"

"Just lovely," Mick replied, pulling his hood back over his head. "Can we go home now?"

8

I PUSHED BACK my plate of scrambled eggs and fried potatoes. I wasn't quite full, but the bitterness of something green that had been chopped and added to the eggs dampened my appetite.

With the remnants of uppers burning away in my nervous system and no alcohol to counteract their effects, I had slept fitfully, my mind ticking off an endless list of worries. We needed to unload the equipment, set it up, run a soundcheck, play through the new songs, figure out how to extend some of the solos to fill five hours, get the set list straightened out. And the hotel hadn't helped my sleep. Floorboards creaked, and I thought I heard voices above us, but I may have been dreaming. Oh, yeah, and the room smelled like a wet shoe. Mick didn't seem to sleep any better on the floor, tossing and turning in his sleeping bag. Only Sam succumbed to the bliss of unconsciousness, snoring softly most of the night.

During my few moments of sleep, I had dreamed of Pete Townshend and his damn perfect chord. Over and over and over he played it, shouting, *Can you see the real me?* Behind him stood the woman from the bar, grinning conspiratorially. I remembered straining to figure out the chord he was playing, but I couldn't make out the tangle of fingers and strings, just like I couldn't untangle the voices and impulses that made up the Real Me. Especially with that woman grinning at me. I was better off awake.

Now I sat in the hotel restaurant, still trying to wake up. I nursed my third cup of coffee, feeling like I was practicing to be old. The restaurant was empty. Maybe it had something to do with the time, almost 11:30 in the morning, but maybe it had something to do with the food.

Yogi, who had been missing all morning, joined us half-way through and ordered his second meal of the day. Before ordering, he had pulled off his plaid hunting jacket, revealing a Cal sweatshirt.

"Boy, you guys sure sleep a long time," he said, smiling away like a kid at a carnival. "I was up at seven." He had already said the same thing three times. Mick squinted at him over the cup of coffee he was desperately gripping between his hands.

"Yeah," Yogi continued, his rusty crewcut looking redder than usual, "it was a beautiful morning." I feared he was about to break into that Young Rascals song.

"Was it?" Mick asked dryly. "Sorry we slept through it."

"Totally beautiful. The fog burned off and the sun came through. And I had a great breakfast at that coffee shop down the street on the corner. Pancakes, eggs, hash browns, orange juice. It was great. And the place was really friendly, especially my waitress."

Yogi was absolutely wired, his eyes big and bright. He didn't drink coffee, so it must've been the sugar from the pancakes he had eaten earlier and the milkshake he was now working on.

Rob, Sam, and I shoved some dollar bills and the check toward Mick. "It's your turn. Have fun with the bear."

* * * * *

ROB AND I stretched out our legs and leaned back against the hard slats of the unvarnished bench. Gazing out at the choppy ocean, we listened to the rhythmic lapping of the waves against the wooden dock. I put down my book and grasped the collar of my Army surplus jacket, pulling it closer to my throat, wishing that I'd brought something heavier and warmer. I felt the smooth metal of the dog tag against the skin of my chest.

While we killed time until dinner, the other guys were off hunting down a music store for Sam, who needed backup reeds for his sax. Mick had also mentioned something about looking for Bowie's latest album at a record store we'd seen coming into town. They wanted to explore the town; I wanted to collect my thoughts. I knew I wouldn't relax until we played the first night. We had spent most of the afternoon unloading the van, setting up the equipment, sound-checking, and running through some songs. The brief rehearsal had gone well, and we were all happy with the warm acoustics of the lounge, which smoothed the rough edges of our sound. We were ready to play. But now we waited. This was the part of being in the band that I hated.

Against the backdrop of a fog bank developing offshore, I saw something, maybe a seagull, bobbing on the water thirty yards away. Turning my head, I focused on the long point of land that curved out into the strait, protecting the harbor. Sally's Hook. That's what the road sign called it.

This was where our music had finally taken us, and it was a lonely place: the mocking lap, lap, lap of crazy dreams at the edge of the world. I suddenly wondered if there ever could be salvation through music. My mind drifted to the original quadropheniac, Townshend's alter ego, Jimmy, perched high on a rock in the ocean, waiting for a wave to take him, to wash over him, like the perfect chord that would wash over us all. It hadn't. And like Jimmy, I knew even if I sat out on Sally's Hook forever, that ocean would never take me.

My brother, Kevin, had called me "Mr. Spaceman" whenever I slipped into one of my moods, but then Kevin never had a melancholy moment in his life. He was the eternal good vibe, believing in all those hippie-dippy '60s notions like give peace a chance, love being just a kiss away, all you need is love. He didn't understand other people's fears, and he didn't understand why I would crawl inside myself until the darkness lifted. He was always confident in the ultimate outcome, the ability of the unified human spirit to triumph over our worst instincts. How wrong he was.

It was during one of my moods when Kevin gave me my first guitar—a cheap nylon-stringed acoustic that he'd received as a Christmas gift—and suggested, laughingly, that I take it and use it to get in touch with myself.

After Kevin's head got blown off along the Cambodian border, my moods deepened, especially on Friday nights. For a full year after we got the news about Kevin, I couldn't face going out, and I couldn't stay in the family room with my parents, waiting for the fight that would inevitably break out, so I would go to bed early, shut off the lights, and turn on the radio. I would lie there with my eyes closed, the radio near my head, listening to whatever came on the AM rock station. If I was lucky, something like the Who's *See Me, Feel Me* would start playing, and I would forget about myself and free-fall through the musical darkness. I was no longer Daniel Travers. I became Tommy, that kid in the song, float-ing through space, out of touch, out of mind. *Listening to you, I get the music.* Those were the good nights. But that was before I discovered cross-tops, before I became Dr. Daniel, medicating myself out of the trough of my later depression.

Rob shifted position on the bench, and I again pulled my coat tighter. I knew I needed to fill the emptiness now before it became complete and the voices arrived. I looked down at my paperback and fingered the bookmark that Nita had given me. I thought about her, about calling her, but the thought made me nervous.

I looked sideways at Rob, who, with his head tilted back, his Stetson over his eyes and his blond hair draped over the back of the bench, appeared characteristically serene.

"Rob, you awake?"

"I am now," he said without opening his eyes or chang-ing his expression.

"Are you gonna call Candi today?" I hoped his response would answer the question growing in my mind.

He leaned forward and gazed at me, his blue eyes focusing. "Funny you should ask that. I was just having this weird dream about her. She was flying above me, like one of those Carlos Castaneda birds, like a Don Juan vision."

"She didn't crap on you, did she?" I asked, checking the sky for seagulls.

He laughed. "No, but it was a pretty cool dream."

"Whatever you say, Rob. So are you gonna call her?"

"Man, you're such a cynic." He took off his hat and shook out his hair. "Well, let's see. We've been gone two nights, right? I've been giving Candi some space to cool down, but maybe it's time to check in."

"Maybe so," I said, but as I did I wondered if Rob was being completely honest with me. Hadn't he tried to call Candi from that phone booth near Portland on the way up to Puente Harbor? And then he had disappeared for a while after dinner the night before, presumably to try her again. At least, that's what the rest of us figured.

Rob checked his watch. "She should be finished with her classes by now, if she isn't hanging out with one of her professors. Anyhow, maybe I should give her a call."

I shook off my thoughts about Candi and made a quick decision. "I've been thinking of calling Nita."

"Who?"

"That girl I met at the party the other night. The one from Berkeley."

"Really? You're gonna call her in Berkeley?" Rob grinned. "You really dig her, huh?"

"I don't know. Yeah, I guess so." My face suddenly felt hot, even against the cold breeze. "She's . . . well, she's interesting. I figure, what the hell, I might as well check her out."

He laughed. "What about all that stuff about girlfriends being bad for the band." He raised his eyebrows. "You changed your mind?"

I paused. He was right. My muddled but growing feelings about Nita weren't consistent with my vision of the future, my plan to ride our music out of Creedly. Assuming she was even interested in me, Nita would only complicate things, divide my focus. Still, the emptiness I now felt had something to do with her.

I looked at Rob. "You're right, and, anyhow, it doesn't make much sense, does it? She's in Berkeley, so how's that going to work?"

"But you're thinking about her."

"Yeah, I guess so."

He stood. "Well, hell, let's find a phone."

We walked back toward the hotel, stopping at a dirty Laundromat stocked with ancient washers and dryers to get change for the phone. Many of the depressing stores along the street had small American flags hanging outside. The sight of them had baffled me earlier in the afternoon until I remembered it was election day, Jerry Ford versus Jimmy Carter. I felt sorry for whoever would have to take over this mess of a country for the next four years.

We found a phone booth next to the post office on First Street, down the sidewalk from the hotel. Rob went first while I waited, leaning against the outside wall of the post office. He lowered his head and turned his back on me a few moments after feeding a number of coins into the phone and dialing. He had apparently reached Candi.

I started thinking about what I would say to Nita. I wished I could better recall her face, somehow knowing that it would help me find the right words, but I could only remember her punk clothes and her brilliant blonde hair. Suddenly I heard Rob's voice rise. I turned and looked through the glass of the phone booth. Our eyes met momentarily before he turned his reddening face away from me and lowered his voice.

Three minutes later, he pushed his way out of the booth.

"How's she doing?" I asked. "Everything O.K. at home?"

Rob forced a grin but looked distracted. "I guess I should've given her another day."

"I thought you looked a little tense in there."

Rob shrugged and gazed down the street. "It's cool. She'll be fine once I get home. No big deal. Everything's fine."

As usual, Rob wanted to keep his problems to himself, but this time I decided to press him a little harder. "Look, Rob, is something else going on between you and Candi besides the band? I'm sensing a lot of tension, at least on your side."

Rob paused and rubbed at his nose. He finally shook his head and said, "No, man, like I said, everything'll be cool once I get home. It's just a week, right?"

When I didn't say anything, he added, "She's just dealing with some shit at school that she wanted to talk about. In fact, she said that she's missing all of you guys. Can you believe that?" He laughed, but there was no humor behind it.

"O.K., Rob," I said, not sure that I believed anything he had said. "Just thought I should check."

He pulled me toward the phone booth. "You're up, man. Get in there and leave me alone." He gave me that hollow laugh again.

I closed the door and paused for a minute to collect my thoughts. I pulled out the bookmark with Nita's phone number. My heart pounded as the phone rang at the other end of the line.

A woman's voice came from far off. "Hello?"

I wasn't sure if it was her. "Nita?"

"No, she's out right now. Can I take a message?"

"Uh, no. I mean, yes. . . . Can you tell her that Daniel, Daniel Travers, called? She can't call me back, but could you just tell her that I called?"

The line went quiet. For a moment, I thought the woman had hung up. Then her voice came back on, and this time it had a warmer quality. "Oh, hi, Daniel. I'm Suzanne, Nita's roommate. Nita told me about you. You're the one in the rock band, right? Anyhow, she's off some place, the library, I think. Or maybe at her art group. Can you call back later?"

I thought for a second. "No, I'll be playing until late tonight. Tell her I'll try her later in the week. I'm not sure when, but tell her I'll try. Thanks, Suzanne."

I hung up and pushed out of the phone booth. Rob was waiting for a report. He listened to me, grinning and shaking his head. "Don't you see, man? She digs you."

"How do you know?"

"She told her roommate all about you. She must like you or she wouldn't have said anything."

I wasn't sure, but the loneliness had momentarily disappeared. There was even a little spring in my step as we walked back to the hotel, ready for our first night in the Mai Tai lounge.

9

"HELLO OUT THERE, ya punters."

Mick's voice echoed around the near-empty room. In response, the half-dozen regulars at the bar swiveled on their stools, stared at us, and then rotated back around. Mick squinted into the stage lights, peering out as if he could actually see without his glasses. He shook his head, noticeably unimpressed by their lack of enthusiasm. "Let's try this again, shall we." He pressed his lips against the mike. "Attention Kmart shoppers, rock band in lounge. Special price. Five superb musicians for the price of two American dollars, right?"

This brought a few groans from the direction of the bar, a reaction that seemed to satisfy Mick.

"Get on with it," I hissed at him.

With an exaggerated shrug, Mick wagged his glitter-painted fingernails at me, tugged at the belt of his blue-and-white striped flares, worn especially for election night, and turned back to the mike. "O.K., mates, we're the Killjoys. We're here all week, so get ready, 'cause we came to your town to help you party down!"

With this cue, Yogi counted it off and we launched into Grand Funk Railroad's *We're an American Band*.

Finally, finally, we were playing again. Everyone had been edgy and quiet waiting for nine o'clock to approach, as if we had never played before, and in some ways we hadn't. Standing on this stage was different. I saw the scuffs and old masking tape left on the stage by countless bands who had played before us. Old broken picks, bits of guitar strings stuck in the stage's cracked plywood. Splintered drumsticks, initials etched into the floor. A shiver ran down my back. Jimi Hendrix had stood on this stage; Ann and Nancy Wilson of

Heart had played here. Who the hell were we? What was I doing here?

Suddenly, as I chopped down at the strings, my chest emptied, compressed. I missed the chord. Fear came over me in a big wave, my legs, arms, fingers suddenly thick and heavy. My left hand shook in an attempt to hold down another simple bar chord. *Keep breathing, keep breathing.* I forced myself to step forward, to look beyond Yogi's drum set toward Rob and Sam, but my view was blocked by Mick, who came bouncing sideways past me with a demonic grin on his face, his chartreuse silk scarf trailing in the breeze. He spun and started back across the stage, slowing as he passed to throw me a gaped-mouth Jaggeresque grin. And then he floated back to the mike for his next bit of vocals.

I took a gulp of smoky lounge air. The wave broke at my feet and washed away, over the scuffs, the broken picks, the legendary footprints, out into the night. I took another breath, stepped forward, and windmilled the hell out of the next chord.

✳ ✳ ✳ ✳ ✳

THE SMALL TUESDAY NIGHT crowd was a blessing of sorts. After my initial jitters and some erratic playing by Yogi, the band relaxed and worked off the rust, knowing that all the bullshit was out of the way and we could do what we came here to do. The string-worn grooves in the calluses of my fingertips felt familiar and reassuring. Undoubtedly, I was more comfortable onstage than anywhere else in my life, despite the occasional bouts of stage fright.

I leaned back, closed my eyes, and slid into the familiar riff behind the bridge of Cream's very cool *Badge*. (Imagine, a song titled simply because Eric Clapton misread George Harrison's written word *Bridge*!) I could feel the band working toward its groove, toward the rhythmic pocket created by bass, drums, and rhythm guitar that gave us our tightness, our sense of forward motion. At our best, the Killjoys could do something most local bands I'd heard never achieved: We could simultaneously play inside and outside of the pocket, keeping a rock-steady groove in place while Mick's vocals and my guitar jumped all around the groove—a screaming, vibrating train steadied by the constant chug-chug of our powerful, deep-throated engine.

I credited Yogi with our ability to reach this unique musical state. He had the steadiest bass drum foot I'd ever heard, laying down a precise, predictable beat that allowed Rob, with his slithering bass lines, to settle down deep into the pocket. In contrast, Yogi's hands were incredibly busy, clattering crazily across his snare and toms, his crash and ride cymbals, in a Keith Moon–like high-wire act of constant motion. Sometimes he played too much, sometimes he would completely lose the beat, but when he was on, and when Mick, Sam, and I were able to grab onto the throbbing electric wire he threw out and hold on without falling, we were truly something special.

The band was already nearing this groove, something that usually happened only when we fed off the energy of a big crowd. Tonight, the room was maybe a third full, and only a dozen or so people were dancing, but it didn't seem to matter. Nobody expected a big crowd on Tuesday night. It was enough just to blast away all the tension that had built up over the past few days.

Now pumping my way through Blue Oyster Cult's *Don't Fear the Reaper*, with the room slowly filling, I scanned the flannel shirts and black leather jackets clustered at tables throughout the lounge. Beyond those sitting, at the back near the door, stood two guys, one tall and gawky, the other short and muscular. Without the requisite flannel shirts and leather jackets, they looked out of place, and I watched them for a moment, noticing how they seemed more interested in the crowd than in us. I wondered who they were, but forgot about them as I punched my distortion pedal for more sustain and volume before launching into my solo.

Minutes later, Mick let out a whoop as we crashed to the ending, and we left the stage for our eleven o'clock break. Heading for the bar, I pulled out a bandanna and wiped sweat from my brow, wondering if we'd be able to sustain our energy level through the final three sets. I was almost to the bar when I saw the woman who'd been sitting on the same bar stool the day we arrived. I tried to veer off before she noticed me, but she pointed a long ring-enshrined finger at me and motioned me over. Sitting beside her, just as the day before, was the guy with the bushy sideburns and red face. He stood up and stuck out his hand. Surprised, I reached out. He gave me a cheerful smile, then angled his hand, attempting to give me one of those hip half-handshakes. Flustered by the presence of the woman, I flubbed it.

"Hey, man, cool set," the guy said, untangling his hand from mine and motioning for Mr. Tom behind the bar. "Sit down and lemme buy you a brew."

I breathed out and plopped down on the empty bar stool next to the woman. Tonight she was decked out in a tight orange granny dress and smelled of cigarette smoke and pungent perfume. Charlie, maybe, based on the strangely outdoorsy, spicy scent I was now picking up. One of my few ex-girlfriends had worn it. I didn't like it.

The woman leaned close to me. "Yeah, kid, you surprised me. You guys sound good for a bunch of young punks. I've seen a lot of bands, but you guys rock pretty good. Maybe you got a future." The whiskey on her breath cut through the perfume. Beyond the clink of beer bottles and glasses, I heard Harry Reasoner's voice giving election returns from a TV mounted on the wall behind the bar. Sam and Rob had moved to the end of the bar and were watching the news report.

"Yeah," the woman continued, "you're gonna do O.K.

here, but you'll have to crank it up some by Saturday night."
And then she winked at me.

I tried hard not to react to the wink. Was she messing with
my head again? "Saturday night?" I said. "What about it?"

"Wait and see, kid." She smiled and blew a ring of smoke
in my face. "Wait and see."

Her friend handed me a bottle of Budweiser. "I'm Kyle,
man, and this here's Kitten." He tilted his head toward the
woman.

I looked at her. Kitten, eh? This woman was no cuddly
pet. "That's really your name?"

"Yeah," she said, her smile shifting to a knowing grin.
"'Cuz I *purrrrrr* if I like you."

I looked around for help, but Kyle had me blocked
off. "You guys are from California, huh?" he asked, apparently oblivious to the vibe being thrown off by his girlfriend.
"Look, you guys need anything while you're here, you let
me an' Kitten know, O.K.? We can get anything . . . know
what I mean?"

Anything? Hmnn. I thought I knew what he meant. Then
I wasn't so sure. Drugs? Women? I nodded at him. "Thanks.
We'll keep it in mind."

"No, really, man," he persisted. "I mean it. Really, just
name it. Anything."

I wasn't ready to get busted for buying drugs from a
stranger, and I wasn't financially or emotionally prepared to
buy sex, but he seemed so eager to be helpful, and there was
something we all could use. Even as I wondered if it was wise
to get involved with those two, I replied, "Yeah, no biggie,
but we're all under 21. If you could buy us some beer, we'd
really appreciate it. We'd pay you back."

Kitten leaned in, glancing sideways at Kyle. "Oh, he can
do better than that. Look, you come with us when you're
finished tonight, and Kyle'll get you all the beer you need.
Gratis, kid."

"We can pay—"

Mr. Tom reached across the bar and tapped his watch. His cloud of Old Spice blew past Kitten's Charlie.

"Guess we gotta get back to work," I said, standing. "I'll look for you after our last set. Thanks for the beer, Kyle." I retreated to the stage.

✳ ✳ ✳ ✳ ✳

THE CROWD HAD thinned by the time we finished at just before two, but I felt elated as the last chord of Bowie's frenetic *Suffragette City* faded away. I packed up my guitar and helped unplug the equipment. The week was off to a good start, and I knew the crowds would grow as we got closer to the weekend. Large crowds always meant a happy club owner and a contented booking agent.

I looked out toward the bar and saw Kyle and Kitten waiting beside the door. I told the guys where I was going, and Mick surprisingly volunteered to go along. "I needs me a cold lager," was all he said by way of explanation.

A bracing middle-of-the-night breeze hit my overheated face when we stepped outside, and I remembered Mr. Tom's warning about how the front doors were locked at three o'clock. "This is Mick," I said to Kyle and Kitten. "Should we follow you?"

"The store's at the far end of town," Kyle said. "You guys ride with us, and we'll bring you back with the beer." He led us over to a battered orange Volkswagen van sitting at the curb.

We piled into the back, and Kyle, with Kitten beside him, started the van on the third try. He wound the van through and beyond the empty, wet streets of downtown Puente Harbor, disorienting me in the process. After five minutes of driving, he pulled around the back of a small liquor store at the end of a short commercial strip. Kitten stayed in the van and waited with us, smoking another in an endless stream of cigarettes, while Kyle unlocked the door and went into the back of the closed store.

"Kyle works here?" I asked hopefully.

Kitten ignored my question and turned to look at us, black strands of hair falling across her right eye. "So your band—" She paused to flick a match out the window. "Your band, like I said, it's a lot better than I thought it would be. Sounds like you've been playing a lot. You been on the road much?"

"We've played mainly around Northern California," I replied, keeping an eye on the back of the liquor store. "This is our first trip out of California."

"And it's lovely to be here," Mick added.

Kitten breathed out smoke. "So you're not on the circuit yet?"

"The circuit?"

"Oh, y'know, the Northwest club circuit. The rock clubs. Portland, Seattle."

I shook my head. "Like I said, we've played mainly around where we live in California. But we're hoping Astley will book us into more clubs."

"Sure, kid," she said as she continued to peer through the smoke and darkness at me. "Tell me, you the leader? Or is it Mick here?"

Unsure about where she was going with her questions, I kept my mouth shut. Most of the people we met in bars were harmless, only wanting to impress us with the bands they knew, the drugs they had, the parties they could invite us to. But Kitten was definitely different. I could see it in the aggressively large Indian turquoise rings she wore on every finger, the glint thrown off by those rings when she cupped her hands to light a cigarette, the persistent aura of her Charlie perfume. From way back in my skull, I heard Pete Townshend whisper, *I knew her at the Marquee, mate. She nearly killed me.*

In the silence, Mick glanced at me and then leaned forward until his thick-lensed glasses, which he had slipped on the minute we left the lounge, were only inches from her face. "Daniel runs the show, but I do all the bloody work, right?" He winked. "If you want the star, I'm your man."

Kitten smiled lazily, but her gaze shifted from Mick back to me. She stared at me for a long moment, and in that time I had the uncomfortable feeling that she was looking right through me. "Daniel, your band can do better than this shit-hole town." Her tongue flicked at her upper lip. "Maybe I can help you guys play better places."

That took me aback. How could *she* help us? With her still staring at me, the only thing I felt was that I didn't want to get involved with this woman in any way. I was about to change the subject when Kyle reappeared, carrying a case of beer.

Kitten saw him and quickly said, "We'll talk more about it later."

Kyle opened the side door of the van. "Olympia O.K.?" he asked, sliding the box onto the van's floor.

"Lovely," Mick answered. "Beggars can't be choosers."

Kyle returned to the store. I purposely angled away from Kitten and scanned the parking lot, half expecting a police car to pull up at any moment, but everything remained dead quiet. Although Kyle apparently did work at the store, it seemed obvious that he was stealing the beer for us. And from a state-franchised liquor store at that.

But under the circumstances what could we do? We helped Kyle load up three more cases—"Two more for you and one for us"—before he locked up the store. We piled back into the van and drove to the hotel, arriving a few minutes before three. Kyle threw the van's door back, and Mick and I each carried a case through the deserted lobby and up to our room, where Sam and Rob were waiting. We trudged back downstairs to get the last case and to say goodbye, but when we hit the street we had to pull up as an old, blue Ford pickup truck sped by us, exhaust roaring. It was the only vehicle in sight besides the van.

We crossed over to the van and Mick grabbed the last case. "Thanks for the beer," I said. "We're heading back in." I paused, then thinking I should at least be polite, added, "You interested in joining us?"

To my relief, Kitten shook her head. "Me and Kyle've got things to do. We'll catch you later in the week. Enjoy the beer, boys."

Suddenly I heard tires squeal, the roar of an engine being violently accelerated, and I turned. The blue Ford pickup came ripping around the corner. Mick, in the middle of the street, looked up, startled, squinting into the headlights.

"Watch out!" I yelled.

But Mick looked frozen in its path. I saw him squint into the oncoming headlights, and when he finally started to move, the case of beer must have thrown him off-balance, because he staggered sideways, falling hard on the far edge of the asphalt. Beer cans skittered out onto the pavement. His glasses had fallen off, and his hand flew out, searching for them.

The truck was headed straight toward him. I stepped into the street but stopped short as the truck bore down, silhouettes of two cowboy hats clearly outlined in the cab. Tires screeched and Mick threw himself into the gutter. The truck's half-crumpled bumper was only yards from him, but at the last moment the truck swerved.

Above the sound of the roaring engine, I heard a man yell out, "Faggot! Get the fuck out of. . . ." Then his voice was eaten up by the noise.

I ran across the street. Mick had rolled into a sitting position and was peering down at the palms of his hands. "What the hell. . . ."

I grabbed his arm. "You O.K.?"

"Yeah, I think so." His accent was totally gone. "But where are my glasses?"

He started to say something else, but Kitten yelled, "Here they come again! Mick, Daniel, get up!"

I looked up the street and saw the truck making a U-turn. I pulled at Mick. "C'mon, c'mon!" He struggled up as the truck accelerated toward us. Looking over my shoulder, I saw Kyle, waving a baseball bat, dash into the street straight toward the oncoming truck. Mick and I scrambled up onto the sidewalk moments before I heard tires squeal.

The cowboys, thank God, weren't totally insane; they swerved to avoid Kyle. But they came close. As they did, Kyle swung the bat, shattering the truck's left headlight. The blow slowed the truck, and Kyle stepped back and swung again. Wood banged against metal.

We could hear the cowboys cursing. For a second it looked like they were going to stop and get out. But Kyle stood there, unmoved, the bat at his shoulder, a fierce look on his face; and finally the truck sped up and lurched down the street. This time it ran a stop sign, continued down the street a couple of blocks, and made a hard left. Would they circle around and come back? I held my breath and listened. But the roar of the truck simply diminished, then disappeared.

Kyle and Kitten ran across the street to join us. My hands shook as I retrieved Mick's glasses from the gutter, but Mick seemed surprisingly calm. The palms of both hands were bleeding and the left knee of his pants was torn, but he was otherwise O.K.

Mick turned to Kyle. "Those geezers friends of yours?" The accent was back.

"Just a couple of rednecks," Kyle said, peering down the street. "They have it in for the dopers. This kinda shit happens once in a while around here."

"Well, that's reassuring," Mick said.

I followed Kyle's eyes down the street. "You think they'll be back?"

"You never know," Kitten answered for him. "Kyle whacked 'em pretty good. Maybe you kids should get inside."

They helped us gather up the beers before driving off. We slipped inside the hotel, where Mr. Tom was waiting for us just inside the door. He glanced at Mick's torn pants and shook his head. I nodded to him and hurried by, hearing the click of the door lock as we headed up the stairs.

Sam and Rob were still waiting for us when we reached the room. Everyone popped open an Olympia and listened in disbelief as Mick told them what had happened. I sat on the bed, barely listening. I suddenly felt nauseous, partly from residual adrenaline, but more from the hate I felt coming from the truck as it spun past us the last time. I lay back on the bed and stared up at the grimy, peeling ceiling, wondering if it was all worth it. Was this where rock 'n' roll had taken me, to this place that now seemed more loveless and hateful than the one I was fleeing? Shit, did the music offer no true redemption, no future? But how could that be? My head—my whole body—reeling, the thought spun through my mind that Townshend's Universal Chord and its promise of a shared truth was a lie; a possibility that made the nausea in the pit of my stomach grow worse.

10

WE ALMOST BUMPED into Mr. Tom when we stepped out of the hotel the next morning. With barely a glance at us, he continued to sweep jagged shards of glass from the sidewalk near the front door. A piece of plywood covered a large section of the front window.

"Holy shit." Rob shielded his eyes from the sunlight reflecting from the remaining sections of glass.

Mr. Tom stopped and looked over at us. "Not good boys."

I stared back at him. "Hey, we didn't do it."

He gestured toward the broken window. "After you come in last night, the window is broken. Who do that?"

It wasn't hard to guess what had happened: The two guys in the truck had come back later to make a point. I considered trying to explain the circumstances to Mr. Tom but gave up on the idea. "Look, we don't know anything about the window. Like you said, it happened after we came in."

He shrugged. "I dunno. You boys, you play good, but. . . ." He turned away and started sweeping again.

We left him and started down First Street into the bright morning sun. I walked behind the other guys, listening to Mick tell Yogi about our run-in with the rednecks.

"Yogi, me lad," he said, "you should've been there. Tires were screeching, beers were exploding. I thought the Hen was going to have a heart attack." He looked back at me and grinned.

Yogi examined the scrapes on Mick's hands. "Aren't you worried they'll come back? Maybe when we're playing?"

"Not bleedin' likely after what Kyle did to their truck. It was like batting practice at Candlestick." He took a couple of imaginary swings. I didn't share his confidence, but, as

Mick would have explained, it was in my nature to worry.

We approached Pam's Cup O' Coffee Café on the corner of First and Washington Streets, three blocks down from the hotel. Yogi's rave review of the café, combined with the bad food at the Mai Tai, had convinced us, despite the café's corny name, to give Pam's a chance. Outside the door, I paused at a newspaper rack to buy a Seattle paper. The front page headline—CARTER EDGES FORD—jumped out at me.

"Hey," I said, nudging Rob, "Carter won."

"Yeah, I heard that last night. Where were you, man? Everybody was talking about it."

His question stopped me, and I thought back to the previous night, which ended sometime around four in the morning. "I dunno," I finally answered, tucking the newspaper under my arm before following Rob inside.

Unlike the hotel, the café looked clean and smelled friendly—good coffee and fresh bread, like my mom's kitchen used to smell before everything went to hell. Sunlight crept through the café's spotless east-facing window, brightening the room, and seascape pastels hung on the creamy white walls. A late-morning scattering of customers were seated around tables casually arranged across the checkerboard floor. Two elderly women sipping coffee together at a table in the back glanced at us as we stood at the entrance, waiting to be seated. Their looks were not hostile, curious maybe. A group of men in out-of-date sport coats and ties—probably Realtors or used car salesmen on break—sat at a table in the corner and generally ignored us in all our hairy, bleary rock-band glory.

A young woman with a stack of menus approached. She carried herself erectly, her straight black hair tied back, exposing high cheek bones and an olive complexion. Her proud carriage was enhanced by her neatly pressed blue-and-white striped blouse and knee-length denim skirt. A blue beaded choker encircled her neck.

"Good morning, Edward," she said, smiling at Yogi, who immediately blushed. She scrutinized the four of us. "I see you've brought the rest of your band this time."

Mick cocked his head. "*Your* band, Edward?"

Yogi ignored him and pulled himself up a little taller. "How are you this morning, Evangeline?"

Rob and I exchanged glances. I peered at the name tag pinned to her blouse. Sure enough: YOUR WAITRESS IS EVANGELINE. We followed her to a large table in the middle of the café, where Mick yawned loudly as we arranged ourselves around the table.

"Coffee?" Evangeline asked.

"Yeah, yeah, yeah, yeah," four of us grunted.

"Orange juice for me, please, Evangeline," Yogi said.

Mick perked up as she moved off toward the kitchen at the rear of the café. "Hey, Yogi, I see why you fancy this place. She'd keep a bloke warm at night. I imagine she'd find the lead singer of a rock band a lovely change from the grotty geezers around here, wouldn't she?"

Sam groaned. "Christ, Mick, you're full of it. You think anyone wearing a skirt is hot for you. Give it up."

"But she *is* hot, mate. Look." He removed his glasses and held them out for us to see. "She's fogged 'em up."

Rob reached across the table and swatted him with his menu. "Hey, man, women aren't objects. Show some respect."

Mick raised his hands to ward off the attack. "Hey, mates, you've got me all wrong. My respect for the fairer sex knows no bounds. I love the girls, just like I loves me mum. I'm here to bring a little joy into their dismal lives. They probably think all blokes are like you wankers. But after they've been with the Mickster, they know better."

"They ought to," Sam said.

We quieted down when Evangeline returned to the table with a pot of coffee and Yogi's orange juice. I took a closer look at her as she leaned across the table to pour Rob's coffee. She had a strong face with dark, penetrating eyes, but her makeup failed to disguise circles beneath her eyes. She wasn't pretty in any usual sense of the word, but her American Indian features gave her an intriguingly exotic appearance.

Mick, who had slipped his glasses into a pocket, also followed her with his eyes. "Allow me to introduce myself," he said when she reached him, "especially since Edward's too rude to do it. Me name's Mick, and I'm the lead singer in *Ed's* band." He glanced sideways at Yogi, who kept his eyes on his menu.

She arched her pencil-thin eyebrows. "O.K. Well, welcome to Puente Harbor, Mick."

"Splendid to be here." He gave her his best come-hither look. "Our first time, you know, and we don't know a soul, except you, of course. By the way, you have lovely hair."

I shook my head in amazement. Sam was absolutely right: Mick was a pathological hound. When Mick first joined the band, his behavior around girls—the constant flirting, the manipulating, the pressuring—had irritated me, but, slowly, I had developed a grudging respect for his intentions, if not his methods. Mick had been telling us the truth. Unlike most guys, he didn't view women as mountains to be conquered, conquests to be compiled. No, he really and truly loved women, just like he treasured his helpless mother. He wanted to comfort them, protect them, admire them, make them feel good about themselves. Unfortunately, his good intentions almost always surrendered to his compulsion to sin, and he had left a trail of ugly one-night stands in his wake. In that way, I guessed, he was just like his father.

Mick's eyes stayed on Evangeline. "Have you lived here long, sweetheart? Perhaps you can show us around your lovely town."

A certain wariness crept into her eyes. Perhaps she was

already on to Mick. "I've been here a few years. But I grew up in Clallam Bay, about fifty miles west of here."

"So, what are the cultural attributes of this burg? For example, where would you take a bloke like me, who's new in town, if you wanted to show him a good time?"

"Christ on a crutch," Sam muttered.

Evangeline smiled, but the wariness in her eyes remained. "Oh, it's pretty dull here, really. I'm sure California's a lot more interesting."

"Oh, certainly," Mick said, "California's lovely, idn't? Beaches, movie stars, Rice-a-Roni, all that rubbish. Unfortunately, we're from Creedly, which is about as exciting as—"

"O.K., Mick," Sam said, "let her do her job. I'm sure she's got better things to do than stand around listening to you all day."

She glanced at the other tables. "I do have other customers." She brightened, back to doing her job. "What can I get you guys?"

We ordered and Evangeline moved over to the table of sport coats and ties. Mick and Sam began arguing about something, and I ignored them and handed Rob all but the front section of the newspaper. I lit a cigarette and glanced across the table at Yogi. He sat staring out the window, softly whistling to himself, his expression oddly sad and disconnected. I sighed and started in on the newspaper.

Evangeline soon returned with our food. Yogi started to speak to her, but Mick cut him off. "I don't mean to take you away from your other customers," he said, with a pointed pause and glance at Sam, "but I was wondering if you ever go to the Mai Tai Hotel to hear the bands?"

"Sometimes," Evangeline replied, placing a plate of ham and eggs in front of Sam. "It's the only place in town for dancing, except for the Bull 'n' Bash. But that's a country-western bar."

"Well, you should come hear us, don't you think? We're playing there every night through Saturday. And we're quite good—"

"I don't—"

"Yeah, you should come," Yogi interrupted her.

She smiled at both of them. "O.K., I'll try to make it by some night this week. If I can."

"Splendid," Mick purred. "I'll watch for you."

"I will, too," Yogi said. Then as if realizing that Mick's position out front gave him an advantage, he added, "I'll be the one behind the drum set."

After watching Evangeline return to the kitchen, I glanced first at Yogi and then at Mick. "You two are pathetic."

"You're giving them the benefit of the doubt," Rob said from behind a section of the newspaper.

"Look," I said, leaning across the table, "I don't care what you two do offstage, but I don't want her getting in the way of the band's business. We're only gonna be here another five days, so stay focused. O.K.?"

"I saw her first," Yogi said, glaring at Mick and completely ignoring me.

"So what?" Mick shrugged, his accent suddenly disappearing. "It's the one who sees her *last* that counts. Know what I mean, *Edward*?"

"Help me, Sam," I said.

With a glint in his eye, Sam leaned toward me. "Which wanker do you want me to kill?"

11

HARSH, SOUR NOTES leaped from my amplifier, jarring me out of the stupor induced by the repetitive riff of *Whole Lotta Love*. I knew what had happened—I'd felt the snap and the zinging release of tension—even before seeing the broken B string dangling from the neck of my guitar.

Out of the corner of my eye, I saw Rob grimacing at me from across the stage while I attempted to retune my bottom four strings on the fly. Barely in tune, I stayed down low through my solo, killing time until Yogi launched into his extended drum solo, which gave me the chance to grab my backup guitar—a cheap Les Paul knockoff—and jump back into the song. Judging from the continual motion of the dancers on the floor, few people had noticed my frantic movements, but I was still irritated.

The ruined string said it all. This night was fast becoming as bad as the previous night had been good. We'd started the night by trying to track down the source of an irritating buzz coming from the P.A. system. Then Yogi missed the ending of our first song and Sam cracked a reed during his sax solo on Jethro Tull's *Locomotion Breath*. Mick was uncharacteristically lethargic, and an added touch of surliness had slowly crept into his song introductions. Even our stage lights weren't cooperating. Twice they had blinked out when Sam stepped on the floor switch controlling the banks of lights sitting atop the P.A. cabinets.

Even the crowd seemed out of it. With a few exceptions, none of the familiar faces from the previous night had returned. We were already halfway through the night and had seen no sign of Kitten and Kyle, and Yogi and Mick were disappointed that Evangeline hadn't turned up. I squinted through the smoky haze of the bar as I started *Taking Care of Business* and saw the two guys I'd seen standing near the door the night before. They were there again, one short, one tall.

Stifling a yawn, I kept pounding out the chunky chords, feeling, perhaps correctly, that I'd played them a thousand times before. Familiarity definitely bred contempt when it came to Bachman-Turner Overdrive.

As we clattered through the song's ending, I looked out through the lights and saw Kitten, laced up tight in a white bodice-hugging leather vest, smiling at me from the edge of the dance floor. Before I could check my inner voices, and just happy to see a friendly face, I smiled back.

✳ ✳ ✳ ✳ ✳

KITTEN SWIVELED on her bar stool and reached across me to grab the pack of Marlboros I'd left on the glossy surface of the bar. Her face brushed against mine as she leaned back, and I could almost taste the lingering, incenselike smoky essence of Charlie on my tongue.

"D'ya mind?" she asked, not waiting for an answer before tapping out a cigarette. She held it between her lips, as if daring me to light it. I steadied my hands and brought the lighter up to the cigarette, holding it there until she had it going. She leaned forward on her elbows, took a puff, and gazed sideways at me through the rogue strands of inky black hair hanging across her eyes. "So whatta you think, kid?"

I willed my pulse to slow. "Let me get this straight. You're saying that you've got connections to promoters booking the Northwest club circuit?"

"Not just the Northwest. I can get you in anywhere between here and Chicago. Denver, Kansas City, you name it. All the rock clubs on the touring circuit."

I gazed back at her in disbelief. She unblinkingly returned my gaze, and I again had that weird sensation that she was looking right through me, that she knew just how badly I wanted to make it with the band. "Thanks for the offer," I finally said, "but I think we're in pretty good shape with our agent."

"Nasty Astley?" She laughed and flicked the tip of her cigarette toward the ashtray.

My pulse picked up again. "You mentioned him before. How do you know him?"

She smiled and leaned into me. "Like I said, kid, I know 'em all. They all come through here once in a while to check out their bands and to see Tom. Astley's O.K., but he can't take you where I can." She blew more smoke. "And you might not wanna trust him, know what I mean? He's ripped off some bands." She leaned back. "So, do you wanna make it or not?"

I looked around the lounge for Kyle, but Kitten had come alone. Sam, Yogi, and Rob were at a table near the stage; Mick was across the room, talking up an overweight young woman in a clingy, red Lycra disco dress. My eyes came back to Kitten. She was probably right about Astley. He was too slick to be trusted too far, and he was likely just using us to get himself out of a temporary fix. But would Kitten be any better for us, and could I trust her? Not bloody likely. Still, somehow I sensed that she wasn't lying to me. "So what are you saying? You can get us bookings?"

She ground out the cigarette. "I've been thinkin' about it since I heard you play last night. I know what you want, and I can help you get it. It's all about connections, kid, and I've got 'em."

My pulse, overheated by a recent dose of cross-tops, ticked up, and I fought giving in to the lie of trust produced by the drugs. Up to this point, I'd figured Kitten was just another groupie who got off on sexually manipulating every-one around her. But, looking at her now, I knew better; there was something else going on here. She wanted something from me; she wanted to use *me*. I just didn't know how or why. I searched my mind for the cautionary voices, for Sam's, for Rob's, but only Pete Townshend's urgent tone came through: *She sees the real you, mate; she knows what you want.* His warning brought me back down. "Look, I'm not saying that I don't believe you, but why would promoters book us on your word?"

"They all owe me," she said simply, a businesslike look suddenly in her eye. "And, like I said, your band's good. I've heard all the groups on the circuit, but you guys have somethin' different going. Something raw but tight."

"Yeah? How do you know so much about it?"

She ran a hand through her tangled hair. "Look, kid, I was with a guy for a while, played in a pretty good band outta Chicago—that's where I'm from—and I toured around with 'em. They played all the clubs on the circuit. I got to know the club owners and promoters." She leaned back again, that same hard but confident look on her face. "I know how the business works."

"Then how'd you end up here?" I leaned toward her. "What happened to your boyfriend?"

She stiffened. "Him? I don't wanna talk about that asshole."

For once, I felt like I had the upper hand. I decided to push her. "C'mon, what happened to him?"

She gave me a weary look and sighed. "Shit, you ask a lot of questions, Daniel. Look, turned out he was just another loser. When they were playin' here last year, I found him in the sack with some local groupie, O.K.?" Her eyes slitted. "And nobody fucks with me." She kept staring at me, then finally shifted her gaze, upward, away from me. "Anyhow, I cut him loose and decided to stick around for a while. I help Tom out with the bookings now." A light shrug, then her eyes right back on me. "But I'm not stayin' in this shithole long."

"I don't blame you."

"Look, Daniel, I really can get you into better places.

Take it from me, the promoters are lookin' all over for young acts like you guys. And they want a strong front man. You got Mick, and you got a cool groove." She nodded to herself. "You need to do some of your own stuff to move up the ladder, but you got time to worry about that later. Trust me." Her eyes brightened. "I know what I'm talkin' about."

I knew she was right about one thing: We *were* good, even on a bad night. And I now understand why she seemed to know so much about the business. But I was still unconvinced by her claim of connections. And I definitely didn't trust her motives. "What's in it for you?"

Her thin smile returned. "I'd think of something, kid."

For a moment, through the haze of cigarette smoke, I saw her clearly. She was like the snake in the garden, tempting me with the forbidden fruit; and, sure, I wanted to reach out and taste it. But could I really believe her? I needed time to think, and I made a show of checking my watch. "I've gotta change a string before the next set. Maybe we can talk later."

I slid off the bar stool and started to work my way through the maze of tables. A hand touched my shoulder. "Slow down, kid." Kitten took my arm and steered me away from the tables. "I wasn't finished."

"Look, I said we'd talk about it later."

"That's what I wanna get straight." She pushed me to a dark stretch of the wall adjacent to the dance floor, keeping her hands on me while she circled around to face me. As she leaned back against the wall, her pin-prick eyes beamed into mine. "What're you doin' after the show tonight?"

"Hanging out with the guys, I guess."

"How 'bout you hang out with me instead?" A faint smile. "We can, um, talk more business."

I felt a line of sweat work its way down my neck. "Can't we just talk here after the show?"

"I'm not talking about just talkin'." Her smile hung there lightly.

"Don't bullshit me," I said, but my voice faltered. I felt the sweat pool at the base of my neck. "What do you really want?"

Now her smile broadened. "What do you *think* I want?"

"That sounds like a trick question." I started to edge back toward the stage.

"You think so?" Catching me off-guard, she tugged at the front of my shirt, pulling me against her. I felt her breasts through the thin fabric of my T-shirt.

"What about Kyle?"

"What about him?" She moved her right leg between my knees and pressed her thigh against my groin. My mind told me to move back, but I didn't.

"I thought you were with him," I managed to get out, my voice hoarse.

"Sometimes I am." She pressed her leg harder against me. "Sometimes I'm not. So, whatta you say, kid?"

This was all too much. I fought for time. "If we did, I mean . . . where would we go?"

"Don't worry about it. There's a room upstairs Tom lets me use." She put her hand on my butt and pulled me closer. "We could go there right now if you want."

Sure, part of me wanted to follow her right then, but more of me didn't. "You know I gotta play," I said, stepping back. "We have two more sets."

Her eyes darkened. "Later, then," she finally said, a curious hint of threat in her voice.

"Maybe." I caught my breath. "Look, let's see what happens the rest of the night, O.K.?"

She shoved me away, shaking her head. "That's not the right answer."

I heard Mick's voice over the P.A.: "Would all Killjoys please come home. And that means you, Daniel."

"Gotta go," I said. I turned and limped toward the stage, smelling Kitten's Charlie all over me.

"Your loss, kid," she called out after me.

I looked back at her and swore to myself that I would not let her fuck with my head again. And, all my senses back in order, I decided I definitely would not let her fuck with the rest of me.

✳ ✳ ✳ ✳ ✳

WE FINISHED *Sweet Jane*, and I squinted down at the song list taped to the top of my amp. One more to go—Kiss's *Rock 'n' Roll All Nite*—and then we were finished. To my relief—or was it?—Kitten had disappeared midway through our fourth set, and I hadn't seen her since. But she was still messing up my head. Despite the vow I'd made to myself two hours before, I couldn't stop thinking about her. I couldn't stop thinking about the way she felt against my chest, the way she'd rubbed her leg up against me, the way she seemed to look clear-eyed and knowing into my rotting soul. Pete Townshend was right: This woman could kill me. For whatever reason, she wanted me, or maybe it was more accurate to say that she wanted to use me. But . . . maybe I was willing to be used, at least until I figured out what she really wanted.

I looked down at the song list again. Regardless of any lingering desire for Kitten, the thought of going upstairs, having a beer or two, and hitting the sack by myself sounded more appealing. The uppers I'd taken earlier had started to wear off, leaving me jittery and anxious, in need of the soothing effects of alcohol. I needed a house call from Dr. Daniel.

Only fifteen or twenty people remained in the bar, but a group sitting at a table near the center of the room had become progressively louder as we worked our way through our final set. Their voices now dominated the room. I heard a shrill laugh from one of the women in the group. I tried to peer through the glare of the lights but couldn't see who it was.

Mick stepped to the mike. "We've got one more for you, right? A little something from Kiss—"

Again came the irritating laugh, followed by another. Normally Mick would have ignored them, but with so few people in the bar, he was competing with their noise. And Mick didn't like competition. He dragged his mike stand to the edge of the stage and squinted through the lights. "Hey!" he yelled out, pointing at the group sitting at the table. "Yeah, I'm talkin' to you prats. Shut your bleedin' gobs!"

The chatter in the bar stopped. Rob and I looked across the stage at each other. Sam leaned over to whisper something in Rob's ear. I stepped forward. "Let it go, Mick. It's not worth it."

Too late. One of the men at the table yelled back, "You got a problem, man?"

Mick pointed at the table again. "Problem? Is that what you call it, ya bleedin' twit. Your mum forget your manners lessons, did she?"

He paused, letting his remark linger, and the bar remained quiet for a few seconds. Then one of the women shouted, "Up yours, you little punk."

I tried to break in. "Hey, Mick—"

But he wasn't through. "Oh, my. Such an articulate comeback. Had to look those words up in the dictionary, did you, dear? So literary. Perhaps you should try out for *The Gong Show*, sweetheart."

The man sitting beside her threw back his chair and came striding toward the stage. He was big and he was pissed. "Fuck you, you little dork. You wanna take this outside?"

Sam and I started forward, but we weren't needed. Before the man got halfway to the stage, the stocky guy I'd seen near the door was on him. He grabbed the man's arm, twisted it behind him, and had him out the door before he knew what was happening.

"Out!" I heard the stocky guy say to the others at the table. They slowly got up and followed him.

At the door, the woman turned and looked back at us. "We won't be back to this dump. You guys are a piece'a shit."

"Good night, sweet princess," Mick murmured into the mike, waving at her. "We'll miss you."

"Shut the fuck up, Mick," Sam said, grabbing his arm. The mike picked up his words, and the lounge became dead quiet.

"Let's play the last song and shut it down," I said, exhausted tension draining from my arms and legs.

"Good idea," Rob added from back near his amp.

Not waiting for Sam and Mick's agreement, Yogi clicked his sticks together, and we half-heartedly launched into *Rock 'n' Roll All Nite*. The song's party-hardy attitude now seemed ridiculous in the context of the Mai Tai's leaden atmosphere, and I stayed in the background shadows of the stage until the song ground to a halt. And then the night was mercifully, finally over.

With eyes burning from cigarette smoke and ears dulled by noise, I slowly placed my guitar in its case, unplugged my amp, disassembled the floor pedals, and wound up my cords. Sam, muttering at Mick, quickly left the stage with his sax cases. I watched as Mr. Tom stepped from behind the bar to stop Sam before he got to the door. I couldn't hear what was said, but they exchanged words, and Sam nodded repeatedly before turning and leaving the bar.

Mick, Yogi, and Rob finished squaring away their equipment and trudged upstairs. As always, I did a last check around the stage to make sure everything was unplugged and secured before heading for the door with my guitars. I glanced at Mr. Tom, but he was busy washing glasses and putting away liquor bottles. Pushing through the swinging doors into the lobby, I almost bumped into the short, stocky guy who'd come to our rescue. The tall, skinny kid stood beside him.

I set down my guitars and stuck out a hand. "Hey, thanks. That guy would've killed our singer if you hadn't stepped in."

The short guy gave my hand a painful squeeze, his biceps bulging against the blue fabric of his T-shirt. No wonder those people had left when he ordered them out. "No problem," he said with a shy gruffness. He let go of my hand and rubbed the top of his black hair, which was cut almost to the scalp. His unshaven face, close-set eyes, squared-off chin, and fighter's nose gave him a tough appearance. "We were just doing our job."

"Your job?"

"Sure. We're the bouncers here."

I stared at him, surprised. But of course. Why else would they be hanging around the door? Still, these guys didn't look like bouncers. At least the skinny kid didn't. His wispy blond hair barely covered his skull, and reddish acne spotted his vertical, pale face, marring his otherwise delicate features. He wore a flowery Hawaiian shirt that hung untucked over jeans that were three inches too short for him, and the black-canvas tennis shoes that anchored his sticklike legs looked impossibly big, like clown shoes.

"Well, anyway," I said, "I'm glad you guys were here."

"That was nothing," the skinny kid said. "Just wait till the weekend."

His high, girllike voice startled me, and I tried not to smile. "Someone else told me that. By the way, I'm Daniel."

The kid stuck out his hand. "Allen. And this here's Cecil." He motioned toward his friend.

"Allen?" Cecil snorted. "Just call him Beanie. Everybody else does."

I looked at our two new allies and grinned. "Look, I'd like to buy you guys a beer, but I guess it's too late and Tom wouldn't sell 'em to me anyhow. How about coming up to our room? We've got some brew up there, and you can meet the rest of the guys."

"O-kay!" Beanie said, his voice cracking on the second syllable.

"Sounds good," Cecil added, "but we've gotta clean up the bar first. It'll probably take us fifteen, twenty minutes."

"Room 204 on the second floor. Come on up when you're finished."

I left the lobby, almost regretting that I had made the invitation. Fatigue was eating away at me, and a quick beer and sleep sounded better than ever. I trudged up the stairs, banging my guitar cases against the wall as I went, hearing angry voices coming from somewhere nearby. It didn't dawn on me that they were coming from our room until I entered the second-floor hallway. I approached the door and heard Sam's voice, loud and threatening. I pushed the door open.

Sam and Mick stood facing each other in the narrow space alongside the queen bed. The look on Sam's face made me stay in the doorway. His eyes, narrow and dark, were focused on Mick's face. Neither of them seemed to be aware of my presence.

"Another thing," Sam said, jabbing a thick finger into Mick's chest, "I'm sick and tired of cleaning up your shit."

"Bugger off," Mick retorted. "I told you, I didn't start that row down there. You deaf, mate?"

"You think you're so fucking clever, don't you? And knock off that stupid accent."

"Hey, I don't have to take your shit, right."

I tried to break in. "Look, guys—"

Sam barely glanced at me. "Listen up, Mick. I'm the one who had to take it from Mr. Tom. He was pissed, man. He doesn't like having to throw out paying customers."

"You think I care?" Mick turned his back on Sam.

"You'd better, because I've had it with your big mouth.

You think you're some fucking prima donna. We could've gotten fired tonight. You listenin' to me?"

Mick spun, and now he stuck a finger in Sam's chest. "Sod off, mate. I carry this band on my back, and that includes you. What the hell do you do, anyhow?"

I knew what was coming, and Mick deserved it. I closed the door behind me, stepped back, and watched. With barely a flick of his wrist, Sam shoved Mick, sending him staggering backward. Mick fell on the bed and stared up at Sam with wide, unfocused eyes. I started to step between them, but Mick sprang up and ploughed into Sam, wrestling him backward. Backpedaling, I managed to stay out of their way. The two of them banged hard into a dresser and knocked over a half-empty beer can, which rolled off the dresser and crashed to the floor in a puddle. Sam, showing more restraint than Mick deserved, pushed him away again. Mick stepped backward onto the beer can, lost his balance, and fell hard on his butt, right into the puddle of beer.

Knowing that Sam's restraint would only last so long, I finally got between them. "O.K., that's enough!" I put a hand on Mick's shoulder to keep him from getting up. He pushed my arm away and tried to stand, but I pushed him back down. From the other side of me, Sam shoved to get at him. "Hold it!" I yelled. They both stopped, noticing me for the first time.

"That's it! That's the end of it. Both of you just back off." I took my hand off of Mick's shoulder. He struggled up, the rear of his jeans soaked with the beer.

Sam pointed at Mick. "I'm outta this band unless he cleans up his act. Poundin' nails is better than *this* bullshit."

"Who bleedin' cares," Mick said.

I stayed between them. "Just shut up, Mick. Sam's right. We get fired from this gig and we're dead. You can go home to your father with your tail between your legs. You got it?" My face was suddenly hot with anger. "Don't fuck this up."

"Hey," Mick said, "I was just saying it wasn't my fault, right?"

I pushed down my anger. "O.K., let's drop it then. You cool, Sammy?"

"For now."

I took a breath. "Mick, you better change your pants. I invited a couple of guys up from the bar." I started to the cooler. "Sam, you look like you need a beer."

With a shrug, Mick grabbed another pair of pants and stomped off toward the bathroom. I tossed Sam a can out of the ice chest. He caught it with one hand, popped it with the other, and turned his back to stare out the window.

Left alone in the middle of the room, I kicked off my boots and plopped down on the unmade bed. Kitten's offer to help the band came to mind, but now I wondered if we would even make it through the week. Maybe we were too much like the Who. I recalled that Keith Moon had quit the band after only three days, Roger Daltry had been forced out of the group right after they recorded *My Generation*, and everybody fought with Townshend all the time. Like them, we could blow apart at any moment. Maybe I had made a mistake forcing the band into this gig so far from home. But my mind went back to what Kitten had asked me earlier in the night—"Do you wanna make it or not?"—and the answer was clear: Playing here was the key to our future. And, at least for me, there was no way back.

I lit a cigarette and gazed around our shabby little room. At least Mick and Sam hadn't wrecked it or thrown the furniture out the window, like the Who did in Montreal during their *Quadrophenia* tour. Hell, by now the Who would've absolutely trashed this fuckin' place.

12

TWO ASPIRIN, chased by a gulp of Oly, were sliding down my throat when someone knocked at the door. Coughing, I took another sip and glanced over at Sam, hoping he would deal with it. No way. Frozen at the window like a statue, he continued to stare down at the darkened parking lot. He was still dressed in his stage clothes, consisting of a Giants baseball jersey, embroidered jeans, and brown platforms. Mick was still in the bathroom changing his beer-soaked pants, so I pulled myself up from the bed and opened the door, expecting to see Beanie and Cecil. Instead, Rob and Yogi strolled in. I told them what had happened while Sam and Mick maintained their positions.

A few minutes later another knock came at the door. At the same time, the bathroom door swung open and Mick straggled out in a pair of tight royal-blue corduroy flares, shining with newness. The pants made a zip-zipping sound as he walked over to the ice chest to get a beer. Sam glanced at the pants and frowned. I pushed off the queen bed and let Beanie and Cecil in, quickly introducing them to the band. As I sat down on the edge of the bed, Mick stiffly zip-zipped back to the other side of the room and slid onto a wobbly wooden chair propped against the wall near the bathroom door.

"Hey, Mick," Beanie said, his eyes getting big, "those pants are bodacious. Where'd you get 'em?"

Mick scowled and we all broke out laughing. Beanie looked around the room. "What'd I say?" I waved him off, trying to catch my breath.

Sam passed out a round of beers, and Beanie and Cecil sat down on the floor with their backs against the wall next to the door. Sam straddled the only other chair in the room on the far side of the bed as Rob plopped down on one end of the roll-away at the foot of the bed. Yogi, whose black high-tops were untied, settled down on the other end of the roll-away and ripped open a bag of Fritos. Our room was suddenly crowded.

I watched Beanie struggle with the tab of his beer can. He finally tugged it off, and foam boiled out and ran down the sides. He took a long swig. "Man, this is righteous brew. We haven't had any for a coupla days."

"But you guys work in the bar," Sam said, breaking his silence. "You must get all the beer you want."

"Nah. Tom'll only give us two a night if we can pay for 'em. We're supposed to be sober in case a riot breaks out or something." Beanie giggled out a burst of squeaks.

I pushed back a smile. "We must be on Tom's shit list after what happened to the window last night. And after the hassle in the bar tonight."

"Don't worry about it," Cecil broke in, his deep voice and serious demeanor demanding our attention. "Tom likes you guys. He's just giving you a hard time. He actually wanted me to throw those assholes out tonight." He shifted his legs and studied his worn work boots, seemingly uncomfortable that the conversation had found its way to him. "We talked to him while we were cleaning up tonight. He thinks you'll bring in a good weekend crowd once the word gets around town. Most of the bands we get in here are pretty bad—just loud and obnoxious."

"But we'd heard this place gets some name acts," I said, "like Hendrix and Heart."

"Yeah." Cecil almost smiled. "We heard that rumor too. Anyhow, Tom thinks you guys are a good change, but don't expect to hear that from him."

"See!" Mick said.

Sam threw him a dirty look. "He didn't seem too happy when I talked to him after the last set."

Beanie giggled again. "You think tonight was bad? Wait till you see Saturday night."

"What about Saturday night?" I asked, leaning forward on the bed. "That's the second time you've mentioned it."

Beanie glanced at Cecil, who shifted position, dislodging white flakes of paint from the wall behind his head. A few landed on his dark hair, like flecks of dandruff. He tried to swat them away, but they were stuck.

"What about Saturday night?" I asked again.

"Haven't you heard?" Beanie was giving me a crazy kind of smile. "Saturday night is Hell's Angels night."

"You're kidding."

"No, really. There'll be fifty Harleys parked out front. Man, you won't believe it. The place'll be fulla motorcycle dudes and their mamas." He jumped up and started shadow-boxing. "We try to stay outta the way, but, man alive, we usually have to break up a coupla fights, at least."

Cecil reached up and tugged at the tail of Beanie's Hawaiian shirt. "Sit down, buddy."

"You get fights in the bar?" Rob turned a tight face toward the two bouncers. "What happens to the bands?" Everybody now leaned forward. This time Beanie remained silent.

Cecil looked around the room and started to speak, then paused as if trying to think of a good way to deliver really bad news. My mind raced. I'd read Hunter Thompson's book on the Angels and remembered the stories of crazy brawls and wanton mischief. Hell, they'd even beat Thompson to a pulp just for being around 'em. Then there was the Stones at Altamont, where the Angels beat a guy to death on camera just for being in the wrong place at the wrong time. A shudder passed through me.

"Look," Cecil said, "don't worry about it, but to tell you the truth—and we've only been working here a couple of months—almost every band has had problems on Saturday night."

"Problems?" Beanie interrupted, unable to contain himself. "That's one way to put it. Man, they chucked bottles at the last band."

"But," Cecil added quickly, "they don't throw them at every band, only the ones they think are shit—"

"They threw bottles?" Rob's face had tightened into a wedge of disbelief.

Cecil shrugged his thick shoulders. "Yeah, but they weren't trying to hit 'em. They were just havin' fun."

"Jeez, it was freaky!" Beanie said. "The singer was dancing around the stage, dodging Olys right and left."

I heard Mick muffle a groan and mutter, "Oh, bloody hell." He crossed the room—*zip, zip, zip*—to get another beer.

"Hey, Mick," Sam said, "you probably shouldn't wear those pants Saturday night."

"Don't be a prat," Mick replied, but his voice lacked its usual bravado.

"Look," Cecil said, moving his legs to let Mick by, "you guys shouldn't worry about it. Me and Beanie'll take care of things if they get outta hand. That's what we get paid for." He smiled for the first time.

I tried to return his smile, but, knowing the effect this information would have on the band, I couldn't. Instead, I glanced around the room. Rob and Mick were clearly rattled by the news, and Sam's eyes had returned to the darkness outside the window. Yogi was starting to nod off. I looked back across the room and repeated Cecil's words to myself: *Me and Beanie'll take of it.* Cecil, maybe, but Beanie? I pictured him taking on some burly bikers coming at us with bottles. They would kill him. Then they would kill the rest of us.

But Beanie giggled, oblivious to the tension in the room. "Some of 'em are actually pretty nice."

"Oh, I bet," Rob said, his fingers tapping out a furious rhythm on his knee.

"No, Beanie's right," Cecil added. "Most of 'em are O.K. They just look scary."

"My favorites are Butch and Whiskey." Beanie was shadowboxing again. "Butch's got a red dagger tattooed on the back of his hand and this big scar across his cheek. Whiskey's his woman, and she kinda looks like Butch, only a little shorter. She always wears this leather thing"—he drew his hands across his concave chest—"and she has a rose tattooed on her boobs. Anyhow, they're pretty nice." He danced a little more "Butch usually buys me a beer when they come in."

"Her boobs are nice?" Mick asked with sudden interest.

Beanie's eyes lowered, his face going bright red. "I mean Butch and Whiskey. *They're* nice."

"Oh." Mick squirmed in his chair. "Not to change the subject, but how'd you blokes end up at a grotty place like this?"

Beanie gave him another one of his weird grins. "Probably the same way you guys did. We just drifted in, you know, like turds blown by the wind." He giggled at his vivid imagery. "Actually, we came in one night to get a beer, and Cecil broke up a fight between two guys. Tom offered him a job, and my buddy here talked him into hiring me, too. We only get ten bucks a night, but we get our room free."

"You're staying *here*?" Mick asked, surprised. I was, too. I hadn't seen anyone going up or down the stairs.

"We're on the ground floor, just off the lobby."

I crossed the room to get another beer and brought back a couple more for Beanie and Cecil. "So then you guys aren't from around here?" I handed them the beers.

"Hell, no." Cecil ripped the metal tab from the beer can like it was a piece of paper. "Me and Beanie got outta the Navy about three months ago and got discharged at the shipyard in Bremerton, over near Seattle. We didn't know what the hell to do, so we decided to hitchhike up the peninsula. Then we were going to hitch down the coast to Frisco or L.A." He stopped for a moment and grinned self-consciously. "Well, hell, we didn't get very far did we, Beanie? I left my wallet at a gas station toilet in Sequim, and somebody ripped it off with almost all the money we had. So when we got here and Tom offered me the job, I figured I'd better take it. We're trying to save up so we can get outta here."

We all nodded at him. The Mai Tai Hotel had a way of making you want to flee.

"Why's nobody else staying here?" Sam asked. "And where's the maid service? We've been here since Monday, and nobody's even brought up fresh towels. And the bathroom stinks."

"We wondered the same thing at first," Cecil said. "The bands usually stay here, but outside of them, hardly anyone else does. Strange, huh?"

"Pretty weird," I agreed.

"At least no bleedin' rednecks have tried to kill you," Mick said. "Some sods tried to run me down last night."

Cecil didn't look surprised. "We heard about it from Tom. We helped him put the plywood in the window. He seemed to know who did it."

"He sure didn't let on," I said. "He seemed to think we'd caused it."

"Yeah, that's Tom," Cecil said. He looked at Beanie, who yawned, and then at Yogi, who lay slouched over the end of the roll-away, his hand in the bag of Fritos. "I think we'd better get goin'. Beanie needs his sleep. He's a growing boy, you know."

Cecil got up and yanked at the shoulder of Beanie's shirt. "Come on, buddy. Time to go." Beanie unraveled his arms and legs and stood up unsteadily.

I followed them into the hallway. "I'm glad we finally met you guys. At least we'll have a couple of friends in the bar. By the way, do you know Kitten and Kyle? I met them last night. They got the beer for us."

Cecil nodded. "Yeah, I saw you and Mick walk out with 'em. They're real regulars. Kyle's kinda clueless, but he's a good guy, I guess. Kitten's another story. She hangs around here a lot and seems to know Tom pretty good. If I were you, I'd watch myself around her."

I was starting to give Cecil a nod, but he must have taken it as a question.

He shrugged. "She's a little scary, that's all."

"I know what you mean. I've been trying to figure her out myself."

"Well, watch yourself, man." Cecil shook his head. "I get the idea that she wants outta here bad. Maybe even worse than me and Beanie. She's tried to hook up with more than one band that's come through here."

"She told me she knows all the promoters who book the bar."

"Yeah, I've seen her talk to 'em when they come in. She's real friendly when she wants to be, and I think she's screwing some of 'em."

My mind started to race. "Rick Astley? Is he one of them?"

Cecil's brow furrowed. "Astley?"

"Out of Denver? Big Country Productions?"

"Sounds familiar, but I'm not sure. I know she's pretty tight with this one local promoter, but I think he's named Beeber, or something like that—anyhow, he's a real asshole. Ol' Kyle doesn't have a clue what's going on." Cecil shrugged again. "Anyhow, we'll see you guys tomorrow."

I watched Cecil guide Beanie the ten steps to the stairwell, then disappear.

13

LATE THURSDAY MORNING the four of us ran down the sidewalk with our coats pulled up over our heads. Rob trailed behind, too cool to run, his battered Stetson shielding his head and face. The rest of us were getting soaked.

The rain came down at an angle, driven sideways by a north wind blowing off the strait. When we turned into Pam's Cup O' Coffee Café, my tennis shoes, sopping wet, squeaked with water. Ducking beneath the covered entryway of the café, I stopped to brush off my jacket and rub water out of my ears. Since leaving the hotel, I'd been hearing a peculiar hissing sound, like radio static, coming from somewhere near my head. At first, I'd thought it was the sound of raindrops hitting my jacket, but now I realized it was internal. I yawned to pop my ears, but it didn't help.

Rob caught up with me before I went through the door and shook water from his hat. "A nice day if you're a duck, huh?"

"Another beautiful day in paradise."

We entered the café in time to see Evangeline seating the other guys. She nodded in our direction as we took our seats before turning back to Mick. "No, like I just said, it's too late. We stopped serving breakfast an hour ago."

"Be kind, will ya, sweetheart? I have me heart set on some bacon and eggs."

Sam scowled. "She said she couldn't already."

Evangeline looked back and forth between the two of them, who were separated only by Yogi. "Well, I'll see what I can do, but you should've gotten up with Edward. He was in here at, what, Edward, nine?"

Yogi nodded, prompting a cold stare from Mick. Evangeline walked back toward the kitchen.

"You've already eaten?" I asked Yogi. I noticed that he was wearing a white puka shell necklace, something I'd never seen on him before.

"I was up before nine. Didn't want to waste the day."

"Waste the day? It's fucking raining." My words came out edgy and irritated, and I suddenly knew why my ears were hissing. Before leaving the hotel, I had taken four cross-tops in an effort to push away my hangover, and I had overestimated what I needed to get through the day. They were too much. As if on cue, my mouth went dry, my heart began to race, and the hissing in my ears grew louder.

Evangeline returned with glasses of water and then left us again to get coffee. Mick and Sam disappeared behind their menus, and I lit a cigarette and gazed across at them, the smoke burning my throat as I inhaled. They had been sniping at each other all morning.

"Mick, Sam," I said, "are you going to do this all day? I think it's time to kiss and make up. We're a band, remember? All for one, and one for all?"

Yogi leaned back in his chair as if to give them room to shake hands, but neither of them took the hint. Instead, Mick reached out to inspect the salt and pepper shakers, and Sam turned his head to watch raindrops strike the window.

"Look." I leaned forward, my face already warmed by a rapidly accelerating pulse. "We've got bigger things to worry about than your fucking little disagreement. Like making sure the switch box for the lights is working before tonight's show. And we need to start thinking about how we're gonna handle this Hell's Angels thing. So why don't you two guys cut out this shit."

Sam eyebrows went up, apparently surprised by the sharpness of my voice. "Hey, like I said last night, I'm willing to drop this if Mick is. I just want him to clean up his act."

I looked over at Mick. "Well?"

"Yeah, whatever," Mick said with a shrug. "I couldn't suss out his problem anyhow, y'know?"

It wasn't an apology, but I figured it was close enough. "Great. We're one big, happy family again."

Evangeline returned with the coffee, and we sat in stony silence while she circled the table filling cups. I took another drag on my cigarette, again feeling the irritation in my throat, and watched Evangeline pour Sam's coffee. Moving from him to Mick, she seemed to sense the lingering tension, sneaking a glance at Mick while filling his cup.

He looked up at her. "Cheers, sweetheart. By the way, I watched for you last night. I fancied you'd be there."

"I said I'd *try* to come." She smiled at him and her features softened. "I promise I'll try to get by before the end of the week." She took our orders and returned to the kitchen.

I pulled another Marlboro from the red pack in my shirt pocket but dropped the match trying to light it. My hands were shaking. I returned the cigarette to my pocket and took a series of long, deep breaths until my heartbeat slowed a notch. "O.K.," I said, "let's talk about a few things before the food gets here. Maybe Beanie and Cecil were exaggerating about the Hell's Angels—"

"Born to be wild," Yogi suddenly sang out.

"What's that supposed to mean?"

Yogi grinned at me, apparently pleased by his timing. "Well, they weren't exaggerating. Evangeline told me that the Mai Tai is known as a biker's bar."

I took another deep breath to fight off the flutter in my stomach. "Well, then, I guess we need to have a plan in case bottles really do start flying."

"Yeah, I agree," Rob said, leaning forward. "I don't really care what Mr. Tom thinks. I'm beatin' a retreat if shit starts hitting us."

"How about me?" Mick asked. "I'm gonna be a bleedin' target up there."

Sam glanced at him and smiled.

"That's why we need to talk about it," I said.

"Look," Rob said, "I've been thinking. . . ." He paused and glanced at Sam.

"What? You've been thinking what?" I heard the impatience in my voice.

Rob avoided my eyes. "Well, I was thinking that maybe we should consider pulling out of this gig. I'm getting really bad vibes about this place. We can get shows in Creedly; we don't need to put up with this shit." He stopped and looked around the table, his gaze halting at Sam.

"Yeah," Sam said, "I think I'm with Rob on this."

My head whipped toward him. "You're what?"

"Rob's right. I've had enough of this. This place is pretty much a dead end. And I'm tired of carryin' the load for certain people in this band." He gave Mick a darting look. "I'm ready to hit the road."

Again, I caught a flicker of eye contact between Sam and Rob. My mind raced and I realized what had happened: They'd already discussed it and had agreed to pull out of the gig. "So what're you saying? You really want out?"

"Don't get excited," Rob said. "We're just talking about this one gig."

"The hell with that," I said. "You guys pull out of this gig and we're finished."

"Jeez, Daniel—" Sam started.

"No. I mean it. I'll find other people to play with. How about you, Mick? Yogi?"

Mick removed his glasses and rubbed at the lenses. "I dunno."

"I'm having a good time," Yogi said. "And I don't think anything too bad will happen—"

"Easy for you to say, idn't?" Mick muttered. "You're protected by your drum set."

"Look," Rob said, looking sideways at me, "I just want to talk it over, O.K.?"

Anger surged through me. I knew I wasn't thinking straight, that the drugs had sped up the firing of my mental synapses, but I was suddenly tired of working so hard to keep everybody happy. "So you're willing to throw it all away just because of a few bikers?"

"It's not just the bikers," Rob answered, his fingers tapping the tabletop. "It's everything. This doesn't fit with my long-term vision, you know?"

"Your vision? Fuck that, Rob. It's really about Candi, isn't it? You just want to get home."

Rob's face tightened. "Watch what you say about her, man. This has nothing to do with her. The band's just as important to me as it is to you. I'm just not sure this gig's worth it."

"That's just fucking bullshit." The hissing in my ears intensified and my fists clenched. I knew I might hit him if I stayed. I pushed away from the table, knocking over a glass of water. Grabbing my jacket, I headed through the door.

Two blocks of wet sidewalk were behind me before I slowed, chilled by the rain, my ears still hissing with unspent adrenaline and amphetamines. I pulled up under the awning of a shuttered department store and lit a cigarette, exhaling painful smoke as I stared out through the rain at the blackened sky. The band had betrayed me. I traced the outline of the dog tag through the fabric of my shirt and felt moisture in my eyes. Emptiness followed, but I couldn't stop the blood from surging through my veins.

I closed my eyes and saw Townshend's Jimmy on the rock in the ocean, the water inching up, the waves covering his shoes, his knees, his waist. I was wrong; the water *would* take me if I let it. The sound of rain striking the awning filled my head, echoing back and forth between my ears like individual notes, fighting, jostling, forming small groups, joining together into larger ones until they finally became a single harsh sound roaring in my ears.

Was this finally it, the perfect chord? If so, then it was not the beautiful sound of unified notes but the discordant noise that separated me from everyone else. Was this what Townshend had ultimately discovered? Was this what had nearly sent him over the edge?

I took another painful drag on the cigarette, leaned back against the outside wall of the store, and tried to fix my mind on what I now understood. Up until now, Rob had been my best friend, but if he did leave, he could be replaced. The same with Sam. I recalled how the Who had changed their original lead singer and drummer, how Roger Daltry and Keith Moon had both left the band in anger, only to return. The Who had survived. Perhaps the Killjoys could, too. Maybe Mick and Yogi would stay with me. I owned the Blue Bomb and most of the P.A. equipment. But we had to get through this week or we were finished. Hell, *I* might be finished.

"Hey, Daniel."

I looked up. Rob ducked his head and stepped under the awning.

"What do you want?"

He shoved his hands down into his pockets. "Look, man, I didn't mean to piss you off. I just wanted to discuss things."

"Yeah?" I threw down my cigarette and stubbed it out.

"We talked it over after you left. We're willing to stick it out the rest of the week if you are. I don't want to screw you guys. Sam feels the same way."

I stared at him until his gaze shifted downward.

"What about after that?"

Rob looked up. "After that?"

"When we get home. Are you and Sam gonna stay with it? I need to know because I'm going on with or without you."

Rob gave me a long look. "It's that important to you?"

"It is."

Rob let out a long sigh. "Hell, I don't know. You know how I feel about the band, but I need to talk to Candi about it. It'd be different if we had a future, but Candi's right, playing clubs like this isn't going to get us anywhere."

I started shaking my head slowly, and Rob added, "Look, I'm not saying I'm going to quit. I just need time to think about it."

"You're wrong, Rob." I stepped on the cigarette again. "We're going places, and this is how we pay our dues." I cocked my head. "You just don't have the stomach for it, do you?" I paused for a second, then went in with the needle. "Or is this just all about Candi?"

His face jerked away, pale-blue eyes shooting into the rain.

"Shit, man, I told you it's not just about her." He was stepping awkwardly side to side. "Look, it's about a lot of things. It's about my future, O.K.? I have to make some decisions. Candi's just the one forcing me to make them right now."

I stared at him. Once again it struck me that he and I were now on different paths, that, for him, music was only a boyhood distraction. I had found what I thought was the perfect chord, and now it stood between us. Deep down, I felt bad about what he was going through with Candi, but I knew that I could go on without him, and I would if I needed to.

"O.K., Rob," I finally said, "let's finish the week and see what happens."

14

STEPPING OVER dark puddles forming in street inter-sections, I followed Mick back to the hotel. The others had already left in the station wagon in search of parts for our malfunctioning switch box, a convenient excuse to escape the tension from our argument in the café.

As soon as we were inside the room, Mick fell onto the unmade bed and announced, "I'm bloody knackered."

With my heart still tapping out a steady beat and my brain reeling from the implications of my confrontation with Rob, sleep was the furthest thing from my mind. "You're tak-ing a nap? You only got up three hours ago."

"Naff off." Mick pulled a pillow over his face.

"Look, we need to talk about the band."

"You're all pilled up, mate. Go do something. Leave me alone."

Mick was right. The hissing in my ears had stopped, but the electrical charges pulsing from every nerve ending kept going. I sat on the roll-away, fidgeting, pondering my options. It was only 2:30 in the afternoon, but the day already felt lost. I moved over to the window. Rainwater streamed down the outside of the fogged-up pane of glass, making it impossible to see the decaying town outside our room.

Mick was asleep within minutes. I listened to his breath-ing and paced the room, pausing periodically to rub a new spot in the window. Nothing moved in the hotel's empty back parking lot. Finally, I pulled out my Graham Greene novel and started to read, but I couldn't concentrate. The place was so damp. God, it was depressing.

I remembered seeing a library near the county court-house just up from the post office. I knew I'd get soaked, but I could no longer remain in the room. The van would be drier, but it was only four or five blocks. Hell, I was already wet. I swapped my soaked tennis shoes for boots, pulled on my jacket, and stuffed the book into an inside pocket.

The rain had slowed by the time I got outside. Turning at the first corner, I looked up at the mountains behind town, seeing that the dark clouds that had piled high against the steep ridge to the south were starting to lift. I jaywalked across the street and cut between the courthouse and the police station. A cop glanced at me as he slid into a patrol car parked in front of the station.

I ran up the ten steps of the old brick library, almost slipping on the top step, and pushed through the heavy front door. The library smelled of damp books and furniture polish, but the hardwood floors and rows of bookcases gave off a comforting sense of solidity. An older woman wearing a simple print dress stood behind the semicircular checkout counter sorting through two stacks of books. She stopped and stared at me with a startled expression. My hair had exploded in the humidity. I pulled the tangled mess back with both hands and held it there, hoping to look less threatening.

"May I help you with something?" she asked.

"No, thanks. Actually, I was just looking for a quiet place to sit down and read for a while." I pulled out my book and showed it to her, as if it proved what I was saying.

Her expression relaxed a bit. She pointed down a corridor lined with bookcases. "There are tables at the back. You're welcome to read there."

I walked down the passageway, scanning book titles as I went. My father had kept his home library stocked with hardbound books, buying a couple every month, and he had left many of them behind when he moved out of the house. I'd read most of them during the solitary months following Kevin's death.

I slid out of my jacket and sat down at a long, gleaming table at the back of the library. An older couple slowly worked their way down a row of books; otherwise, the library seemed empty. I heard the faint ticking of a clock on the wall behind me. Quiet. I needed quiet.

I opened my battered paperback copy of *The End of the Affair* and pulled out the bookmark. The name on the bookmark startled me: Nita Annstrom. I hadn't called her back. Closing my eyes, I tried to remember how she looked, how she sounded. I tried hard, but I couldn't remember. I could picture her punky clothes but not her.

I started in on the book and slowly got pulled back into the story that I'd started two weeks earlier. World War II London. A tortured, obsessive love affair between a married woman and a novelist. All jealousy, darkness, pain, and guilt. As I read, I kept wondering why all my relationships ended up feeling that way. Then I almost laughed out loud. What a ludicrous comparison.

I paused and followed a scratch in the surface of the table with my fingernail, thinking about the few girls I'd dated. Besides the one or two one-nighters I'd had with women I'd met playing local clubs, my so-called relationships had been limited to dating a girl for a few weeks during my junior year of high school and another for a month or so the summer after I graduated. Both relationships had ended with the girls complaining that I wouldn't open up to them, that the band was more important to me. And I knew that what they also said about me was true: I trusted nobody. And why should I? Would they be there for the long haul? Would anyone be there when I needed them? Kevin, my parents, Rob? I shook my head. So how would Nita be any different?

I continued to follow the scratch in the tabletop until it flowed into a set of initials within the scratchy outline of a heart. For the first time on this day, I couldn't answer one of my own questions. Kitten suddenly entered my mind, but I pushed the thought of her away.

I read on. The book's love affair became more complicated.

A German bomb had struck the apartment in which Bendrix, the novelist, and Sarah, the married woman, were making love. Sarah thought Bendrix was killed by the bomb and made a deal with God that she would give him up if God brought him back to life. Well, poor Bendrix had only been knocked unconscious by the bomb's blast. He was alive, but he had lost his lover in a deal with God. Right. That's what trust got you.

I looked up when I heard grinding footsteps on the hardwood floor. The librarian approached my table, glancing up at the clock on the wall above my head. "I'm sorry, sir,"— *sir?*—"but the library closes at five o'clock on weekdays." She paused, looked up at the clock again, and then turned on her heels and headed back toward the front of the library.

I heard her, but my mind was still in rainy London. I looked at my watch, then twisted to look at the clock on the wall. Could it be that late already? Sure enough, it was a quarter to five. Big chunks of time often got lost when I was pilled up. I knew the guys would soon be gathering for dinner, so I closed the book and pulled on my jacket. At least for the moment, Bendrix and Sarah would have to work out their own problems.

Emerging from the library, I stepped into near-darkness. A large drop of water hit the top of my head while I carefully made my way down the concrete steps. By the time I reached the sidewalk I realized that the drop had fallen from the library's eaves; it had stopped raining.

I started back the way I'd come but got only halfway down the block before seeing the telephone booth in front of the police station across the street. The booth, lit from within, glowed in the mistiness of dusk. I stopped at the edge of the street. I could wait until I got back to Creedly to call her. But I had enough change in my pocket, and she would probably be home by now. I had told her roommate I would call back later in the week. Was this late enough? No. But I was like Bendrix in the book. I knew the distrust he felt and the obsession that drove him when Sarah would no longer see him. And . . . I needed to answer my question.

Like a metal ball drawn by a magnet, I crossed the street and headed for the telephone booth. Slamming shut the door, I pulled a fistful of coins from my pocket and counted the change. After sliding the coins into the slot, I carefully dialed the number. I took a deep breath, waiting to hear the ring on the other end of the line. One, two rings, three. I waited for the click of an answer. Four, five, six. Two more, I thought. But I let it go four more before I hung up. Quarters, dimes, and nickels jangled down into the coin return box as if I'd won a jackpot.

With the rain coming down once again, I started back toward the hotel, certain that Bendrix would've let it ring at least two more times.

* * * * *

A FEW MINUTES later, I was following snaky rills of rainwater down the sidewalk toward Main Street when a familiar orange VW van pulled up at the curb beside me. The passenger-side window rolled down, and Kitten leaned across the empty passenger seat.

"Hey, kid." She motioned me over with one of her ringed fingers. "Get in."

"What?"

"Get in. We need to talk."

"What for?" The scent of Charlie, now smelling like damp weeds, drifted through the open window.

"I've got news for you, and it's about your future. Just get in." From inside the van, she popped open the door. I glanced around before sliding in beside her. She kept the engine idling and smiled across at me. "I was just coming to look you up. This is your lucky day, kiddo."

"Oh, yeah?" Water trickled off my jacket and onto the seat. "It hasn't felt like it so far."

"Get ready, then." She brushed strands of hair away from her face. "How'd you like to open for Heart? They're playin' at the fairgrounds on Sunday."

I shook my head. "What're you talking about?"

"I told you I know the promoters who do bookings around here."

"Yeah?"

"So, the opening act dropped out and they need someone to fill in."

My mouth dropped open. "And they want us?"

"Doesn't matter. I can get you in." She slipped the van into gear. "Let's go to my place and talk it over."

"Wait. Can't you just tell me here?"

"Jesus, kid, you're dripping all over the place. Let's go."

She swung the van around in an illegal U-turn and chugged up the hill past the police station. With one hand she lit a cigarette, took a puff, and handed it to me. I considered it for a moment before bringing it to my lips.

"Where's Kyle?" I asked, curious but at the same time suspicious about where this might be heading.

She motioned back toward the ocean with her thumb. "Out there getting wet, as usual."

"He's what?"

"Kyle's crew on a fishing boat. He probably won't be back for a week."

"But I thought he worked at that liquor store."

"Naw, that's his buddy's gig."

I stubbed out the cigarette in the overflowing ashtray. Now I knew for sure: Kyle *had* stolen the beer. It figured. I settled back and wrapped my arms around myself. The rain had soaked through my jacket, and I was beginning to shiver in the drafty van. I glanced sideways at Kitten, bound up tight in her Levi's jacket, peasant blouse, and hippie skirt, and considered the situation. I had nothing to lose by hearing her out. The band was about to bust up unless something good happened. An opening slot for Heart would be a damn good start.

Kitten drove a few more blocks before pulling into the parking lot of a ratty little two-story apartment building. She stopped near the back of the lot and cut the engine. "C'mon," she said, stepping out onto gravel. "We're upstairs."

I hesitated. "The guys are waiting for me at the hotel."

She tucked her head back into the van. "You afraid of being alone with me?"

"No," I lied. "Should I be?"

"You're a big boy. I'm sure you can take care of yourself. Let's go."

Kitten didn't wait for a response. Turning, she started for the stairs. I followed her up to the unit at the back corner. She unlocked the door and we stepped onto burnt-orange shag carpet. A kitchen was tucked behind a counter at the back of the living room. A hallway led off to the right. The apartment was sparsely furnished with an armchair and sofa, both covered in the same tone of dull brown, and a smudged glass-topped coffee table, littered with ashtrays and empty cigarette packs. A stereo was set up on the floor next to an old television set, and a red lava lamp gurgled away in a corner of the room beneath a felt black-light poster of a tiger.

"Cozy place," I said.

She ignored me and reached down to flip on an FM rock station. Pink Floyd's *Wish You Were Here* came softly through the small speakers on either side of the stereo receiver. "Take off your jacket and sit down. I'll get you somethin'."

I assumed she meant a blanket or towel, but she came back with a bottle of Jack Daniels and two glasses. She took off her Levi's jacket, sat down beside me on the sofa, and poured two fingers of whiskey into each glass. "Here." We clinked glasses, and I took a sip, letting the smooth liquid etch its way down my throat.

"So tell me about this gig," I said, now noticing, with her jacket off and the light behind her, the absence of a bra beneath her gauzy blouse. I forced myself to recall the vow I'd made to myself about her.

She downed her whiskey in two gulps. "I know the guy who's workin' the show from the local side. Bob Beeber."

I took my eyes away from her blouse, remembering that Cecil had mentioned someone with a name like that the night before. "Did you say Beeber?"

"Yeah. He's a friend of mine. Anyhow, he told me that the opening act's singer got busted up in a wreck yesterday. They need someone who can do a thirty-, forty-minute opening slot. You guys are finished at the Mai Tai Saturday night, right?"

"Sure, but we're leaving the next morning."

"Plan on sticking around, and I'll see what I can do to get you in." She kicked off her red clogs and put her bare feet up on the coffee table.

As I rolled the whiskey around in my glass, I again wondered if she was for real. Opening for Heart would be an incredible break, the kind of opportunity a band gets once, if it's lucky. I didn't know how Rob would feel about sticking around for another night, but I figured the other guys, including Sam, wouldn't give him much choice.

"How much would we get paid?"

She laughed and poured more whiskey into my glass. "You'd get taken care of, kiddo. They were gonna pay the other band five-hundred bucks."

I gulped down more of the Jack Daniels and felt the fumes rise to my head. The sudden lift brought by the combination of the high-octane alcohol and the uppers was unmistakable. But, recalling Cecil's warning about Kitten, I kept my guard up.

"So why are you doing this?" I peered at her through my glass. "What's in it for you?"

She shrugged. "I like you, kid." Then she laughed again. "You don't trust nobody, do you?"

"Depends on who I'm talking to."

"O.K., let's get down to it, then." Her eyes slitted. "What I want is a manager's cut. Fifteen percent."

I tried to calculate the potential fee. Sixty dollars? Seventy? The damn whiskey had already muddled my thinking. Whatever it was, it would be worth it. "I think we can handle that."

"And there's one other thing."

"Yeah?"

She leaned toward me, her face close to mine. "If I get you this gig, you gotta take me on as your manager."

I pulled back. "You're kidding."

"You think so?" She took a sip of whiskey and smiled.

"We've already got an agent." I shook my head. "What do we want with a—"

"Don't fuckin' fool yourself, kid. Astley'll use you and move on. If you wanna move up, you need someone who's got access to *all* the promoters."

I gazed at her face, one that would be pretty if it wasn't so tough. I saw nothing but confidence, or bravado. "Maybe so," I said, "but I don't see it. What? You're gonna travel around with us and do the bookings?"

She nodded. "That's the idea."

I took a minute to picture the situation but couldn't. I searched my mind for a way to put her off without endangering the possible Heart gig. "You could do the bookings from here," I suggested. "We'd be happy to pay you fifteen percent for any gigs you got us."

Kitten's smile faded, replaced by a fierce hardness around her eyes. "Look, kid, I want outta this fucking town. I've been waiting for a band that has the stuff to hook on to." She leaned toward me. "We can be good for each other, if you're smart."

I shook my head and tried to think. "I doubt the other guys will go along with it. I mean, I'd have to talk to them about it."

Now she leaned back. "That's your problem to work out. You take me or you don't get the gig."

"How do I even know this is for real?"

Her eyes lit up. "Let me worry about that. You'll know one way or the other by tomorrow."

I downed the rest of my whiskey and lit a cigarette. The price for getting this gig was becoming high. But did I have a choice? I knew there was a good chance Rob would quit the band when we got home, and even though I was willing to replace him, I knew it'd be a difficult and lengthy process. Playing this gig might provide me with the glue to hold us together. We could always dump Kitten later.

She emptied the Jack Daniels bottle by pouring equal amounts into the two glasses. "Well?"

I took a deep breath. "You get us the Heart gig, and I'll talk to the guys about the management thing. But it's limited to getting us gigs, right? No one tells us what we play."

"And dealing with the club owners."

I suddenly wished I was sober. Still, I knew it was all talk until we signed something. "I guess we can work out the other details if the gig comes through."

She smiled and hooked a leg over mine. "You won't regret it, kiddo."

I moved my leg away. "I should get going."

"You should, but you won't."

She tugged her skirt up above her knees and moved her leg back over mine. A warm flush ran the length of my body. The damn whiskey. She twisted a little, and my hand found its way onto her leg. "What about Kyle?"

"Kyle ain't ever leavin' this town, and I ain't stickin' around to wash his clothes." She leaned close to me and my hand slid farther up her leg. She put her arm behind my head and in one fluid motion pulled herself onto me. I let myself sink backward into the couch. As she loosened my belt, I couldn't miss the gleam of triumph in her eyes.

✳ ✳ ✳ ✳ ✳

I MADE IT BACK to the Mai Tai at 8:40, more sober than I deserved to be, knowing that I was cutting it way too close. And I felt absolutely dirty.

Hurrying through the lobby toward the stairwell, I heard Mick's voice coming from the P.A. in the lounge. I stopped and stepped inside. Mr. Tom was behind the bar, and the guys were already up on the stage, running through a sound-check.

"Test, one-two-three . . . test, test." Mick's voice echoed around the near-empty room. "I'd like to welcome you to tonight's meeting of Alcoholics Anonymous."

"Cut the shit," I heard Sam say.

I walked across the floor toward the stage. Mick leaned below the stage lights and squinted at me. "Who's that poofter? Why, it's Pleasant! Good to see ya, mate."

I ignored him and stepped up onto the elevated platform. "Sorry I'm late."

"I brought your guitars down," Rob said from the other side of the stage. "We just got started."

Seeing Rob's hopeful expression, I intuitively knew that he wanted to make amends for this morning's argument. In a way, knowing what I had to tell him later, it made me feel worse. I'd decided to wait on saying anything about Kitten and the Heart gig until I knew we had it. I pulled out my guitar, plugged in, and tuned it as fast as I could. "Let's get this over with," I said, checking my watch. "I still need to change clothes."

Mick sniffed the air and followed his nose over to me. "You smell like a poncy petunia, mate. And a rank one at that. Where've you been?"

"Nowhere. Get out there and let's play."

He gave me a knowing grin and hopped down onto the floor. Yogi clicked his sticks together and we started into an instrumental version of *Sweet Emotion*. Mick moved around on the dance floor, checking the volumes of the instruments. He pointed at me and lifted his thumb. I turned up a notch. He caught Rob's attention and had him turn down his bass, then listened for another thirty seconds and waved us to a stop. "Lovely, but you're a little sour, Daniel."

I strummed an open E chord and twisted the tuning pegs until the guitar was back in tune. We started the tune again, and this time Sam walked out onto the dance floor to check the vocal levels on the song's three-part harmonies. He adjusted volumes on the mixing board, had us do it again, and then shut us down.

I stripped off my guitar and jumped from the stage. "I'll be back in fifteen minutes."

Beanie and Cecil were at the door, checking the IDs of a group that had just come in, and I waved at them as I sped by. The bar was starting to fill, and I knew I had little time to waste. Within seconds, I was up the stairs and into the room. I had my boots off and was unbuttoning my shirt when I noticed something odd: My tennis shoes had been neatly placed on the seat of the chair next to the bed, and an unopened can of beer had been stuck in the opening of one of the shoes. I walked over and peered at the second shoe. Two neatly rolled joints were woven into the laces. Peace offerings from Sam and Rob.

I smiled and worked one of the joints from the laces. I lit it up and paused between removing articles of clothing to take occasional hits. After taking one last, long draw on the tightly rolled reefer, I pinched it out and stepped into the shower. The water ran over me in sheets of warmth, and I let it run, along with the scent of Kitten, down into the drain of the filthy shower.

15

MY EYES FLUTTERED open, then closed, confused by the blurry whiteness of the ceiling. Slowly, I opened them again. Somebody had raised the blinds and left them up; gray light filtered through the dirty window. Friday morning. I rolled over and looked at my watch on the nightstand. Barely seven, only four hours after we had stopped playing cards with Beanie and Cecil. Mick and Sam were still asleep.

Unwilling to be cheated out of sleep time in the big bed, I forced my eyes shut and pulled the covers up to my chin. But it was no good. My brain latched on to one image: Kitten. What the hell had I done? I shivered, again yanking on the mildewed sheets. I recalled little of her darkened bedroom, but I remembered everything about her: the wild look in her eyes, the clutching grip on my waist and legs, the guttural sounds from deep in her throat. It wasn't just about business; it was more intense, more personal. In the pit of my stomach I knew I was in trouble. I had fucked up big time.

I tried to get the image of her and her thrashing black hair out of my mind. My eyes wandered around the room. Cobwebs in a corner of the ceiling. Empty beer cans on the dresser and floor. Mick sprawled on the roll-away at the foot of my bed, one hairless leg hanging over the side. The plaid sleeping bag containing Sam's body bunched against the wall near the door. His brown-suede platform shoes lying sideways on the chair next to the window. But it wasn't any good: the rancid smell of Charlie, of Kitten, was still in my nostrils.

I quietly rolled out of bed and tiptoed to the window. Through the dirty pane, I looked out into the smudgy dawn and tried to convince myself that what I had done was O.K., that I had to do whatever was required to keep the band together. I realized Pete Townshend was right: Kitten had easily seen what was important to me, what I was willing to sacrifice to avoid returning to Creedly with the band in splinters. I had nothing but music to hang on to.

Suddenly cold, I turned to go back to bed. My foot side-swiped a couple of empty beer cans sitting on the floor and the clank of the cans awakened Mick. I heard him groan and turn over. He opened one eye. I knew he couldn't see me clearly; his glasses were nowhere to be seen. "What're you doin'?" he asked, his accent still asleep. "What time is it?"

"It's nothing." I crawled back into bed.

"What?" Mick reached out with his hand, searching the floor for his glasses. I saw them on the dresser.

Sam kicked at the bottom of his sleeping bag. "Shut the fuck up," he moaned and rolled against the wall, pulling his pillow up over his ear.

"Go back to sleep, Mick," I whispered, but he had collapsed back on his bed and seemed to be already gone. I pulled the covers over my face and closed my eyes.

✳ ✳ ✳ ✳ ✳

I DIDN'T SLEEP LONG. Or maybe I did.

Bam! Bam! Bam!

I shot upright, my heart pounding. Mick half-fell off the roll-away. Sam struggled to free his head from the sleeping bag.

Bam! Bam! Someone continued to pound on the door.

"Hold on," I yelled, rolling out of bed and trying to make my way around Mick to the door. Sam finally freed himself and scurried into the bathroom. I glanced out the window as I went by, noticing that the sky was lighter but still gray.

I opened the door a crack, partly to conceal my nearly naked body and partly because I wasn't sure who was on the other side. I peered through the crack to see Mr. Tom standing in the hall-way with his fist raised, ready to strike the door again.

"You have phone call," he said, peering at me curiously. I realized my hair was sticking out sideways.

I wasn't sure I'd heard him right. "I have a what?"

"Phone call. They waiting. You better hurry."

He started down the hall toward the stairs.

"Hold on," I called after him. "Where? Where's the phone?"

"In kitchen. Phone in kitchen. Better hurry. Long distance."

I nodded as he disappeared down the stairs. My brain started spinning. Who could possibly be calling me at this hour—whatever hour it was. And: Where were my clothes?

Mick was now up, hiding in a corner of the room; he'd found his glasses. "Bloody hell," he said, standing in his tight underwear. "I nearly pissed me knickers. What'd he want?"

"I've got a call." Hurrying around the bed, I almost tripped on the covers that had slid onto the floor. I steadied myself and grabbed my jeans off a chair.

Sam, still in his boxer shorts, emerged from the bathroom. "Who has a call?"

"Daniel does," Mick said. "Maybe it's me mum."

I pulled on my shirt and fumbled with the buttons. "Why would your mom be calling me?" I finally got the shirt buttoned up. "What time is it?"

Sam grabbed his watch from the dresser. "About a quarter after eleven."

I didn't bother to put on socks. I slipped on my tennis shoes, loosely tied them, and went out the door. I tried smoothing down my hair as I went down the hall. So, who could be calling me here? Kitten? But she wouldn't be calling long distance. And then Nita flashed through my mind and my heart pushed upward.

I ran down the stairs, through the lobby, and into the restaurant. As usual, no one was eating there. Mr. Tom, standing at the cash register, pointed at a phone attached to the wall beside the doorway to the kitchen. I grabbed the receiver dangling from the end of a long cord.

"Hello?"

"Goddamn, Daniel, what took you so long? You still sleeping?"

I recognized the nasal voice, the DJ-like patter, but couldn't immediately put a name or face to it. The momentary confusion had a déjà vu quality to it, like a conversation from my past. "I was upstairs in our room. Who is this?"

"It's Rick Astley, dude. I was just calling to see how you guys're doing."

The sense of déjà vu became stronger. "Rick. Yeah. Hi."

"So how *are* you doin'? Are you trackin' me, man?"

I finally caught my breath. "Yeah, sorry. I was just surprised to get a call here."

"Well, I'm callin'. So, how's it goin'?"

"Fine, I guess."

"Cool," he said. "Look, I've been gettin' good reports on you guys."

I caught my breath. "Really? From who? Mr. Tom?"

He laughed. "I've got my sources in every club. I always like to get a report when I send a new band out on the road."

I leaned against the wall and rubbed at my eyes. "Well, what'd they say?"

"Relax, man. You guys passed the test." He paused, and I heard papers being rustled. "Let's see here. I hear you've got a pretty tight sound"—he was reading now—"and that your lead singer puts out a lotta energy. She also said your drummer's a little erratic, but he kicks out the jams pretty good. Anyhow, my source thought you guys could go places with a little seasoning."

My head started to pound. I heard only one word: *she.* I rested my forehead against the wall, sure that Astley was referring to Kitten. I considered that a moment. On the up side, I now knew that her claim of knowing the promoters was legitimate. On the down side, with Astley's ear, I realized she now had some true power over us.

"Hey, man," Astley said, breaking into my thoughts, "this is good news. I'm not hearing much enthusiasm on your end."

I lifted my head. "Sorry, Rick. No, it's great to hear."

"That's better. Everything else cool there?"

"Sure." I paused and looked around. Mr. Tom had left the restaurant. I lowered my voice. "By the way, Rick, you didn't tell me that this place is, like, a biker's bar."

Astley cackled with pleasure. "I booked you guys in there on purpose. I wanted to see if you could hack it."

My face grew red and I resisted the urge to curse him.

He laughed again, but he seemed to sense my anger. "Chill out, friend. Nothin's gonna happen. Just finish your week. Then you're outta there."

"Right."

"And, look, I've already got another gig for you, and I think you'll like it." He paused, but I remained silent. "You hip to Heart's big show there on Sunday? At the county fairgrounds?"

I almost dropped the phone. "What about it?"

"How'd you like to open for 'em? They need an opening act." I could see his eyebrows go up. "Pretty good, huh?"

"*You're* booking that show?"

"It's a professional courtesy thing, ya know? Bob Beeber, the guy promoting it, called me and wanted your band. He knows I book you guys, so he wanted to go through me. So, hey, you Killjoys ready for the big time?"

So Kitten *was* behind this. She knew Beeber, and she knew Astley; hell, she was probably screwing them both. Clever girl, she'd gotten Beeber to agree to use us, then had steered him to Astley. Like that, one day after she'd screwed me. I was a little pissed for a moment, then had a better thought. Now I could tell the guys that the offer had come through Astley and wait on discussing the management issue. I thought about how to play this on the phone now. "The promoter specifically asked for us?"

"He asked for the Killjoys. That's you boys, right? He said he's working with someone who saw you at the Mai Tai. He needed somebody fast, and you were there. It's a huge break, dude, so I told him you'd do it."

Smart, Kitten, smart. She had me boxed in and was calling my bluff, but we had to take the gig. It'd be crazy to let this chance pass by. "Yeah, O.K., sounds like we have no choice. So what's it pay?"

He paused for a second. "Three hundred bucks, man. That's top dollar for an opening gig for someone like you guys."

From the shifty tone of his voice I knew what was happening: Astley was planning to pocket the difference between the three hundred he'd pay us and the five hundred he'd get from the promoter. Kitten was right: The guy was a bastard. No surprise, but still I proceeded carefully. "So, we'd get three hundred before your fifteen percent cut?"

Again, he paused. "No, man. No charge since it came in from another promoter. You get the whole enchilada." Now I saw him rubbing his hands together. "That's the way I treat my bands."

My anger rose, but I pushed it down. So this was the game we were playing. Still, I felt empowered knowing that Kitten had already fixed it with the promoter. But I wasn't ready to squeeze Astley out of the picture. "Tell them we'll do it for four hundred."

Astley snorted. "Look, Daniel, three hundred's top dollar. Like I said, this gig is a huge break. You don't wanna lose this, man."

"But they need a band now, right?" I was breathing fast, but I felt I had him. "And they want us."

"Yeah, right." A pause. "I don't know. Look, I'll see what I can do."

"I'm sure you can work it out." I felt myself start grinning. "In the meantime, we'll get ready for it."

"Yeah, sure." Astley suddenly sounded distracted, disinterested. "I'll be back at you with the details."

"Great. Thanks, Rick." I hung up. Right then, Mr. Tom reentered the restaurant and headed for the kitchen. I intercepted him. "Mr. Tom, we'll need our rooms for an extra night, through Sunday. Is that a problem?"

He shrugged. "Sure. You got rooms." He glanced up. "Plenty rooms here."

"How much?"

Without answering, he disappeared into the bowels of the kitchen. I headed back up the stairs, realizing with every step that we were really going to do it. In two days, we were opening for Heart, one of the country's hottest new bands, a group with a song in the Top 40. Most likely, we would be meeting Ann and Nancy Wilson and their manager, and God knows who else. Astley was right: This could be a huge break. Unless we embarrassed ourselves, we'd be taking a huge step up the rock 'n' roll ladder. *Like playing the Marquee, mate.*

Sam was in the shower when I got back to the room, but Mick sat half-dressed on the bed. "Who rang? It wasn't me mum, was it?"

I closed the door behind me. "Man, you won't believe it." And for the second time that morning, I got that weird you're-about-to-do-it-again déjà vu feeling.

16

ROB SAT ON THE EDGE of the windowsill with his fingers tapping away on the worn-out right knee of his Levi's, click-click-clicking like he was sending out an SOS to home or thereabouts. And the message was that our tenuous peace treaty, in place for less than a day, had been broken by my news of the Heart gig.

Directly across the room, I stood braced against the wall, looking over the heads of Mick, Sam, and Yogi, who were sprawled on the beds between us. Rob slid off the windowsill and tried to pace along the short, narrow strip of carpet between the queen bed and the wall. I watched him, noticing how his frustrated gait contrasted with the hang-loose stride of the *Truckin'* dude on the front of his Grateful Dead T-shirt.

He turned and shook his head in annoyance. "I can't believe you'd take this gig without talking to us first. I told Candi I'd be home Monday morning.

"C'mon, Rob," I said, "it's not that big of a deal, and it's Heart, man."

He stared across at me. "Shit, I agreed to stay here for the rest of the week for the good of the band and because I knew it was important to you, and then you turn around and do this. How long have we been friends? I guess loyalty only goes one way, huh, Daniel?"

"Rob, I didn't have any choice." I kept my voice calm and patient, but Rob's barb stung. "Like I said, Astley couldn't wait for an answer. And I didn't see how we could pass this up."

Rob started pacing again. "Christ," he said, the exasperation in his voice kicking up another notch, "I didn't agree to it, and Sam didn't either. Right, Sam?"

All eyes swung to Sam, who had remained silent up to this point. He thumped a pillow and tossed it to the far end of the queen bed.

"Shit, Rob," Sam said, "I was ready to pull out yesterday, but this is different. It's Heart, and it's only one extra day. And the money would come in damn handy."

"And, more important," Mick added, a leer passing across his face, "we mustn't deny the Wilson sisters."

"Can it, Mick." Rob's gaze bounced from Sam to Yogi. "What about you?"

"Jeez," Yogi replied, his eyes getting large, "I'd kinda like to hear my drums miked through a big P.A. system. That'd be cool."

"That'd be cool? To stick around this dump for another day?"

"Sure. Why not?"

Rob's hands flew up into the air, his face contracting tight into a vertical line of nose and chin. I waited, guessing that, now standing alone, he would give in. Sure enough, after another series of short-legged steps along the wall, he stopped and glared across at me.

"Fuck it. I guess I'm outvoted again."

I maintained a diplomatic expression even though, for a moment, I wanted to throw my fist into the air and bring the fingers of my personality together, showing everyone that I could do it. But I stopped myself, knowing that only Townshend would understand.

Instead I said, "Tell Candi it's my fault. Tell her we'll leave as early as we can Monday morning. If we drive straight through, we'll be home sometime in the middle of the night."

Rob just shook his head in disgust. It was clear that he felt betrayed. He had attempted to make peace and I had manipulated him. Although I understood Rob's interest in getting home, I didn't understand why he was so agitated about staying another day. I sensed something other than just wanting to get home by Monday was bothering him.

"Let's go eat," I finally said. "Maybe we can work out the song list for the gig."

Yogi jumped up. "I'm going to Pam's. Evangeline won't believe this."

"She will if I tell her first," Mick said, heading toward the door, with Sam close behind.

Rob slowly followed. I paused to pull on my jacket and caught up with Rob just outside the room. Knowing that I needed to make some kind of conciliatory gesture, I put my arm around Rob's shoulder.

"It'll be O.K. Tell Candi you'll be coming back a star. Maybe that'll make her feel better about you staying with the band."

Wrong move. Rob shoved my arm away and spun to face me.

"That's it for me, Daniel," he hissed. "I've fucking had it. I don't know how much you're willing to sacrifice for this damn dream of yours, but you've just lost your bass player."

I stepped back, surprised by his physical response. "I don't get it, Rob. I know Candi thinks you're wasting your time with the band, but what's the big deal about staying one more day?"

Rob stared at me, his face flushed a deep red. "Candi's threatening—no, fuck it. Look, this has nothing to do with the band. I told you that I needed to get home, and you just ignored me. That's what this is about."

I heard something in his voice. "Candi's 'threatening' what?"

Rob paused and then shook his head. "It doesn't matter now. I'm out, man."

My momentary elation over getting the band to go along with the Heart gig faded. "So what're you really saying? That you're going to quit the band over this?"

"Exactly, man." Rob's face hardened. "I'll play the show, only because we used to be friends, and I owe it to the other guys, but that's it. I want you to know now: I'm definitely out when we get home. You'll need to find someone else."

"But Rob—"

"Look, man, it's over. You know it, I know it. We're not on the same wavelength anymore. You want this shit too much, way more than I do." He turned and started down the stairs, but he paused after a few steps and looked up. "And those pills you're taking are fucking you up."

Standing at the top of the stairwell, I watched him until he reached the bottom and disappeared from sight. I took one step down and then stopped. I had lost my appetite.

✻ ✻ ✻ ✻ ✻

THE DAY, SPENT wandering along the waterfront, poking into local shops, basically avoiding the rest of the band and Kitten, had dragged on like few before, but by the time our Friday-night show rolled around I was properly pilled-up and illogically full of optimism about life in general and the band in particular.

To my relief, Rob was amiable during the sound-check, acting as if nothing had happened this morning. He even tossed off a few jokes about Mick's red-satin jacket and skin-tight baseball pants, observing, with deadpan accuracy, that Mick had balls. Adding to the unexpectedly good vibes, the rest of the band seemed giddy at the prospect of using these last few Mai Tai shows as a warm-up for the Heart gig. I concluded that Rob had kept his decision to himself, and I cautiously joined in with the chatter, reminding myself, as I had all day, that the Who had almost broken up dozens of times. Perhaps Rob could still be kept on board.

Following the sound-check, I hopped off the stage. Beanie and Cecil stood at the back of the bar next to the door, and Beanie, wearing the same gaudy Hawaiian shirt as the previous two nights, waved me over. "Daniel, my man! How's it hangin'?"

I winced at his voice and grinned. "It's hangin'. Good to see you guys at your station."

Cecil snapped off a salute. "On duty, sir."

I peeked through the door into the lobby. "Any bikers tonight?"

"We'll maybe get a few," Cecil said, "but not like there'll be tomorrow night." He stepped back to allow a group of women to enter. Beanie took two dollars from each and stamped the backs of their hands. They passed by me in a blur of makeup and perfume.

"Dogs," Beanie said, giggling.

"By the way," I said, making my voice sound as casual as possible, "did you hear that we're opening for Heart on Sunday?"

Their faces spun from the departing women to me. "No shit?" Beanie said.

"We found out this morning. The original band had to drop out."

"You're really not kidding?" Cecil said. "Heart?"

"Yeah, we're really doing it." The rush I got from simply telling them was startling.

Beanie clapped his hands together. "Awesome!"

Cecil shook his head. "You guys are gonna be famous someday. Maybe we should get your autographs while we can."

"Yeah, right."

"We're off Sunday," Cecil said. "If you want, maybe we can help you move your gear over."

"For sure," Beanie added, "we'll be there."

I grinned and bobbed on the balls of my feet. "Thanks, guys. We should get a few comps, and, if we do, they're yours."

"Awesome!" Beanie cried out again, causing heads to turn throughout the lounge.

Cecil glanced in the direction of the bar, where Mr. Tom stood mixing drinks for two of the women who had just entered. "Keep calm, buddy."

I stepped back to let two more women come through the door, including a cute young brunette wearing a black miniskirt and thick-soled go-go boots. Beanie took their money, and the go-go dancer unzipped her leather bomber jacket, revealing a body packed tight into a Danskin leopard leotard topped by a man's white shirt open halfway down the front and tied by a scarf at the middle. I tried not to stare.

Cecil leaned over and whispered, "You better check her ID, buddy."

The go-go dancer heard him, frowned, and dug into her purse. Beanie, with shaking hands, held her driver's license up to the light and gave it a good inspection before handing it back. She passed into the bar.

"Whoa," Beanie said, watching her wiggle away, "she's bodacious."

"Yeah," Cecil said. "How old is she, Beanie?"

"A perfect twenty-one." Beanie continued to watch her move to a table near the dance floor.

"Twenty-one, my ass. That's gotta be a fake ID she's using, or she's the youngest-lookin' twenty-one-year-old I've ever seen." He cocked his head. "I'd run her out, but Tom wouldn't like it."

I smiled. "Mr. Tom likes 'em young?"

Cecil snorted. "Nah, he likes their money. If they've got some kinda ID, he wants us to let 'em in." He gave his head a quick shake. "We're gonna get busted someday."

"I've noticed this place gets some dangerous women."

"You ain't shittin' me."

"Speaking of which, could one of you guys let me know if Kitten shows up?"

Lifting an eyebrow, Cecil said, "Whatta you want with her?"

"Nothing in particular. Just let me know, O.K.?"

Cecil folded his arms. "Whatever you want. I'll send Beanie over if we see her."

I moved out of the doorway as Yogi, chewing on a Baby Ruth bar, strolled in from the lobby. He had slipped upstairs and changed out of his sweatshirt into a shirt I hadn't seen before, a white, loose-fitting smock with three-quarter-length sleeves. The shirt's V-neck and cuffs were embroidered with wide swaths of green paisley border material, making him look something like a chubby acolyte ready to light the candles before Sunday-morning service. Only this acolyte was wearing a puka shell necklace.

"That's different," I said to him. "I've never seen you play in anything other than a tank top. And where'd you get that necklace?"

He smiled. "Evangeline gave it to me. Cool, huh?"

"Evangeline? Why?"

"She said it was for being so sweet to her." He shoved the rest of the candy bar into his mouth and threw an imaginary drum roll across the air with his hands. "You ready to play?" He seemed as wired as me, only as a result of a different substance.

I checked my watch. "Yeah, let's do it." We started toward the stage. "Keep the riffraff out," I called back to our protectors. Beanie grinned idiotically and waved.

* * * * *

APPARENTLY INSPIRED by the thought of strutting his fine stuff in front of the Wilson sisters, Mick absolutely swaggered through our first set, shaking his rear, twirling the mike, posing with one foot up on the monitors. In between poses, he'd dance to the edge of the stage and abruptly stop, teetering on the edge, a move he'd been perfecting all week. Occasionally, yells of "Jump!" would come from the crowd, which was hilarious considering the stage was only a few feet above the dance floor. Even so, I held my breath every time he did it, worried that Mick, his eyes blinded by bad genes and bright stage lights, would eventually end up sprawled face-first on the dance floor. But I finally stopped fretting. The strings felt too good beneath my fingertips, and the high-octane blood pumping through my veins carried too much energy to be wasted on worrying about our lead singer.

We plowed through Steve Miller's suggestive *Rock'n Me* and Alice Cooper's sneering *No More Mr. Nice Guy* before slowing it down with Elvin Bishop's *Fooled Around and Fell in Love.* Mick had already noticed the little brunette in the miniskirt sitting at the table behind the dance floor, and he aimed the ballad right at her.

The bar continued to fill with Friday night partyers as we stretched out and cranked up the volume and tempo. Near the end of the set, Beanie appeared at the edge of the stage and, grinning and gesturing toward the bar, mouthed the word "Kitten." I caught my breath and nodded a thanks. We finished the set with *The Boys Are Back in Town*, and I hurried around the far side of the lounge, then up the stairs to our room. Wanting to be well-fortified when Kitten tracked me down, I chugged a beer, smoked a cigarette, and popped two more of my cross-tops before returning to the bar just in time for the next set.

The second set went even better than the first, and the crowd grew to the point where the dance floor became a permanent sea of undulating polyester and grinding denim. My adrenaline continued to pump, and, with Yogi's help, I pushed the tempo as hard as I could. Cecil kept busy taking money and stamping hands, and Beanie danced along the back wall of the lounge, arms akimbo like a puppet being played by a drunken marionette. Kitten stayed hidden somewhere behind the wall of bodies gathered near the bar.

A murmur of approval came from the crowd as I pounded

out the opening chords to *It's Only Rock 'n' Roll*, and the dance floor soaked up even more bodies. From out of the middle of the writhing mass came the little go-go dancer, boogying with a skinny guy in an Angel's Flight suit. Mick saw her. We all saw her. With her shirt flapping open, she spun across the dance floor on the toes of her boots, looking young, available, and sleazy. She twirled circles around her dance partner, sneaking glances up at Mick, who needed no additional prompting to take hold of the mike and move to the front of the stage until, with hips gyrating, he was almost on top of her.

Following Sam's ripping sax solo on ZZ Top's *Tush*, we finished the set, and the go-go dancer moved off the floor and back into the maze of tables. Mick, his head zigzagging and eyes squinting, jumped from the stage, hot on her heels. Sam nudged me as I set my guitar in its stand. "You see that?" he said, nodding in the direction Mick had gone. "I thought he was gonna blow a gasket when that little bimbo shook her ass in front of him."

"She's Mick's type all right." I switched my amp to standby and lit a cigarette.

"Jail bait, for sure," Sam said. He stepped off the stage and headed for a table nearby already commandeered by Rob and Yogi.

I dawdled on the stage for a few minutes to finish my cigarette and to work up the courage to face Kitten. I then took a deep breath and started weaving through the tables toward the bar, heading in the general direction of her usual barstool. But halfway there, Mick, face flushed red and breathing hard, came out of the smoky haze and grabbed my arm. "Daniel, I want you to meet somebody."

I shook him off. "I've got some business to deal with."

He reattached himself to me. "Sorry, mate, I need your help." He steered me diagonally across the floor to a table. "Daniel, this is Rita," he said, indicating the little dark-haired go-go dancer sitting across the table.

"Hiya, Daniel," she said in a high voice. A word came to me: *bubble-gummy*. I shook her hand, which she offered like a limp rag. Up close, she couldn't be more than seventeen, if that.

Mick pulled me around the table to a woman sitting beside Rita. "And this is Tanya. Tanya, this is me mate, Daniel." He left me and hurried back around the table to the chair on the other side of Rita. I continued to stand, realizing why Mick had dragged me over: He needed me to keep the friend busy while he worked on Rita.

"Why don'tcha sit down," Tanya said in a breathy voice, motioning toward the empty chair next to her. As ordered, I dropped my pack of Marlboros on the table and slid into the chair. Unlike Rita, Tanya, who appeared to be three or four years older than her friend, was a big-boned girl with feathered-back brownish-blonde hair that looked as if it had been dyed in the distant past. Her brown eyes were surrounded by heavily applied aqua makeup, which distorted rather than flattered her plain features. A half-full glass of something pink sat on the table in front of her.

She leaned toward me. "I like what you're playin'. You're a really primo guitarist."

"Yeah? Thanks."

"Look." She held out her right hand and wagged a ringed finger in my face. "It's my mood ring. See? The stone's blue, so I must be groovin' to your music."

"Glad you like it." I reached for a cigarette and glanced at Mick. He and Rita, giggling about something, had their heads together. Mick's hand was on her arm. Above the jukebox sound of *Jim Dandy*, I heard Rita ask him, "Are all of you British guys so funny?" My eyes involuntarily rolled up into their sockets.

Tanya ignored the happy couple and slurped from her drink. "You're from California, huh?"

"That's right." I stole a look at her bloodshot eyes. "North of San Francisco."

"That's cool. I'm gonna move there someday when I get it together. California's where all the righteous music's at. We got nothin' up here, except Heart. You heard of 'em?"

I smiled to myself. "Sure. They're playing here Sunday, aren't they?"

"At the fairgrounds. You guys going?"

"Maybe." Right then I decided to keep the news about the gig to myself. "Someone told me that they played here when they first started out."

"Here at the Mai Tai?"

"That's what I heard."

She laughed. "No way. They opened for someone at the fairgrounds a coupla years back, but they never played here."

I took a drag off my cigarette and squinted at her. Was she right? Who knew? "I guess I got bad information."

"I guess so."

"But what about Hendrix? He played here once, didn't he?"

"*Jimi* Hendrix?" She laughed again. "Who told you that?"

I suddenly felt foolish. "Our agent."

"But Hendrix, he's, like, dead, isn't he?"

"Yeah, well, I meant in the Sixties."

"Your agent must've been loaded. I think I woulda heard about it if Hendrix had ever played around here."

"I guess you would've," I said. I felt myself sag in the chair. Astley was a bigger asshole than I thought.

Tanya ratted a strand of hair with a finger, looked at me, and furrowed her brow. "But, hey, they get some good bands in here once in a while. I mean, like you guys. You're the real thing."

I perked up. "You think so?"

"For sure. You guys are heavy." She smiled and her plain features lit up. "Especially you."

I saw the warning signs and knew I had to be careful; eventually everybody looked good to me when I was pilled up. And for some reason I couldn't imagine, I was apparently looking good to the women around here. It probably had something to do with the bad lighting. Still, Tanya was no way my type, and I couldn't think of a simple way to leave without being rude, so I said, "You're friends with Rita?"

"Actually, she's a friend of my little sis, but she's pretty cosmic, so I let her hang out with me."

Oh, yes, the lovely, very young Rita. I saw my opening and lowered my voice. "So how old *is* Rita anyway? She doesn't look old enough to be in here."

Tanya grinned and her eyes fluttered. She was drunker than I thought. "Oh, she's old enough, if you know what I mean. I'm old enough, too, in case you're interested." Then she winked at me.

That was it; time to go. I looked around for an exit.

"Ooh," Tanya suddenly said, again flinging her hand into my face, "look at my ring now. It's dark blue. You know what *that* means?"

I had no idea, and I didn't want to stick around to find out. I took an exaggerated look at my watch. "Hey, look, I'm sorry, but I've gotta get back on stage." I stood, and she stopped smiling. "Hey, Mick, I'm gonna tune up. I'll see you on stage in five minutes, O.K.?"

"Lovely. Five minutes." His right hand had crept under the table.

I turned to leave, but Tanya put a hand on my arm. "I'll see you later, Daniel?"

"Oh, sure. I'm not going anywhere." I pulled away and maneuvered around the table, picking my way through the maze back to the stage. My temporary self-assurance, the product of four cross-tops and a couple of beers, had been reduced to a jittery mess by my encounter with Tanya. I shook my head. First Rob, now Tanya. I couldn't seem to avoid disappointing people, and the guilt was starting to catch up with me.

I stepped up on the stage, flicked on my amp, and reached for my guitar.

"Hey, kid, you been avoiding me?"

I turned to see Kitten standing at the side of the stage and sucked in a breath. Dressed to the teeth in a blue-velvet blazer over a white Western shirt and tight jeans, her black hair flaring out, she looked dangerously attractive, even to my jaundiced eyes.

I stepped down and she hooked my arm, guiding me to a dark corner near the stage. "Where you been, kiddo?"

"Um, looking for you," I answered half-heartedly.

"You were heading in the wrong direction." She gave me a thin smile and tugged a cigarette from the pack in my shirt pocket. "Who was that?"

I lit the cigarette for her. "Who?"

"That girl you were sitting with." She blew smoke in my face; accidentally, I thought, but I wasn't sure. Kitten looked drunk, too. Or maybe stoned.

"Nobody. Some girl Mick just introduced me to."

"That right?" She loomed closer to me. "The poor little thing looks like she has the hots for you."

I forced a laugh. "She's nobody in particular. We were just talking."

Kitten's grin hung there, but her eyes burned hot. "Don't fuck with me, kid. I can take that Heart show away from you just as easy as I got it."

I shifted from one foot to the other.

"You got the call, right?"

I nodded. "Astley called me this morning."

"Well, then, you and me are in business, and we got some details to work out. Right?"

I suddenly realized that all day long I'd been avoiding the one thing that was now totally obvious: The gig was in place, and as far as Kitten was concerned, she was now our manager. I leaned against the wall and looked at her, picturing myself as a promoter or club owner; and for the first time I flashed on the advantages of having her as our manager. Unlike me, she had the brutal toughness to survive in the business, and with her looks, she would get what she wanted out of them, every damn time. Maybe she would become our oversexed version of the Who's manager, Kit Lambert, pulling us up the ladder on the sheer strength of her nerve and willingness to use whatever it took.

I heard myself say, "You free after we're finished tonight?" The words came out of my mouth without much thought, possibly encouraged by the lure of the tiny buttons of her taut shirt begging to be released.

She slipped an arm around my waist. "Wish I was, kiddo, but I got more business."

"At two o'clock in the morning?"

"That's why I'll be a great manager for you guys. I do my best work at night." She pinched the flesh above my belt and I pulled away. She tugged me back. "Keep your pants zipped, and we'll talk tomorrow night after your show."

"Keep *my* pants zipped?"

She smiled saucily, then lifted her chin in a gesture toward the stage. "They're waiting for you."

I looked over my shoulder and saw Rob, Sam, and Yogi up on the stage. "Guess I should go. I'll see you tomorrow."

As I started to turn, she hooked a hand behind my neck and pulled my head toward hers. Her lips locked onto mine and her tongue pushed between my teeth. Against all judgment, I let my tongue find hers. Then she shoved me away. "That's all you gotta remember, kid. Don't fuck with me."

Kitten slid back into the darkness of the lounge, and I climbed onto the stage. Swallowing hard, I picked up my guitar. Rob, his bass dangling from his neck, was staring at me, his head shaking ever so slowly, as if every back-and-forth motion brought forth a brand-new word describing how big of an asshole I had become.

17

KITTEN HAD DISAPPEARED into the night air, but that didn't mean that the night was over. Far from it. I had other problems to deal with, and they didn't have anything to do with finishing off our show. In fact, we blazed through our final sets with the crowd surging back and forth between the dance floor and the tables in waves of pulsing movement. No, the problem was avoiding Tanya. She had spent most of the evening lingering at the edge of the dance floor, gazing up at me with an expression that alternated, depending upon the song, between reverence and desire. My precious picking on *Stairway to Heaven* brought forth a solemn swaying of her head and shoulders, whereas my distorted riffing on *American Woman* elicited grinding hip shakes and pelvic thrusts. Through it all her eyes stayed on me.

Unnerved by the attention, I managed to avoid Tanya most of the evening by hitting the john and sneaking upstairs with Sam for beers between sets, but I couldn't avoid her following our last set. Knowing Tanya's eyes were on my back, if not on my heretofore unappreciated backside, I took my time packing up my guitar, unplugging cords, and checking to make sure everything was turned off. When I finally stepped from the stage, I nearly bumped into her.

"There you are," she said, fumbling with the buttons of her quilted, brown, Chinese-style jacket. "I've been waiting for you."

"Have you?" My eyes darted around. Besides Mr. Tom behind the bar, only Beanie and Cecil remained in the lounge.

"How 'bout we go do somethin'?" She continued to work at the buttons. "I got a place up the hill." Her murky eyes focused and latched on to my face. "Nobody else is there, and we could listen to music or something."

"Um . . . where's Rita?"

"Oh, she's upstairs with Mick." Finally finished with the complicated process of buttoning her coat, she looked at me and smiled. I thought she might give me another wink, but instead she said, "C'mon. Let's go. I've got some killer pot. We can get high, and . . . you know?"

Kitten notwithstanding, I wasn't used to getting what I assumed was a straight-up proposition, and I certainly wasn't used to turning one down, but I knew messing around with Tanya would be more trouble than it was worth. She was drunk—that probably explained her interest in me—and I wasn't drunk enough. And who knew where Kitten lurked.

"Look, Tanya," I said, half-feigning a yawn, "thanks for the invitation, but I'm exhausted. I think I need some sleep."

She stuck out her lower lip and frowned, her smudged aqua eye shadow cracking a bit. "Oh, come on, Daniel, loosen up. We could have some real fun."

I took a step back. "Maybe we could do it some other time." Another yawn, this one more genuine. "I'm really beat."

In a flash, her face changed from a sloppy, drunken pout to an image of tight, scrunched-up anger, a frightening transformation that stiffened my back. "Some other time? Like when? I mean, you've been staring at me all night, then you expect me to just go home when Rita's up there in the sack with your buddy?"

"Staring at you? What're you talking about?

Tanya huffed and swung away, taking a couple of tipply steps backward toward the door to the lobby. "If you wanna be some big loser, that's *your* problem. What are you, a homo or something?"

I picked up my guitar and started after her. "Hey, hold on."

She stumbled to a stop. "What?"

"Look, it's nothing personal. I'm just really burnt out, and I wouldn't be much fun tonight." I gave her as genuine a shrug as I could manage. "You know?"

She obviously knew I was lying. "Whatever you say."

"Can I at least walk you out?"

She shrugged and started toward the door. I followed and received a sly thumbs-up from Beanie when we passed from the lounge into the lobby. At the hotel's front door, she turned toward me, and, thinking she was either going to kiss me or slap me, I stepped back. But, instead, she said, "Are you sure you don't wanna come over? You could sleep at my place."

I paused, not to reconsider her offer but to think of something safe to say. "Look, Tanya, you're really nice. And I'd come over in a second if I weren't so beat." I tried to smile. "But I don't think it'd be a good idea tonight." This was ironic. How many times had girls said the exact same thing to me?

Her face darkened again, going through that quick transformation from soft to flinty. "I guess you'd rather be with Rita or someone like that hardass woman I saw you talking to earlier." Up went her mascaraed eyes. "She's probably waiting for you, isn't she?"

"Hey, look, it's not that."

"You think you're a hot-shit rock star, don't you?" She started to turn. "Well, there'll be another band here next week, so see ya around, loser." Then, presciently it turned out, she added, "And you know where Rita is. Guess you won't be getting much sleep tonight."

She walked through the door but abruptly stopped, turned, and thrust her mood ring into my face. "Look!"

I glanced at the stone, which, like Tanya's face, had darkened.

"It's turned black!" she said. "And it's all your fault."

With that, she shoved through the door, slamming it on the back swing. I turned and trudged upstairs, wondering what the hell was going on. Why was everyone suddenly trying to get something from me? Was I being too distrustful? Was I just being a cynical jerk? Or were we all just trying to exploit each other? Wasn't that, in essence, what Nita had jokingly asked me in the van the night of the party?

But at least Nita had been smart and honest enough to say that out loud. As I hit the top of the stairs, I suddenly missed her, and it was like a sudden blow to my chest. But how could I miss somebody I'd only met once, whose face I had a hard time remembering? My eyes closed, and I tried hard to recall Nita, her blonde hair, her eyes . . . but try as I could, it was only Kitten's face that came to mind.

✳ ✳ ✳ ✳ ✳

SAM AND ROB were sitting against the far wall of the room with their feet up on the ice chest, drinking Olys and talking, when I walked through the door. Perpendicular to them on the bed, Mick and Rita lay sprawled out with their backs against the headboard. Rita had one bare leg lying across Mick's; he had his arm around her. Oh, boy. I grabbed a beer and sat on the floor near Sam and Rob. Mick caught my eye, arched his eyebrows, and tilted his head toward the door, like "Why don't you blokes get the hell outta here?"

With Tanya's angry face in mind, I didn't need much prompting. "How 'bout we go down to your room, Rob? This one's getting a little crowded."

Rita giggled, and Mick said, "Brilliant idea."

We grabbed the ice chest and carried it down the hall to Rob's room. Yogi was lying fully clothed on one of the twin beds, his nose stuck in a copy of *Popular Mechanics*. "What's up?" he asked, looking up from the magazine.

"Mick wanted to be alone with Lolita," I told him.

"And he better watch where he puts his pecker," Sam

said. "Her daddy could be the chief of police for all he knows. Man, she's barely outta her diapers."

"That's crude," Yogi said, his ears reddening.

"You want crude? Just go down to the room in a few minutes."

Rob ignored us and pulled a plastic baggie out of the toe of his spare pair of shoes. He rolled a joint, twisted the ends with a flair, and lit it. Sam and I sat on the end of the bed, and Rob pulled up the room's only chair, and we passed the joint among the three of us, with Rob and I eyeing each other with each pass. We finished the first joint, and Rob, his face starting to relax into his preferred hippie nonchalance, started rolling another. With a casual lift of his eyes, he asked me, "You found another bassist yet?"

I leaned back on the bed. "I don't think I'll need to."

Sam's eyes darted between the two of us. "What're you talking about?"

Rob fattened up the reefer. "Didn't Daniel tell you? I'm getting out when we get home."

Overhearing us, Yogi tossed his magazine aside and slid down the bed. "You're what?"

"He's getting out," I answered for Rob. "At least he thinks he is. I think he'll change his mind after we play the Heart gig."

Rob grinned. "I don't know, man. Maybe you're planning to replace me with that woman from the bar. She looks like she'd keep the band happy."

"What woman?" Yogi asked, looking suddenly concerned. "You're not talking about Evangeline, are you?"

"No, Yogi." I reached across and took the joint from Rob. After taking a long hit, I changed the subject. "You're losing your mind, Rob. The truth is you can't live without us."

Rob took back the joint. "We'll see. But I know I won't miss places like this."

"Maybe," I said, "but I know you'll miss all this fun." I barely attempted to hold back the sarcasm. "Who else you gonna get loaded with on a weeknight at two a.m.?"

Rob just smiled and said, "It's Friday, or have you lost track?"

Sam shook his head and cracked his knuckles. "Shit, Rob, maybe you better hold off until we see how the Heart gig goes. We won't be staying in shitholes like this forever."

"It won't matter. I'm out. Daniel's plans are too big for me."

Sam and Yogi looked at me. I shrugged and said, "Let's see where we're at when we get home. Things may change."

With the sense that everyone was still staring at me and waiting for me to say something more, I stood up and wandered away, leaving Sam and Rob to finish the joint and for Rob to explain his reasons for quitting. The room had a small balcony extending over the back parking lot and I stepped out onto it. The cool air slapped my stoned face and the humidity worked at the rubber band holding back my hair. I sucked in the coolness and held it, released it, and pulled in another, forcing the oxygen into every cell of my body, but I couldn't hold on. Too many thoughts ran through my head for me to grab on to one.

Within a few minutes my hands were lifeless, cold and white. I stepped back into the room, and the scene had changed. Rob was still in his chair, but Sam was hovering over Yogi on the bed. "O.K., give it up," Sam demanded. "I know you've got a stash in here somewhere. Where you hiding the picnic basket, Yogi?"

Yogi tried to hide his round face and protruding ears behind the magazine. "I don't know what you're talking about." But I saw a paper bag stuffed under the edge of his bed and pointed at it with one of my stiff fingers.

"Aha! You Bogart." Sam sprang forward. Yogi rolled over

to grab the bag, but Sam was quicker, pinning him to the bed with one hand and clutching the bag with the other.

"No!" Yogi yelled, pulling the bag away from Sam and rolling toward the far side of the bed. But Sam went with him, thrusting himself onto the bed in pursuit of the bag. He was about to put Yogi into a headlock when the whole thing—the bed frame, the box spring, and the mattress—collapsed sideways, sending Yogi and Sam onto the floor on top of each other in the space between Rob and Yogi's beds.

From his chair, Rob looked down at them and asked dryly, "Would you two like us to leave you alone?"

Sam ignored Rob and pushed himself to his feet. "Yes!" he exclaimed, hoisting the bag in triumph. He turned it over and shook it. Two bags of potato chips, a bag of animal cookies, and various candy bars spilled onto the collapsed bed. "Bingo!" he said, ripping into a bag of Ruffles. Yogi flopped back onto the floor and groaned.

✳ ✳ ✳ ✳ ✳

SIX BEERS AND two joints later, the empty remains of the potato chip bags and three candy bar wrappers littered the floor. Yogi surveyed the damage from the mess of his bed. "When're you guys leaving?" he asked, apparently hoping the carnage was over.

"Good idea," Sam said. "Let's go see if lover boy is finished." We wobbled down the hallway and around the corner to our room and listened at the door for a second. Then I knocked. Nobody responded. I knocked harder.

"What?" came Mick's voice, laced with irritation, from behind the door.

"Hey, Mick, it's late, man."

We heard some rustling and the door opened a crack.

"Bloody hell," Mick said through the vertical opening. "What do you sods want?"

Sam pushed his face against the door. "Whadda you think we want, you moron? We wanna hit the sack, O.K.?"

The door opened a little more. Mick's shag haircut was standing straight up and a blanket was draped around his bare shoulders. "Don't be wankers. Can't you see I'm busy?" A high-pitched giggle came from the darkness behind him.

"What's the problem, Valentine?" Sam asked. "You're usually done in, what, thirty seconds?"

"Sod off, chubby." Mick slammed the door, and the lock clicked shut.

Sam looked at me and I shrugged. "You can't rush art," I said. "Let's give him thirty more minutes."

"And then I bust down the door and smack him."

"Right."

"Thirty minutes, asshole," Sam yelled through the door.

We returned to the other room. Yogi was just getting under the covers of his flattened bed and Rob was half undressed. "That jerk," Sam announced upon entering their room. "We've gotta hang out here till he gets rid of her."

Yogi groaned. "You guys already ate most of my food and wrecked my bed. You're not gonna keep me awake all night, are you?"

Rob belched. "And good food it was, Yogi."

"Shit," Sam said, "this sucks. Maybe Rob's right about all this bullshit." He stomped off through the door to the balcony. I followed him outside, where Sam stood with arms braced against the balcony rail, peering out into the night. An almost full moon burned through spotty clouds, eerily lighting up the back wing of the hotel and the parking lot.

"What'd you mean, 'Maybe Rob's right'?"

Sam continued to stare across the parking lot. "Don't worry about it. I'm not gonna quit, unless Mick keeps fucking with me." But he seemed distracted by something off in the distance. He pointed left, toward the end of our wing of the hotel. "You know, you can see the window of our room from here." Sure enough, you could see the window, the last one on the wing, maybe forty or fifty feet away, clearly illuminated by moonlight. The blinds were shut and no light came from the room. I stared at the window but didn't understand the significance of Sam's discovery.

The door to the balcony opened, and Rob's head poked through. "Damn, it's cold out here. Look, why don't you guys sleep in our room. There's plenty of space on the floor."

"Might as well," I said. I'd be on the floor anyhow. "Let's go get our sleeping bags, Sam."

We went back down the hall, but this time Sam got to the door first. He smacked it with his fist loud enough to be heard throughout the hotel. "Open the damn door, Mick!"

"Naff off!"

"We want out damn sleeping bags!" Sam pounded on the door again. "And we're not going away."

"Bollocks," we heard Mick mutter. A couple of creaking steps came toward the door, then a bump, followed by, "Ow! Shit!" Then came a giggle, some rustling sounds, and the door cracked open.

"Here're your bloody bags." Mick pushed mounds of sleeping bags through the halfway-opened door. "Now piss off." He slammed the door shut.

Sam pounded on the door again. "And we want our damn pillows!"

"The pillows!" I yelled, stifling a laugh. "Out with the pillows!"

The door yanked open and two fluffy objects came flying through the opening. We ducked, and the pillows smacked against the wall behind us, and suddenly I was in a dream-like tunnel of whispy whiteness. Slowly my pot-addled brain hooked onto the fact that the threadbare pillows had burst open, filling the hallway with an explosion of feathers. "It's snowing," I heard myself murmur as I squinted across at the door, where I saw Mick's head poking through.

With the feathers continuing to swirl through the dank air of the hallway, Sam sprang into action. He grabbed one of the pillows, still partially filled with feathers, and started to jam it through the cracked doorway above Mick's head. Mick threw an arm into the air to block it, but the arm and the pillow met directly above his head, and rest of the feathers spilled down all over him.

"You wanker!" Mick yelled out, frantically brushing feathers away from his face. Rita's head suddenly appeared behind Mick's shoulder.

"Hah!" Sam yelled back, turning to grab the other pillow, which was on the floor at my feet. Mick saw him and sprang backward, crashing right into Rita. Somehow he managed to slam the door shut before he and Rita went down, followed by two thumps on the floor and a high-pitched scream.

We jammed our ears against the door, forcing down our laughter so that we could listen to the scuffles and curses coming from behind the door. When things finally quieted down, Sam turned and looked at me with the biggest grin I'd ever seen on his face.

"Sweet dreams, Valentine," Sam called through the door before we brushed the feathers from our hair and clothes, gathered up the sleeping bags, and started down the hallway.

"Quick thinking with the pillows, man," I said. "You really got him."

Sam lips curled up crookedly. "Whatta ya call that?" he asked as we turned the corner at the end of the hallway. "Boner interruptus?"

I thought about that for a second, but the comment was gone before I could fix on it. "I'm really loaded," I said.

Sam grinned at me. "Me too."

We burst into Rob and Yogi's room and tossed the sleeping bags into the air. One of the sleeping bags landed on Yogi's head.

"Shut up," he pleaded, but he couldn't have been sleeping with the light still on in the room.

Rob, sitting cross-legged on his bed in his boxer shorts with a copy of *Rolling Stone*, looked up and grinned. Elton John, wearing a silly sweater and sillier eyeglasses, also grinned back at us from the magazine cover.

I surveyed the room with a surge of pride. The destroyed bed, the littered floor, the feathers floating in the air from our sleeping bags: We were truly becoming more like the Who every day.

Sam crossed over to the remains of Yogi's bed and peered down at him. "Where are those animal cookies? I'm still hungry." He leaned over and grabbed the paper bag that Yogi had stuffed under the sheets.

"I give up." Yogi sighed and pulled a pillow over his head.

After taking a handful of cookies, Sam handed the bag to me, and I took a couple before handing it back. They were the good kind of animal cookies: iced pink and white elephants, rhinos, and bears. We stood in the middle of the room, munched the cookies, and looked at each other. Going to sleep now didn't seem possible. What to do, what to do?

Sam's face suddenly took on a demonic look, an evil grin emerging from beneath his bloodshot eyes. "Let's go out on the balcony."

Since he had the cookies, I had no choice but to follow him out into the cold. Sam leaned forward against the rail of the balcony and shielded his eyes with his hand, like a sea captain searching for dry land. "Yeah," he said to himself.

I wrapped my arms around myself to keep warm. " 'Yeah', what?"

He turned toward me. "You know, I wouldn't be so pissed at Mick if it wasn't my turn to sleep in the big bed. But after what he's doing in it tonight, I'll never be able to sleep there again." And then he grinned. "It's payback time."

He looked into the bag of cookies and selected what appeared to be a pink frosted bear. I thought he was going to eat it, but he instead took careful aim and flung the cookie in the direction of the room window. The pink missile bounced off the brick wall about two feet left of the window.

With a sense of loss, I watched as the shattered frosted fragments of the cookie dropped into the shadows of the parking lot. Sam pulled another cookie out of the bag.

"What are you—"

The cookie went flying toward the window.

Smack! This one landed squarely in the center of the lower window pane.

"Hah!" Sam grabbed my arm. "Down, down!" We knelt on the platform and watched the window through the vertical iron bars of the balcony. Nothing happened.

"Hmm," he murmured. "I thought that'd get his attention for sure." He peered into the cookie bag. This time he pulled out two, one pink and one white. He licked each one and then pressed them together, twisting and turning the cookies until the sticky icing held. "O.K.," he said, surveying his creation in the moonlight. Once again he wound up and flung the cookie bomb at the window.

Whack! This one bounced off the top pane. For a second I thought he'd cracked the window, but I couldn't tell for sure. We knelt again on the balcony, watching the window. After a few seconds, the window blinds started moving. They parted and Mick's eyes and forehead appeared. Moonlight framed his pale face, a face that turned one way and then the other. Without his glasses, I knew Mick would never see us, especially in the crisscrossed shadows created by the railing and the balcony above us. Mick's face disappeared back into the room.

Sam was choking with laughter. "That's . . . that's"—he finally caught his breath—"that's worth another beer."

"Good idea. I'll get a couple." I stepped back into the room.

Rob was still sitting on the bed. "What're you guys doin' out there? What's so funny?"

"Sam's launched an attack on Mick. A cookie attack."

"Good Lord," Yogi murmured from beneath his pillow.

"A cookie attack?" Rob looked puzzled. "This I gotta see." He grabbed his coat and pulled it on over his T-shirt and boxers. I went out with him, a beer in each hand. Sam was at the rail again, readying himself for another attack. The cookie went sailing through the night, this time missing.

"Wide right," Sam declared. I gave him a beer.

"You hit it yet?" Rob asked.

"Oh, yeah. Twice. But I've missed the last three times. It's a pretty good toss to that window. Guess that's why I was never a quarterback." He took a long swallow of beer. "I've got an idea. Let's all try at the same time. One of us is bound to hit the fucker."

He handed out cookies: a white elephant to me, a pink camel to Rob, and a pink bear for himself. We braced ourselves on the small balcony, and Sam counted down the launch. On "blastoff," we heaved the cookies. I heard two smacks against the brick wall, but the third cookie found its mark, rattling off the window. I knew it was mine.

"Down!" I whispered. We all knelt, jockeying for position. This time it didn't take long. The blinds shot up and Mick's face appeared at the window. He seemed to be struggling to put on his glasses.

"Oh-shit, oh-shit, oh-shit," Sam whispered.

Mick finally got the glasses perched on his nose, and his head jerked around as he searched for the source of the attack, training most of his attention on the parking lot below. I thought Rob's bare white legs might give us away, but Mick apparently couldn't see us or didn't know where to look.

Rita's face appeared briefly at the window before both faces disappeared. This time Mick left the blinds up as they retreated into the darkened room.

"We got the bastard that time!" Sam said. "Let's let 'em stew."

We sat on the balcony for a few minutes drinking our beers. With my back against the wall, I glanced across at Sam, who was leaning against the balcony railing, a look of deep concentration on his face as he apparently contemplated his next attack on Mick. Beside me sat Rob, smiling to himself in an amused kind of way while he peered into the bag of cookies to see how many were left.

Despite the bitter cold, I felt myself grinning, realizing how great it was to be in a band. What other job provided you with friends who went with you everyplace, friends who loved the same things you loved, friends who would go crazy with you when the time was right? And then, in a moment of mental clarity, the good feeling evaporated as I remembered that Rob was on his way out.

I sipped my beer and looked upward at the gloomy night sky.

Sam finished his beer first, crumpling the can between his hands. "It's time to finish the bastard off," he said, standing.

He took the bag of cookies from Rob and held it up to his face, studying the contents. "We're runnin' outta ammo. I think the shotgun approach is our best chance."

He gave Rob a few cookies, handed me five, which were reduced to four after I ate one, and then emptied the remains of the bag into his right hand.

"O.K., this is the plan." Sam's tone was hushed. "On the count of four, we throw all the cookies at once. You got that?" He looked at the two of us.

"You're not gonna ask us to synchronize our watches, are you?" Rob asked.

Sam ignored him. "All at once, right?"

We nodded, exchanging looks of determination, our feet set, right hands bulging with cookies. "Ready?" Sam asked. "One, two, three . . . four!"

I heaved mine as far as I could. Then I gazed out, where I saw, with a mixture of shock and glee, that Mick's head was sticking out of the window, something that none of us had noticed as Sam counted down. Mick was looking down into the parking lot, apparently unaware of what was coming at him from our direction. With the sky raining cookies, I held my breath, but not for long. The little iced projectiles hit everywhere, including the brick wall on both sides of the window and the pane of glass above Mick's head.

His face was right there, and at that moment the last of the cookies came flying down through the night air, smacking Mick right in the middle of his forehead. His hands flew up, his head pulled back, and his glasses went sliding off sideways into the night.

Knowing that Mick would see us for sure, I opened the door to the room and we all tried to shove through at the same time. Rob bumped me from behind and I slid on the nylon sleeping bags lying in a heap on the floor. We all went down in a convulsed mound of twisted nylon.

"Good God!" Yogi exclaimed from beneath his pillow. "Is there no end to this?"

I gazed across the mound of sleeping bags at Rob, who looked back at me with a lopsided grin.

"You're gonna miss this," I said to him.

18

FROM WHERE I sat in the backseat of the station wagon outside of Pam's Cup O' Coffee Café, Yogi's round head was a sickening sight. It wasn't so much that the view of his head was particularly nauseating, although it was a little too circular to be human; it was just that everything had been making me sick today, from my coffee-and-cigarette breakfast at Pam's to the smell of our bedroom when Sam and I had finally gotten into it earlier in the afternoon. And now this. Why, at Yogi's urging, we'd ever agreed to dinner at Evangeline's was well beyond me, especially considering our looming date with the Hell's Angels in a few hours.

I hung my head out the window and breathed in the soggy air, opening a bloodshot eye every few seconds to watch for Evangeline at the front of the café. A fat lady walking a pink poodle drifted down the sidewalk, saw me, and scurried by.

I shifted back inside. "Yogi, move your head."

He turned around. "What'd I do?"

"Nothing. Just move your big head outta my way."

"God, Daniel," Rob said from the other end of the backseat, "take some more aspirin or something. And maybe you should've eaten breakfast."

I grunted back at him and sagged into the seat. What good was it having a hangover if you couldn't bitch about it?

Sam glanced back at me from the driver's seat. "I guess we shouldn't have had those last two beers, huh, Daniel?"

Yogi turned and handed me a small paper bag. "It's half a sandwich. It might make you feel better."

I pulled out the sandwich and unrolled the paper wrapping. Roast beef. It smelled O.K. I carefully took a bite. Not bad. "Someone got a Coke?" I asked. Yogi handed me one out of another bag he had on the front seat.

"Where do you get all that food, Yogi?" Rob asked from beside me. "You're like a walking grocery store."

Sam leaned forward to look toward the café. "Shit," he said, "where is she?" Evangeline had told us that she'd be off by five, but we'd been waiting in front of the café for twenty minutes. "Yogi, go see what's keeping her."

To my relief, the back of Yogi's strangely balloonlike head slid from view. I closed my eyes, wondering once again how the Who survived their nightly hangovers as I nibbled on the sandwich. But my eyes soon reopened at the sound of approaching footsteps, and I saw Mick's cocky face coming down the sidewalk toward us. He slid into the seat vacated by Yogi.

"How's it goin', mates?" Mick said, flashing us a cheesy smirk. "Get a good night's sleep last night? Mine was about perfect, thanks to lovely Rita. By the way, sorry you two had to do without your pillows."

Glances flew around the station wagon with the realization that Mick apparently didn't know who had launched the cookie attack on him.

"So where've you been?" Sam asked, trying to keep a straight face.

We hadn't seen Mick all day. He was gone by the time Sam and I returned to our room to shower and change clothes following our late breakfast. The bed had looked like a war zone: covers and sheets all over the place. Sam had left a note, incorporating a few choice phrases, on a stained spot in the middle of the bed, telling him where we'd be.

"I've had an absolutely splendid day," Mick said. "Took Rita out for a bit of lunch. Then I walked the lass home."

"Home?" Rob said. "Is she old enough to have her own place?"

The smug look faded. "Well, not exactly. She still lives with her mum and dad."

"You mean you just walked her up to the front door? You've got balls."

"Yeah," Sam said, "I can just see it: 'Nice to meetcha, Mr. and Mrs. Jones. Here's your daughter. . . . What's that? Oh, yeah, she really puts out.' "

Mick scowled. "You think I'm daft? I left her at the corner near her house."

I rallied my strength. "So, Mick, how old *is* she?"

He didn't answer. Instead, he gazed out the car window toward the front of the café.

Sam elbowed him. "Yeah, Mick, come on. How old is she?"

He mumbled something into the window.

"What?" we all asked.

"Bloody hell. Sixteen, O.K.?"

Sam let out a howl. "Sixteen? Oh, man, your ass is grass. You ever heard of statutory rape?"

"She won't tell anybody."

"Sure, Mick." Sam nodded, his head moving up and down with exaggeration. "I hope it was worth it."

The smug smile returned. "Aye, it was worth it. She had a lovely time."

Groans filled the car, but Sam's expression suddenly changed. "Hey, Mick," he said, glancing back at me, "sorry about the pillow thing. Hope we didn't mess up your timing."

"My timing?" Mick looked sideways at him. "What're you talking about?"

"Well, we felt kinda bad intruding on you. I mean, you're kinda known as the Rembrandt of love. We wouldn't wanta screw up one of your masterpieces, right, Daniel?"

"Right," I answered.

Sam started in on him again. "So the rest of the night went pretty smoothly, huh? No interruptions?"

"Why d'ya ask?"

"Oh, I dunno. You know, I've heard there's ghosts in the hotel. . . ." He finally broke out laughing.

Mick's face shifted from suspicion to realization. "You yobs! You were the ones, weren't you? I knew it. You almost scared Rita away." He looked around at our laughing faces and then threw himself back against his seat.

"They were only animal cookies," I pointed out. "We thought you and Rita might be hungry after all that activity."

"You too?" Mick said.

"So what happened to your glasses?" Rob asked.

"They're O.K.," Mick replied glumly, "no thanks to you yobs. I found them in a dumpster in the parking lot." He looked around at the three of us, shaking his head and breathing out an exaggerated sigh. Then he went silent. Rob leaned forward and glanced past me toward the café. I followed his eyes and saw Yogi and Evangeline coming out the door. We all piled out of the car, except Sam, who stayed behind the steering wheel.

"Hi, guys," Evangeline said. Her clean dark hair was pulled back; her genial face looked bright and cheerful. I saw her name tag still pinned to her waitress outfit. "Thanks for picking me up. Sorry I'm late."

We played musical chairs, with Mick and Yogi angling to see who would sit next to Evangeline. I didn't care; I just wanted to be next to an open window. I returned to the back seat, and Rob got in on the other side. Evangeline slid in next to Sam, and before Yogi could react, Mick grabbed the seat beside her.

Yogi stood on the sidewalk for a few seconds, and then he tried to slide in next to me. "No way," I told him. "If you don't want your sandwich back, I suggest you sit in the middle."

Yogi immediately climbed back out of the car and waited for me to get out before sliding in beside Rob. I got back in and shut the door.

Sam turned the ignition. "Everybody ready?"

"Ready, Dad," Rob answered.

Sam popped a Fleetwood Mac tape into the eight-track and we were off.

Evangeline guided us south through town. I watched the passing scenery, soon seeing Kitten's apartment complex slide by, reminding me of my appointment with her after tonight's show. A few blocks beyond, in an area confused by a jumble of small subdivisions and older strip malls, Mick turned his head, caught my eye, grinned, and nodded toward an unusually bright blue house sitting beneath a streetlight on a corner. "Rita," he mouthed.

I ignored him, cracked my window, and rested my chin on top of my forearm on the window edge. Closing my eyes and yawning, my ears popped. Above the sound of the wind whipping by my ears, I heard Evangeline's voice.

"I don't know how long I'll stay here," she said in response to a question from Sam. "I used to think I needed to stay near my hometown because my mother was alone, but she remarried, so there's nothing holding me here. But so far I really can't afford to leave. And where would I go, especially by myself?"

I opened my eyes and looked over at her. In the green glow of the dashboard I could see her simple but sweet face, a little puzzled but determined. The air through my open window blew long strands of her dark hair across her face. Yogi leaned forward, putting his head almost between hers and Mick's. "You could come to California," he said.

Evangeline smiled back at him. "I've thought about it, but I'm not sure my car would make it. That's why I usually take the bus to work. Besides, I like the mountains and the ocean."

"We've got mountains," Yogi said, "and we've got lakes where we live. Lots of lakes."

"Maybe someday, Edward. But tell me more."

I stopped listening. My stomach churned as the car swung around a corner and chugged up a hill, then ran halfway down another before pulling over in front of a large Victorian.

"Lovely place," Mick said, pulling himself out of the car. "You live here alone?"

She followed him from the car. "It's a fourplex," she answered, searching her purse for keys. "I rent one of the units."

We followed Evangeline around the left side of the house to a porch. She flicked on a light as we filed through into a small living room alive with the warm smell of incense. A dining area and kitchen were located immediately to the left.

"Make yourselves comfortable," she said. "I'll be right back." She went through the living room into a back bedroom separated from the rest of the apartment by a rainbow curtain of beads.

At first glance, the living room was notable only for its lack of furniture and haphazard arrangement of spider plants. A greenish couch and a simple end table were set against the left-hand wall. Opposite the couch, a cheap stereo and a few record albums were stacked on brick-and-board shelves resting on the brown shag carpet. A small television sitting on a metal stand in the corner, with a stained-glass swag lamp hanging above, completed the furnishings. But on closer inspection, it became clear that the room held much more.

Candles of all shapes, sizes, and colors were arranged on every flat surface in the room, including the end table, stereo shelves, television top, and the window ledge in front of the macramé curtains. Candles that looked like trolls, candles shaped like mushrooms, animal candles, short candles, tall candles, white candles, yellow candles, rose-colored candles, even black candles. I glanced at Rob, who was standing near the stereo studying the waxy collection, and he looked back with raised eyebrows. We both could have been thinking the same thing: She's a witch.

Evangeline's voice came through the beaded curtain. "I know the furniture's ugly, but it's not mine. It came with the place." O.K., that explained the furniture, or lack thereof, but what about the candles?

While Yogi, Mick, and Sam settled down on the couch, Rob continued his tour of the candle exhibit, and I slowly followed him around the room. On the end table, cone-shaped incense lay in a brass dish next to a copy of *Jonathan Livingstone Seagull*. A framed Kahlil Gibran poem hung on the wall over the stereo. I stopped to read it. Some tepid sentiment about accepting the "thunder and lightning." What choice did we have, I wondered? I knelt and rifled through the ten or twelve albums stacked on the stereo shelf. James Taylor. Joan Baez. Joni Mitchell. Cat Stevens. Seals and Crofts. Carly Simon. And, of course, Melanie's *Candles in the Rain*.

Evangeline reemerged from the bedroom, looking relaxed in jeans and an oversized wine-colored sweater. "Put on something if you want," she said to me. For lack of a better choice, I selected Cat Stevens's *Tea for the Tillerman*. Evangeline continued into the kitchen. "I'd better get started with dinner so you guys can get out of here in time. Anyone want to help?"

"I will," Yogi called out.

"Why are you always so nice to me, Edward? O.K., you can do the salad. And Mick, can you help me open the wine?" The two of them followed her into the kitchen.

"Marvelous," I heard Mick say, "this thing has a cork. Screw caps are more our cuppa tea." Evangeline's laughter drifted from the kitchen.

I sat down on the couch next to Sam, who rolled his eyes around the room and whispered, "This place is kinda spooky, isn't it? What's with all the candles? Is she planning to hold a séance or something?"

"I hope not," I said. "All these candles burning at one time would suck the oxygen right outta our lungs."

✳ ✳ ✳ ✳ ✳

EVANGELINE SLID the big bowl of spaghetti across the table toward me. The motion caused a long river of wax to run down one of the two tall candles in the middle of the table. Thank God she hadn't lit the ones in the living room. The dining area felt clammy enough, with condensation from the pasta streaming down the windows.

I served myself a large pile of spaghetti, splattering sauce on my yellow T-shirt in the process. "Damn." I dabbed at the spot with a napkin.

"Tsk, language, me lad," Mick scolded me. "A lady is present."

"That shirt needed a little color anyhow," said Sam from the chair next to me.

"Now it's tie-dyed," Rob noted.

I gave up and took a bite. "Hey, this is pretty good."

Evangeline beamed back at me.

The dinner had taken on a formal air. Maybe it was the wine, the darkened room, the candles. Maybe it was the presence of Evangeline. Whatever the reason, we all sat board straight, trying to use our best table manners, which weren't particularly good. It was weird; in two hours we would be playing in front of drunken bikers, but here we were now, napkins tucked in tight, elbows off the table. The thought of what might come later tightened my stomach.

Mick refilled Evangeline's wine glass. She glanced in my direction and said, "I think Daniel may need some." I had refused the wine up until now.

Mick reached across Sam's plate with the bottle. "Here's

a spot of the hair of the dog that bit your arse. It'll do you good, mate."

So much for good table manners. I sipped the bitter red wine, craving something sweeter, something easier on my hangover, like a vintage Boones Farm or Annie Green Springs.

Yogi, sitting on the other side of our host, took a sip from his wine glass—the first time I'd ever seen him drink alcohol. With his pinky stuck out, he tilted the glass to his lips. This was definitely getting weird. He glanced sideways at Evangeline and gestured toward the candles. "I like all this—it's all very romantic."

Mick snorted, but Evangeline gazed back at Yogi with glasslike eyes and said, "I'm a bit of a romanticist, I suppose; I knew you'd appreciate it," which caused our drummer to blush about three shades of red.

"Speaking of which," Rob said, glancing in my direction, "take Daniel there. Now he's your true romantic."

Surprised, I looked across the table at him, only to see him grinning back at me, his face, like Yogi's, red with wine.

"Our Daniel?" Mick said. "Since when?"

"Ask him," Rob said, pushing his hair back behind his ears. "He's got a girl in every port."

But it was Evangeline, smiling at me like the Mona Lisa, who asked, "Is that right, Daniel?"

I squirmed in my chair and gestured at Rob with my fork. "I don't know what he's talking about."

"Sure you do," Rob said. "Let's see. There's that girl in Berkeley—I think her name's Nita—and then there's Kitten right here in Puente Harbor."

"What?" Sam asked. "Kitten?"

"You sly dog," Mick said with a wink. "The queen bee herself."

"Rob's crazy." My voice came out louder than intended. "I've just been doing some business with her."

"Is that what you call it?" Rob glanced around at the other guys. "I saw him kissing her—or was it the other way around?—between sets last night."

"My, my, Pleasant," Mick said. "I thought you smelled a wee bit fruity when you came back the other night. You've been a busy lad, haven't you?"

"No busier than you, Jack," I shot back.

He glanced sideways at Evangeline and put a finger to his lips.

"So," Rob said, "which one is it going to be, Nita or Kitten?"

"Shut up, Rob. You know damn well I don't have anything going on with either of 'em."

"Thou dost protest too much, me thinks," Mick said. "I sense true love with one of the lasses."

"My guess is that it's Nita," Rob said, his lips pulling back into a wry grin. "Which brings up why he's hanging out with Kitten."

I kept my mouth shut. Everyone but Evangeline was now grinning at me. She leaned forward and, with eyes reflecting the candlelight, said, "I think Daniel should follow his heart."

All heads turned toward her.

"I always do," she said, her voice dropping into a dreamy whisper. "Your heart's never wrong. My mother told me that. Follow your heart, no matter where it takes you. Being with someone for any other reason is wrong." She said these last words looking directly at me, as if she knew that I, more than anyone else here, needed to hear her simple kind of truth.

"This is ridiculous," I said, flashing on the thought that she really was a mind-reading witch.

Evangeline's gaze did not waver. Across the smoking candles, she repeated, "Being with someone for any other reason is wrong."

With all eyes slowly rotating from her to me, I felt my

face grow warmer. I pushed away from the table. "I gotta use the bathroom. Where is it?" I didn't wait for directions, instead heading through the living room toward the only possible location.

"Did I say something wrong?" I heard Evangeline ask, sounding way too much like Nita.

I pushed through the veil of beads and found the bathroom just to the right of the inside of the doorway. Candles burning on the counter lit up the mirror, so I didn't bother turning on the lights. I splashed water on my face and stared into the mirror, looking hard for the telltale signs that I knew were there, but found nothing that Evangeline could've read, nothing that would've revealed the secrets that were beginning to eat away at me. She didn't understand: I was following my heart, right into the soul of the music, and Kitten was only a vehicle to help me get there. Nita? Not a factor. Fuck Rob.

But Nita pushed her way back into my head. For a moment, I saw her in the mirror, her beautiful brown eyes gazing at me, searching my face. *Follow your heart. Follow your heart.* But I knew that following my heart wouldn't lead to Nita. She was gone, and it was pretty unlikely that I'd ever see her again. My salvation was through music, not love, and this was the moment and the place where I would find salvation. And who ever said that salvation would come in a neat, pretty package, all wrapped up in a big bow? Kitten was now part of the package, and that's the way it was.

I rubbed at my throbbing temples until the blood worked its way back into my brain, soothing the parched membranes connecting the elements of the plan that had emerged day by day, piece by piece: finish out at the Mai Tai, play the Heart gig tomorrow night, and don't look back. I stared into the mirror, willing Nita's face away. Kitten had made herself necessary to the plan; love was not. There was nothing to unite me with anyone else, no magical chord, no lost note. My path was my own, just like Pete Townshend's was his. That's what he had been telling me. He was leading me to the Real Me, and I was almost there. I let the breath flow in and out, my body capturing the waxy, incense-laden air until it filled the empty spaces.

After splashing my face again, I fished around in my pocket for my pills. The small tablets slid out of the vial and down my throat, helped by a handful of water. I took one last look in the mirror, blew out the candles, and returned to the table.

19

AN HOUR LATER, and fifteen minutes behind schedule, the five of us pushed our way into the lobby of the Mai Tai Hotel. My nerves, stoked high by my cross-topped buddies, were beginning to tingle, and, better yet, my hangover, wiped out by the food, the drugs, and the wine, was now only a bad memory.

I started to follow everyone upstairs before changing my mind. "Mick, grab my guitar, O.K.? I'll start plugging in things."

"Right-o, mate."

"And grab that flannel shirt lying on top of my suitcase."

"Aye."

He and the others disappeared up the stairs. I retraced my steps and headed into the lounge, where a few dozen customers, some familiar to me, some not, were already scattered among the tables. I waved at Mr. Tom behind the bar and began winding my way through the tables toward the stage. Near the edge of the dance floor, a woman dressed all in black sat alone at a table, her back to me, an empty glass in front of her. I glanced at her as I passed by. Then I fell over a chair.

Awkwardly scrambling up, my face reddening, I looked at her again. It was Nita. She stood, smiled, and tucked her chin.

"Remember me?"

"Nita?" I felt myself blinking, looking into that pure face of high cheekbones and upturned nose. Brushing off my clothes, I stepped toward her, taking in the black turtleneck sweater, charcoal straight-legged jeans, and black lace-up boots. "What are you doing here?"

"Um, I wanted to see you." Her smile started to fade, the small chin tucked deeper, and the brown eyes rolled up. "Is it O.K.?"

"God, yes. I'm just shocked to see you." I tried to smile, but the surprise had frozen my expression.

She ran her fingers through her choppy blonde hair. "I've been waiting for you."

"We were having dinner. God, I can't believe you're here."

She lowered herself into a chair, and I followed into the one beside her, the smell of her leather jacket, slung over the back of her chair, coming to me. With an impulse that could only be explained by the drugs, I took her hand. "How'd you get here?"

She laced her fingers through mine, her eyes downward. "I decided to use one of those plane tickets my dad kept sending me."

"You flew to Seattle? When?"

"Yesterday after classes."

I swallowed twice to lubricate my throat, which had gone bone dry from the uppers. "And you came all the way up here to see us?"

"I wish I could say yes." With her left hand, she tugged at the neckline of her turtleneck, her throat porcelain white against the black of the sweater. "I mean, I thought about it. Especially after I missed your call the other day. I thought you'd call back."

I looked down at my hand, locked up with hers. "Things have gotten pretty hectic around here." My eyes lifted to scan the room before settling back on her face. "So then you flew up to see your dad?"

"I thought I'd try spending the weekend with him, but it didn't work out."

"No?"

Nita removed her hand from mine and started tracing a deep scratch in the varnished surface of the table. "He has a girlfriend living with him. He didn't tell me about her until I got there." She turned up her chin, closed her eyes, and shook her head. "I freaked out. I couldn't help it. I took one of his cars and drove over here."

"Wow." I realized I knew very little about her. "Does he know you took it?"

She opened her eyes. "I left him a note. I told him I'd bring it back."

"But how'd you know where to find us?"

"You told me. Remember?"

My mind stretched back to the party but found no recollection of telling her where we'd be. I shook my head.

"Well, you did." The shy smile, the one that had remained somewhere in the back of my head all week, emerged. "I didn't remember the name of the club, but I knew it was something unusual. I asked somebody at a gas station, and they said the Mai Tai. And then I saw your picture on the front window."

"You're a regular Columbo."

"I wanted to keep track of you." Her brown eyes locked onto mine. "I need a friend right now. And, remember, we share a secret."

At first I didn't know what she meant, and then I remembered the thread of punk music that connected the two of us. My heartbeat clicked up a notch. I gazed back at her, but in the background I saw Mick and Sam coming through the door of the lounge. "Look, Nita, we start our show in about fifteen minutes and we've still gotta sound-check. What're your plans?"

Her eyes dropped to the table. "I don't normally ask guys this question, but what do you want me to do?"

Her question brought everything back into sudden focus, and I saw what would happen if she stayed. She couldn't be here when Kitten arrived. "I hate to say this, but maybe you should take the car back."

"You mean, go back to Seattle?"

I nodded, but, as I did, the unknown consequences of her leaving stretched out in front of me, and I feared they might be worse than if she stayed. I needed time to sort everything out, but with the clock ticking, the guys gathering onstage, I had none. Still, I knew I couldn't send her away. I was too fucking weak to do the right thing, even with the mood-elevating drugs pumping through me. My mind jumped to the heroic assumption that Kitten could be put off until tomorrow. "No," I finally said, "don't do that. It's too late. Why don't you stay here at the hotel? It's pretty grungy, but I know they have rooms."

She cocked her head sideways as if studying a picture frame that needed straightening. "I already checked into a Travel Lodge out on the highway. I wasn't sure you'd be happy to see me. Are you?"

Out of the corner of my eye, I saw that Mick and Sam had made it to the stage and were watching us. From the other end of the room, Rob and Yogi came through the door, where Beanie and Cecil now stood. "Are you kidding? I'm really glad you're here, but I've gotta get to work. You'll stay?"

"Don't worry about me. I'll get dinner, and then I'll be back later, O.K.?" She paused and stared hard into my eyes, as if there was something more that needed to be said but couldn't be verbalized. "I'm glad I found you," she finally added.

"I'm glad you did, too."

She squeezed my hand, and my heart took a tumble sideways. I held her hand for a few moments more before we separated and she left the lounge.

Mick met me at the edge of the stage with eyes arched in a rare expression of admiration. "My, my. I thought Rob was a bit dodgy, but, bloody hell, you're a regular Romeo. You've got two birds in this port?"

"Didn't you recognize her?"

"From where?"

Sam walked over dragging a monitor cable. "From the party last Saturday night. Right, Daniel?"

"You got it."

"That's Nita?" Mick asked.

"That's her," Sam answered for me.

Rob had overheard and joined us. "She came all the way up here to see you?"

I shrugged. "Why not?"

Mick squinted out toward the door through which Nita had just gone and then back at me. "Lemme suss this out. That bird I just saw you with—that punky blonde with the tight trousers—she came all the way to Puente Harbor to see *you*?"

"That's what she said, more or less." I suppressed my grin and pulled on the flannel shirt Mick had brought down for me.

"I hope Kitten likes her," Rob said, wiping the beginnings of the grin from my face. I stopped buttoning the shirt and looked out into the lounge, searching the gathering faces for the woman who now had me tethered to an ever-shortening leash.

Mick put an arm around my shoulder. "Just remember what Evangeline said, me lad. Follow your heart." And then he laughed, long and loud, his voice echoing around the room that would soon be filled by the unholy trinity of Nita, Kitten, and the Hell's Angels.

* * * * *

I STOOD STOCK-STILL three feet in front of my amplifier, alone, waiting for the stage lights to burn my shadow into the stage. I knew every song on the set list by heart. I knew them better than I knew my own fragmented family, but I had no understanding of how to deal with the rest of what was now spinning toward me.

My thoughts were interrupted by Mick, who came bouncing across the stage from where he'd been huddled with Sam and Rob. "You ready, Daniel?"

I took a deep breath and nodded.

"Relax, mate. I've seen neither hide nor hair of Kitten or the bikers. Of course, the night is still young, idn't?" With a tight grin, he turned back to face the crowd waiting in the lounge. He motioned toward Sam, and the stage lights jumped at me, throwing everything into a blue-yellow haze, including the cymbals and drums right behind me, where Yogi sat, clicking his sticks together at the tempo of the first song.

"Evenin', mates," Mick said into the mike, his voice bouncing around the room. In the stage lights, he looked almost elegant in his chartreuse scarf, satin burgundy shirt, and the infamous navy-blue cords, which clung to him like a wet suit. The constant murmur of voices in the lounge dropped down as I sensed all eyes turning toward us.

"Hey," Mick called out to the crowd. "It's Saturday night, and, as you bloody well know by now, we're the Killjoys. You can catch us tomorrow night opening up for Heart at the fairgrounds, but it's our last show here at the Mai Tai, right? So get warmed up, 'cause you know what they say: *Saturday night's all right for fighting!*"

He pointed at me, and my head suddenly cleared. On cue, I windmilled my arm and attacked the strings, banging out the first in the biting series of chords that started the Elton John song. Yogi and Rob jumped in after my second pass, and we were off.

We hurtled through the first songs at a blinding pace, our screws tightened by the repetition of the nightly shows. I forgot about Kitten and Nita and leaned into the skittering groove laid down by Rob's deep-throated bass and Yogi's crash-and-burn drums. We were halfway through the set before my consciousness left the confines of the stage and took in everything that had become so familiar to me after five nights at the Mai Tai: the heavy sweet-and-sour blend of cigarette smoke, stale beer, cheap perfume, and tangy sweat; the dark forms of Beanie and Cecil standing at the door; the green Rainier sign glowing on the wall behind us; the shadowed heads arranged around tables beyond the dance floor; Mr. Tom working mechanically behind the bar. I took it all in, sensing that my world was about to change, but not knowing what would change it. Nita? Kitten? The Hell's Angels? Or the entire unholy trinity framing my world at this moment?

On *Brown Sugar*, Sam moved up to blow a solo, the red stage lights glinting off his tenor sax, his shoulders twitching to the high notes, the embroidered back pockets of his jeans swaying to the thumping beat being laid down by Yogi. I looked past him to Rob, who, as usual, seemed deep in thought, lost in his world of fingers and strings. His blond hair fell down the back of his longsleeved blue work shirt, and for that moment the world seemed near perfect . . . until I remembered that our bass player would soon be gone.

The lounge was already packed, with the regulars at the bar overwhelmed by the dozens of guys on the make and girls ready to be made who only came out on weekends. The heat in the bar was becoming unbearable, and I could almost feel the steam rising off those who had just come through the bar doors. A drop of sweat rolled down the side of my face. I moved back toward Yogi and away from the hot bank of lights angled at me. Unfortunately, this drew Yogi's attention to the crash cymbal near my left ear, which he attacked as Sam was ending his solo. Grimacing, I looked over at him, but he stifled a yawn, probably feeling the aftereffects of the wine.

I moved back up to my mike for the *"yeah, yeah, yeah, woos"* at the end of the Stones' song, and the familiar spiced, weedy aroma of Charlie hit me. Of course, Kitten. I knew she was on the dance floor even before I squinted through the lights to see her ten feet away, midnight-black hair flying, body moving in a sheer white blouse with an elastic midriff. She looked up and gave me a long, penetrating stare. I felt a shiver run down my back.

She melted back into the jammed lounge as we continued through the set, knocking off *Bang a Gong*, *Easy Livin'*, and *Dream On*. The pressure-cooker feel of the bar grew more intense, and I felt like I was performing in a sauna. I kept searching the crowd for any sign of the rest of my unholy trinity, but neither Nita or the Hell's Angels had arrived.

Near the end of the set, Evangeline, dressed in a long-sleeved black T-shirt with a scoop neck, appeared at the edge of the dance floor and stood watching Mick move around the stage, her head nodding to the beat of Frampton's *Show Me the Way*. She stayed there until she had gained Mick's attention, then smiled and stepped back into the darkness of the lounge.

Rob started the bass line of Golden Earring's *Radar Love*, the final song of our first set. The pulsating bass notes, joined by the drums, again filled the floor with sweaty, jiggling dancers. I edged out to the front of the stage, ready to spin out the guitar licks that slid between Mick's vocal lines. As I did, I thought I noticed something different in the air, a slight chill, and perhaps a trace of the oily sea air that permeated Puente Harbor, mixed with something else. Gasoline fumes? Had the doors to the bar and the hotel been left open? I squinted and peered out through the haze hanging thick in the bar. From beyond the glare of the lights, the blur of bodies and faces in the lounge became more distinct. Through the dancers, through the jumble of tables and chairs, I saw an uneven line of men—large men with long hair, beards, black leather jackets, studded belts, and motorcycle boots. They stood facing us, arms crossed, surveying the lounge like a conquering army. The Hell's Angels had arrived.

20

I FOLLOWED Sam and Rob through a lounge that now smelled distinctly of leather and gasoline fumes, edging my way through the locals at the tables and the bikers milling around near the bar. I looked for the holy part of the trinity, with part of me hoping that Nita had wised up about her dad and the car and left town.

The bar, where Kitten was presumably holding court, was walled off by bodies, and I headed for Beanie and Cecil's post at the doorway, figuring they'd know if a blonde girl with an odd-looking haircut had come through the door.

But I didn't get there. Kitten, who always seemed to know where I was, suddenly appeared out of the crowd and cut me off.

"Hey, kid," she said, with a flip of her head, "what's up?"

"Just heading out for some fresh air."

"We gotta talk." She pulled me over near the jukebox, which was blaring Chuck Berry's *My Ding-a-Ling*, and I found myself staring at the white of her exposed belly.

She fingered the elastic hem of her blouse. "I talked to the promoter about tomorrow night."

"Yeah? Everything O.K.?"

She turned sideways to let someone pass by, and the light from the lobby revealed an outline of everything underneath her blouse. She caught my gaze and smiled. "Oh, yeah. Everything's cool. I'll give you the lowdown when we get together later." A glance toward the stage. "You told the other guys about our arrangement?"

"Um, kind of—"

She cocked her head. "What do you mean, 'kind of'?"

"Not all of—" I stopped. God, she'd know I was lying.

The way she looked at me—it was like she was all over me, in my head, like she knew what I'd say before I said it. "Well, I didn't tell 'em anything much yet—"

Kitten nodded sharply. "I figured." A trickle of sweat ran down the side of her neck and disappeared into the black tangle of hair touching her shoulders. "Well, you better deal with it."

I shifted my eyes to the doorway, where Rob and Sam stood talking to Beanie and Cecil. "Kitten, look, Rob's getting cold feet about things. I think he's got a girlfriend at home who's putting pressure on him to quit the band. And he's already pissed off that he's gotta stay to do the Heart gig, so I don't want to spook him about anything else right now. I thought it'd be smart to wait until after we do the gig."

She shrugged. "That's your problem, kiddo. Just make sure you do it." She leaned toward me. "Or I'll do it for you."

"Hey, I will. Don't worry about it." I was relieved that Kitten hadn't pressed me harder. I had no idea what I was going to do about her once we'd played the Heart show, and I didn't want to be forced to tell the guys about her until I had to.

She squinted at me, again seeming to read my mind. "Look, Daniel, don't double-cross me on this. Just remember that I've got the promoter for this show wrapped around my finger. You guys won't be on that stage unless I let you."

"Christ, I said I'd deal with it."

She nodded slowly and swept strands of hair away from her face. "Anyhow," she said, "I got you some comps for the show."

She handed me four tickets. I glanced at them. The Killjoys weren't listed—not a surprise considering we weren't on the original bill—but Heart's swirling name ran across the top. It was weird, but seeing that made it all real, and helped me buck up my courage. I stuffed the tickets in my back pocket and took a deep breath. "Look, about tonight, I'm not sure I can make it." I took a step closer to her. "Maybe we can go over the other details tomorrow morning."

She frowned. "Tomorrow?"

"Yeah, I've got something I need to do after the show."

"Put it off." Her hands went to her hips.

"I said I can't."

"You're comin' over to my place."

An unfamiliar surge ran through me. "Hey, look, you don't own me."

She grabbed a button near the top of my shirt, then with a flutter of her ringed fingers, she ran her hand down to my belt buckle and gave it a sharp tug. Her eyes blazed at me through the haze of the bar.

I felt a quick shiver, of dismay, anger. I pushed her hand away and shoved past her toward the door, but she went right after me.

"Hold up," she said, grabbing my arm.

I stopped but kept my body angled away from her. Kitten released her grip. With a tired motion, she again swept hair away from her face, a gesture that proved futile as strands fell back across her left eye. The juke box paused between songs, and I heard her sigh. "Look, Daniel, I'm not lookin' to mess with your head. I just want outta this town. I never meant to get stuck here, y'know?" She sighed again. "I've got plans, just like you do. You're not gonna screw that up for me—for us—are you?"

I was caught off guard by her vulnerability, but I still chose my words carefully. "As far as I'm concerned, we've got a business deal." I almost reached out to touch her shoulder, to brush the hair away from her face, but I willed my hand to stay where it was. "I'm not backing out of it as long as you keep up your end. But that's it."

She seemed to flinch, or maybe she was just trying to fling hair away from her face. I wasn't sure. But when she next spoke I had to lean forward to hear her.

"I don't know what you think about me," she said in a hissing whisper. "Maybe you think I'm a bitch. A lot of people do." Her eyes were on me, searching. "But I think we're kinda alike. Maybe you don't think so, but I feel it. Know what I mean?"

"Alike?" I shook my head. "I don't know what you're talking about." But of course I did. Kitten was messed up, this town she was stuck in was messed up, Creedly was messed up, and *I* was messed up. Maybe we did, in some way, want the same thing. And once again I was struck by the thought that she knew exactly what I'd give up to get what I wanted.

Her next words confirmed it. "What I'm sayin' is that we both know what we need, and we can get it together." She reached out and took my hand. I was struck by how different it felt from Nita's, rougher, colder, the metallic bands of her rings pressing against the flesh of my fingers. "I can be good for you."

There was a nakedness about her expression that almost got to me, but I resisted the notion and pulled my hand away. "I said I'd stick to the deal."

The dark glint came back into her eyes. "You think you're pretty smart, don't you?"

I forced a grin. "No smarter than you, I'd guess."

"Fine," she said, crossing her arms. "Don't worry about me. But we do have business, so I'll see you later."

"We'll see." I turned and left, and this time she didn't come after me.

Sam and Rob were still standing with Beanie and Cecil at the doorway. Using my bandanna, I wiped sweat from my forehead.

"What happened to you?" Sam asked.

"I got detained." I looked back toward the jukebox, but Kitten had disappeared.

Sam started to say something else, but Beanie suddenly

reached between us and pointed a skinny finger at a table
near the bar. "There they are."

We all turned and followed the line of his finger.

"Remember?" Beanie said. "I told you about 'em, Butch
and Whiskey. They're my buddies."

At a table, a burly couple sat facing each other, two
pitchers of beer, two mugs, and a pack of cigarettes between
them. A red scar ran across Butch's stubbled right cheek,
and tattoos decorated his arms. The oversized brown-haired
woman with him was stuffed snugly into a black leather hal-
ter top, a large red rose tattooed on her bulging bosom.

"You remember?" Beanie asked, and then he giggled.
"She's the one with the big you-know-whats."

"Yeah," Sam said, "we remember."

"I put in a good word for you." Beanie grinned at us.
"They're pretty heavy with the other bikers."

I took another look at their table. At the same time,
Butch glanced back and caught my eye. Discolored teeth
emerged from the bushy beard, and he raised his mug in our
direction before draining it.

Cecil finished stamping the hands of another group of
bikers. "Butch bought Beanie a coupla beers and he's flying."
He winked. "You know Beanie; he's a cheap date."

Rob, his face paler than usual, shifted to let the bikers
pass by. His gaze followed the group, and he murmured,
"Man, you weren't kidding about the bikers."

"Yeah," Cecil said, "they all kind of showed up at the same
time, didn't they? I'm surprised you didn't hear 'em arrive. You
really oughta take a look outside. It's pretty amazing."

"Let's check it out." Sam started toward the door.

Glad for any excuse to leave the lounge, I followed Sam
and Rob through the lobby. We stepped outside, our breath
suddenly bursting into little clouds of mist, and gathered
on the sidewalk. Tires and gleaming chrome stretched the
length of the block.

"Holy shit." Rob stared up and down the street. "It's like a friggin' Harley-Davidson lot out here."

Sam let out a low whistle and strolled down the sidewalk, inspecting the various choppers angled in to the curb. I knew nothing about motorcycles, but Sam understood the meaning of these bikes, ticking off the model names and numbers to himself as he moved past each one. Halfway along the line he said, almost reverently, "These are serious machines. Custom choppers."

After another pass down the line of bikes, Sam finally satisfied himself. "My dad would love to see these bikes." His eyes were wide. "He really would."

I nodded but said nothing, knowing that Sam's father had permanently messed up his leg in a motorcycle accident. "Maybe we'd better get back inside before the natives get restless."

Rob and Sam nodded and reluctantly headed back up the steps to the front door. I was about to follow them inside when I stopped and looked down the sidewalk. As if I had willed the vision, Nita emerged from the mist near the end of the block, her blonde head caught by a streetlight. The vision seemed to waver and shimmer as she came nearer. I held my breath, wondered if I was hallucinating, watched her come closer, and, convinced that she was real, stepped back down to wait for her.

"It's you," I said when she got near. "I thought you'd left."

She smiled back at me. "Not so lucky, mister. No place was open around here, so I had to drive out to a coffee shop near my motel."

My wide smile surprised me. "I'm glad you're back."

She scanned the motorcycles and raised an eyebrow. "Everything going O.K.?"

"So far, I guess."

"So, then, I finally get to hear your music. I'm excited."

"You sure you want to go in?"

She put her fists up like a boxer. "I'm sure. I've been to punk shows in San Francisco worse than this. And I've got my club boots on."

I looked down at her heavy-soled black shoes. "You might need 'em. But stay close to the stage where I can see you. I might need your help."

"Yes, sir."

She grabbed my arm and we walked into the bar, where Kitten and the Hell's Angels were waiting.

The unholy trinity was now a reality.

✳ ✳ ✳ ✳ ✳

I REUNITED WITH Sam and Rob on the stage, which now seemed like a fragile little island in a sea of bodies and drifting cigarette smoke. The background growl of bikers swirled around us, and my adrenaline, which didn't need much additional stimulation, kicked up higher. I lit a cigarette, strapped on my Strat, and checked the tuning. Sure enough, the heat in the bar had put me out of tune, but I quickly retuned and tried to steady my racing mind. A few moments later, Yogi and Mick walked up with Evangeline. She lingered at the edge of the stage, shooting glances back into the lounge. Nita had found a table near the front of the stage off to my right, but I couldn't see her unless I stepped to the edge and squinted through the lights.

While Yogi slid behind the drums and warmed himself up with a few rolls, I quickly reviewed the list for our second set. I worried we didn't have anything fast and hard enough for this crowd, and, with a glance out toward the bar, I wondered if and when the bottles might start flying.

We started off with Blue Oyster Cult's ominous *Don't Fear the Reaper*, and I thought I heard a mild buzz of approval coming from the tables beyond the dance floor. By the second verse, Kitten had returned to the floor with some of the other locals, but the bikers remained at their tables. Kitten danced around till she was sure I had a clear view of her swaying butt. She was getting it on, pretty obvious. Did Nita notice the bumps and grinds being sent my direction?

We worked our way through a blistering set of *Hey Baby*, *You Ain't Seen Nothing Yet*, and *Movin' On*, and despite the sense of danger that came at me from every corner of the bar I began to relax again. My guitar, which had finally adjusted to the heat, felt natural in my hands, the strings doing what I needed them to do, my pick slashing through the air with ease.

Few bikers had hit the dance floor, but I felt good about our momentum and was growing confident that we'd be able to pull the crowd along with us. No doubt Mick, again testing the edge of the stage with his blind, dancing feet, felt the same way.

Then it all changed. And when it did, the end came quickly.

Like a car running out of gas, our forward motion, which had propelled us nicely into Steve Miller's *The Joker*, slowed and stalled, killing the song's drop-dead-cool attitude. Measure by measure, then note by the note, the tempo of the song, kind of tepid to begin with, petered out. By the time we crawled to the final verse, the song had become a regular dirge.

It soon became apparent that the problem was Yogi, who suddenly sounded like he was playing in a vat of molasses. His beat had become a tortoise race between the snare and bass drum, with the bass drum losing ground to the snare each lap around the verse. I glanced back at him several times before realizing what was wrong. The droopy eyelids, the flinching brow, the reddened face—they all said the same thing: Yogi had sunk into a wine hangover.

When we finally, mercifully, reached the end of the song, the dance floor cleared. Once again I saw the ragged line of bikers standing along the back edge of the floor. Rob cast a worried look in my direction moments before he and Yogi started into Ace's sinewy *How Long*.

We weren't more than halfway through the first verse before we were in trouble again. Usually, we'd slide down easily into the song's sultry groove and let it carry us forward, but again Yogi was dragging the beat.

I drifted back from my mike to the drums. "Pick it up," I yelled at him.

He looked at me in surprise, then jerked the tempo much faster than needed. I bobbed my head, trying to get him locked into the right tempo, but he couldn't find it. His beat skittered back and forth like a tape player with a wow-and-flutter problem.

Back on the dance floor, one couple tried to fast dance, then gave up. Another attempted to slow dance before quickly moving back to their table. Even Mick was having trouble following us. His movements became jerkier by the minute as the beat slowed again. Rob and I tried to force the tempo, push it forward, but against the drums we were swimming upstream. By the end of *How Long*, we were almost drowned out by the growling voices coming from the dark edges of the dance floor. I stepped through the lights to look over at Nita, but her head was turned toward the bikers.

"What's bloody wrong with him?" Mick yelled at me, squinting back at Yogi. Sweat beaded his face.

"Too much wine, I think. He's already hungover."

"Tell him to get his arse in gear before these yobs start chuckin' bottles at me, right?"

I retreated and leaned over Yogi's floor tom. "C'mon, you're dragging everything."

"I can't help it," he said, followed by a gaping yawn. "I'm pooped."

"You've gotta pick it up." Someone in the crowd yelled for us to start playing. "Get focused or we're gonna lose this crowd."

"I'll try," he said, but I could see in Yogi's slumped shoulders and blank eyes that he was almost out of gas.

Then inspiration struck; I knew what would help him. I turned my back on the crowd and dug into my pocket, fishing out the vial. Tapping out two cross-tops, I said, "Here, take these."

He leaned over and peered into my palm. "What are they?"

"They'll keep you awake."

Behind us, I heard Mick announce the next song, Traffic's *Rock & Roll Stew*. The voices in the crowd grew louder.

"No way," Yogi said. "How do I know what they'll do to me?"

"Just take the damned pills, O.K.?"

Mick came up from behind and grabbed my shoulder. "Hey, let's go! They're gettin' pissed out there, right?"

I kept my eyes on Yogi. "Look, the pills won't hurt you. Trust me."

"C'mon, c'mon," Mick said over my shoulder.

"You owe me, Yogi."

I watched him roll the idea around in his head for a few more seconds before he reached out, took the tablets, and downed them with a slug of Pepsi.

"Hey!" Sam yelled across at us. "Let's play!"

Mick glanced at him and then back at me. "You got any more?"

"What?"

"The cross-tops."

"C'mon, Mick. You don't need 'em."

"Oh, I do, mate. Believe me."

There was no time to argue. Again angling away from the lights and the eyes of the crowd, I dug out two more white tablets and dropped them into his outstretched hand. He grinned, swallowed the pills, and bounced back to his mike stand.

Turning to Yogi, I counted out the tempo and together with Rob hit the three chords starting out *Rock & Roll Stew*. Throughout the first verse, I held my breath, knowing that we'd have to survive at least twenty minutes—the time it'd take for the uppers to kick in—before we could count on much from Yogi. But twenty minutes was way too long. Before we even got through the first verse, Yogi's drumming had deteriorated into a plodding, listless shuffle. Any sense of groove was long gone, making every note, every beat a struggle, like trying to haul a heavy rock up a mountain.

Rob shot another tense look at me from across the stage. Sam jabbed his sax in a frantic motion to speed up Yogi's beat. Mick kept his back to us, but I could tell from his stiff posture and violent swipes at the mike that he was furious beyond belief. The dance floor remained empty, and the sluggish, bluesy song seemed to go on forever. Then, nearing the end, a thick voice cut through the smoke of the lounge: "Play some Black fuckin' Sabbath!"

Another voice rose up in support: "Yeah, man, screw this lightweight shit! Sabbath! *Iron Man!*"

"*Paranoid!*"

"Fuck that! *War Pigs*, man."

We ground to a halt, and the beer-soaked voices rattled off more Black Sabbath songs, arguing among themselves about which one was best. Mick squinted back at me and then down at the set list taped to the floor near his monitor. "Sorry, mates," he said to the crowd, "we're a little short on Sabbath, right? How about some"—he paused to glance at his set list again.

I looked down at mine and saw the Doobie Brothers' lightweight *Listen to the Music*. Immediately, my eyes jumped across the list, looking for something, anything, that might work better. Steppenwolf jumped out at me. "Hey, Mick," I yelled at him, "let's do *Magic Carpet Ride*."

He squinted, sweat dripping off his face, before return-ing to the mike. "Right, mates," he said, shouting to be heard above the bellowing crowd, "be cool now. We've got some Steppenwolf for you."

The crowd hooted back at him. "Sabbath!" somebody yelled again.

Stiffening, Mick pointed his finger in the direction of the bikers. "Listen up, mates. We play what we wanna play, right?"

"Oh, shit," I muttered to myself.

Somebody in the crowd laughed, but it was a low and menacing sound. I knew I couldn't let this go on. Without waiting for Mick's cue, I looked at Yogi, who had his face in a towel, and yelled out, "Stay with me!" and started up *Magic Carpet Ride*.

The song seemed to work. A few of the bikers gathered at the edge of the dance floor and bobbed their shaggy heads. And Yogi more or less kept up with us. Maybe my cross-tops were starting to kick in; maybe they would save us. For five minutes—the time it took us to play the song—I thought we'd survived. Then I wasn't so sure. We finished and the place settled into an ominous quiet. More men, shadowed through the stage lights, gathered at the edge of the empty-ing dance floor and stood staring at us.

"Play some fuckin' metal," one of them growled.

"Judas Priest!"

Beer bottles started tapping in unison to the stomp of motorcycle boots.

"*Genocide*!"

"Sabbath!"

I felt panic setting in, as if the room had closed down and was squeezing the breath from my lungs. Across the stage, Rob had turned away from the crowd and was fiddling with knobs on his amplifier. Next to him, Sam nervously mouthed the reed of his sax. A beer bottle rolled across the dance floor and banged against the edge of the stage. I jumped back toward my amp, and Mick, his eyes wide, followed me. "Bloody hell! What now?"

"Don't ask me. You're the one who pissed 'em off." I scanned the set list, but the titles seemed to merge together.

"Whatta we do? Whatta we do?" He was gasping, hyperventilating.

"You O.K.?" I yelled in his ear.

"The pills," he yelled back, "they're kicking in, man. They're makin' me. . . ." He fluttered his fingers near his head.

The pounding continued. Another bottle hit the stage near the monitors, and someone screamed out, "Deep Purple!"

I looked at Mick. None of us was big on the song, but we all knew it. We had no choice. "*Smoke on the Water*!" I shouted.

"What?"

"*Smoke on the Fuckin' Water.*"

Mick just stood there staring at me.

"Get up there," I yelled at him. He turned as if to move forward but stayed put. Without waiting for him, I started the song. My left hand shook as I tried to hold down the anthemlike progression of bar chords leading up to the verse, and I held my breath until Yogi came in on the closed high-hat. But when he did, he was right there, right where he should be, square on the beat, sending out a sizzling series of triplets. Then he hit the snare smack on the second beat. Rob came in way down low with the chugging distorted eighth notes, and we were suddenly locked in. I glanced at Yogi, saw his wide, bright eyes, his happy smile, and knew that he was wired.

Mick, too. Now he came back alive. He pumped his fist at me, moved up to the mike, and started barking out the lyrics. I looked beyond him to the dance floor, where couples crawled out of the shadows and began moving, shaking, throwing out their arms, kicking their feet. A group of bikers came out, and the plywood floor of the stage began to pulse, seeming to rise and fall in rhythm to their stomping boots. I watched, simultaneously fascinated and terrified.

Now up at the mike for my background vocals, I saw Nita standing at the edge of the dance floor, chin tucked, eyes on me. With sudden confidence, I hit my foot switch for maximum distortion and lit into the solo, my fingers humming on the strings, working chromatically up the neck into the cutaway. I slid back down for eight bars, then back up again. I rode up as high as I could, found the note I wanted, and stayed there, bending all the noise out of it that I could. I glanced at Mick and saw him bouncing up and down as if trying to touch his head to the ceiling. He kept going, and I watched him, holding the note, amazed, knowing that he, too, was fired up by the mixture of fear, adrenaline, and amphetamines.

The crowd caught the action and started pounding in time to Mick's bounces. The entire room shook. Someone turned on the disco ball, and a strobe light shot out from the ceiling. Everything became glittery shards of light. Bodies and faces became fragments. I turned, knelt on my left knee, angled my guitar into the amp, scratched up the volume, and coaxed a blue line of feedback from my speaker cabinet. It enveloped me and traveled from my guitar, through the pick, up my arm, past my closed eyes, into my brain.

And I was suddenly out, free, rising above the stage, looking down, my eyes closed but still seeing the tops of Rob's and Sam's heads, the flashing hands of Yogi across the cymbals, the shape of Mick bobbing along the edge of the stage, the hands of dancers clapping high above their heads. In the flashing strobe, I saw Evangeline, Kitten, Beanie and Cecil, Mr. Tom, and Nita smiling up at me. And, in the moments between darkness, I saw a single drunk biker near the back edge of the dance floor lift a bottle above his head, pause, and then fling it toward the stage.

My eyes popped opened. I raised, turned, and, in a flash of light, saw it. The bottle smashed against the front of the stage, inches from Mick's feet. As if a grenade had exploded, Mick lurched sideways, arms flying upward. He spun, staggered back. We moved toward each other. He looked at me, his eyes rolled up, turning white. And then he collapsed.

21

WITH MICK SPRAWLED on the stage next to the drums, everything came to a grinding halt. Suddenly the houselights came up, shocking my eyes to pinpoints. We struggled out of our instruments while the crowd began to whistle and clap, either thinking Mick's collapse had been part of our act or celebrating because they had managed to take one of us down.

I got to Mick first and rolled him over. He was out cold, but I saw no cuts on his face, no blood, nothing. I put my hand on his chest and felt it rise and fall. The others arrived at the body a moment later.

"Christ," Rob said, "is he O.K.?"

"I dunno. He's breathing."

Sam felt for a pulse just to be sure. "Should we get a doctor?"

In his bare feet, Yogi knelt and peered into Mick's face. "I don't think anything hit him."

Rob went down on a knee beside him. "Then what's wrong with him?"

Before anyone could speculate, Yogi reached back, grabbed a cup of water from the floor near his drum set, and flung the contents into Mick's face.

I started to push Yogi away, but Mick's eyes popped open. The eyelids fluttered three or four times before the pupils rolled down into place. His eyes shifted from Yogi to me, and in a blurry voice, he asked, "What happened?"

I heard feet on the stage and looked back to see Evangeline and Nita. "Can I help?" Evangeline asked. Nita stayed behind me. I felt her gentle hand on my shoulder.

"What happened?" Mick asked again, his accent disappearing in the blurriness of his voice. With Evangeline's help, he pushed himself into a sitting position and woozily looked around at us.

Sam shifted back, and Cecil edged his way into the circle around Mick. "You O.K. up here?"

"He fainted," Yogi said.

"I what?" Mick asked.

"You fainted. My sister did the same thing once in a school play."

"Oh, shit." Mick rubbed at his eyes.

Cecil glanced back into the lounge, and I realized people were now hooting, hollering, stamping their feet. The juke box had been started up—I heard Rod Stewart singing *Tonight's the Night*—but it didn't cover up the noise.

"You gonna be able to go on?" Cecil asked.

I looked at our singer. "How about it, Mick? Can you finish out the set?"

"Fuck that," Rob said, standing and glancing toward the mayhem on the dance floor. "This is fuckin' crazy. I'm finished."

Cecil shook his head and glanced back into the lounge again. "I threw that fucker out, but the rest of 'em are gonna tear this place apart unless you keep playin'. It's happened before. Tom's freakin' out."

As if on cue, a bottle came whizzing out of the crowd, missing Rob's head by several inches before smashing against the wall behind the drums. Rob went back down on a knee, his eyes wide, his fingers furiously working at the bridge of his nose.

"The hell with Tom," he said, his voice rising with hysteria. "I'm not going back out there."

"You walk off," Cecil told him, "and they'll trash your equipment. I guarantee it."

"Somebody needs to call the cops," Sam said, his voice steadier than Rob's but still strained.

Cecil shot him a hard look. "You know how many of

these guys are packin' drugs and guns and knives and shit? It'd be a war in here."

From behind me, I heard Nita murmur, "I think he's right."

My gaze rotated from Mick, who was still trying to shake the cobwebs from his head, to the dance floor, where a dozen bikers had gathered near the foot of the stage, stomping their black boots, creating a steady, ominous sound. Faces with bristling beards and red eyes glared up at us.

"Yogi," I said, "help me get him up." I got under one of Mick's arms, Yogi grabbed the other, and we pulled him to his feet.

"How're you feeling?" I asked Mick, propping him up.

He turned his head and squinted at me. "Me head's light, mate."

His accent was back, so I took hope. "Can you sing?"

"Sing?" He shook his head back and forth. "No, mate, I'm knackered."

"C'mon, let's walk it off."

Evangeline shoved her way between us. "Stop it!" She put her hand on Mick's cheek. "Can't you see he's hurt?"

"Christ," Rob said. "Look at him. He can't even stand up."

They were right. Mick was finished. I knew that if I pulled away, he'd fall back down. "Over there," I said to Yogi, motioning with my chin toward the back of the stage, behind my amp, where our cases were stacked. We dragged him over and laid him out. Evangeline found a towel and put it under his head as Nita left to get him some water.

Our moving to the back of the stage encouraged more chaos out front. I heard glass breaking and a shout, and I knew that we'd never make it out of the bar if we stopped playing. Cecil, who had been standing to the side while we dealt with Mick, grabbed my arm. "You guys better do something fast, O.K.? I'm goin' back out there to make sure Beanie doesn't get killed."

I watched him leave the stage, shoving his way through

the bikers on the dance floor, and motioned Rob, Sam, and Yogi over. "We need to play something, at least until things calm down in here. Maybe Mick'll come around."

"Play what?" Rob asked, his voice still higher than usual. "Who's singing?"

"You can."

"No way. I don't know the lyrics. You do it."

I shook my head. *My* voice out there? Uh-oh. "I don't know 'em either," I told them.

"Maybe we can just jam," Sam said. "Do something over a blues pattern."

"How long are we gonna get away with that?" I asked.

Sam shrugged.

"I know what we can do," Yogi said, brightening. "Let's play your songs, Daniel. You know the words."

All eyes turned to me.

I shrank back, my stomach churning. "Fuck that. I'm not the singer."

"You are now," Rob said. "Either that or our stuff gets trashed, and I ain't going back out there to dodge bottles."

"C'mon, Daniel," Sam said. "We know the changes enough to fake our way through. Right, Rob?"

He nodded. "I can watch his hands if I get lost."

I looked at Rob, finding it hard to believe that he would go back onstage, even if I was the one singing. "You're really willing to do this?" I asked him.

Rob stared at me for a long moment before his face shifted into a twisted grin, the kind of mirthless expression I imagined you'd see on someone going to the gallows. "If you've got the guts to do your songs, I'm willing to back you up," he said. "I guess I'm calling your bluff, Daniel. Weren't you the one who told me last week that we're all in this together? It's up to you now, man."

Sam and Yogi nodded in agreement. I stared back at them and realized my choices were down to what Nita had called our little secret. It was punk or nothing. Could it save my life? I hoped so. But the thought of being up there alone, with no control, nothing to hide behind, scared me shitless. I instinctively searched my pocket for the vial, but even if I swallowed a pill, it wouldn't kick in for at least twenty minutes. No, I was on my own.

"This is crazy," I said, breaking off eye contact. "I can't do it."

Rob shook his head and took a step toward the side of the stage. "I'm not taking a bullet for you."

"Wait." I took one last look back at Mick, who was still flat out on the floor with Evangeline and Nita beside him, and forced down the cold gut fear. "O.K., let's do that last one I brought in. *Thrill.*"

"That crazy thing you wrote?" Rob's eyes narrowed. "You sure?"

"Yeah."

He took a long look into the lounge. "O.K." A pause. "What are the chords?"

I grabbed my guitar, turned down the volume, and went down on a knee. The feel of the strings calmed me. "You remember? It starts on an E and walks down in half steps to the D. See? And then it drops to the B, slides up to the G, then drops to an F-sharp. Then it repeats. That's the whole thing." I played the elemental chord progression quickly. "I'll start it out, and you can come in on the turnaround."

Rob rubbed his forehead and blinked at me.

I saw his confusion and my momentary resolve faded. "This is never gonna work."

"No." Rob looked again at the Hell's Angels lined up against the edge of the stage. "It's all major bar chords, fifths, right? I can follow you."

"I hope you're right." I looked at Yogi. "Remember, this thing goes fast, so hit everything as hard as you can, and above all else, make sure it doesn't drag."

Yogi's head went up and down in quick, jerky motions. I realized he was still cross-topped up, but at least he was energized. He tapped his sticks, fast. "I'm ready."

Hearing the madness in the background, I looked around at their faces, feeling the acid eating at my gut. "Let's do it."

Our huddle broke up. Seeing us back on the stage, the crowd quieted and someone cut the juke box. Bikers at the edge of the stage, all still in their leather jackets despite the steamy atmosphere, trained their eyes on us. One of them, a hulking dude with a red bandanna draped over his skull, caught my eye and with a glare flicked the stub of a lit cigarette toward one of our monitors. The guy standing beside him followed the arc of the cigarette with a gob of spit. They both missed the speaker, but they made their point.

I turned my back, cranked up the gain on my amp, hit a chord, then adjusted the gain upward again. I needed to be as loud and distorted as I could; something had to cover up my vocals. I slowly ran through the chords to *Thrill* once just to make sure I remembered them. For a moment, a surge of crazy hope ran through me. Maybe the song would work with these violent rebels without a cause. Somehow I knew how they felt; somehow I knew that the song, written during one of my darkest periods following Kevin's death, spoke to the alienation that connected me to these people. Maybe they would feel the connection, too.

Someone kicked at the front of the stage. I looked over my shoulder and saw the bandanna guy grinning at me. "Where's the little homo?" he growled, his grin freezing me in place.

I had to force my eyes away, my neck stiff, vertebrae grinding. Christ, I had no connection to these people. What was I thinking? The floor of the stage continued to vibrate as the biker kicked again and again at the plywood, sending splinters of sparks through my head. Was the Marquee like this? How much shit did Townshend have to take from the crowd? Did the Who get bottles thrown at them, have people spitting at them?

"What the fuck you playin' next?" one of the bikers yelled.

"Better be Sabbath," came from somewhere.

Oh, shit. My throat, dry and tight, hurt like a son of a bitch, but we couldn't stall them any longer. I took a gulp of water, looked across the stage at Rob to make sure he was ready, and then turned to Yogi. "Keep it fast!"

I hit the first chord of *Thrill* as hard as I could and literally felt the displaced air rush from my amp and fly past my ears. I saw the heads of the bikers jerk back. My eyes jumped to the neck of the guitar, to my hand moving up and down the spaces between the frets, blocking down on the buzz-saw chords. At the same time, my mind leaped ahead, trying to remember the words of the first verse.

With a cymbal crash, Yogi was in, hard and fast, no syncopation, no accents, every beat smacked hard. He was soon joined by Sam's tambourine. And then at the next turn-around, Rob's bass slid into the pattern. For a moment, we were all in together, but halfway through the chord progression Rob missed a note and stopped. I angled to show him the neck of my guitar, the position of my index finger on the top string, and he nodded, locked back in, and had the pattern sorted out by the third pass through.

With the band roaring behind me, I edged up to the mike, glass from the broken bottles crunching underfoot. A larger crowd, now dotted with a few women, had gathered at the foot of the stage. Heads, only a few feet lower than my own, were pumping in time. The stage lights shifted from blue to yellow, the faces before us became a blur, and I could no longer see beyond them. I damped the strings with my palm, closed my eyes, and suddenly saw the words, just as I'd written them in my bedroom back home. I opened my bone-dry mouth, ready to go, but nothing came out. I gasped for air.

Keep breathing, keep breathing, keep breathing.

The chord progression worked its way around again. I took another deliberate gulp of air, swallowed, and told the words to come. This time, through the monitors, I heard my voice out in front of me even before I seemingly formed the first word.

The real me
Ain't the one you see.
The real me
I don't dare let free.
The voices tellin' me to kill
To keep the thrill alive.

It was all around me. My disembodied voice was bouncing off the walls. I was shocked by the power, the exhilaration, of it. I'd blown out so much air a dizzying wave passed over me. I opened my eyes and sucked in what my lungs could hold.

Sam punched the lights back to blue, and I could see again. Yogi kept the beat pounding, but people weren't dancing yet. But they were moving—milling, heaving, surging forward. I stepped back from the mike and glanced around the stage. Sam and Rob were still back near the bass amp.

The chord progression wrapped around again and I put my lips to the mike.

They killed my brother,
They messed up my mother.
I'm lookin' for another
To help me recover.
And I'm poppin' pills
To keep the thrill alive.

I spun away from the mike, stumbling back toward Yogi, powering the chords, windmilling as much noise as I could out of the Strat. My eyes caught Nita, still standing in the dark area behind my amp where it was relatively safe, and a thought darted through my head. This was it: She was seeing the Real Me, pilled-up, screaming out things I wouldn't even tell my best friend.

We stayed on the chord pattern, picked up speed and volume, five times, six times through. With no clear arrangement, I just kept pumping the chords, letting Yogi, crashing cymbals and firing bass drum beats, virtually solo over the top. He built the volume and momentum up to an impossibly high level, then dropped it, locking back in. Disoriented, I careened toward the mike stand, the sea of bodies at the stage's edge pulling me toward them. The words of the last verse moved to my mouth. I took a lungful of the Mai Tai's searing air, closed my eyes, and let it go.

The real me
The voices all agree.
Gotta let him be,
Can't set him free.
There's nothing left that's real
To keep the thrill alive.

My eyes, sensing motion near my face, flew open. Three feet in front of me, I saw a clenched black-gloved fist pumping upward, beating at the air in rhythm to the beat. And at the bottom of that fist was Butch, dirty beard, red scar, tattoos. Beside him was Whiskey, her rosy bosom heaving up and down.

Butch's fist came flying up again. "Fuckin' A!" he screamed at me, spit flying, eyes huge. "This is righteous shit!"

Shocked, I stepped back. He screamed it out again, this time to the bikers around him, and I watched as more clinched fists, one at a time, then all together, sprouted and filled the air like a field of black-headed poppies.

My mouth fell open.

22

NITA LEANED BACK against the outside wall of the Mai Tai Hotel and pulled her jacket cuffs down over her hands. "Man, I've never seen anything like that," she said, "not even in San Francisco."

I tried to smile, but all I could do was shake my head. "One minute I thought they were gonna kill me, and the next everything changed." I cupped my hands and lit a cigarette. "Pretty amazing."

Except for the motorcycles parked along the curb, the street and sidewalk were deserted. Fog had crept in tight around the hotel, making it seem as if we were alone in a cocoon of brick and mist, and it was silky quiet except for the distant static hiss, like a seashell echo, in my ears. I checked my watch. We had ten minutes left before the next set.

Nita hugged herself for warmth. "Do you remember what I asked you at the party?"

I thought back, but it was a long time ago. "As I recall, you asked me a lot of things."

"You know, about why you play music?"

My tortured explanation now sprang to mind. "Barely."

"Well, now I really know why you do it." Her brown eyes sharpened. "And I was right."

I stared at her. "What're you talking about?"

"Transcendency, Daniel."

"What?" I laughed, but I clearly remembered what she had said, even if I hadn't understood it.

From behind a slightly parted veil of hair, her eyes burned back at me. "You know what I mean. You must've felt it, too."

I stopped laughing. And then I understood. I wasn't crazy. At least, not entirely. Minutes earlier I had stood at the microphone in a world reduced to my ears and my eyes, a collapsed little world where nothing else existed except me, the crowd, and the incredible noise pulsing around us. And all those strangers—people I had feared moments earlier— were taking my song, raising it up with their hands, holding on to it, and, by extension, holding on to me. I pulled in a deep breath. So that was it. We'd all been linked by that chord, that Pete Townshend Universal Chord, and for that moment it was perfect.

And Nita understood it.

She reached out and poked my arm. "You're a star."

I rolled the cigarette between my fingers. The perfection of the moment, held together by Nita, me, and my music, couldn't last, I feared, but I smiled at her. "I'm just glad we survived."

"Survived?" She giggled. "You were like the Ramones up there. The energy was almost scary."

"Well, Mick can take it from here. I don't have any songs left." I was almost disappointed that Mick had recovered by the end of our set.

She poked my arm again and tucked her chin. "So what was that song about?"

"Which one?"

"The first one—what do you call it?"

"*Thrill*."

"Yeah." She leaned toward me. "I couldn't hear all the words clearly, but there was something about your brother." She stopped, and her eyes came up, steady on my face. "I didn't know you even had a brother."

Pulling in a painful line of cigarette smoke, I thought back to when I had written that song, sitting on my bed at home, with Kevin's beat-up acoustic guitar with the nylon strings. I remembered it being dark, late in the afternoon or at night in the dead of winter, months and months after Kevin died, around the day my father left. From Kevin's gentle folk guitar this venomous song had emerged, spilling out like it had been there all along, waiting for me to find it.

And I had found it. I had let it out into the light, and this piece of me had been embraced. My brain still couldn't quite get around the idea that maybe I could open myself up. This realization thrilled me, but it also made me nervous.

I dropped the cigarette and stubbed it out with my foot. Could the moment last? I knew it couldn't. But, then, this was Nita. Maybe I could tell *her*. I reached out for one of her hidden hands. "My brother, Kevin—"

I heard the scraping sound of the hotel's front door being pushed open. Nita's head turned, and I followed her eyes to see Kitten standing at the top of the steps, arms crossed, staring at us.

Kitten gestured down toward Nita. "Who's this?"

Caught off-guard, I didn't answer. Kitten's eyes bounced between the two of us. "I said, Who's this?" She came down the steps toward us.

I moved into the space between the two women. "Her name's Nita. She's a friend of mine from home."

Nita came up beside me and hooked my arm.

Kitten stopped and smiled, aiming her sulfurous expression straight at Nita. "Oh. You're Daniel's girlfriend, huh?"

"That's right," Nita said. I glanced at her, startled by the forcefulness of her answer.

"So, Daniel," Kitten said, shifting her gaze to me, "Nita's why you're busy tonight."

"Look—"

"You didn't tell me about *Nita*, Daniel." In her mouth, Nita's name became a dirty, bitten-off thing.

"Why don't you leave us alone?" I said, knowing there was little hope that she would.

She ignored me and turned back to Nita. "You just get in?"

I felt Nita's grip tighten on my arm. "This afternoon," she answered, leaning into me and looking up with an expression that asked, *Who's this?*

Kitten threw off a throaty laugh. "Well, you're too late, honey. I've had Daniel to myself all week."

"Shut up," I said to her. I felt Nita stiffen beside me. "She doesn't have anything to do with our arrangement."

Kitten pulled a pack of Camels from her jacket pocket and tapped out a cigarette. "'Our arrangement'? Is that what you're calling it?"

"I know what you're doing, Kitten. Just cut it out."

She looked at Nita. "Did he tell you about"—she struck a match and lit the cigarette—"'our arrangement'? Did he tell you we . . . sealed it with a kiss?"

Nita's grip loosened. "What's she talking about, Daniel?"

I pulled her toward the steps. "Let's go back inside."

But Kitten backed up and stayed between us and the door. "We've been having a pretty good time, haven't we, kiddo?"

"She's lying." I looked at Nita, but I knew that she'd see that I was the one not telling all of the truth.

Kitten's smile grew wider. "Good try, Daniel."

Nita pulled away from me and looked at me with cloudy, accusing eyes. "You've been with *her*?"

"Look, Nita, I was going to tell—"

"Don't worry, girl," Kitten interrupted. "I checked out his equipment. It's all still working."

Nita took three steps backward down the sidewalk away from me. I went after her. "She's exaggerating," I said. "Believe me."

From behind me, Kitten laughed again. "Why would I 'exaggerate'?" She flicked her fingers around that last word.

Nita took another step backward. "I saw the way she looked at you from the dance floor."

"Shit," I muttered to myself, carefully moving toward her. "Let's talk about it, Nita."

Her eyes suddenly flashed fury. "Then it's true," she said, jerking at one of her sleeves. "You—damn you! You're . . . you're just like my father." She turned and, pulling her keys from her purse, headed down the sidewalk toward the corner.

"Nita!" I started after her. In the glare of the streetlights, I thought I saw tears glistening on her cheeks.

She ran across the street. "Leave me alone!"

I stopped at the corner and watched her slide into an orange Datsun 280Z. The car lurched away from the curb and spun off. I followed her taillights until they grew small and disappeared into the darkness.

When I returned to the front of the hotel, Kitten was still there, standing on the bottom step, smiling with dark triumph, the vile smell of her Charlie perfume all around her.

"Get the fuck out of my way," I said, restraining an urge to punch her.

Her smile took on a wicked twist. "Kiddo, you think I'm gonna let some amateur screw up my gig?"

"You're a real bitch." I pushed by her and headed for the door.

"Maybe I am," she said, grabbing my arm, "but I'll be the one who's leaving with you on Monday."

I shook loose. "Go to hell." But even as I said it, I knew that I was the one heading there. There was no avoiding it. I'd made a deal with the devil—something I knew the minute I'd allowed myself to be enticed into Kitten's bed—and now I was simply paying the price.

The unholy trinity had been shattered.

✳ ✳ ✳ ✳ ✳

I WALKED BACK through the lounge to the stage, suddenly sick of the stink of beer and cigarettes, tired of the loud music and drunken voices, angry at everyone, especially myself. Bikers patted me on the back and offered me beers, but I didn't care. So much for the power of the Universal Chord. Could the moment last? Did the chord really exist? Had I really thought it possible? What a stupid shit.

I stood alone on the stage, my back to the crowd, waiting for the rest of the band to return for our next set. I popped a couple more cross-tops—how many had I taken?—then closed my eyes and tried to block out the noise. I pictured Nita driving back to Seattle, leaving me like everyone else who had left before and would leave in the future. Leaving me like Dad, like Kevin, like Rob.

Mick appeared at the edge of the stage with his usual entourage of Evangeline and Yogi and stepped up onto the littered platform. "Waiting for the professionals to take over again, are you?"

I glared at him. "Think you can handle it?"

His eyebrows arched up. "You O.K., mate?"

"Sure. Just don't fucking faint on us again, O.K.?"

"My, my." He turned away and bent to readjust his mike stand.

From across the stage, Rob strapped on his bass and wandered over to me. "Nice job on the songs, man."

"Thanks."

He glanced out into the lounge. "I guess it should be easier from here on out. They seem to like us now." He grinned and pulled a fat joint from the pocket of his shirt. "One of them gave me this."

I tried to smile. "Guess it beats having bottles thrown at us."

"Sure does."

"So, are you still going to quit?" I hadn't meant it to sound like a challenge, but an ugly edge had worked its way into my voice.

He apparently caught it and his grin disappeared.

"Nothing's changed, man." With that, he palmed the joint and slid back over to his side of the stage.

I shielded my eyes and peered out into the blur of the crowd, knowing that Nita wouldn't be there, but I saw Evangeline standing near the edge of the stage. She caught my eye and waved me over.

"Where's your friend?" she asked. "I thought I'd sit with her."

"She's gone."

"Oh." She gave me a worried look. "For good?"

"I dunno." I shrugged. "Looks like it."

She frowned. "That's too bad. I liked her."

"Me, too," I said as I faded back toward my amp.

✳ ✳ ✳ ✳ ✳

For what it was worth, Rob was right: We now owned the place.

Every time we started a new song or one of us stepped forward for a solo, a roar would come from the tables beyond the dance floor. Beers kept arriving at the edge of the stage. Even the occasional screwup didn't break the spell. Rob's mike stopped working, and later our stage lights blinked out, but it didn't matter to the crowd.

And, for once, it didn't matter to me. I was numb to it all. Part of me, lit up by my cross-tops, buzzed and tingled, shook and sweated, but everything from my skin outward had become distant, apart, as if I were watching it on TV. I played our songs, heard the music, saw the dancers, but I felt none of the intensity from earlier. And as we worked through the next set of covers a muted desperation grew within me, a hollow fear generated by the knowledge that when the drugs wore off, I'd be alone again, with the Real Me. Nothing had changed, man.

We finished the night with *Won't Get Fooled Again*—Pete Townshend's unneeded reminder to me that I was a fool to buy into the lie that everything could be different, that things would be better. But as I angrily bashed my way through the chords, taking out the ultimate frustration of the night on the strings of my guitar, the song, as always, worked its way under my skin. Slowly but surely, I felt the irrational hope that lurked somewhere beneath Townshend's cynical lyrics build within me, lifting me up on the rising tide of Townshend's impassioned insinuation that things *could* change. In the midst of the song's chaos, I closed my eyes and heard Townshend's whispered voice, telling me: *You can't change the world, mate, but you can change yourself.* At that moment, I understood what he meant. And shortly after Mick let loose with the second of the song's two screams, I realized what I had to do.

23

IT WAS A FEW MINUTES after two and raining when I made it to the phone booth down the street from the hotel. Breathing in the cold, leaden air, I looked up the number, ripped the page out of the phone book, and rolled a dime into the slot.

The phone rang at least eight times before an annoyed voice answered, "Puente Harbor Travel Lodge."

"I'm trying to reach someone there. I don't know her room number."

The operator sighed. "Name?"

"Nita Annstrom." I spelled it for her.

"Hold on."

I waited, hoping Nita hadn't checked out, knowing that she could've without telling them. The voice came back on. "I can patch you through."

"Hold on. Look, I just realized how late it is. I'll call back tomorrow. What's her extension?"

Another sigh. "One-fifty. Goodnight."

Without a jacket to protect me, I ran through the rain to the parking lot behind the hotel and slid into the Blue Bomb. While the engine warmed, I looked up through the wet windshield and watched the silhouetted figures of the band and whoever else they were drinking with pass back and forth behind the blinds of the room. When the sound of the engine dropped down into its normal sputter, I let out the clutch and pulled into the alley.

The asphalt of Puente Harbor glistened in my headlights. I now knew these streets, and while they looked strange in the dead-of-night stillness, I had no problem finding my way across town. Three turns brought me to the highway along the waterfront, and I turned east before slowing as the lights of motel row came into view. The Travel Lodge had the largest sign, lit in yellow-and-blue neon. I drove through the parking lot and found Room 150 on the ground floor at the end of the east wing. With my heartbeat accelerating, I shut off the headlights and pulled into a parking spot almost in front of the room. Thinking about my next move, I cracked the window and lit a cigarette, wondering if Nita was still here.

Exhaling smoke through the window opening, I saw an orange 280Z parked two cars over. Looking at the darkened window of her room, I considered just leaving a note on the windshield of her car, but then I pictured Nita simply scrapping the wet paper off the glass in the morning without bothering to look at it. And, anyhow, what the hell did I have to say that could be put into a nice, neat little note? Shivering, I ground the cigarette into the ashtray and got out.

For a long moment, I stood beneath the shelter of the second-floor balcony thinking about what I'd say to her. Finally, I knocked softly on the door and stepped back, watching the curtained window for any sign of light or movement. Seeing nothing, I took a breath and knocked again, this time louder.

A dim light switched on, and a moment later "Who's there?" came from behind the door.

"Nita, it's me, Daniel." I waited for the door to open.

"It's late," she said through the laminated surface. "Please go away."

"I need to talk to you." I moved closer. "Can't you open the door?"

There was a long pause. Then, quietly: "It's not your fault. I made a mistake coming here. You should go back to your hotel."

Something in the sleepless tone of her voice betrayed an opening. "I'll leave if you want me to, but I need to say something first. And I can't through this door."

No answer came back, but a moment later the door cracked open the width of the security chain, and a sliver of her upturned pale face glinted through the opening. "What is it?"

I started to speak, but a light flicked on and a curtain moved in an adjacent room. "Look," I whispered, "I'm gonna wake up everyone in this place if you don't let me in."

One of Nita's brown eyes blinked. "Hold on for a minute. I'll come out." The door shut, and I lit another cigarette and waited. After a few minutes, Nita slipped out, clad in her black jacket and jeans.

"Let's talk in the van," I said.

Her eyes moved from me to the van. "No. Let's walk."

Without waiting for my reaction, she started into the parking lot, sliding through the shadows with quick, stiff steps toward the highway. I caught her at the sidewalk, and side by side we headed in the direction of town. Nita swept at her disheveled hair and kept her eyes straight ahead, as if trying to see something off in the distance. The rain had lessened, turning into a heavy mist, and a car roared by us through the shimmering moisture. I breathed in, tasting its fumes.

I tried to order my thoughts before speaking, but Nita beat me to it. "We don't know each other very well, do we," she said, maintaining her forward gaze.

I wasn't sure if she was asking a question or stating a fact. I glanced at her. "I guess not."

She shook her head. "I don't know what I was thinking coming here. After what happened with my father. . . ."

"Look, Nita—"

"Let me talk first." She shoved her hands down into her pockets and rushed on. "It wasn't fair to you, showing up without telling you first. I know that. But I thought I saw something at the party, and—" she paused for a moment "—I always trust my senses." Then with one swift, heart-wrenching shake of her head she added, "But I guess I was wrong."

I took a quick breath. "Let me explain about her."

She took a step ahead of me. "No, don't. You don't owe me anything. I'm the one who showed up unexpectedly, and—" She stumbled on a crack. I caught her arm, but she wrenched away. Watching her put space between us, a wave of fatigue swept over me. I turned my face upward into the falling mist and let the moisture hit my eyes. Thinking through what I could say, voices filled my head, calling out words, suggesting lies, concocting excuses. Sorting through them, I searched for my own voice. There was something about her that demanded the words that lurked below the surface, the ones I knew I didn't know how to say. But I had to find a way to say them.

I caught up to her. "Nita, there's something I should tell you."

She glanced at me. "Do you mean about the drugs?"

I stared at her. "What do you mean?"

"I have friends who do uppers. I can hear it in your voice, Daniel. I'm not being critical. How could I? I smoke grass. I just guessed that you do 'em."

My stride broke and I fell a step behind again. An echo of a voice came from way back in my head: *She sees the real you, mate. Tell her the bloody truth.*

I took a deep breath and lengthened my steps until I was beside her again, searching for a way to get a handle on the truth. "Listen to me, Nita. That's not what I wanted to tell you. I don't know how to put it, but have you ever listened to *Quadrophenia*, the Who album?"

"*Quadrophenia*?" She squinted at me like I was crazy. "I know it, but what about it?"

I swallowed hard. "I know this sounds stupid, but sometimes I think I'm like the kid in those songs on the album. It's like I . . . it's like I can't seem to find myself. Like there's nothing there but these fragments of other people, these pieces of things. Like I'm four people at once, and they're all about to fly apart." I shook my head. Could this make any sense to her? "I guess what I'm trying to say is that music's the only thing that holds me together." I shrugged. "And the drugs—well, they do sometimes, too." I got in front of her and faced her straight on. "Do you understand?"

She stopped and looked at me. "Are you trying to explain why you were with that . . . that woman? You don't have to make up excuses."

"Christ, I'm not making up excuses." I clenched my fists in frustration. "I'm telling you that there's something wrong with me. That's why everything I do, except the music, gets messed up." I realized my head was violently shaking back and forth. "I can't explain it."

Her eyes strayed from my face. "We all do things we don't mean to do." She gazed down the street. "You know, Daniel, you don't owe me anything. You don't have to explain it to me."

I rubbed at my damp forehead, realizing once again that the truth was no good. But I also knew that nothing else would work with her. "Look," I said, searching unsuccessfully for the right way to put it, "I slept with Kitten. I know it was a big mistake. But at the time it made some kind of weird sense. I mean, no, that's not what I mean. Look, she got us a gig opening for Heart. They're playing here. Tomorrow night. She has connections. She knows promoters, people in the business who can help us. This gig is really important, and she—" I shut my mouth, realizing I was going on like a speed freak.

Her eyes latched onto mine. "You're opening for Heart tomorrow night?"

"Yeah. At the fairgrounds. And Kitten got us the gig, and—I don't know—one thing led to another. I screwed up. It was like this other part of me took over. . . ."

Her eyes broke away. "You can sleep with anybody you want. I don't make those kind of demands on anyone, especially someone I hardly know." She started back toward the motel, then abruptly stopped again. "Daniel, I, well, I don't care that much that you slept with her—it's not important to me—but I hate thinking that you would compromise yourself, your music, just to get better gigs. That's what you did, isn't it?"

With amazing clarity, she saw what lurked beneath the surface. I posed like an artist, but at the first opportunity I was willing to sell out. And Nita knew it.

"Yeah," I said, "I guess that's what I did."

She started down the sidewalk. Stuffing my cold hands into my pockets, fingers touching the comforting glass of my vial, I followed her. The rain suddenly started again, bringing with it the earthy smell of her damp leather jacket. I caught up with her and looked at her face. Streaks of water ran down her cheeks, looking like tears, but I guessed this time they weren't.

"Nita." I tried to catch her eye, but she wouldn't look at me. "Look, you said that you didn't know me, but you do—you really do. That's why I came here tonight. I need to be with someone who really sees me. And you do. You know all about the drugs, you know about the music, you know I'm screwed up." My voice, high and breathless, scared me a little; but I pressed on. "You know all that, so why'd you come here?"

She snuck a look at me and lowered her chin. "Because I trust my heart too much." She said it in a voice so muted that I barely heard her, but I was immediately struck by how much her words sounded like Evangeline's from earlier in the night. At least we were in agreement on one thing: Trusting your heart, like telling the truth, was a bad idea.

We walked on in silence, and my legs, which I realized I'd been on for hours, ached. Still, I watched her out of the corner of my eye, seeing her transparently blonde hair, as if by magic, stray from yellow to blue to red, reflecting the neon lights of the motels we passed. I shivered and rubbed a sleeve across my face.

Nita glanced at me. "Don't you have a coat? You're getting soaked."

"I forgot it."

"You should go back to your hotel and get dried off."

We turned into the parking lot of the Travel Lodge. Breaking apart from each other, we circumvented puddles and cars on the way to her door. My mind raced for something more to say, but only echoes of fragmented thoughts bounced around my skull. The only concept that blazed out with clarity was that Nita—this girl who somehow saw the Real Me—was going to leave me and that I would be alone.

She unlocked the door and turned toward me. "Daniel, I came here because my father *didn't* tell me the truth. I was . . . well, I simply needed someone to—" She shook her head. "I see it wasn't fair to lay it on you." She tilted her head back, looked above me. "Dishonesty, it always makes me do crazy—"

"Nita, I'm being honest with you."

She sighed. "I know that. But right now, I need to go back to Seattle and get things straightened out with my father." She put a hand on my arm but pulled it away after a moment. "Good luck with your music, Daniel. You have a lot of talent. Just stay true to it."

She turned and disappeared into the room, and the void she left in her wake was immediate. I felt myself slipping into it, knowing that words—my words—were weak and useless. Music was the only way I could connect with anyone. Suddenly remembering the Heart tickets in my back pocket, I pulled one out and knelt down in front of her door. "Nita," I whispered as I slipped the ticket under the door, "don't go back yet. Come see us play tomorrow night."

I waited for something, anything, but there was no response. I stood outside in the boundless darkness until the light shut off in her room.

Finally, I lit up my last cigarette, pulled myself into the Blue Bomb, and headed back through the rain to the hotel.

24

THE POUNDING at the door—*thump, thump, thump*—was another one of those weird déjà vu moments.

I shot straight up in my sleeping bag as Mick and Sam did the same thing. We all looked at each other as the pounding continued.

"What the fuck," Sam sputtered from the roll-away. "Who's that?"

"Hey!" Mick yelled at the door. "Sod off!"

After a pause, the knocking started again. This wasn't the sharp, nervous rap of Mr. Tom; this was the measured thump of authority. I crawled out of the sleeping bag and pushed off the floor. Sunlight filtering through the window blinds created a series of wavy gray-and-white bars across the floor, and I hip-hopped across the streaks and cracked open the door. Peering out, I looked directly into the big, square face of a cop, a face blurry with heavy, sandy-colored eyebrows and a thick mustache. Behind him stood a shorter, dark-haired policeman.

"Is your name Mick?" the cop asked. His voice was calm, but his wedge of a jawbone jutted out toward me like an accusing finger. The badge on his cap seemed to shine directly into my eyes.

I blinked. "No."

"Is he here?"

"Um—" Momentarily confused, I blurted out, "Yeah. But he's still in bed." My mind, foggy with sleep moments before, cleared. Was any grass out in the open? Any pipes, roaches? I had slipped in after the others had gone to bed. Who knew what they had left lying around.

The cop craned his neck in an attempt to look above and around me, but I kept my face and frizzed-out hair between him and the interior of the room. He gave up. "Look, sir, we're with the Puente Harbor Police Department. We need to talk to this Mick person."

All of a sudden sounds of scurrying feet came from behind me, and I heard Mick hiss out, "Oh, bloody hell."

Hearing the commotion, the smaller policeman pushed forward. "You need to open up," he demanded.

"Look," I said, hoping to stall them while Mick and Sam hid anything that needed hiding, "none of us are dressed. We just woke up. Can't you hold on a second?"

The smaller cop's hand moved to his holstered revolver. "Now, sir."

I turned sideways and swung open the door. The two cops pushed into the room, forcing me back against the door. Mick, naked except for his red bikini underwear, froze near the bathroom door. On the other side of the room, Sam shoved something under the queen bed and straightened up. My eyes flew around, seeing scattered beer cans and a package of rolling papers beside an ashtray on the window-sill. The policemen also scanned the room, but Sam wisely shifted to a spot between them and the ashtray.

"Which one of you is Mick?" the big-jawed cop asked.

Mick and Sam looked at each other for a moment before Sam said, "He is," pointing across the room.

The cop trained his steely-eyed gaze on Mick. "Is that right?"

Mick faded back against the wall. In his near nakedness, he seemed smaller than usual. "Why do you want me?" His accent was gone.

The big cop stayed put but kept his eyes on Mick. "We need to ask you a few questions. You'll need to come down to the police station with us."

"What for?" I shifted off the wall. "What's he done?"

The two cops exchanged glances. The larger one licked at his mustache and, looking from me to Mick, said,

"Someone has lodged a complaint against him. We need to check it out."

"A complaint?"

"Yes, sir."

"What kind of a complaint?"

The big cop paused, looked at his partner again, and then said, "Contributing to the delinquency of a minor."

"Shee-it," Sam said under his breath.

"And possibly statutory rape," his partner added, the corner of his lips curling up.

A hiss, like air escaping a balloon, came from Mick's direction. He slid halfway down the wall, his hands dropping to cover the front of his bikini briefs. I looked from Mick back to the cops just as the big one said, "We need you to get dressed and come down with us."

"But she—"

I cut Mick off with a wave of my hand. "Can it, Mick. Get dressed and go with them." I knew anything Mick said would make it harder for him later. And, now noticing a baggie of pot sticking out of one of Sam's shoes, I wanted to get these cops out of the room as quickly as possible.

"Am I . . . am I under arrest?" Mick reached for the glasses lying on the floor beside the bed.

"No, sir," the big cop answered. "But we'd like to ask you some questions, and your cooperation would be appreciated."

"Don't you have to read him his rights?" Sam asked.

Both cops turned toward him. I held my breath, wondering if they'd notice the baggie sticking out of the shoe. "He'll be advised of his rights," the big cop said, "before we take his statement."

"Mick," I said, "you'd better go with them."

"And," the cop said, "please bring some identification with you."

Mick looked at me and then at Sam before grabbing a

pair of jeans and a shirt from the floor and starting to dress. We all stood and watched him go through the fumbling motions of buttoning his fly, pulling on his socks, tying his tennis shoes. Finally finished, he looked at us, his face colorless and devoid of the squinty arrogance that always passed for his charm. "I guess I'm ready."

The two policemen stepped to either side of the door, and Mick started forward. "Wait," I said to Mick, "you forgot your jacket." I grabbed it from the floor, and with my back to the cops, handed it to him, whispering, "Don't admit *anything*." He nodded and straggled out the door with the cops.

I shut the door and listened until the sound of their footsteps disappeared down the stairwell. "Rita," I said to Sam.

He nodded. "Lovely Rita."

* * * * *

BY NOON—an hour later—Mick hadn't returned. And now we had lost Yogi.

Sam, Rob, and I sat at a table in the Mai Tai's empty restaurant, drinking weak coffee and waiting for our breakfast to arrive, all eyes on the open door leading to the lobby.

"So Yogi was just gone when you got up?" I asked Rob.

"MIA, man. Nothing, except for a Snickers wrapper on the bathroom counter."

"Knowing Yogi, he's probably over at Pam's having lunch."

"Screw Yogi," Sam said. "What about Mick? Shouldn't we get him a lawyer or something?"

"Where are we gonna get the money to hire a lawyer?" I asked.

"We could call his folks. Maybe they could wire some."

"Yeah, right," I said. "Like his father's gonna send us money to get him outta jail on a rape charge. Calling him's a last resort. And, anyhow, we don't know if they've even charged him." But all the implications of what was happening went through my mind again. Not only could Mick be charged with rape, which was too stunning to even consider, but if they held him in jail, we'd be out a lead singer for tonight's show and, maybe, for all future shows. We'd be screwed. I'd be screwed.

"By the way," Rob said, "your friend Kitten came by the room last night looking for you."

"Yeah?"

"Oh, yeah. And this might be a moot point now, but she said we need to be at the fairgrounds by five to set up and sound-check. She said she'd meet us over there."

"Five. Right."

"That's five hours from now. So when're you telling her that we're not making it?"

"I dunno. Let's see what happens with Mick." At that moment, I couldn't even contemplate the remote chance that we'd be ready. My mind drifted to Nita. She'd probably left town by now. . . .

Rob tapped out a rhythm on the table. "So what's the deal with Kitten, man?"

"What do you mean?"

He snorted, and the irritating tapping continued. "What do I mean? Well, we were a little fried to hear that Kitten's involved with this gig."

Now recalling that I had never explained our arrangement, I avoided his eyes. "Yeah, I was going to tell you."

The tapping stopped. "Kitten already did. And what's this shit about her coming on as—well, as you guys' manager."

"Oh. She mentioned that, huh?"

"It's true?" Sam said. "We thought she was fulla shit."

My face reddened. "She's got connections to the promoter. It was the only way we could get the gig. I was gonna tell you after the show tonight. But nothing's in writing."

Rob shook his head in disgust. "You're a real dick, Daniel. Anything for a gig, huh?"

I pulled out a cigarette and tapped it down on the table. "O.K., I'm a dick, but I got the show, didn't I?"

"Look, I'm out after tonight, so it doesn't matter to me, but the other guys were a little surprised to hear about your secret little arrangement with her."

Sam leaned forward. "Why didn't you just tell us, Daniel?"

"I said I was going to after the show tonight."

Rob laughed. "What show? If Mick's not back by five, you guys are cooked—we're cooked. You're not planning on carrying it yourself, are you?"

"I dunno. I hadn't gotten that far in my thinking."

Rob shot Sam a look, and something seemed to pass between them. "Well, here's the deal, man. Sam and I talked about it while you were in the shower, and we're outta here tonight if Mick doesn't show. We got lucky last night, but we're not going on tonight without him. We don't have anything close to enough songs."

I looked at Sam. "Is that right? You're gonna blow off this gig? And you're just gonna leave Mick sitting in a jail cell? Well, I'm not."

Sam lowered his eyes to his coffee cup. "It's not fucking worth it. I knew Mick would pull this kinda shit eventually. And now this thing with Kitten." He shook his head. "I've had it. Sorry, Daniel, but we're taking off if he doesn't show."

I slumped down and let the unlit cigarette drop onto the table. Christ, maybe they were right. I didn't have enough songs to fill out a thirty-minute set—not even close—and playing the Heart gig without Mick wouldn't do our future any good. I looked around the table and realized the ridiculousness of the situation. What future?

"Look," Rob said, "I'm sorry about Mick. We don't want

to leave him hanging, but he brought this on himself. And it's not gonna do any good for me and Sam to hang around here while this thing gets sorted out."

"I agree," Sam added. "And we thought it might be better if we were back in Creedly anyhow. That way you could give us a call if Mick doesn't get out tomorrow, and maybe we could go over and talk to his parents. It might save you an ugly call, and it might be better if they heard about it in person."

"O.K.," I said, too weary to argue, even though I doubted the sincerity of their offer to deal with Mick's parents, "if that's the way it is. . . ." I looked at my watch. I had less than five hours to pull all the pieces of the band back together again or I might as well leave town with them. "You guys can have my breakfast. I'm going over to the police station to see what's going on with Mick. When you're done here, get started breaking down the stuff and get it loaded, O.K.? Beanie and Cecil said they'd help. Give them these."

I handed Rob two of the three remaining comp tickets. A tight little smile appeared on Rob's face. Maybe he was thinking about seeing Candi sooner rather than later. Or maybe he was pleased to have jammed me. I couldn't tell; I had lost touch with him. And, for whatever reason, he had changed. Confrontation didn't seem to bother him anymore.

"We'll load up," Rob told me, "but like I said, if Mick's not back by five, we're outta here. We'll drive the station wagon back. You and Yogi can take the Bomb."

"What about Mick?"

"Like I said before, I feel bad for him, but he's your problem now."

＊ ＊ ＊ ＊ ＊

Our lead singer seemed to be shrinking. From across the table in a tiny room off the jail corridor, he sat slumped in a cracked vinyl chair with his head tilted sideways, arms wrapped around him, his legs crossed tight. "What took you so long, mate?" The British accent was back, but his voice sounded fragile.

"I'm lucky I got in. Told them I was your brother. Fortunately they didn't check my ID." I kept my voice low even though we were alone, locked into the room.

"They believed you with all that hair?" Mick tried to smile, but his lips pulled back into a twisted grimace.

I leaned forward. "Look, we only have five minutes. Have they charged you?"

"They're holding me on suspicion, right? My arraignment's tomorrow."

"Tomorrow? Shit." I gazed up and saw a square grill in the center of the ceiling. Was the room bugged? I dropped my voice even lower. "What'd you tell them?"

"Nothing. But, look, mate, I'm screwed. They know everything. Rita's old man told them she was with me all night."

"I knew she was bad news the minute I saw her."

Mick twisted in his chair. "It wasn't her fault. They said a friend blabbed to her old man about it, and she's gonna testify. It must be that chubby bird. What was her name?"

I lowered my head and closed my eyes. "Tanya. It was Tanya."

Mick unraveled and started squirming. "Bloody right! That Tanya bitch! Look, Daniel, you've gotta get me outta here, right? There's a grotty bloke back there in the cell who's taken a fancy to me." He winced. "And what about the gig tonight?" An expression of excitement momentarily crossed his face before he caught himself and smacked his forehead. "What the hell am I talking about? They're not gonna let me outta here."

"Maybe we can bail you out. You want me to call your folks?"

"Hell no! They'd go through the bleedin' roof." His face suddenly went blank. "God. Rape. Maybe you should call them. . . . No, shit, look, talk to Rita. Maybe she'll change her story, right? If she doesn't go along with it, they don't have a bloody case, do they?

"Not unless one of us talks."

He rolled his eyes. "Just get me the hell outta here, will you? Talk to Rita."

"That's crazy." I half shook my head. "What would I say to her?"

"I dunno. She's a bird, right?" He shook his shoulders Jagger-style. "Just play her up."

"Play her up?"

"You know, flatter her." Mick leaned across the table, forced a grin, and tapped the side of his head. "Just think like the Mickster, mate. It'll come to you."

I sighed. Maybe he was right. Maybe we didn't have any other options. "Where does she live?"

His face lit up. "Remember? On the way to Evangeline's? That big blue house on the corner. Bright blue, ugly, right? You can't miss it, mate."

I pushed away from the table and stood. "I'll see what I can do, but don't get your hopes up."

It took a minute, but Mick slumped back into his chair, and the shrinking process started again, arms clutching his narrow shoulders, one skinny leg crossing over the other, head lolling forward. He looked so small and unhappy that I actually felt sorry for him. And to my surprise, I realized that I liked him better the other way, cocky and brash. Even so, I couldn't resist taking a shot.

"Hey, Mick."

He looked up at me.

"If I were you, I'd keep my back to the wall. Know what I mean?"

"You're a regular sod, Daniel." His face dimmed even more. "Just get me the fuck outta here."

25

I KNEW I COULDN'T just walk up to Rita's house and ring the doorbell. Wasn't there a law against witness tampering or something like that? And even if there wasn't, I wasn't stupid enough to think I could just waltz into her house. And so, parked across the main boulevard alongside the cinderblock wall of an old neighborhood grocery store, I waited, slunk down in the driver's seat of the station wagon. Tommy Bolin's *Teaser* played on the eight-track, and I squinted out through the dirty windshield, the clock ticking toward a time when I'd have to risk ringing the doorbell. Forty-five minutes had already passed and no one had come or gone from the bright-blue house on the corner.

At least it wasn't raining. But that was about the only thing going right today. I checked my watch again. Almost three o'clock. We'd never make the gig on time, if at all. And when we didn't show up, Kitten would go ballistic, Astley would hear about it, and that would be that. No agent, no Kitten, for better or worse, no nothing. I'd be back in Creedly with the remains of a failed band, moving back into Mom's house because I was broke. And Nita. . . . I shook my head. She was already history.

I looked over at a phone booth near the entrance to the grocery store. What the hell. Slipping out of the station wagon, I made my way over and tried to look up the number. No phone book. I searched my pockets and found the wadded-up piece of paper—the page I'd ripped out of the phone book the night before—jammed down along with my cross-tops vial, spare guitar picks, and coins. Keeping one eye on the house across the street, I flattened the page against the glass side of the phone booth and dialed the number.

"Puente Harbor Travel Lodge." It was the same flat, genderless voice from the night before.

"Extension one-fifty."

"One moment, please."

The line went dead, then rang again. After seven or eight rings, each telling me what I already knew, I started to hang up. Then the ringing stopped.

"Hello?"

A man's voice. I flinched, dropped the receiver in the cradle, then thought for a second and redialed the Travel Lodge number.

"It's me again," I said. "I'm calling for Nita Annstrom. You just put me through to her room, but someone else answered. Could you please tell me if she's checked out?"

A pause, and then, grudgingly, "Hold on."

My stomach churned. I braced myself against the corner of the phone booth. The house across the street looked miles away.

The operator came back on. "She left this morning."

"Are you sure?"

"Look, are you the one who called in the middle of the night last night?"

"I—" Through the dirty glass of the phone booth, I saw someone emerge from the front door of Rita's house and walk across the lawn.

"Sir—"

I hung up. The small figure reached the sidewalk and turned toward the corner. It was Rita. She had on the same black-leather bomber jacket she'd worn at the club, but this time she was wearing jeans instead of the miniskirt. I kept behind the door of the phone booth and watched her. She reached the corner at the main boulevard, looked both ways, and began walking diagonally across, coming straight at me.

I waited for her to reach my side of the street and start

for the front of the grocery store before I stepped out of the phone booth. "Hi, Rita."

She stopped and stared at me.

"Remember me? Daniel, from the Killjoys?"

"Oh." Her jaw started working frantically at a wad of gum. "Hiya." Without the heavy makeup and go-go boots, she looked like a typical fifteen- or sixteen-year-old on her way to buy a copy of *Teen* magazine. Mick would be dead meat if she ever got on the witness stand.

"Can I talk to you for a second?" With my heart pounding, I had difficulty keeping my tone conversational and casual.

Her gaze darted around, stopping on the blue house across the street. She giggled nervously. "I can't, y'know. I would, but I'm like really, really grounded, and I'm just supposed to get some things and be back at the house, and I'm not supposed to talk to anybody, especially someone like you."

"C'mon, Rita. I just came from seeing Mick at the jail." I held her small brown eyes. "He asked about you."

Her chewing stopped. "He did?"

I nodded. "Look, he knows you didn't turn him in. We all know it was Tanya. But they're holding him for statutory rape. You know what that is, right?"

Rita paused, then gave me a tiny nod.

I went on. "And he could get, like, fifteen or twenty years." For some reason, that didn't sound bad enough. "And they might send him back to England."

Her eyes grew big, white space around brown pupils. "But I thought—"

"Look, let's talk for a minute, O.K.? We can sit in my car. That way nobody'll see you."

Her gaze flew around again before resting on me. "Well, O.K., I guess, but I gotta get back home soon, y'know?"

I walked her over to the station wagon and held the front

passenger door open. After looking around again, she slid in, and I checked my watch. Shit, three-twenty. I didn't have any time to screw around. My mind spun. What would Mick say to her? What words would make this scared little girl recant her story? Standing beside the station wagon, I conjured up Mick's smirk and listened for his voice. *Bloody hell! Play her up, mate.*

I got in on the driver's side and popped out the Tommy Bolin tape. "Rita," I said, leaning toward the young girl, "Mick wanted me to tell you that he really likes you. In fact, he thinks you're pretty special and really hot. That's what he said. And I can see why—" I stopped. The words sounded ridiculous coming out of my mouth.

But to my surprise, Rita smiled, and it was oddly grown-up and knowing. Then her eyes narrowed and her lower lip pushed out, making her look again just like a pouty little kid. "But he didn't call, he didn't come by or nothing. How could I know?"

"Look, Mick wanted to, believe me, but we've been really busy. We had to play last night, and we've got this Heart gig tonight. But now Mick's in jail, so. . . ."

Rita popped her gum. Frown lines appeared below her dark bangs. "But they . . . the police, they made me tell them. I didn't want to, y'know, but Tanya, she told my daddy everything, and. . . ." Her hands fluttered up like frightened sparrows.

"Rita, you've gotta help Mick. He wanted you to be there at the Heart concert tonight. He wanted to see you before we left tomorrow."

"He did?"

And then true inspiration hit me. I reached into my back pocket and pulled out the last of the comp tickets. "He insisted I give you this."

She took the ticket and studied it.

"It's our last comp ticket—gets you in for free. But, with

Mick sitting in jail, it's no good now, I guess. It's too bad, though, because Mick thought you might get the chance to meet Ann and Nancy Wilson of Heart."

She kept looking at the ticket. As she did, my attention was caught by the sight of a man coming out of Rita's house. He strolled across the lawn and peered toward the grocery store. Worried that he would see us, I flipped down both visors. Rita started to look up, but I pointed to the face of the ticket. "See? The show starts at eight, but we have to be there by five." I clicked the face of my watch. "That's only a little more than an hour from now."

As I talked, I kept one eye on the figure across the street. To my relief, the man, probably Rita's dad, returned to the house after taking a long look at the grocery store.

I reached across for the ticket, but she pulled back. "You have to be there at five?"

"To set up and sound-check. But we won't make it unless you help him."

She continued to clutch the ticket, and her eyes became watery. "How can I? I'm grounded, and the police already wrote everything down."

"You could retract your statement."

"Retract?" She frowned. "What's that mean? Like, lie?"

I paused for a second. "No, not really. Just take it back. Tell them that you were pressured by Tanya to say everything, that you just hung out in the room with Mick and that nothing happened." I looked at her; she was considering this. "But you'll have to do it now, or we won't be able to play tonight. And Mick . . . one way or the other, you'd never see him again."

"But my daddy—" Her eyes froze. "He'd absolutely kill me."

"Mick needs you, Rita. The whole band needs you. Don't you want to see him again?"

She turned away and pressed her forehead against the side window. "I can't do it. I've . . . I've gotta go."

With the comp ticket still in hand, she flung open the door and started out. I reached out and caught the sleeve of her jacket. "Mick's going to prison without your help. He'll never sing again, and you'll never see him again. *Please* help him."

Rita started to cry. "It's not my fault. I don't know what to do." Her head shook from side to side. "I don't know what I can do!"

I tugged at her arm, and she suddenly quieted and looked across the interior of the car at me, as if hoping that I would give her the answer. Her young face became red and scrunched up, shedding years by the moment, and my heart dropped away at the sight of it. *Charm her, play her up.* Yeah, sure. But, shit, that wasn't my skill. Driving people away was what I did best.

Christ, I couldn't do this anymore.

I searched my brain for another voice, a voice that spoke the truth—at least, the form of truth that a sixteen-year-old would understand—simple, direct, no bullshit. And what other truth was there, really? I sorted through my mess of a mind for the voice that came from a knowledge of the perfect notes, the Universal Chord. It had been there for a moment last night, I was sure now. For that moment I had felt the connection, and then it had disappeared into the chaos of crashing glass. And then later, when I had played my songs, I had felt it again, but. . . .

I shook my head. That's what had driven Pete Townshend crazy. It wasn't that the Universal Chord didn't exist. It was just that you couldn't hold on to it. The notes formed, pulled together in perfection, and then they faded away, note by note, decibel by decibel, to a whisper that you could no longer hear. It was there, but it wasn't. But, now, from somewhere, someplace, I heard the ringing, sustained purity of the chord again; and then I heard Evangeline's words in Nita's voice.

"Rita," I said, "I can't tell you what to do. All I know

is that you can't go around hurting people you care about, even if you'll never see them again. I lied to you about what Mick said. He likes you—I think he really does—but I made some of those things up. I don't know if he wants to see you again. And maybe you don't really want to see him again. But you've got to follow your own heart. People connect for a reason." I looked into the distance through the windshield. "I don't know why."

She gazed at me, her brown eyes, like Nita's, swimming in pools of watery whiteness, and suddenly a great sob burst from her. She pulled away and ran from the car. Without looking, she dashed across the boulevard.

As she reached the other side of the street and disappeared into the house, I slammed my palm against the steering wheel. I'd fucked up again, hadn't I? Christ, why hadn't I learned? The same damn mistake, over and over: Honesty, the truth, was no fucking good.

✳ ✳ ✳ ✳ ✳

THE BLUE BOMB was parked on the street in front of the Mai Tai's side load-in doors. I pulled up behind the van and walked into the lounge, still trying to think through a last-gasp plan. Rob and Sam were sitting on the front edge of the stage, suitcases and rolled-up sleeping bags at their feet. Behind them, Yogi was down on his knees, tunelessly whistling while taking his drum set apart. Nobody else was in the bar, and nothing but broken strings, strips of masking tape, and bits of glass were left on the stage. The bar no longer looked anything like the Marquee. Maybe, I thought now, it never had.

Sam saw me first. "Did you talk to the little bimbo?" His voice echoed around the hard wooden edges of the lounge and came back to me. He held out the van keys.

I exchanged them for the station wagon keys. "Yeah, and she's not a bimbo. Anyway, she wouldn't do it."

"Shit," Sam muttered, shaking his head. "Mick really bit the big one this time. I actually feel sorry for him, and I never thought I'd say that."

"He could be looking at some serious jail time," I said, my stomach churning. I shifted my gaze to Rob. "So you're O.K. with just leaving him?"

Shrugging, Rob replied, "Like we talked about before, we can probably do more good for him in Creedly than we can here, so what's the point in staying another night?"

I didn't have a good answer for him, so I just sighed, rubbed at my eyes, and searched my mind for some way to keep the band together.

Rob exhaled, rocked on his heels, and sprang to his feet. "Well, that's it, man. We've got the van packed. We only need to get Yogi's drums in the station wagon, then we're rolling. Your stuff's still up in the room. So's Mick's."

For the hundredth time, I checked my watch. "It's not five, yet. Let's talk about it some more."

He flipped his hair. "Talk about what?"

"I've been thinking. Maybe we can still put a set together. We only need thirty minutes or so. And we've got my three songs. That's—what?—fifteen minutes if we stretch 'em out? Maybe we can—"

"Christ, Daniel, give it up. I told you, we're outta here."

As if on cue, Sam picked up a suitcase. "Let's get these things in the wagon."

"Hey!" Yogi's head popped up from behind the bass drum. "You're not leaving without us."

So it was a done deal. They were all ready to split and just assumed that I'd go with them. "Screw that," I said. "Yogi's right. I'm not leaving until I see what happens to Mick. We just can't leave him."

There was a long silence.

Yogi finally came over to the edge of the stage and looked down at me. "When I said 'us,' I didn't mean you, Daniel. I'd stay for sure if we were playing. I was talking about *us*, not you or Mick."

Irritated, I stared up at him. "Us? What the hell are you talking about?"

With his free hand, Sam hoisted a sleeping bag and looked over at me. "You're gonna love this."

"Love what?"

"He's talking about Evangeline." Sam shook his head in a slow, weary motion. "Yogi says she's going with us."

"I don't get it." Now I was shaking my head. "Going where? To the Heart gig?"

Rob grabbed the other suitcase and sleeping bag. "Yogi's taking her home with him."

"He's what?" I looked up at Yogi. "But—"

"Save your breath," Sam said. "We've already tried to talk him out of it."

My forehead creased. "She's going to Creedly with you? Why?"

"We talked about it this morning," Yogi said, grinning down at me. And then he sang out, *"I think she loves me, so what are you so afraid of?"*

"C'mon, Yogi," I said. "wake up. Look, I hate to break this to you, but it's pretty unlikely that she loves you."

But Yogi kept grinning. "Maybe she does, maybe she doesn't. But I know she likes me—she told me so—and she's ready to get out of Puente Harbor. She said she's going to follow her heart."

Hearing those betraying words again, I grimaced. "Look, Yogi, that's totally crazy. What about her stuff? And where's she gonna live? In your folks' house?"

"He's got a plan," said Sam. "You should hear it."

"That's right." Yogi was still grinning. "She's going to get a—"

I waved him off. "Not now. I've got bigger things to worry about."

Sam and Rob started for the door.

"Hey, hold on!" I yelled. They stopped and looked back at me. I searched my mind for hope, for some Who-like vision of resurrection. "You promised you wouldn't leave until five. We've still got a half hour. Mick could still show up. Maybe they'll let him out."

"Fine, man." Rob sighed. "We'll stick around until five if it makes you happy. We've gotta wait around for Yogi, anyhow."

"By the way," Sam said, "we could use some change for the trip home. We get paid yet?"

I stared at him and felt my face go red. "Where's Mr. Tom?"

"Last time I saw him, he was in the restaurant."

"I'll be back in a minute." I started weaving through the lounge, and then I stopped and pointed a finger at the two deserters. "Don't leave before I'm back."

✳ ✳ ✳ ✳ ✳

ALL THREE OF THEM were outside on the sidewalk with Beanie and Cecil when I returned. Rob and Sam were sitting on the fender of the station wagon, and Yogi, humming to himself, was standing across from the two bouncers. It was almost dark and the air had become dank-cold again, but I was more aware of the dampness under my arms. I looked at the guys and knew that I wouldn't tell them what had just happened inside. It didn't really matter. The Heart gig had slipped away, Mick was in jail, and the band was breaking up. What did a few dollars matter at this point?

Rob made a show of checking his watch. "Five-fifteen, man. We need to get truckin'. We get paid?"

"Sure." I pulled up next to Yogi. Beanie and Cecil nodded a greeting in a way that told me they knew what was going down.

"Cool." Rob held out his hand.

I pulled out the wad of cash and counted out four twenties each into the palms of Rob, Sam, and Yogi. Turning away so they wouldn't see how few bills remained, I stuffed the rest into my pocket.

Sam fanned out the four bills and angled them into the streetlight until Andrew Jackson's face lit up. "Eighty bucks? Shouldn't it be more like a hundred and fifty?"

I shrugged. "We've gotta figure out expenses before divvying up the rest. We'll do it when I get home." The truth was that Mr. Tom had deducted $240 for the rooms—twenty bucks per room per night—which had left us with a net of $510 for the week. I had argued with him, had told him that Astley said the rooms were included, but he wouldn't budge. $510. Not much for five nights of dangerous work.

"When're you heading home?" Sam asked.

I shrugged again. "I'll see how tomorrow goes."

"Let us know," Rob said. "Like Sam said, we'd be willing to go over and talk to his folks."

"I'll keep that in mind," I said, still doubting that they'd be willing to face Mick's father.

"Well." Rob looked at Sam. "We still need to pick up Evangeline, so we'd better get going."

"I'm ready," Yogi said, still sprouting that goofy grin.

Beanie, who had been uncharacteristically quiet, started bobbing around. "I can't believe you're gonna blow off playing with Heart. Ann and Nancy Wilson." His eyes bloomed. "Man, oh, man."

"I can't, either," I said under my breath. Then louder: "They gave you the tickets, didn't they? You can still go."

"We've got 'em," Cecil said, "but it won't be the same."

"That reminds me," I said, looking directly at Rob, "I better call over there and see if I can reach someone. At least I can give them a heads-up that we're flaking out." Rob shifted from one foot to the other, turned away from me, and glanced down the street. All other eyes went this way and that, avoiding each other, avoiding mine.

The momentary silence hung there, glances still darting around in the almost-dark. Sam finally broke it, turning to Beanie and Cecil and saying, "Well, look, you guys take it easy. I hope you get outta this shithole soon. And look us up if you ever get to Creedly."

Then Sam looked at me. "Give my regards to Mick, huh? I hope you can spring him, but I bet they let him off easy. That girl was asking for it."

"Sure, Sam."

"You guys ready?" he asked the others.

Yogi opened the back door of the wagon.

Rob shifted and faced me with lowered eyes. "Sorry it came down to this, man. I guess some things aren't meant to be."

"I guess not." The moment felt strangely like a breakup with a girlfriend. With events now rushing forward out of control, I felt myself starting to grin from the sheer weirdness of it all.

"If I don't hear from you tomorrow, call me when you're back," Rob said. "We'll settle up the bills, and I'll get my gear out of the house."

Now I *was* grinning. I couldn't help it. "Take it easy, Rob. And give my love to Candi."

His eyes came up angry, and he stared at me before looking away again. "Sure, man."

Stepping out of the circle, I watched as handshakes were exchanged. Sam climbed in behind the steering wheel and started the engine. Rob climbed in beside him, and Yogi slid into the back. With Beanie and Cecil waving, they started away, and I turned my back and headed for the door of the Mai Tai. Hearing the sound of the station wagon rumble away, my stomach double-clutched and the trap door of my depression began to open up. I forced my mind to move forward. I had to get the stuff out of the room and figure out where I was staying tonight. No way I was spending another night at the Mai Tai, especially by myself. And I really had to go by the jail again. . . .

I was pushing through the door when the sound of screeching tires stopped me. I spun around and looked down the street, immediately recalling the episode with Mick and the blue truck, and flashing on the sensation that this had all happened before. It had, but it was not what I thought.

26

HERE HE CAME, déjà vu all over him. The shit-eating grin, just like the one I saw the day after his conquest of Rita, spread across his face, his teeth gleaming in the streetlights like a set of miniature white Christmas bulbs.

At first, after hearing the station wagon scream to a stop, I thought Sam had hit something. But that wasn't it. They had just seen him first, strolling down the side street from the police station. And it wasn't until he rounded the corner and I saw his cocky, bouncing steps that I knew what had happened.

I came down off the Mai Tai's steps and watched Mick breeze down the sidewalk. Beanie and Cecil moved up beside me.

"You," Mick yelled out, pointing at me, bouncing, bouncing, bouncing on the balls of his feet, "you are a bloody genius!"

"They let you out?" I threw my head back and exhaled. "For good?"

"I'm a bleedin' free bird!" He threw his arms around me. "You did it, mate!"

He squeezed the breath out of my lungs, but I managed to mutter, "Rita?"

He let go. "She took it all back! I heard her old man screaming at her out front, but she wouldn't budge, right? Not my Rita!"

Beanie raised his skinny arms to heaven. "Now you can play!"

I looked over Mick's shoulder and saw the taillights of the station wagon blink red as Sam backed into a parking spot near the end of the block.

"Can you do the gig?" I asked him.

"Is the pope bloody Catholic? Just need to change me clothes, mate."

We were already a half-hour late, but we could still make it. Who else would they use? I looked up to see Sam and Yogi joining our little knot on the sidewalk. Rob stopped a few paces short of the rest of us and folded his arms. "So the prodigal son returns."

Mick's lightbulb grin flashed around. "Bloody right, and I'm ready to rock 'n' roll. Where were you blokes headed?"

"Uh, well." Sam shifted uncomfortably from one foot to the other. "We thought you were cooked, man. We were, um—"

"Hey, not the Mickster!" He went into a little dance, throwing punches into the night air like a prizefighter. "I'm ready to play!"

"Forget it," Rob said, his jaw tight. "It's way too late."

I stepped around Sam to get a direct line on Rob. "Why's that, Rob? The equipment's all loaded and ready to go. Mick and I just need to change clothes."

"We'll help you unload over there," Cecil offered, glancing from me to Rob.

"I said forget it." The redness of Rob's face could be seen even through the gathering darkness. "I'm not doing it."

Mick stopped shuffling and jerked back as if slapped. "What?"

"I said I'm not doing it. I told Candi I'd be home tomorrow."

"Don't be a bloody poofter, Rob. The bird's not worth it."

"You think so?" Rob said through gritted teeth. "And Rita was?"

Mick bounced forward. "At least she leggo my balls when she was done."

"Fuck you, man. At least *I* can manage an adult relationship."

Mick took another step closer. "Bollocks to that, mate.

You think Candi's so sweet? I'll take Rita anytime over a ballbuster like Candi."

I saw Rob flinch. He took a step toward Mick. "Is that right, Mick? And you're going to introduce your little rape victim to your precious mother, huh?"

Mick met Rob and moved right up into his face. "Watch what you say about me mum, right?"

"I'm sure she'd like to know how you treat women. Just like your old man."

"You cunt!" Mick grabbed a fistful of Rob's shirt.

Sam tried to shove his way between them, but they were locked up, chin to chin. I edged in from the other side and pushed Mick away. Suddenly my head went sideways, my ear on fire, my knees buckling. The sidewalk rose up and smacked me, and all breath left my lungs. Stunned, I lay on the sidewalk for what seemed like several seconds before rolling over and rubbing the side of my head, heat slowly receding away to a throbbing numbness. Forcing my eyes open, I looked up into the faces of Rob, Sam, and Mick.

"Man, you O.K.?" Rob's voice sounded muffled. I rubbed at the ear again and struggled into a sitting position. Rob was flexing his right hand as he looked at my ear. "God, man, I'm sorry," he said.

Yogi, Beanie, and Cecil edged into the circle. Rob was now on his knees beside me. "I didn't mean to hit you, Daniel. Are you O.K.?"

I looked up blankly for a minute, then said, "Yeah, I think so." I touched my swollen ear. "What'd you hit me with? A brick?"

"It wasn't meant for you." He glanced over at Mick.

I shook the numbness out of my head and tried to grin through the pain. "Violence, Rob? I didn't know you had it in you."

Rob looked chagrined and embarrassed. "Yeah, well, shit. He shouldn't have said that about Candi."

Mick leaned down. "Hey, sorry, mate."

Rob took my arm and helped me up. I stepped out of the circle to brush off my clothes, and Rob came up beside me. I heard the breath coming hard through his nose. "Look," he said, lowering his voice and glancing back at the others. He was about to continue, but he paused, rolled his eyes upward to the night sky, and rubbed at the bridge of his nose. His eyes finally came back to my face. "Candi . . . look, man, she's leaving me. At least I think she is. I guess that's why I blew."

I stopped rubbing my ear. "She's what?"

"She met somebody else, a professor at the college, and she's talking about moving out. She told me on the phone the other day."

"Christ, Rob. One of her teachers?"

Rob nodded, his eyes closing for a moment. "Yeah. She thinks he's some hot-shit intellectual, and I guess I'm not, at least not while I'm playing in a band. I've been trying to talk her out of it the last few days. I asked her to wait until I got home before making a decision, but then you booked the Heart gig."

"God, I'm sorry. But why didn't you tell me? I thought she was just jealous about you being away with us."

He shook his head and looked down at the sidewalk.

"So that's why you've been wanting to get back so bad?"

"I thought I could stop her."

I looked at him until his eyes came up. "I guess we haven't been on the same track lately, have we?"

"Not lately, man," Rob said. "But I'm still sorry I hit you."

I checked my ear again. "Maybe you knocked some sense into me."

He breathed out what sounded like a chuckle. "Hope so."

From over Rob's shoulder, I saw the other guys huddled

near the station wagon. They seemed to sense that they
needed to give us some space, so they hung back, watching.
Leaning against the brick wall of the Mai Tai, virtually in the
same spot where Nita had been the night before, I felt my
gaze turn back to Rob, and I realized that he'd been react-
ing to events exactly the way he always had. He was trying
to keep Candi happy, and he couldn't without making me
unhappy—a major quandary for a guy who liked to please
everyone. No wonder he had become so combative and dis-
agreeable. Rob was miserable. He hadn't changed. I had.

This realization, along with the continued throb of my
ear from Rob's fist, jarred something in my head, loosened
another one of those thoughts that had been stuck there
over the past twenty-four hours. What was it that I had said
to Rita earlier in the day? You could not go around hurting
people you care about? Maybe it was time for me to take my
own advice.

I caught Rob's eye and took a deep breath. My entire
body hurt from the effort. "Look, Rob, we go back way too
far to let this kinda stuff come between us, y'know?"

Rob nodded. "Yeah, I know what you mean."

"I guess I've been a real shit about things," I continued,
searching for the right words, "and I'm really sorry about all
the grief I've been causing you."

I paused for his reaction, but Rob only gave me a slight
nod in recognition of my way-too-late apology for the way
I'd been acting.

I took another deep breath. "But, look Rob, I'm dealing
with some stuff myself that's been kind of fucking with my
head lately. It just seems like all this crap's been building up
in me for years, this urge to get outta Creedly, to stay outta
Creedly. Man, you know, this gig—I guess I see it as my way
to finally leave it behind. But I know it's not like that for you.
You've got things back home that are important to you."

He was listening carefully, his head turned, an ear angled

toward me. "By any chance," he said slowly, "does this have anything to do with Kevin?"

I felt myself flinch inside at the mention of my dead brother's name, and I suddenly visualized Mom rubbing at the stain on Kevin's khakis. Why couldn't I get that memory out of my head? "I dunno," I finally answered. "Yeah, I guess maybe it does. I've always seen the band, the music, as my way of getting away from all of that shit."

"I didn't know that, man." Rob reached out and put his hand on my shoulder. "You never talk about it."

"It's . . . it never goes away." I closed my eyes for a moment. "Listen, Rob, go on home and deal with Candi. This gig isn't worth losing her. The music doesn't matter *that* much."

He started to nod.

I saw Mick break away from the huddle near the station wagon and come toward us. "Hey, Rob, I didn't mean any of that stuff about Candi, right? It's just that I wanna do this gig. Candi's cool. So nothing personal, O.K.?"

Rob's pale blue eyes seemed to fade back into his head. He looked at Mick with a blank stare. "You really mean that, Mick?"

"Sure," Mick said, breaking into a grin. "We're best mates, right? And a little row between mates don't mean shit, right?"

Rob seemed to roll that around in his head before he answered. "Yeah, I guess you're right."

"And, look, Rob," Mick said, "I always want me mates up there on the stage with me. Can't do my thing without my favorite bass player, right? And you gotta be up there when I shake me bum for the Wilson sisters. Like Daniel's always saying, we're all in this bloody thing together."

Rob's face finally relaxed a bit. "Yeah, and it seems like I said that last night, didn't I?"

Mick looked at him blankly. "Last night?"

"That's right," Rob said, smiling to himself. "You were out of it when we were trying to talk Daniel into doing his songs."

"And I never thanked you for that," I said. "I wouldn't have done 'em if you hadn't pushed me."

Rob nodded reflectively.

"So, Rob, you forgive me, mate?" Mick persisted.

"Don't sweat it," he answered, still with that reflective look on his face.

Mick turned and gazed back at Sam and Yogi, who were standing with Beanie and Cecil near the station wagon. "Speaking of the Wilson sisters," he said, "the guys are wondering what we're doing."

I pushed myself off the wall. "We're not doing the gig. Rob needs to—"

"Yeah, we are," Rob broke in. "We're doing it."

"What?"

"We're doing the gig."

"We are?"

Rob's eyes locked back in. "What you said a minute ago, Daniel, you're wrong. The music matters. At least, I know it matters to you. I don't want to get sentimental about this, but I wouldn't have ever gotten to know any of you guys if it wasn't for our music." He half-smiled, but his forehead creased with strain, giving me the impression that it took all his strength to go on. "Maybe it's the only thing that really does matter when you get down to it." He spat on the ground, punctuating his next words. "The rest of it is pure bullshit."

"You sure?"

His face relaxed into that serene hippie smile of his, the one I hadn't seen for days. "Hell, what's one more night here in paradise?"

Mick threw his arms around the two of us. "We're just like the bloody Who. Like I said, what's a row between mates, right? Let's rock 'n' roll!"

✳ ✳ ✳ ✳ ✳

Sitting in her orange VW van facing out toward the road, Kitten was waiting for us just inside the gated entry into the fairground's parking lot. Mick was beside me in the van; the rest of the guys, including Beanie and Cecil, were jammed into the station wagon behind us.

On Kitten's hand signal, a security guard swung the gate open and we pulled in. My headlights caught Kitten flush in the face, and she squinted and rolled down her window. I pulled up beside her.

"You're way late, kid," she said, flicking cigarette ash toward us. "The promoter's pissed."

"I had to get our lead singer outta jail first," I said, motioning toward Mick.

"Jail? You playing Monopoly?"

"It's a long story. Where do we load in?"

She shook out her mane of tangled midnight-black hair. "Follow me. By the way, where's your little friend?"

I knew who she meant, and I wanted to tell her to stuff it, but now that we were here, the gig was the only thing that mattered. "She's gone."

"Too bad." A tight-lipped grin came back. "Hope it wasn't on my account." She tossed out the cigarette and spun the wheels of the VW in a wide U-turn.

"Lovely lass," Mick said. "How's she in the sack?"

"Scary as hell."

"And she's going to manage us?"

"I haven't signed anything yet."

"Right." Mick nodded. "Well, if she can get us gigs with Heart, maybe she's worth it." He cracked a smile. "And, look, I can take her off your hands if she's too much for you."

I followed her van across the muddy parking lot. On the far side, cars were flowing in from a separate entrance. We drove past what looked like a rodeo arena and around an exhibition hall to the rear of an old brick auditorium. A tour bus, emblazoned with the swirling pinkish Heart logo from their *Dreamboat Annie* album, was parked next to two panel trucks alongside a loading dock. A surge of red-hot energy shot through me.

I must've muttered or sighed or something because Mick glanced over at me. "You know," he said in a musing tone, "I feel sorry for those Wilson sisters."

That caught my attention. "How so?"

"Cuz, look, mate. We're gonna show 'em what rock 'n' roll's all about, right? And after I give 'em a little of *my* magic man routine, just wait, see. Those poor sisters'll go crazy on the Mickster. Know what I mean?"

He waited for my nervous face to react, and then he gave me that smirky Jaggeresque grin. Christ, I could've kissed him.

✳ ✳ ✳ ✳ ✳

WITH A GUITAR CASE in one hand and a canvas bag of cords in the other, I stood and stared out across the vast expanse of the stage's hardwood flooring. It was easily the largest stage we'd ever played. An amazing and expensive array of amps, speakers, keyboards, and drums had been set up and awaited their now-famous owners. The name Heart had been stenciled on everything but the drums. Enormous P.A. speakers, stacked four boxes high, anchored both corners of the stage near the front edge, and in between stood a row of three microphones, with 15-inch monitor speakers aimed at each. Cecil had already rolled my Fender Twin Reverb onto the stage, and it looked pathetically inadequate next to the Marshall stack looming over it.

My bowels started to tighten. I peered into the auditorium and watched a crew of eight men work at pulling out a set of bleacher-style seats along the right-hand wall. A matching set of seats had already been moved out from the opposite wall. In between, running from the stage to the double-wide set of doors leading to the lobby, lay a wide swath of open concrete flooring maybe six feet below the level of the stage.

I heard footsteps behind me.

"Hey-ho, Puente Harbor!"

Mick's voice echoed around the empty spaces of the auditorium. He stopped in the wings, hands on hips, jeans tight, chartreuse scarf wrapped around his neck and flowing down over his shoulders. Behind him, Rob and Cecil came up pushing Rob's Peavey amp toward the stage. Sam and Beanie trailed them, each lugging one of Yogi's floor toms.

In four bouncing steps Mick pulled up beside me, cupped his hands, and called out, "And God save the queen and the Royal Albert Hall!"

The workers stopped and looked up at us.

"Can it, Mick," I said. "Let's get set up."

A bearded roadie dragging a set of cables appeared from the far side of the stage and motioned Rob, Cecil, and the Peavey toward him. Our equipment was being set up in front of Heart's, which gave us an immediate and clear sense of our place in the order of things. When we finished our set, our gear would be quickly shoved aside, clearing the way for the main attraction. Still, I figured being pushed out of the way for Heart beat the hell out of commanding the stage at the Mai Tai.

I headed back out to help with the rest of the drums but stopped when I saw Kitten, a sheaf of papers in her hand, coming toward me. Walking with her was a man sporting a huge ball of brown permed hair.

"Daniel," she called out, "this is Bob Beeber. He's promoting the show." Beeber looked to be about forty, my height, skinny in the chest but paunchy at the gut. A roll of flab bunched up at the stomach of his too-tight Allman Brothers T-shirt. If Kitten was allowing this guy to sleep with her, as Cecil had suggested, then I could see why he owed her.

I stuck out my hand, but Beeber ignored it.

"You know what time it is?" he asked in an agitated nasally whine, sounding a lot like Rick Astley. Did these guys grow on trees?

I dropped my hand. "About six-twenty?"

"Damn right, smart-ass." The kinks in his hair jiggled. "And you're way fucking late."

"Sorry." I put a remorseful look on my face. "But, look, we can set up fast."

That didn't satisfy Beeber. "Who the hell do you think you are? My sound guys have been waiting around for an hour."

"Beeb," Kitten broke in, "give the kid a break. They had to deal with some unexpected shit in town, O.K.? They're here now."

Beeber's beady eyes shifted to Kitten's face, dropped to her half-unbuttoned shiny black polyester blouse, and then rotated back to me. "Look, buster," he said, poking a finger at my chest, "I'd flush you guys down the toilet right now if Kitten wasn't your manager. You fuckin' missed your sound-check, and we're opening the doors in a few minutes, so you'll be mixed on the fly. But that's your problem. You got thirty minutes of stuff?"

I shoved down my rising anger. "Yeah."

"Well, keep it at thirty. These kids are here to see Heart, not you."

"Got it."

A bespectacled kid with a clipboard came out of nowhere and grabbed Beeber's arm. "Heart's wondering where their food is."

"Shit!" Beeber spun and waddled off with the kid toward a dressing room door at the rear of the stage.

"See, kid," Kitten said, squinting one eye at me, "it pays to be a bitch sometimes. You'd be shit outta luck without me."

I faked a grin. "You're still a bitch."

"Still pissed off about last night, huh?"

"Could be."

"Well, just cool off, kiddo. You and me, we're goin' places, and that chick would just be baggage."

I ignored her and pointedly turned my attention to the loading door, where Beanie and Cecil were hauling in what looked to be the last of Yogi's cymbal stands. "I need to get back out front."

She held out the papers. "You need to sign these first."

"Sign what?"

"It's a contract for tonight. Beeb says you gotta sign it."

I took the papers and flipped through the four pages of tightly packed print. "Why so long?"

"It's the usual bullshit." She pulled a Bic pen from a rear pocket of her jeans. "Just sign it."

"Hold on." I glanced at the first page. Just the expected stuff about the date, location, fee, etc. Everything looked O.K.. Pages two and three seemed to have canned verbiage about liability, copyright issues, the promoter's right to withhold payment for nonperformance. I turned to the last page and took the pen from her, positioning the signature line over the flattened palm of my left hand. I was about to sign when a dollar figure in the middle of the page caught my attention. I raised the page to my eyes.

"Hurry up," Kitten said. "You don't have time to fuck around."

"Wait a second." I read the line and the rest of the paragraph.

> Upon payment for the stipulated performance, the undersigned, as sole representative of the musical group known as the Killjoys, agrees to pay Kitten Wertz a sum in the amount of $60 per her prior oral management agreement with the undersigned. Furthermore, the undersigned agrees to a one-year manage-

ment contract with Wertz, providing her with
exclusive booking and promotional rights for
the Killjoys. . . .

I looked up at her. "You get your buddy Beeber to put
all this in here?"

"Jesus, kid, it just puts into writing what we've already
talked about." Kitten's hands went to her slender hips.
"What's the big deal?"

Bells went off in my head. But what was the big deal?
Kitten had come through on the Heart gig, just like she said
she would, and Nita was already gone. So what was I worried about? But I looked at the contract again and saw the
future with Kitten stretching out in front of me, and it didn't
include Rob and Sam. Deep down, I now knew that Kitten's
fifteen percent management fee wouldn't include the true
price of any success she could bring us. I had already paid
part of the price last night when Nita shut the door on me.
What other hidden costs would be included in this deal? I'd
felt that the four parts of my quadrophenic self had been
coming back together again, but I knew that Kitten could
blow them apart in a second.

I shook my head. "I'm not signing this now."

She pointed at the signature line. "Sign it. You ain't
playin' tonight unless you do. Beeber'll pull the plug on you
if I tell him to."

I thought quickly. "Look, I'll sign it after we get paid. I
don't trust Beeber. And why should I trust you after what you
did last night?"

She crossed her arms and stared at me. "Don't you learn,
kid? Last night was about something else."

"Yeah? Well, how will it help you if Beeber pulls us?" I
glared at her. "Then you'd have nothing."

Her chin jerked up, and the vein running along the side
of her throat tightened. After a long pause, she reached out
and snatched the contract out of my hand. "Still think you're

a smart guy, huh, Daniel? O.K. After the show then. But if you don't come through, you're history with Astley and every other promoter who books this circuit. Got it?"

She spun on the heels of her white cowboy boots and stomped off. I realized I'd been holding my breath and sucked in a gulp of air.

✳ ✳ ✳ ✳ ✳

HEART GOT THE big dressing room at the rear of the auditorium. None of us ever saw it, but we assumed it was huge based on the platters of cold cuts and cartons of booze being carted in and out of the room. People came and went through the door to the dressing room, but we never saw the sisters Wilson.

We Killjoys got five pink molded plastic chairs in the wings, where the roadies and sound men tromped around us, taping down stray cords and checking connections. The chairs were circled and we had our instruments out, empty cases on the floor within the circle. We were going through the motions of tuning, but what we were really doing was sweating collective bullets.

Ten minutes till showtime. I'd tossed back a couple of cross-tops, and they were kicking in. I already had that twisty feeling of way-too-high optimism and out-of-control terror. Evangeline had shown up a few minutes earlier and disappeared into the crowd at the foot of the stage with Beanie and Cecil. Balancing my guitar on my lap, I lit a cigarette, my last until our set was over, and peered out into the narrow slice of the auditorium visible from my chair. The floor area was packed with people sitting cross-legged on coats and blankets. Some spaces remained in the bleachers, but they were filling up fast. Kitten had told me that the place held 1,200 people, but it looked like way more than that were already packed into the auditorium. A haze of tobacco and marijuana smoke hung in a misty layer above the audience.

Led Zeppelin's *Immigrant Song* blasted from the P.A. speakers, and the stage vibrated to the rhythm of John Paul Jones's thumping bass line.

Sitting across from me, wearing his thick glasses and studying our seven-song set list with a pen in his hand, Mick was hunched over, his foot tapping away much faster than the tempo of the Zeppelin song. Beside me, Rob was plugged into our small battery-operated tuner and was making adjustments to his bass. On the other side of him, Sam sat slumped down in his chair, nervously opening and closing valves on his tenor sax. Sitting next to Mick, a barefooted Yogi was staring vacantly up at the ceiling, whapping a drumstick against his thigh with one hand and clutching a half-eaten Big Hunk bar with the other.

Mick looked up from the set list. "This bleedin' thing needs to be changed."

"What?" I breathed out a lungful of cigarette smoke. "Now?"

"Why not?" He held the list out for me to see. "Look. Here in the middle. *Radar Love*. Doesn't work."

I glanced at the list. Except for my songs, which we weren't doing, we had no original material, so our idea was to play lesser-known covers, hoping that we could pass ourselves off as something other than a straight covers band. The one exception was *All Along the Watchtower*, which we were doing as a set opener in tribute to native son Jimi Hendrix. After that, things got more obscure, with the New York Dolls' *It's Too Late*, Bowie's *Rebel Rebel*, the Velvet's *Sweet Jane*, and Roxy Music's *Both Ends Burning*. We'd decided to end with an amped-up version of the Monkeys' *Steppin' Stone*, which sounded nothing like the original. But Mick was on to something. Right in the middle, between *Rebel Rebel* and *Sweet Jane*, we had the way-too-predictable *Radar Love*.

"Maybe you're right," I said. "But it's crazy to make changes now. And what would we do instead?"

Mick's eyes brightened. "Let's put in that song of yours. The first one you did last night, right?"

My heart began strumming against my sternum. "No way."

"C'mon, man, it kicks bloody arse. And we could really use an original in the set, see."

The pounding in my chest increased. "I thought you hated that punk stuff, and, anyhow, how do you know? You were passed out when we did it."

"I heard it," Mick said. "And maybe I'm changing me mind about the punk stuff."

"Yeah, let's do it." Yogi stopped tapping. "That song was a blast."

"See?" Mick said.

"You want me to sing it? What'll you do?"

"Play tambourine and shake me little bum for the birds." He smiled. "What else?"

I glanced at Rob for help, but he shrugged. "I'm with Mick on this one. It's better than *Radar Love*."

"Bloody right." Mick scratched out RADAR LOVE and wrote THRILL in big block letters.

I started to protest again, but a huge roadie lugging a thick bundle of cords plodded past us and called out, "Five minutes, dudes. Be ready to go."

My bowels suddenly churned again. Was there time to use the john? I stood and took a step in that direction, but the door to Heart's dressing room suddenly swung open. Two women, one dark haired, the other dishwater blonde, came through the door and looked in our direction. My bowels froze up, but my pulse took off at a gallop. They were coming right at me. Ann and Nancy Wilson.

I managed to grunt out a warning to the other guys. The chairs behind me squeaked and slid and suddenly they were beside me. I couldn't take my eyes off the two women.

Ann Wilson, wearing a flowing black blouse, open at the

throat and belted at the waist, reached us first. Her hair, cut in a long shag, feathered along the edges of her neck, was impossibly black and silky. "You must be the Killjoys," she said in a throaty voice, her hooded eyes smoky cool.

Nancy Wilson came up beside her and stopped with hands on boyish hips, waiting for one of us to say something. In the high cheek bones and rounded chins, I could see the resemblance between the two sisters, but Nancy was younger, lither, somehow looser. And where Ann's persona, her aura, was darkness, Nancy was all light, from her blondish hair and pale eyes to her long-sleeved pearl-white blouse and faded jeans. She looked relaxed, ready to strap on a guitar and jam.

Among the five of us, only Mick, who had slipped off his glasses, had the presence of mind to speak. "Aye, that's us," he said, grinning, "the Killjoys. And we know who you are."

Nancy frowned and glanced at Ann. "I thought Beeber said they were from California."

"The rest of us are," I said, pushing my heart back down into my chest. "We don't know where *he's* from." I tilted my head toward Mick and then shut my mouth. Christ, a lame joke. I didn't know why I had said it.

A look bounced between the sisters, and a smoldering half-smile appeared on Ann's face. "Well, wherever you're from," she said, "thanks for opening for us. We heard you stepped in at the last minute."

"Yeah," Nancy said, "we know it's a tough gig opening for a name act. We were doing the same thing a year ago."

"Oh, please," Mick said, going into an exaggerated bow, "it's our pleasure."

I glanced at the other guys, and except for Yogi, who was staring at the sisters with a dazed expression, they appeared horrified by Mick's cocky gesture. I looked back and noticed Kitten standing off to the side in the shadows. She was staring at me and frowning.

But Nancy giggled at Mick's gesture, long vertical dimple lines flashing below her fine cheek bones. "So what are you doing up here in Puente Harbor?"

I angled my body between Mick and the Wilson sisters. "We just finished a week here at the Mai Tai Hotel."

One of Ann's eyebrows arched high. "Oh, really? We know *that* place, don't we, Nancy. Is Tom still there?"

"Oh, yeah, he's there." I smiled, now knowing that Heart *had* played the Mai Tai.

"Cheap as ever, I bet," Nancy said. "Look, there're better places to play around here. Check out the Aquarius Tavern in north Seattle or the Hatchcover in Bellevue."

"And Deeter's," Ann added.

"And tell them we sent you." Nancy dug into a pocket and pulled out a white guitar pick. Handing it to me, she said, "If they don't believe you, show 'em this. They'll treat you right."

The pick was embossed with a small heart encircling the initials NW. I grinned. "Thanks. We'll definitely check 'em out." I glanced over at Kitten to make sure she had heard the offer. Her scowl told me she had.

Beeber suddenly appeared at Ann's elbow and glanced around at us with a sour expression indicating that he wasn't too happy his stars were fraternizing with the likes of us. "Everything O.K., Ann?"

Her eyes narrowed on him. "Sure, Bob. Just wishing the guys luck."

"Right." Beeber glanced at his watch. "It's about time for 'em to go on."

Nancy raised a fist of solidarity. "Knock 'em dead, guys."

"Yeah, do that," Ann said, pausing to give us one more of her Mona Lisa smiles, "but leave a few breathing for us." Nancy's laugh trailed her as she followed Ann back to their dressing room. Beeber watched them leave.

When the door to their dressing room closed, Kitten came up out of the shadows and put a hand on Beeber's shoulders. "Everything cool, Bob?" she said.

"Yeah, fine." His tone was detached, as if his mind had left with the Wilson sisters. One hand rubbed at the belly of the T-shirt. "Your guys ready?" he asked Kitten. We had apparently become invisible.

"They're ready."

"O.K. I'll announce 'em, then they're on. The Killbobs, right?"

"Killjoys, Beeb," Kitten answered. "And they're gonna kick butt, right guys?"

Her question went unanswered.

Beeber turned away and signaled toward a technician wearing a pair of headphones at the edge of the stage. Without another word, Beeber walked off in that direction and Kitten went with him. We headed back toward the plastic chairs to retrieve our instruments. The recorded music and the houselights lowered, and as they did, the sound of a thousand voices rose up in a pulsing, expectant hum.

27

BEEBER STOOD in the middle of the stage, a single white spotlight trained on his permed hairball of a head. Even from the side of the stage, where I stood with the others, my Fender strapped on tight, I could see the sparkling lines of sweat running down the side of his face. As if taking a cue from Beeber's free-flowing perspiration, my entire body went damp and my arms and legs grew heavy and numb. Only my heart seemed to be working properly, and it was trying to rip its way through my chest.

Beeber had just said something about Heart, and the crowd was shrieking in response. He paused while the noise abated. Our name was coming up. I took one last look around. Mick was bouncing up and down on the balls of his Adidases, but the other guys looked like they were waiting to go to the gas chamber. Somehow their ghastly expressions made me feel better, but not much. My hands were shaking, and I wished that I hadn't taken the uppers. Rob was right: They were making me a mess.

Sweat pooled above my eyebrows. I ran a sleeve across my forehead and looked out into the crowd, picturing myself in front of that dark mass of buzzing bodies. A breathless panic hit me, squeezing my heart. What were we doing here? We were nobodies. A wave of dizziness washed over me. My head started to float away. *Keep breathing, keep breathing, keep breathing.* I tried to conjure up Pete Townshend's voice, straining to hear his assuring words—*Just play these chords, mate*—but instead the chords to *The Real Me* ripped through my brain. The Real Me. Maybe this really was it.

And then I heard Beeber's overamped voice start into our introduction:

> *. . . and straight from California, an up-and-coming band . . . some calling them the new Rolling Stones . . . days away from recording their first album . . .*

Christ, the bastard was making up shit about us! My brain slid sideways.

> *. . . here to get you warmed up for Heart, as if you needed it . . . hah hah hah . . . the . . . the . . .*

He paused and looked over at us. Fuck! He had forgotten our name! I started to yell it out, but Kitten's voice came from somewhere on the far side of the stage. Beeber glanced in that direction and then back out at the crowd.

> *. . . Give 'em a big welcome . . . the Killjoys!*

And we were on. Before I could move, Mick was out in front of me, virtually skipping across the stage to the center mike. Rob went by, Yogi, Sam. In slow motion, I moved toward my amp on the near side of the stage. Lights blasted on from everywhere, overhead, from out in front, from the side, pulsing colors, sudden heat. Nearly blinded, I managed to find the jack end of my cord and plug in, vaguely aware that the crowd, waiting for us to start, had already gone quiet.

I accidentally hit my strings. Sound rocketed out, came back at me, went out again. Shocked, I started to turn down, but a disembodied voice came from somewhere: *Don't, we'll mix you.* I looked up, squinted, and saw the dim light of the sound board straight out and elevated in the middle of the floor. One of the sound guys waved at me.

I turned my head and saw Mick with a microphone in one hand, pointing out into the crowd with the other. He was twitching, loaded for action. "Hey, Puente Harbor! Ready to rock 'n' roll, mates? You better, 'cause we're gonna do it to ya!"

A smattering of claps, a few hoots.

He glanced back. Almost in reflex, I nodded at him. The click-click-click of Yogi's countdown cut through, and Mick called out, "This one's for Jimi, wherever he is."

I took a breath. My hand clamped down on an A-minor bar chord, my pick cut across the strings. A huge ball of crunchy distorted sound went shooting out from everywhere.

Christalmighty!

Flicking past the G, hanging on the F, then back up and through again, I looked around in amazement, stunned by how loud my guitar sounded routed from my amp through the P.A. A blue spotlight caught me. I windmilled a chord over the top of a thundering drum roll raining down all around me. Yogi's beat steadied at the turnaround right as Rob's bass slid into the groove. The stage literally shook. God, it was an incredible noise.

Mick barked out the first line, but I could barely hear him. Like magic, his voice came up and the rest of us notched down. Now he could be heard, and he sounded like ten Micks rolled into one, louder than a bomb, more powerful than a speeding locomotive. . . .

So much adrenaline was pumping through me that I thought I might explode. Even so, my feet, planted ten feet in front of my amp, wouldn't move. But my skin danced and tingled with high-decibel electricity. I chanced a glance across the stage and saw Rob spread out wide, head bent, hair hanging, hands crawling all over the bass. Sam was up beside the drum set, pounding the bejeebers out of his tambourine.

Second verse already. Mick had the mike in hand, doing that skipping, hopping jig along the edge of the stage. The upturned faces of kids lined the edge, heads bobbing, hair thrashing, mostly guys, a brave girl here and there. I saw Beanie's head above the rest. Next to him, Cecil, Evangeline.

A drumstick went clattering by me. Yogi went into a one-handed beat for a second before grabbing another stick. We got to my solo. I knew I'd better keep it simple or I'd blow it. Surprising myself, I hit a burst of triplets, repeating them like echoes, moving up an octave, doing the same thing. Mick was now facing me, pumping his fist, his scarf flying in the air. I ran up higher, and then—Pete, forgive me—rolled back my head, closed my eyes, clinched my teeth, and, against everything I believed in, did the guitar god pose of all time. Mick grinned, screamed something in my face, and hopped back to the front of the stage.

In a blur we reached the end of the song, slowing down through the last walk-up and vamping the final chord for what seemed like a minute. Yogi finally ended it with a clattering roll. And all was suddenly quiet.

After a moment, tentative applause leaked out of the crowd. Someone who sounded like Beanie screeched out, "Rock 'n' roll!" And then sporadic cries of "Heart!" were heard. I stood in a pool of sweat. Drops of it were all around me, and my white coveralls were already drenched. Breaths came in heaves. But at least I was still breathing. And now Mick was back on the mike, squinting into the crowd.

"Allllright, now! You all warmed up out there? Get ready to get your ya-ya's out, baby, 'cause we got it live if you want it."

He reached back and gave me the *c'mon* motion with his hand, and I somehow found my way through the bluesy guitar-run intro of *It's Too Late*. Rob and Yogi joined me, and Sam moved up to punctuate the beat with tenor sax riffs. Mick's cock-of-the-walk strut took him up near the edge of the stage, and he leaned out over the crowd, wagging a finger and shaking his butt. The crowd egged him on, hands motioning for him to come closer, but he danced away, only to return and move right up to the edge. I held my breath until he danced back.

Still riding on adrenaline, we skittered through the song, bouncing in and out of the pocket of Yogi's scary, almost out-of-control beat. Sam pumped through his solo, wailing and shrieking over the ten thousand watts of P.A. power, and then I moved up closer to the front of the stage and ripped off my best Johnny Thunders solo, all slop and volume. Another verse, Mick shouted out a dozen "*It's too lates*," and we jammed through the chord progression four more times before skidding to a stop-on-a-dime ending.

Silence. And then the same tepid, scattered applause. My heart dropped. This was it. We couldn't play any better than this. I caught my breath and gazed out into the crowd—a blurry, shadowed mass thirty feet beyond the stage—scanning the faces of the people I could actually see. I found Beanie, Cecil, and Evangeline. They were clapping like crazy, but nobody else was.

I looked down at the set list taped to the floor. Suddenly a girl's voice came shrieking out of the humming crowd. "Mick!"

Who the hell was that? I looked up. Mick shielded his eyes from the stage lights and peered out.

Again the high-pitched, almost hysterical scream: "Mick!"

And then I saw her, pushing through the much-larger bodies near the stage. Little Rita, packed into a tight blue halter-top and black miniskirt. Her hands were up over her head, stretched out toward Mick. I shot a glance across the stage at Rob, whose jaw hung open, and at Sam, laughing and shaking his head. Mick skipped up to the edge of the stage and bent down to grab Rita's hand.

"Bring on Heart!" someone yelled. "*Magic Man!*"

"Get off!" another voice hollered out, followed by scattered boos.

I waited for Mick to return to his mike, but he ignored the crowd and stayed with Rita. The boos coalesced into a rhythmic cascade of hoots and jeers. Fearing a repeat of last night's near-debacle, I caught Yogi's eye and started banging out the opening riff to *Rebel Rebel*. With Rob joining us, we kept the riff going, hard and insistent, until Mick finally pulled away from Rita and got back on mike for the first verse.

I edged forward to help with the background vocals. With the lights pulsing yellow, the sound of the band all around me, my heart thumping away, the scene took on the unreal vividness of one of my dreams. I half-expected Pete Townshend to step out of the blinding lights to show me the chords.

Now up at my mike, I squinted into the brilliance. Christ! Flying pinpoints of color. No, wait! Something was coming at me. I instinctively flinched, but a shower of little somethings hit me and went bouncing all over the stage.

I fell back but not before another shower came down through the lights. This time the cluster of objects landed at my feet and scattered. I kept the *Rebel Rebel* riff going and bent down to peer at the floor. What the hell? Little multicolored heart-shaped Valentine candies were all over the place. In the bright lights, I could actually see B MINE on one of the chalky hearts. Why were they throwing these things at us? I looked over at Rob, whose surprised face undoubtedly mirrored my own. And then, as another handful of the tiny candies came flying up, the realization, along with a few of the candies, hit me. The Heart fans were sending us a message: We want the girls. Get the hell off their stage.

But what could we do but keep on playing? Mick held his ground and swatted at the candies as if they were gnats. The rest of us moved back as far as we could. My retreat brought with it a sinking feeling. This was it, the big time? Was this what all the trouble with Kitten had gotten me? Valentine candies thrown in my face?

Now midway through the Bowie song, with my hands

mechanically running through the riff, I almost laughed seeing all the little hearts scattered across the stage. *Listen to your heart?* I had the bloody things all around me, and they weren't saying anything other than *you fool you fool you fool.* . . . Nita was gone. For this? I stepped forward and crushed one of the candy hearts into dust.

Suddenly a roar came from the crowd. My head shot up. I peered out through the lights. Nothing. Had they run out of ammunition? But now something started happening in front of the stage. I could see the crowd heaving, people jostling, heads turning. What looked like a human wave was pushing forward, flowing toward us, bodies reaching the stage, then spreading out sideways. I saw Rita carried away, off to Rob's side of the stage. Beanie, Cecil, and Evangeline edged off in the other direction. And then I saw a large clot of bodies clad in black leather push up to the very front of the stage and stop. The floor cleared around them. I blinked and shook my head, but they were still there: Butch, Whiskey, and at least two dozen of their biker friends. Their gloved fists came up and starting punching the haze of smoke in time to the beat. Butch opened his mouth: "Fuckin' A! Killjoys!" Whiskey blew us a wet, bosom-jiggling kiss. The Hells Angels had come to our rescue again.

By now we had almost reached the song's end. The bikers fists were pumping hard. One by one, other fists rose up and started shaking in rhythm. Encouraged, Mick spit out the last line, hopped up to the edge of the stage, and started slapping upraised hands. Bouncing back and forth, his scarf flapping behind him, he worked the edge of the stage, teetering on his heels before dancing away and then up to the edge again.

I glanced over at the others to cue them for our last pass through the riff. They nodded back, and I turned to face the audience. Something was wrong. My head swiveled from one side of the stage to the other. Mick was not there. I looked again, squinted into the wings. Gone. Peering out, I saw the crowd heaving again just beneath the lip of the stage.

The last note came. The others hit it and held on while Yogi banged out a crescendo, but I screwed up and kept going. Fortunately Yogi covered me, and I recovered to hit the final crash with the others. But where the hell was Mick? Straining forward until I reached the end of my cord, I looked over the lip of the stage. Shit! There he was, on his back, suspended in the air by the upraised hands of Butch and his buddies.

A spotlight found his twitching body. A roar erupted from the bleachers. Rob and Sam came up beside me, and we watched the bikers pass Mick from hand to hand. Mick's arms and legs were flapping around, seeking traction, like a turtle on its back.

From behind us, Yogi yelled out, "What's going on?"

"He fell in!" Sam yelled back.

Two roadies came out of the wings. When they saw the bikers, they faded back. We were on our own. Sam started toward the edge of the stage, but Rob and I grabbed him. "They'll kill you!" I shouted in Sam's ear. He looked from me to the bikers and nodded.

Mick was twenty feet out, still being passed from biker to biker. I scanned the mob until I found Butch's bushy Neanderthal profile. He had just passed Mick off to someone else and was standing sideways to the stage. In his bulky motorcycle jacket, he looked to be about three hundred pounds. I took a deep breath. "Hey, Butch!"

The biker's head jerked around, lips pulled back, eyes blazing. I pointed at Mick and motioned toward the stage with my hands. The crowd saw my gesture and almost as one roared out, "No!"

Butch continued to stare up at me, his eyes narrowing. I could almost see his greasy mental gears spinning: *Throw him back? What the hell for?* In the meantime Mick floated from hand to hand, squirming, kicking. And the crowd continued to yell. Finally, Butch's head rotated all the way around, his eyes taking in Mick, the crowd behind him, the bleachers, then back to me. Slowly, his expression softened, eyes relaxing, head nodding. And what remained of his teeth emerged through the chaos of his beard. He looked over his shoulder and yelled at his buddies, "Throw him back, boys! He's too small to keep!"

The bikers reacted to Butch's command like a precision drill team. Within seconds, they rotated Mick around and passed him forward until his feet were about a body's length from the front of the stage. Suddenly, en masse, they rushed forward and flung him up, a rag doll tossed by a catapult. We scattered. For a moment, Mick seemed to hang suspended in the air above the stage, his mouth open, eyes wide, scarf flapping lazily in the breeze. And then he came thudding down, feet first, between two monitors. His momentum drove him straight toward Sam and Rob. They reached out and steadied him to a stumbling stop as the crowd exploded in cheers.

We hustled Mick away from the edge of the stage, back toward the drums. He seemed lost, squinting around, his eyes unfocused, muttering, "Bloody . . . bloody . . . bloody hell."

"You O.K., man?" Rob shouted at him.

Mick opened his mouth, but his answer was blotted out by the rhythmic stomping sound coming from the bleachers. From the floor, clapping hands joined the stomping feet. The auditorium—stage, walls, ceiling—started to rock and roll. I felt it. Mick felt it, too. His face went pale, and during that moment I thought he was going to faint again, but, instead, he cocked his head as if listening to the cacophony. His face took on a peculiar twisted look. And then he smiled.

I sensed trouble. "Mick," I yelled, "you all right?"

"Bloody hell!" He started bobbing, squinty eyes radiating heat. Suddenly he spun and thrust both fists into the air. A roar erupted, the stomping, screaming sound ratcheting up until it was deafening. The temperature climbed a hundred degrees, and my hair burst from its rubber band confinement. I couldn't think.

Mick continued to exhort the crowd, hopping up and down and pumping his fists. He had lost his mind. And now I watched a pony-tailed guy in a plaid shirt climb up onto the far side of the stage. Mimicking Mick, he thrust both hands into the air and danced around until the bouncers came out and shoved him back into the melee. I edged backward and heard a voice yell out from the wings. Turning, I saw Beeber, Kitten, the Wilson sisters, and three other guys who must've been the rest of Heart standing there. Their eyes were shooting back and forth between us and the crowd. Only Nancy Wilson seemed to be happy with what was going on. She raised a clinched fist and pumped it in cadence to the crowd.

Beeber was in a hair-jiggling panic. He took a step toward me and yelled, "Play something, damnit!"

I motioned Rob and Sam over and hollered, "What's next?"

"Thrill!" Sam yelled back. "You're up!"

I caught my breath and glanced out into the auditorium. Mick was still dancing around like a fool. I tried to think but couldn't. My stomach flip-flopped. "You sure we should do it?"

Both of them nodded, and Sam yelled, "It's perfect!"

"Yeah, man, it's symmetrical!" Rob said, grinning hysterically.

I wasn't sure what he meant, but something clicked into place in my brain. *Punk is coming!* No, not coming. . . . It was here! My time had come and I had no choice but to play my furious, crazed song. My head seemed to nod on its own. We broke apart.

I moved forward, that one thought in my head: Punk is

here right now. And only one thing was wrong: Nita wasn't here to see it.

I waited until Yogi climbed back behind the drums, and then I let go with a blitzkrieg attack of chords. The sound of my guitar was swallowed up and spit back at me a millisecond later. Yogi and Rob came in, the volume pitched up, overwhelming the roar of the crowd. Mick ran over to his mike and was met by a sea of pumping fists rising above the bodies on the floor. What was he doing? Was he going to sing my song? I wasn't sure, but I staggered toward my mike as if being dragged downhill by the gravitational pull of the bikers at the foot of the stage. Mick was still at his mike, pointing into the crowd. I kept ripping out the chords, waiting to see what he was going to do.

Mick suddenly grabbed his mike stand and dragged it up to the edge of the stage. Feedback rang out for a moment before I heard him scream, "That was bloody awesome! You want me to come back out?"

The crowd roared a response. I kept playing.

Mick threw a fist into the air. "Bloody hell, I'm comin' back out, mates!"

I heard him, but he made no sense. Was I stoned from all the pot smoke in the air? I watched Mick bounce to the very edge of the stage, stop, and, like a diver, bring his arms together over his head. In response, pumping fists below the stage stopped and flattened out, creating a platform of upraised palms. In an electrical flash, I had that déjà vu sensation again. I saw Mick's father, arms raised, at the edge of the Sacramento River, ready to baptize his followers. Mick was doing the same thing. He leaned out over the edge of the stage, his arms extended upward, rocking back and forth on his heels. And then he pirouetted until he faced us. He grinned and, as if in slow motion, drifted backward down into the crowd, leaving behind only a momentary glimpse of his flapping scarf.

I couldn't get the first words of *Thrill* out of my mouth. I had stopped breathing. The chord progression wrapped around again, and I watched a spotlight catch Mick and follow him as he floated out across the hands of the bikers and beyond into the roiling mass of the crowd. As if caught in a riptide, the bikers and the others near the stage followed Mick's body back into the main part of the floor.

For a moment, the area in front of the stage cleared, and Beanie, Cecil, and Evangeline came flowing back into the void. They were grinning up at me. Beanie's entire body was jerking around in a celebration of something none of us had ever seen before. I felt a red-hot uplifting surge shoot through me. Air filled my lungs. I was breathing again. The words of the first verse burst into my head, and, as I took another look down at the foot of the stage, a vision of a girl with choppy blonde hair and tucked chin filled my eyes. Could it be? I blinked and looked again. No, she wasn't really there. Pulling in another breath, I took one last look out into the auditorium, and in that moment, in the blinding illumination of the stage lights, I again saw a vision, a vision of the future that didn't exist without Nita, and I realized that my eyes hadn't deceived me. She was there, just like Pete Townshend was there, and I could see her. Just as Townshend was part of me, just as he had guided me to this moment, Nita had become part of me and was ready to take me the rest of the way home. As real as anyone could ever be, she was standing at the foot of the stage, her bright blonde hair shining like a beacon, her smile asking me to sing the song that we both knew, ready to go with me into the space where the music would change, where the music would save us.

In Nita's upturned, childlike eyes, I saw the Real Me.

28

WE STOOD TOGETHER on the stage, front and center, all five of us, side by side, arms draped over each other's shoulders, facing out toward the roaring crowd. Just like the Who at the Cow Palace. I had one arm hooked around Rob's shoulder, the other around Mick's. Yogi and Sam anchored the opposite ends of our little chain. All connected. And we were all drenched in sweat and grinning.

The houselights came up. I swept the auditorium with my eyes. Everyone on the floor appeared to be standing, as they had since Mick had launched himself out onto the sea of hands. I leaned my head back and glanced into the wings. No Wilson sisters, but Beeber and Kitten were there. Beeber screamed something at us, motioning for us to come off the stage. I ignored him and focused on Kitten. She saw me and stared back, expressionless. One ring-adorned hand came up and swept away black strands of hair from her face. I could tell she knew I would never sign the contract. And I knew that she'd trash us with every promoter she knew. But I had Nancy Wilson's guitar pick in my pocket. . . .

The applause peaked. I looked sideways at the guys and nodded. In unison, we bowed, again just like the Who. As my head came up, I saw the little group standing at the foot of the stage. Rita, Evangeline, Beanie, and Cecil. And in my mind's eye, with her chin tucked, her brown eyes holding me, was Nita. But only in my mind's eye. She wasn't really there, but she was. And finally I knew it was safe to listen to my heart.

Unexpectedly, a sob grew in my chest, building up inside until it hurt. I couldn't hold it back, a half-cry, half-laugh.

Rob glanced at me. "You O.K., man?"

I gasped and nodded at him.

Mick nudged me and pointed out into the crowd. "Hey, Pleasant! Look at all the yobs! Were bleedin' stars, mate!"

I nodded again, but I saw only Nita's face. I saw it as clearly as I could see where the music would take us, together. There she was, ghostly but true. She smiled, and it looked as if she mouthed something. I knew what it was. I heard her voice, soft and steady, inside my head: *Transcendence, Daniel*.

I smiled.

Finally, finally, we were unified. And, in that moment, it was perfect. Absolutely bloody perfect. And from far away, I heard the beauty of the Universal Chord, the combination of notes uniting us all, rippling toward me, coming closer, enveloping me, piercing my ears, swirling inside my head. Pete Townshend heard it. Everybody in the auditorium heard it. I knew it, because they were me and I was them. We were all one, perfect notes in a perfect chord of harmony.

It was an awesome sound.

But could I hold on to it this time, or would it, as always, simply fade away?

ACKNOWLEDGEMENTS

First and foremost, heartfelt gratitude is due Jim Merk, who volunteered hours of his personal time to edit several earlier versions of this novel. In addition to his friendship, I thank him for his unerring eye, patience, and unwavering kindness. Several others provided comments on drafts of the manuscript, and to them I owe thanks for their observations, criticisms, suggestions, and encouragement. These readers included Christy Corzine, Nick Dennis, Cindy Erickson, Kathy Humphrey, Lisa Rea, and Greg Trott. Thanks also to my longtime buddy Jim Freeman (author of *Parade of Days* and others), who helped in so many ways.

I would be remiss if I did not gratefully acknowledge the inspiration, friendship, and great memories provided by all those who allowed me to play music with them over the years, including the guys who took those first crazy road trips with me. I also thank my good fortune in finding Robert Dunn, publisher of Coral Press, who believes in the synergistic power of rock 'n' roll and good fiction. Much thanks also to Linda Root, whose cover design perfectly captures the attitude and flavor of this book.

And finally, everlasting thanks to Pete Townshend and the Who, whose music touched my soul and kept me alive during the darkest days of my youth. No one should ever doubt the redemptive power of music, especially in the lives of those young enough to recognize it.

Roger L. Trott was born and raised in the Sacramento Valley town of Lincoln, Calif., and spent his high school and early college years in Redding, Calif. He studied English, journalism, and economics at Shasta Community College, Sonoma State University, and the University of California, Davis. He is a former rock music critic who has played bass and guitar in bands throughout Northern California. Roger continues to live in Northern California with his wife, Lisa Rea, their dog, Bobbie, and Roger's four guitars and three amplifiers. He is currently working on a second novel of musical fiction and continues to write songs and play music whenever and wherever he can.

298

Coral Press publishes Stories that Rock.

If you enjoyed *Getting in Tune*,

We're sure you'll like our other novels.

Please visit our website, www.coralpress.com. There you will find:

- Downloadable excerpts from all our books.
- Musical selections from your favorite
  Coral Press performers, including:
    The Killjoys (from *Getting in Tune*)
    The Annas (from *Meet the Annas*)
    And more to come.
- Our blog on all issues concerning
  musical fiction.
- Coral Press T-shirts, messenger bags,
  stickers, and other fun swag.
- Many more treats and surprises.

We Love Rock 'n' Roll ✤ We Love a Good Story